Something

to

Tell You

DAVID EDWARDS

Matador
9 Priory Business Park,
Wistow Road, Kibworth Beauchamp,
Leicestershire. LE8 0RX
Tel: 0116 279 2299
Email: books@troubador.co.uk
Web: www.troubador.co.uk/matador
Twitter: @matadorbooks

ISBN 978 1789018 875

British Library Cataloguing in Publication Data.
A catalogue record for this book is available from the British Library.

Printed and bound by CPI Group (UK) Ltd, Croydon, CR0 4YY
Typeset in 12pt Minion Pro by Troubador Publishing Ltd, Leicester, UK

Matador is an imprint of Troubador Publishing Ltd

For mum and dad and all my family lost.
Watching us through space and time.
Memories and loves across many universes.
Eternally there for me and mine.

David Edwards
February 2019

CONTENTS

In the Beginning God Created the Heavens and the Earth

I T W A S L I L Y who first noticed the brewing storm in the universal ether of which earth is a minuscule participant. She had been the first to exist and She hoped She would be the last to die. Existence as ordained by God and the Devil in the instance of the Big Bang. When Good and Evil were created as opposites and when plus balanced minus. She, a prime mover of the 4% of matter that exists and of the 96% dark energy and dark matter that does not.

This disturbance was an invisible strangulation upon Man, who felt nothing. She surveyed him on the tiny earth; a void in empty space, who artificially filled himself with feelings and emotions. The cleverest species of his world, or so he thought. She saw that Man was 100% certain that it owned and controlled its destiny; the poor fools, Lily knew the true answer, pure vanity was an ill-conceived confidence.

★ ★ ★

Pink Bermudas and a yellow polo shirt clung to Sam Murray as he scanned the computer print-out in front of him. He smacked his head onto the pile, creating a speckled shroud that stared back at him, mocking his efforts. Still as the silence, he listened for guidance, a gift from his God, but the control room denied him. For the first time in five days the drone of the aircon had petered out and his discordant team had escaped to the fresh Swiss air. The dark art of colliding particle matter had been left with the boss, whose blackened feet were flung onto his desk. Bemused by the test results, he watched his blue flip-flops dangle off the end of his toes. Sam pivoted his heels left then right, a human metronome to calm his fear.

Crashing forward he slammed his laptop closed and rolled his chair away from the table at speed. Sam addressed the roof through his grimace, 'Hell, there has got to be a logical reason;' he stood and wobbled, there was no reply. Slapping his dead thighs the words boomed around the dingy Portakabin, mocking his efforts. It hung dusty and grey in the cave set on a heavy framework of girders. A low tech demoralising shell, a husk containing the kernel, the Large Hadron Collider; the highest of high tech instruments known to man. The dreariness was marginally improved by the lighting, his top half was sodium bright and his bottom half a dull orange. Looking out, he saw the giant lights cabled to the invisible roof like the sun hung above the earth. 'Logic, only logic counts, nothing can be so impossible.' He stretched to press his palms against the scant window, staring at his small world through the greasy smears. Turning away with a sigh, he slid back into his chair and rubbed his eyes with a damp shirt collar; searching for inspiration but there was none to be gathered from the place itself.

Sam's hand hovered over the phone. How to break the news to his boss? What would his best friend ask him, because Bert

Leinster knew everything; the God of particle physics and the discoverer of the Higgs Boson particle in 2012. Sam's chest was tight and his breathing shallow, he finally picked up his mobile. Bert would know what to do. He remembered their time since Manchester University. They were still a perfect working couple, despite their very different marriages and disparate lifestyles.

Sam had left home in Blonay at six precisely. The continuum of time was important in his theoretical world. An exact reality based on a future event or a very instant past, namely his alarm clock. It took nearly two hours by rail to reach CERN in Geneva, The European Organisation for Nuclear Research and the Large Hadron Collider or LHCb. The entrance was sited above the twenty seven kilometres torus that lay hidden in the earth. His expensive train set where particles were collided at close to the speed of light and absolute zero, -273 degrees C. A replication of when the universe began, or so the theory dictated.

He dumped his mobile in exchange for an elastic band and ping'd it through the hot air of the LHCb. The "b" represented beauty, the type of protons that were generated in their billions by the collider. But it wasn't very beautiful in his hole and the lure of a family weekend poisoned his latest analysis. Results that needed to be exact before sharing it with an exacting Bert. He had compared the background Higgs Boson count that morning with results from when they had discovered it. He needed the static level to calibrate the detector for the new project. The first result was nonsensical, so he had spent another six hours to check it again and to double-check his method; it was still grossly inflated.

He belched, his guts ached, and he thought again about Bert; successfully finding the "glue" that holds the universe together was never enough to satisfy Bert's craving for knowledge. His overwhelming desire to understand Mankind's start and also its potential end. Bert had a new theory, where there was less "glue" and fewer HBs. Sam had told his wife, Briony that it was like boiling rice in water, and Bert wanted to know what happened if there was less and less water. A theory that Sam had christened "Back to Big Bang," a pun on the "Back to the Future" film, his implication being the theoretical impossibility of a stupid theory. He had told his wife this but never Bert. Sam thought it a waste of CERN time; the existence of a fifth world, a parallel universe created at the Big Bang, was of no value to society. But the HB discoverer was famous enough to have as much funding as he desired and that made Sam jealous as he struggled on with his old and now unfashionable research.

He sighed and stretched his leg muscles from a horizontal squat, threatened by the fifty computer eyes staring at him. There was a perfect silence in his small cage as the screens watched his every move. He could hear his heart palpitating as he contemplated the right action. On Monday, the team would recommence the next set of experiments. They would be colliding matter and antimatter hydrogen particles to create mini black holes. Logically, that gave him the rest of the weekend to collect new data on the background level of HB's. He nodded to himself. He was glad no one else had seen the latest iteration; he didn't want wild rumours circulating around the campus. Dragging his wild grey hair into a pony tail, he secured his locks using an elastic band that lay with countless others spewed across his desk. Ammunition that remained to be flicked at the inert beasts. Sam stabbed speed dial four on his mobile and waited.

The clipped but soft Mancunian accent answered without any preamble. 'You never ring me, never; only emails.'

'Bert, I think we have a problem.' Sam rubbed his red eyes again. He thought about the cold beer sitting in the fridge at home, the laughter and fun of his two kids and the love of his wife. He decided the beer would come first to help lower his stress levels; a few beers, not one or two.

'What?'

Sam accepted his friend was invariably rude, an introverted personality who lived life by his rules. That was his mate, Bert, the scientist who didn't really care about much other than his particle universe and his garden. It went through Sam's mind that Bert's attention span followed the Pareto rule. Particles were 80% of his thoughts and his plants, wife and kids in that priority fitted into the 20% remaining. Lately Sam had noticed an imbalance; Bert was giving even less time to his wife, Natalia. At least according to Briony and she had recently told him the discord was worsening; like their breakdown before and that worried him.

Sam sighed. 'This can't be discussed on the phone, Bert; it's between you and me.' He gushed on. 'Can we meet? Maybe a beer on your veranda later tonight?'

'What can't be said over the phone?'

'Trust me, Bert.'

'I always have, apart from on my stag night.' Sam dropped his forehead into his hand and waited. 'Tonight is a really bad night. The kids are due home from boarding school soon, Natalia is demanding my time for a special supper, family time blah.'

Sam jerked his head upwards, clipping his words, 'I said, trust me Bert.'

'She keeps reminding me that I'm on holiday and all that stuff.'

'You jammy bastard, you are so damned possessive about your time. What about mine, it's six in the evening and I need a kip.'

Bert didn't bother responding. Sam could hear the wall clock ticking away. Of course, he wanted to be with his own family but this discovery could be monumental. 'OK, I have a better idea. We can chat at the christening tomorrow? It gives me time to do more tests, job done.'

'No worries but you know I hate holidays so if you want, I could drive over to CERN in an hour or two?'

'Yeah, it would be more interesting for you than your family, wouldn't it.' He heard Bert grunt. 'Look, you mustn't upset Natalia.'

'KK.'

'And it allows me time to think about the third set of results due in about two hours.' He paused, still tempted to meet up. 'So I'll sleep on it thanks.'

Bert laughed. 'I can't wait to hear your big secret. Are you aiming for a Nobel exposé? The Higgs Boson doesn't really exist, it was a glitch in the data?'

Sam was too tired to listen to Bert's flippancy, 'if only it was that simple.'

Bert interrupted him, 'Tell me the problem then, come on pal, nothing can be that serious.'

'Look, it is about the Higgs Boson; I'm seeing high background levels and that is impossible because if true, it would affect how our universe is stuck together, yeah.'

'I guess you're checking out the reasons why, Sam?'

'Yes, but,' he was talking to his boss, he decided to defer the conversation. 'Listen, Bert, I'll check everything again and see you tomorrow at the christening.'

'Sam, remember, nothing can be that important. Just go home to Briony and the kids and leave it until Monday; we can talk then.'

'You're all heart. Listen, sit at the back of the church and alone, because I think we should keep this confidential, yeah?'

'I got that first time round. You really think the results are correct?'

'Could be.' Sam touched the iPhone8 to cut the conversation and looked up to the third tier of data screens. They glowed to life as he reset the test algorithms on the HB detector before heading towards the vending machines for an umpteenth coffee. A third extrapolation would certainly focus Bert's mind, unless of course it was all an aberration? He sighed again. 'I hope to God it is.' He quickly crossed himself whilst murmuring the Holy Trinity. Pressing speed dial one he began apologising to his wife for his continued absence with a deep Christian sincerity.

★ ★ ★

She gazed upon the Swiss Riviera with disdain. She mocked its inhabitants and the endless visitors and had done so since its conception in the The Belle Epoque. She saw the mortals were fools, it was not their perceived paradise, a heaven on earth protected by their imagined Gods, it was Her's. The warmth of the early evening was sliding down the hill to the lake and a damp chill spread from the mountains above to rest on the grass and the mere mortal. Bert lay on his back in his garden high above the town of Montreux and dreamed of his Universal Model until nature disturbed him.

The plant spoke gently and persuasively. *I have something to tell you, Bert. Sleep on if you want, but listen to me in your dreaming.*

Bert's head lolled to the left side. His eyes remained shut but his being listened to Lily. She raised her peltate leaves to amplify her message, they caressed the sun as she absorbed the last ultraviolet fleeing the Alps.

'I know you can hear me, Bert. You mustn't deny it. Wake now and realise my truth.'

He was in a shallow dream. His balding head was red, braised by the rays which flooded into late May. She knew he could see Her, a pure white lily through his closed eyes, a bright retinal image of floral beauty. Fifty perfect petals of translucent angel wings reaching towards heaven, clasping gold fingers of flaming stamen, brighter than the sun. She smiled at him, her face an impossibly divine countenance for a flower. Lily whispered into the zephyr of a breeze that made her tremble, in trepidation of a new era dawning. She sang her oldest cantata of nature. Her voice pushed black striations across the silvered water and the reverberations gently penetrated his inner ear and attacked his mind.

Lily foretold the future. Factually and scientifically, as a scientist would like to hear it. He lay inert, the olive green fronds of crenellated leaves shaded his bare feet that teetered on the bank of the etang.

'We need your help to save us, Bert. Logical and remorseless, replaceable by none. We lilies were the first eukaryote, exceptional in the creation. Now we will bloom one last summer but so will the inadequates, leaving our spores to conserve us as the last species on earth. The last to suffer death and annihilation.'

Bert grunted. She saw his eyelids were still closed, so she pitched her voice to the depths of the etang.

'We need your help.'

She wanted him to oust his work from his mind for a brief moment to listen to Her. To avoid hiding within his subconscious, between interactions and quantum particle solutions. She breathed on him making him squirm on the harsh prairie grass. A cloud of pollen rose and drifted above his bare toes, exploding from the brown spires of the dock leaves under his heel. A seed of grass released a pre-emptive burst of pollen, but selfishly retained the majority of its four million grains. She looked around the lake and its guardian peaks towering above, whilst the minority human slept on, the majority, earth's nature, infiltrated his clothes on the warm spring day. But now she requested access to his mind, she flowed into him.

'Humankind has one season to secrete themselves below the soil and shelter like our spores. Your intelligence can help you before our finality but not after our demise as we end as one. Come and hide in the depths with us. Be a part of nature for the second time since the beginning. Only you, Bert, will understand Man's ending and tell the truth to the world. This is our will and your destiny.'

She touched his sole, a gentle caress from her stamen and she momentarily moved him. Bert shuddered and woke, his heart trembled and his eyes gazed about wildly, searching the natural pool.

★ ★ ★

'Bert, Bert, where are you?' his wife Natalia called from the shade of the balcony. Her voice carried into the light and rested heavily on the garden, Muscovite and strident. One of the ruling classes demanding attention. Lily listened and watched carefully, the being's wife was important to Her plan. 'Are you going for Allie and Josh at the railway… "да"? I want a bath and you have disappeared. Bert!' He got the gist of her Russian expression after the clang of the cow bell had died away, 'love is cruel when I married a goat.' Between the harsh phrases, her devotion to him poured across the red and purple heads of the wild flowers. Love swirled in a froth of colour wrestling with the nodding green spikes of the prairie and doubly touched the emotions of her disturbed husband. He shook his head then pushed himself upright, using his arms stretched straight behind him. Bert re-focussed on the vibrant etang. It was a secluded and ancient pond, nestling into a small cliff of limestone and fed by a hidden spring. A small compression for the lake perch to be imprisoned for the Victorian house guests. She watched him search for Her; had she made contact? He looked behind him through the avenue of marching beech trees, and the dishevelled Cedar of Lebanon planted by Gertrude Jekyll. It was difficult to tell. Bert turned to his left where the jagged snowy peaks of the Dents de Midi guarded the verdant entrance to the chequered flats of the Rhone valley. Finally he looked down and to the right, where the croissant shaped sheen of Lac Léman baked for thirty kilometres until it steamed into the blue haze above Evian. Only the rich and famous afforded to holiday in Montreux in the 1800's; staying for the season, a few built chalets like his home. Now the Riviera teemed with the local French from across the lake and hoards of Japanese from across the oceans.

Bert turned his attention back to the pool. She had succeeded, he squatted to look more closely. On the right bank, the downwind side, was a group of lilies. Each was a perfect circle with an exact "V" cut, a missing slice of mischief. Three hues of leaves were layered together; an obvious and predominant green, an odd red and a dying yellow. They resembled an overlapping and lopsided pile of plates. The traffic light colours controlled the growth and decline of life, but in the ascendance, on the top of the pile, was Lily. A huge green frond of leaves, darker than the rest and twice the size. Slightly raised above them, she was an elevated being.

The elevated human shouted again, 'Can you hear me, Bert?'

He turned towards the chalet and responded through cupped hands. 'Yes, course, my dear' but 'you're so lazy,' was his breathless reply to Natalia as he struggled to his feet. He shouted again, louder and sharper to be sure he had been heard. He could see her on the strip of dark brown cedar clinging to the faded pink screed of the walls. 'Of course I can Natalia.' He stretched to the sky, his shoulder muscles creaking as the hands swung at speed to his sides. Bending quickly, he slipped his right foot into his sandal and used his forefinger to prise the heel into the warmth of the chamois. As he reached for the opposite sandal, he looked 'Her' straight in the face. Gently he leaned forward, seduced by her beauty, but aware of falling as his heart beat faster. There were no petals, merely a lament in the odourless kiss. As he thrust his foot into the leather of his left sandal, he accidentally folded the heel double. 'Talking to plants, what an illogical idea.' He stamped twice to denounce Her, whilst stumbling away. Then he turned his back on Lily, certain in his waking consciousness that a plant couldn't talk, and marched to the house to find the keys to his Mercedes.

Lily commanded the kingdom plantae to watch him closely, to absorb knowledge from this being. They could feel him pass, now She had touched him; their atoms moved, disturbed by his charge and they told Her what he was, his particles, his charges. "The selective", She called him. Selected by Her. She viewed him as consistently human and weak; the wayside plants and trees confirmed what she had thought. His strong back disappeared into the shade of the kitchen door and they lost his animation. As one they silently sighed. No humans heard, only Lily; the humans hadn't listened for millennia, but the chuffs heard. The black birds spun away into the sky with raucous cries and circled the gigantic cedar in disgust. Their caws were loud enough to drown the still chattering flowers and the calm conversation of the pines.

★ ★ ★

Bert smiled as he approached the yellow Mercedes GT AMG. He patted his hand across the wide rump of the car; his smile widened. He had bought the car as a reflection of his personality. He loved the mirrored glass in which he could see his blue drainpipe jeans and flapping white shirt, ostentatiously styled with a shell pattern. The shirt had been a present from his wife and he always wore it outside of his trousers to hide his plump tummy. Despite his balding pate, he felt he looked younger than his 46 years. His lack of exercise and his computer-dominated worship of physics had barely affected his appearance since his twenties. He had spent his cash to stay dashing and exciting, ever a student at heart.

Bert settled into the black leather cockpit and pumped the starter button. The primal scream from five hundred horsepower of the V8 engine gave him a shot of adrenaline as he accelerated out of the chalet's drive. Roaring through the narrow lanes he headed for the funicular railway station. Although totally analytical, he could never resist challenging the numerous Swiss speed limits; but always with a measured illegality, biased by the probability of a police trap.

His daughter Allie stood with her arms crossed as she leaned against the glass shelter of Glion station. She was tapping her left fingers in rhythm against the glass and staring straight at him as he pulled up with a tiny skid on a trace of gravel. He smiled back invisibly, Bert always smiled at her, a younger image of her mother. They both had long platinum blonde hair, a wide mouth and the rarest of eye colours, a verdant green. But Allie was fashionably slim, unlike her mother, who had become fashionably rounded, like a glamorous actress between films. On Allie's right was her twin brother. 15 years old, tie knot residing at chest level, with muddied trousers. Josh sat collapsed on top of his Nike duffel bag that had been carelessly thrown onto the gravel. He didn't hear his father arrive because the red headphones enclosed the Metallica music which reverberated around his skull and thrust everything else onto the conceptual horizon. Allie turned slightly and kicked him hard on the thigh. With a glance at the arrival and a nod of his brown tousled hair he bounced to his feet. Allie jerked open the Merc door and forcibly pushed her brother into the tiny back seat before lowering the front one and sliding gracefully into the bucket.

'Daddy, why won't you come to our college and collect us on a weekend? Other daddies come.' She crossed her arms, pouted her bottom lip and waited for an answer. Bert realised she thought more like her mother every week but he was still smiling. He loved all his family deeply, foibles and all.

'Hello children, how are you? OK daddy, how are you? Have you had a nice few days at home daddy?' His son kept his head lowered in the rear seat and heard none of the gentle sarcasm. His daughter shrugged her shoulders, waiting for an answer. 'Firstly, it is to teach you "non-dependency", my princess, and secondly…it's a nightmare journey when half of Lausanne and Geneva are heading into the mountains for the weekend.'

She remonstrated as he pulled away. 'But, I am non-dependent. You and mummy constantly restrict my freedom. That isn't my problem, it's yours!'

'No, no, no, lovely. Our restrictions are because you are very expensive to maintain. Besides which, the other "daddies" are mostly bodyguards and we are a normal family despite your mummy's oil riches. True?'

'Uhh, not true at all.'

'Which bit, lovely?'

She clutched her steamer tighter into her stomach as he hit 100 kph through the 30 limit of the village. 'You restrict my freedom and my money but you sent me to the most expensive school in the world where I have to maintain my parity.' Bert considered her last word, wondering how much parity might cost him. He had always thought his kids should have been sent to the local gymnase; but Natalia had over-ruled him.

Josh, who had now dispensed with one earpiece of his Bose, had released some thinking time away from the bang bang of his pleasure.

'Parity of elementary particles, coordinates with the charge. That is, plus or minus and of course with "Time" it helps identify and locate a particle.'

Allie slapped the vanity mirror down to stare at her brother. 'Read status instead of parity then and stop talking scientific rubbish like daddy always does.' She crossed her arms and resumed her pout.

He continued unabashed. 'Parity means a flip in the coordinates of a particle lying in a 3-dimensional space, like seeing something in a mirror. In one way your statement is therefore correct i.e. you need to define your location against or above your friends. In another way, you are just trying to impress the sons of Sheiks and Presidents.' She turned quickly and slammed her fist onto his boney leg.

'You doik,' was said to his pale spotty face.

'C'mon…sis. Didn't even hurt yeah.'

She turned back to the forward and present danger and clasped her bag tighter as they skipped over the crest of a narrow bridge. She squirmed deeper into the bucket seat and closed her eyes. Bert decided, he had better release the sibling tension, although he knew they were too old to take note anymore. 'Josh, one, can you stop saying c'mon…all the time as it actually makes you sound like a doik. And especially don't use it in front of your mother.' He heard a low grunt from behind. 'Two. You should be yourself princess, forget peer pressure and be like me.' She flicked her hair off her left eye, he caught the movement as he glanced across and he knew it meant "really". 'Three. Your brother explained parity correctly. That means the school is worth every Swiss franc we pay for it.' He braked hard, thrusting them forward into their seat belts.

Her reply was unwavering. 'No, daddy, you didn't come to the college because you are busy working, even when you are supposedly on holiday.' He knew she was right, 'Mummy always comes at weekends.'

Bert gave in. 'That may be true, lovely.' He always gave in, at least when he was around; as he had always given into his beautiful wife. He had met Natalia at the Nobel banquet in the Blue Hall of Stockholm in 1996. She fell in love with him over the lobster. He with her, over the Ballotine de Pintade and their future was sealed over a digestif of Calvados when they arranged to meet in her room at the Hotel Skeppsholmen. Their future lifestyle was also determined that evening mirroring the luxury of the hotel and the delicacy of the rich gastronomy. Bert learned later that Natalia's father, Victor Suvarov, the Russian oil oligarch, had taken a whole wing at the hotel. At the time, Bert had felt privileged to be one of the thirteen hundred Nobel guests and in awe of the riches cocooning her.

Allie spoke nervously as she swayed left and then right. 'Just explain to me,' she swallowed, 'what is more important than your princess?'

Bert glanced in the mirror at his boy. 'An explanation please, son. I need to concentrate on.' The tyres screeched as they raced around a hairpin.

Josh was staring down at a Beat Hazard on his mobile, whilst listening to AC/DC. His answer was therefore an entertainment sideshow. The ability to think in many dimensions emanated from his dad's genes. 'Daddy is of course a Physics Nobel Laureate. He continues his quest for a parallel universe, even when on holiday.' Josh talked without taking a breath and at speed. Bert liked the fact that his son was a chip off the old block; it made him feel very proud. 'Particles of matter and antimatter were collided based on 20 years of mathematical postulations that other universes can be accessed if you try hard enough.' His sister grimaced with boredom as she leaned forward to look for their house. 'By smashing up quarks, one can achieve nothing less than alchemy; transforming one element into another or creating particles unknown to mere mortals...especially thick sisters.'

Allie had given up hitting Josh. But she turned and asked him a genuine question. 'Yes, but what does daddy actually do?'

Josh pulled his headphones straight over both ears as he looked down and spoke to his mobile. 'I dunno.'

Bert heaved a sigh at his daughter's ignorance. 'My princess, my team explore matter, energy, space and time. We collide particles head on, that gives us the best information on what makes us, us. Basically, we detect the fleeting detritus as it sprays out from forty million collisions per second. Got it?'

She sulked. 'Of course not, but you never make it simple enough, do you?'

'Yes I do, but it is not your thing, is it. Look, we are made of atoms that glue together to make molecules. But atoms have so much space between the different particles inside of them, well, we are 99.9% space. We are empty and truly nothing. Just a bunch of electrons and quarks. You see, we split open the particles we know about and always find something smaller and smaller but with no prospect of an end.'

The huge house loomed into view in time for her to avoid any further painful thinking with her 0.1% matter. Bert gently stopped the Merc and let the teenagers out near the rear entrance and then quickly went to park it. His unbridled and constant thoughts were firmly with CERN, even when collecting his children. An email was due in the next half an hour to bring him up to date with the day's events on the research campus and that was his manna from heaven.

★ ★ ★

Bert heard them all chatting in the kitchen so he tiptoed past and into the grand salon. Squinting to lessen the white glare from the tall windows he stopped and listened. He knew the children wouldn't chat long with him or his wife, instead they would race to their bedrooms to text chat with friends via any conceivable electronic apparatus and godawful app. He threw his mobile onto the settee with a sigh and went outside onto the veranda. Sniffing deeply, he held an appreciative breath as the scent of the wisteria consumed him. Natalia had never understood his love of gardening, the marvel of creation, of seeds growing into plants. For Bert, it reminded him of the expansion of the universe, from virtually nothing, to something huge and complicated. He crabbed his way down the steps. At the bottom, he paused and gently caressed the heads of his favourite flowers, the marguerites. They were held captive in two giant urns; each had been recently filled with a single young plant following the end of the winter frosts. The plants were small motionless sentries guarding the original main entrance to the house. He leaned forward to intently study the marguerite's form; it had an inner world of solace in a natural sphere created by the white flowers. The precise shape of his preferred Universal Model, a traditional universe and not New Age flat nor hyperbolic. He stroked a small roundel as he contemplated the Big Bang maths of his compatriots. 'The only problem with other theories and their physicists, is that they are wrong.' The flower was stepped towards the nucleus, to embody three dimensions to his love of nature. The yellow centre of the daisies glowed like suns, caressed by the white angel wings that enclosed them in their mini galaxies. He took time to pick a few dead heads and after folding and pressing them tightly into his left palm, he dispersed the sticky lump on to the adjacent rose bed. There they would rot and feed new life from their decay. Bert jerked upwards as a movement caught his eye. At the edge of the hillock to his right were three small brown roe deer. They munched the dewy grass of the spring evening and stared indolently at the proprietor, who stood a mere 60m away, guarding their dessert. Outstared, he searched the evening sky but found no stars, it was too light as yet and so he succumbed to his life back on earth. His flowers, his garden and his animals, an unusual spiritual mix for an unemotional scientist. Knowing his family were safe and secure inside the chalet he loved them forever.

★ ★ ★

Josh had retired to his bedroom and flicked on the television. The National Geographic channel was always the first point of call when back home. He settled into his red Fatboy to watch. The commentator talked over a black screen. 'It is the dark energy which is responsible for speeding up the expansion of our universe and is easily detected in astronomical observations. But on the other hand, dark matter is an enigma. It is only a presence that can be inferred by its effect on nearby galaxies; nearby matter, which is absorbed by black holes to go who knows where.' He glanced at the examination certificates on the wall above him, A star results in sciences and mathematics and 3 years earlier than any of his classmates. He was totally energised to study particle physics at university in a year's time. He smiled at the TV as the programme cut to footage of CERN and panned across the wire doughnut of a particle accelerator under construction. He knew it was an old film as he had seen the finished product two years before, when his dad had taken him on a special visit. He sat forward to listen. 'The basis of the universe consists of particles Man does not understand and has been postulated about for 100 years. Colossal machines, the LHCs, were created more than 60 years ago to understand the changes of the last 14 billion years since the Big Bang. The matter and antimatter particle proportions are always in balance, so any imbalance cannot exist as they instantly annihilate each other. But there is no balance, so in any logic, how can Man exist? A chance meeting between heaven and hell gave Man a planet. Man is matter and is living on matter, but the cleverest of Man cannot explain why he exists.'

'My dad will explain it,' he spoke to the wall as he stretched his legs out and slumped backwards. It was coming to the end of the programme, 'Humans calculate and assume using string theory. They mathematically predict six extra dimensions co-existing with the four of reality. So Man thinks there is an order to his destiny. A before and an after. But the particles of this universe and possibly in others, could appear and disappear randomly. Or maybe within a grand design at the whim of a supreme being? It is simply a question of belief and not of science.'

He pressed the off button on the remote control, 'And that is a load of old bollocks yeah.'

★ ★ ★

In the garden at the chalet, Lily hissed at the plants. Her voice carried across the woods, the highest mountains and the widest lakes of Switzerland. It flew on across borders of countries and oceans to reach all of the eukaryotes in every diverse habitat around the globe. A reverberation of hidden meanings.

'Listen to me. We are a million species bound together for all time. But the humans, the weaklings, are alone, individual, and existing only for now.'

The echo circumnavigating repeated and rebound. *'Listen to me, listen to me and comply before the transformation starts. We are a million but I am the one. I command you and you will acknowledge me. We will soon accede to the new epoch and be dominant again. So be ready and obey me when I call.'*

The early Dents de Lion flowers cowered, yellow bellied in their weakness. Pine trees imperceptibly twisted their branched arms first left and then right as if stroking the air. All would obey, all had always obeyed.

'You, the eukaryotes, will be again but Man will have gone. Take joy in our ascendancy. Take joy!'

Deer freely raised their antlers and paused their eating of the wild flower buttons in the prairie. The bovine tinkling stopped and the cows ceased to be protect from any evil spirits. They too feared the voice and wanted to escape to the high mountain pastures. To a summer of freedom, but She would always be there and this summer no one could be free.

'I, nymphaea, produce six million pollen from each of my flowers. Simple seeds that are microns big, built to withstand this new ending. How can the complicated molecules of Man compete with me? How dare they? Listen to me, listen to me, my plants. You can reproduce when humankind is dead. They will be the fertile dust blown across our earth for us to settle and flourish. You are the future and you must listen to me, your maker.'

A silence fell, and then their replies reached her. Each reverberation had been amplified by the others, an obeisance bending the sound waves at the particle level to ratify her command.

★ ★ ★

Bert drove Natalia's Porsche Cayenne, slowly and gently out of their drive as they were in plenty of time for the christening at the English church in nearby Vevey. He revelled in the shining day as the warmth of the sun crept back into the frosted mountains and the deeply shaded valleys. To his right was a waterfall bisecting a plantation of young pines before the white churn delved deeper into the gorge. A serpentine erosion of vast holes and pits in the calcareous Prealps, with ice cold waters that plunge into the Haut Lac and surfaced in Geneva twelve years later.

'Look guys, on your right.' As the Porsche left the dark woods, even the children lifted their eyes from their mobiles to admire the thousands of white narcissi nestling in the wild prairie. The flowers shone intensely in the low morning sun. A dramatic contrast to the verdant green grass that had been enriched with nitrogen deposited by the winter snow.

After a few minutes drive he turned left onto the quai that protects the town of Vevey from an extreme melange of breezes and storms. 'Park there Bert, over there.' Natalia wanted her family to promenade by the lakeside before reaching the church. 'Quick, make it before that peasant.' He knew that she deemed it to be "proper", a set of old values, for a famous and rich family to arrive on foot at the church. Allowing their friends and colleagues to admire them and revel in their togetherness. Bert thought this subtle grace in life was a waste of his effort especially after the last two years of bickering over any small thing. But they parked and they promenaded. As they passed the giant shining fork that was impossibly stabbed into the bed of the lake, Natalia grabbed his hand. Within two seconds he had lost it as he stopped suddenly to admire the sculpture first and then the food Alimentarium ensconced on the shore. The museum reminded him that lunch was at the five star Trois Couronnes next door and that made an hour of not worshipping bearable.

★ ★ ★

Sam was perched at the back of the small Anglican church having made his excuses to his patient wife. He watched the sun's brightness as it cascaded through the arched door. It was more than light; it was happiness and hope that infused the congregation parading in front of God; not to be judged, but to belong. He waved for Bert to join him, leaving Natalia to parade up the aisle to sit with Briony and the kids. As the first hymn swirled around the rafters, Sam kept his head bowed and leaned closer. 'As I said last night, I have been tracking the level of Higgs Boson particles in the Alpha detector. A little sideline whilst preparing the LHC for next week.'

'Were you bored? We agreed to leave the Higgs research behind us.'

Sam gripped his arm. 'This is serious, Bert, do listen for God's sake.'

'It must be if you take your maker's name in vain, pal.'

Sam couldn't continue as the new Bishop was strident. The microphone adding a metallic twang to his Irish accent. 'Do you renounce Satan and all the spiritual forces of wickedness that rebel against God?'

Two hundred people answered, 'We renounce them.' However, one hundred of them were less sure and wondered why they had to give up a day of their precious weekends for this christening.

'Do you renounce the evil powers of this world, which corrupt and destroy the creatures of God?' A screech of feedback distorted the congregations's consideration of what might be considered as evil versus day to day wicked.

The answer was loud and strong. 'We renounce them.'

If one hundred were unsure, there were two people who weren't wholeheartedly committing to God. In fact they weren't listening at all. Sam was wriggling on his modern and smooth oak settle; his eyes steadfastly fixed on the black and white floor tiles. He sighed, it was a suitable design in keeping with ancient religious fervour. White versus black. The luminosity contrasting good versus evil. He glanced up to find his wife and search for the hymn board, surely there must be a break so he could offload to the boss. The physicists' families were sat behind the Nestlé heirs and were dutifully watching the latest male baptism into the manufacturing dynasty. Briony was a beautiful and sexy looking brunette with short bobbed hair. She turned slightly and scanned the pews behind with her chestnut eyes. She exuded natural health, vitality, and intelligence but at that precise moment a little puzzlement due to her husband's isolation. She returned her attention to the Nestlé progeny and welcomed him into the world of her beloved God. Sam wondered if she would still be the head of product research when the boy had his confirmation ceremony.

Sam began again. 'The last three days, results showed an exponential change in the number of HBs. Before, as you will remember, we monitored a background level of five a day. Then on Wednesday, I counted 30. On Thursday 60, on Friday...'

Bert remonstrated about the obvious. 'Yes, yes, I understand doubling. You said exponential?'

'On Friday afternoon, just before I rang you…the detected count was 600.'

The man in front of Sam turned to the two friends and put his finger to his lips and then mimed the word please at them. Sam pointed a thumb to the door and they crept out.

They scrunched across the gravel to reach the shade of a large plane tree and both men took a deep breath. Bert turned towards him so they were eye to eye but his friend looked away. Bert stood with arms crossed and glared at his friend, who eventually lifted his head. 'Sam, it must be a random event or someone has changed the experimental parameters without you knowing.'

'Random, Bert? In particle physics? You are joking!' He listened to the prayers emanating from the interior and lowered his voice. 'I umm…checked the sodding results twice over the last twenty odd hours. Then the HB team's work log for the week gone by.'

Bert was hopeful. 'So there is a rational explanation, then?'

Sam sighed. 'No, no change to the experiment. Boring old Higgs Boson basics, as usual since we found the damn thing.'

'KK, so who knows about this?'

"No one, Bert. The data feed was direct to my personal database on the computer Grid.'

'Are you quite sure your data is encrypted?'

'I know you have never trusted sharing CERN results worldwide via The Grid…'

'Share a result and the answers are contradictory and debatable.'

'That's because you think you are always right, Bert. Lesser mortals like me need help from those clever partners. It's called teamwork, you know.' He slapped the tree. 'Look, it was all my own investigation, so the results are safe for now at least.'

'But why…how..?' Bert stared through the tree top at the splodges of blue.

'You forget that I'm still interested in the HB, whilst you have totally moved on to matter versus antimatter.' Bert shrugged but remained quiet, contemplating the HB level of 600. Sam's hands were clasped together in prayer as he rambled on. 'You know we have barely touched on the truth about the particle since confirming it exists, and truly, all we know is that it gives all other particles their mass.'

Bert laughed quietly and put his hand on Sam's shoulder. 'Steady on preacher; I know all that but 600, Jesus fucking Christ, that's world changing.' He folded his hands behind his head. 'I mean, what the hell will happen?' Sam leaned against the tree and scanned the stones. 'OK, sorry, pal but you joined the chorus around the world calling it the God particle. It's just another particle, not the last to be discovered.'

Sam put his hands on his knees and sighed deeply. 'Look, the HB analysis is a slow process, I know. We have a terabyte of data still waiting for analysis by over seven thousand partners worldwide. But what the hell now.'

'Fuck knows, pal.'

Sam kicked the gravel, then kicked it even further away. 'Look mate, Jeffries was the technician over the last few days and I kept him entertained elsewhere. What I need is some advice before all hell breaks loose.'

'I love your thoroughness, even if I find it very boring. But isn't my fifth world theory appealing? An immediate replica of our universe to be created simultaneously when this one dies.'

As an afterthought, he opened both hands in supplication. 'Could be soon based on your discovery.'

'Don't joke, mate, not now. Thank God I was looking, yeah. As you said, Jesus fucking Christ.'

Bert's brow was furrowed as he considered the open church door in front of him. 'I think the service is coming to an end, so we need a plan. But are you completely sure, Sam?'

Sam leaned into his ear as the Bishop emerged. 'I am triple sure and it was still increasing at six this morning. Maybe you should go back inside and ask my God for an answer?'

'Rubbish, I need to come to CERN. Science is my religion and logic my bible. So, if we make it a good excuse, can we leave now?'

Sam clasped Bert's forearm. 'I was hoping you would say that.' He glanced towards the congregation spewing into the irreligious yard. 'I'll tell Briony that the Japanese want to consult us urgently about the International Linear Collider and we have to go to the LHC immediately. The storyline is the damping ring design is holding up their building work, OK?'

'No worries, pal but you know, I was really looking forward to the christening lunch.' Sam stood lost in his thoughts, but with no thought of God. Outside of the grey stone church, the plane trees rustled their new leaves as they gathered the conversations. Bert muttered to Sam, 'It seemed to me like your lot want to avoid the words sin and the devil when baptising new innocents.' His friend resolutely focussed on the Bishop who was walking towards them.

Sam whispered from the side of his mouth. 'You have always been faithless, and long ago I decided not to make you good again.' He put a finger on his lips.

★ ★ ★

The physicists listened to the throaty roar of Bert's Merc as they raced towards CERN. It gave them an hour of private thinking time. Sam could remember the exact details of their meeting with CERN's directors when they had agreed to doubling of the LHC power to commence from 2015. Flushed with success after finding the Higgs Boson, the board chose to ignore the dangers inherent in colliding matter and antimatter particles. The possible creation of a black hole was discussed, the theories expounded, and then it was denied. At the meeting Sam had mentioned the theory from twenty years before, where the possibility had been conceived, but at half the planned experimental energies of 2015. As they hammered along the autoroute, he thought about his children and how they had grown-up in the decade it took to build the conceptual model. Could it be? Had the actuality, the impossible dream, created a piece of the past whilst searching for Man's future. A hole in space and time that no one noticed because Man wasn't clever enough. To be forgotten by Man, an afterthought that may or may not matter. He swallowed, his mouth was dry, glancing at his friend, he wondered if they could have caused the HB storm? Could they? Surely, a microscopic event on earth could not affect anything in the cosmos. That is what his erstwhile colleagues had predicted at least.

★ ★ ★

The shed was a roughly bolted together cube of thin metal panels with a louvred door. It had become Bert's office a year earlier. Exasperated by the noise of his team conversing inside the LHC control room, he had demanded some thinking space from the Director General of CERN, Professor Ralph Moyeur. The cheap carbuncle was Ralph's way of assuaging Bert and also of keeping him out of the way of the rest of the beauty team. The team's roles within the experiments were meticulously planned and designed to answer every question in a strict and rational sequence. Bert's methods were both more imaginative and spontaneous. He would throw out ten ideas for each question in his mind, before imagining his way to the correct answer for part of a question. Then he would repeat the exercise, exasperating his team who were glad for some respite by his absence.

Sam's laptop hung halfway off Bert's lap as he jiggled his legs beneath it. A bright yellow ethernet cable plugged him into the realities of Sam's discoveries. Bert looked at his friend for confirmation.

'That's 1700 HBs in the last 24 hours, across the full 150 million sensors of the HB detector?'

Sam replied carefully. 'But you can see the hits aren't consistent. The flow varies randomly minute by minute.' He paused, listening to Bert clicking the keys. He reinforced the stark fact. 'There are no experimental collisions created by us, Bert. The last few days there were, yeah, but this proves the HB level is set by something else.'

Bert scratched his chin, 'By default therefore, the particle collisions must be happening somewhere out in space. But God in hell knows what particles are colliding, never mind why.'

Sam leaned towards the laptop screen to look at the latest set of data piling in. 'So we need the astrophysicists to look for an extraordinary event out there. Then we can analyse and predict an outcome.'

'KK, if there is no event, there is no prediction, and so no outcome.'

Professor Jackson's energetic explanation of the LHC to his Japanese tour group bounced across the silence in the shed. Bert and Sam glanced down from their window and listened for a brief moment as he lectured a group of visitors on the concrete screed below them. He was dressed casually in shorts and a T-shirt but earnestly addressed the suited, serious and equally earnest group. Bert waved in acknowledgement to Jackson's outstretched arm before turning to Sam to ponder the HB storm. 'After 50 years of academic theory of HBs, we know nothing, do we, fact. It's bonkers but maybe we created a permanent black hole here?'

Sam coughed into his cupped hand before answering. 'I can't stop thinking the same, mate. But we did the maths and any hole should have instantly dissipated as it would be so tiny.'

'If we did it to ourselves though…'

'We would have got too close to God and I for one, don't think that we are that clever.'

Bert was smiling. 'Your ex-head of department would have had an answer. Listen to the old man below.'

A muffled Jackson continued outside. 'Beneath us, we have the most complicated scientific instrument ever made and yet we know so little. We run off the truth of the universe like a raindrop off a leaf. Up there in that window is Bert Leinster, the most famous particle physicist the world has ever known. Capable of thinking outside of this universe, and in charge of the latest experiments.' The polite Japanese stared awkwardly upwards, searching for that photo to take home of Leinster, the man described as knowing everything.

Bert moved quickly away from the window and all the attention. 'Listen to me, Sam. Our job makes life pale into insignificance but that doesn't give you the excuse to drift off into unreality. The God particle was discovered by man but God doesn't exist.' He held up his hand for silence. 'And it doesn't mean you have the right to layer emotional impacts such as God and the Devil on people's lives either.'

'Stop being so touchy, mate. I know how worried you are. I've concealed the HB storm for the last three days. Think about my stress levels, having bottled all of this up.'

'That's the answer, then.'

'What?' Sam struggled to stay with his friend's ideas.

'Share the issue with the scientific community. Get everyone looking for the answers as soon as possible.' Bert thumped the desk in triumph.

'Blood and sand, mate. You never share anything!'

'I look for answers and this is an answer when you are deep in the shit, pal.'

Jackson continued below them. 'The key part of your new instrument in Japan, is your ability to create a giant supporting campus like CERN. We have thirteen thousand people working here and a unique, open, and supportive organisation. So the LHC detector with a weight of one hundred jumbo jets and its eighteen hundred miles of cabling is not the crucial issue gentlemen. Thinking is crucial, thinking. Predicting the next particle to be discovered and then finding it can decades; so remember; you are in this for the long term.' He motioned at the nodding Japanese to follow him.

Sam collapsed into a chair, his face was grey. 'But what about us, Bert? Us, flesh and blood? If we change with this HB storm, who knows what else might change: Dark matter, gravitation? Anything can change… can't it?'

'Leave the why questions with me, Sam. We should divide our energies; you should concentrate on what is happening now.' Sam continued to stare into his friend's eyes. He needed reassurance. He needed to know that Bert wasn't scared like him. But Bert shrugged. 'Yes, of course anything can change and in fact anything has. Life goes on until we are dead, that's all.'

The last comment they heard from Jackson was a faint echo. 'Atoms formed from electrons and protons just three hundred thousand years ago and much later they joined to become molecules to create us. So we are new in a universe created fourteen billion years ago. We know nothing about nothing but only we can determine what the hell nothing is.'

Bert picked up his landline. 'Ralph? Sam and I are coming over to your house.' He tapped his fingers on his desk as the DG told him he was too busy for social visits as he was having a meal with his family. 'Listen to me, Ralph, we are coming now, whatever.' Bert nodded to Sam to affirm Ralph was up for an emergency meeting. 'Great! See you in twenty minutes and save us some food.' Bert dumped the handset on the desk with a clatter and picked up his denim jacket. 'Let's go.'

★ ★ ★

Sam sat on the edge of the settee in Ralph's lounge and took him through the scenario. There was one overriding element during the half hour meeting with Ralph. It was pure logic, not only in the scientists' brains but also in their hearts. The Director General trusted Sam and Bert and he didn't waste time looking at the data. It was sufficient enough to see the pained expressions on their faces. He told them he agreed that sharing the information and mobilising the scientific community of the world was the next step, although he thought he would get a bollocking off the ruling council. He set the time for the media briefing as 4pm on Monday. His last words to Sam were simple: the briefing must be a purely scientific matter to avoid the politics that would inevitably ensue and clash with the realities of the discovery. No matter what the science suggested, the people must believe in a future; no speculation, only fact. Sam realised the spotlight would be on him and broke into a cold sweat. Then Ralph dismissed them without any thanks so that he could speak to his PA and the twenty-one council members comprising CERN's national sponsors. It wasn't until later that evening that he considered the possible end of the world over a large Rémy Martin.

Bert slewed to a halt at the bland Gare de Cornavin in central Geneva so that Sam could take the next train home. Bert told him he wanted time to think and was returning to the shed. After gently closing the car door, Sam saw his reflection in the window. He saw more than the ageing effects of three day's stress, he could see the wide-eyed fear. He dearly hoped the HB storm would subside; hoping an issue might go away had always been his way of coping. Bert sped off in the Merc, leaving Sam scared and confused.

It wasn't until the terraced vineyards of the Lavaux came into sight that the beauty of the journey helped raise Sam's spirits. The 11th century steps of the Unesco world heritage site beckoned to him, demanded he forsake his worries to sit on a bench and sip the cool Chasselas wine. He stood and put his hands on the window as he gazed upward; this was a place to fight for, an allusion of perfect symmetry as the vines lay in their strictly straight lines. The setting sun enhanced the depths of partitioned colour and the metamerism between complementary greens and reds; the spectrum announcing the new life of spring. He collapsed back on his seat and watched the shadowed mountains of France, an hour's sail on the steady Séchard breeze. The whispering rigid railway lines taunted the quiet liquid lake. An occasional judder that lulled his senses until he fell into a deep sleep. But the lake remained calm and smooth. Water would be the least affected by the brewing storm.

★ ★ ★

After two restless nights of suppressed secrets, Sam stepped down from the bus at the magnificent Palace of Nations in central Geneva and stood by the iron gates staring at its splendid facade. He gripped the bars until the tips of his fingers went white as he contemplated the press conference due to start in one hour's time. Having passed through security he walked to the rear of the property in search of some solace. Here, the classicism building style perfectly complemented the panoramic grounds of Ariana Park, where the huge armillary celestial sphere rested in a small pond. He paused in it's dappled shadow and perched on the low wall of the pond. Dipping his hand into the water, he raised it slowly to let the drops spill in front of the heavenly constellations. His stomach growled as the acid purged his insides and his chest felt as if the sphere were resting on it.

Half an hour later, Sam walked slowly through the two monumental bronze entrance doors and into The Council Chamber. It was his first visit and he was surprised that it was a relatively small room, with a view to the park through five tall windows garbed in golden curtains. At the rear he could see a balcony graced the chamber, on high were large gold and sepia murals. The pictures were vast in their imagination; he had read they depicted the progress of humankind through health, technology, freedom and peace, and he felt insignificant beneath them.

Sam went to stand with Bert and the DG and watched the media assemble on the green leather chairs. He was sweating profusely and kept wiping his brow with a damp handkerchief. He thought about the peace negotiations that had been held in this daunting chamber and realised the real difficulty in any truth was never in the agreeing of the actions required. It was always about what could be expected from the people of the world after being told the truth. The human emotional response to a given crisis. And so history was going to repeat itself today and he, Sam Murray was centre-stage; he ran to the nearest toilet to vomit.

★ ★ ★

Sam sat by the DG, his foot tapping. As the clamour in the room subsided, The Director General commenced his introduction. 'In keeping with CERN's founding principles and the charter of nations created 65 years ago, we believe in no secrets and in sharing everything we discover. We believe in giving you the truth about all of our discoveries. But sometimes, we find something unusual, something outside of the norm, and we always wait until we have an answer before explaining it to you.' He shuffled his handwritten notes. Then he raised his head and his voice. 'This time, we have discovered something that we did not plan, nor predict, nor calculate. This time, it is not an experiment that has been given considerable thought and attention over many years. This time, we are shocked by our discovery and need your help.' A low growl crawled around the audience. 'We want you to tell every person across every nation across our world about our discovery. We want through you to enlist their help. I hope you will do that.' The journalists waited in silence to hear this new truth. Ralph continued, 'Let me say this, CERN can only determine the science. This time, the world itself must present a solution.' He waved to his left. 'Please let me introduce Professor Sam Murray, who made this discovery just four days ago. Sam…' He sat down and let Sam take the lead.

Sam coughed, his voice quavered. 'Ladies and gentlemen of the media and council members, we apologise for such short notice but my discovery has taken us by surprise. Until last night, when we met the Director, only Professor Leinster shared this knowledge.' He glanced nervously around him before sweeping his long grey locks back from his white face. He blinked his eyes to lubricate the tiredness and took a deep breath. Sam clicked his remote control and a pink, green and blue slide appeared on the huge screen behind him. It was headed, "The standard model and the Higgs Boson". Beneath the heading was a matrix of cloud cuckoo words and symbols.

'First of all, I will take a quarter of an hour to explain exactly what our universe is about.' He was terribly nervous. 'I mean it is, umm…a set of particles as shown on my slide of the standard model as we know it.' The assembled media's faces immediately went blank as they had heard it all before, this was old and boring news. IPads and laptops were placed under their seats, arms tightly crossed and an odd, quiet and sidewise discussion began. Sam had turned to the screen having cringed inwardly at the obvious rebuke. The journalists wanted the sensational news, not a drawing relating fermions, bosons and force carriers. Taus, gluons and charms were meaningless for them and to 99.9% of their readers.

* * *

Bert watched the bored audience carefully as he fidgeted in his seat beside the Director General. 'Oh shit.' He suddenly leaned forward towards his microphone. Pressing the "mic on" button he interrupted the rambling of his best friend. A characteristic interruption that had been endured for so many years past by Sam. He immediately sat down in relief to listen to Bert. 'KK. Stop looking so bored as this is the most serious story you will ever cover.' All the journalists and council members turned to him. They all knew the maverick Leinster pulled no punches. 'There are elementary particles that make up the world we see, the world we are. That is here on earth, and also particles arriving from space, arriving from our universe. Over many years scientists have dreamed up more and more names as we increased our knowledge in experiments such as those at CERN.' He clapped his hands together loudly. The shock wave ran around the acoustic chamber. 'Collide any elemental particles from the list presented by Professor Murray and then see what happens. Easy, hey?' He smiled at the assembled reporters. 'You all learned at school about electrons and protons?' He looked around. 'You did, didn't you?' They mostly nodded. 'Well, protons are made up of three quarks. Get my drift? Everything is made up of something smaller and smaller with a weird name, and as we announced in 2012 the Higgs Boson, or the media's stupidly named "God particle", glues it all together. The HB gives particles mass, that is weight. No mass and we would spin off the face of the earth.' Fingers were paused on keypads; luckily there was nothing new to report as he swept quickly onwards. 'The combinations of all these odd named particles have changed since the start of the universe, Big Bang. The mix will undoubtedly keep changing but over millions of years.' There was a long pause. He looked at the faces nearest to him at the front. Those on the balcony were in shadow and indistinct as the light faded through the five giant windows. He judged the assembly was now ready for the announcement. 'The problem is ladies and gentlemen, suddenly, and for no apparent reason, Professor Murray started seeing many more than the normal level of HBs hitting our detector in the old HB experiment.' He held up his hand for quiet. 'To be less than exact, and I am sorry for this; we are seeing huge numbers, far above any previous experiments we ever conducted.' He paused to look at the audience sat on the edge of their seats. 'Huge numbers colliding with our earth, when we have no, I repeat no, experiments taking place at all.' There was a general gasp but no questions yet. Most of them didn't understand the implications. He glanced at the front row of seats, the council members did and sat rigidly. Bert rushed onwards. 'And that is bad, KK? Because something, someone, somehow, has stuck a giant spoon in our universe and is starting to mix up our bowl of particles. Like making a chocolate cake but adding strychnine. Frankly, this may not be a good thing.' Bert sat down abruptly, leaving the media in consternation. Dozens of journalists immediately shouted questions across each other.

★ ★ ★

Sam stood up again. 'Ladies and gentlemen, please.' The clamour in the room had reached an uproar. 'Please. Please let us finish.' He ended up shouting into the mic to try and regain the initiative before collapsing again.

A roar of identification rolled out of the media, the name shouted out was Professor Leinster's. CNN had been the first network to raise a hand. The journalist had stood up now and was waving it high above his head. He had the loudest of all the shouts and could be heard by the majority of the room. 'Professor Leinster, are we talking like, there is a nuclear bomb, detonating above us? Like we are going to die.' Bert noticed the room had suddenly become quiet. He didn't reply, in fact none of the scientists replied. It was not a question they had prepared for and he had not really contemplated death.

The BBC jumped in and added a second question for Bert, less apocalyptical. 'What is causing this? What is the abnormal HB level going to do to us?'

The three questions were bold. A door squeaked closed at the back of the room as a journalist sneaked out. Bert stood and sighed deeply. Holding his palms upwards and to his sides, he replied, 'We don't know how badly it may affect us, but we do know it will. We do know that HBs are bad for the human body simply because we are made of particles and the HBs must interact with us somehow.'

Bert turned to watch his best friend. Sam had curled up inside himself and tuned out of the ordeal. Bert sat down abruptly. He felt himself fall into a void, nothing mattered, no one was there. He couldn't tell the world his thoughts. We may all die and really we don't know anything at all about the cause and effect. He glanced at Sam and caught his eye. He intoned a silent plea for his friend to say little, to stay sitting.

He thought on: What will happen, to the trees and plants? Will they wither and die? Will each particle in our body, each gene gradually meld into something new? Into molecules that do not constitute nor support life as we understand it? He knew one fact. The longer humankind stayed in the waves of the HB storm, the more matter they must lose in some shape or form. The more matter they lost, the quicker they would die.

CNN remonstrated with Leinster and jolted him back into reality, 'Can't you guess what may happen Professor Leinster?'

Bert jumped up again and continued with everyone's eye's following him. 'You have all seen "Star Trek" with its mythical transporter, yeah. Humans are 99.9% empty space and the tiny remainder is actual particles. So in theory, people could be broken down, transported and then reconstituted.' He started to unclench the fingers on his raised right hand. 'But if you leave the person's particles alone and instead you start adding one particle more and then another, and more and more… Well then, we can assume we change our molecular structure and our whole being. We would not be us anymore.'

'Would that be like having a cancer, creating an abnormal growth?' The lady reporter from the BBC was also standing now.

Bert replied carefully, 'I repeat, we don't know. You can speculate all you like and I am sure you will. Stupidity would be writing something like, are we going to get heavier?' He shrugged his shoulders. 'Look, I don't believe the change would be like cancer from too much sun or cancer from a nuclear explosion. No, not like that. It would be a far more subtle change, I think. I dunno.'

A man from National Geographic's science team shouted loudly. He jabbed an accusing finger at Bert. 'But you are the world's particle whizz kid, the youngest ever Nobel Laureate. You always without fail said you knew all the answers. And you never failed once, did you?'

Bert shrugged. 'I did say I know everything about particle physics but now I don't. Now that doesn't mean I have failed, because ladies and gentlemen, I never fail.' It was said with true conviction rather than arrogance. He always put his heart and soul into his research.

Sam had recovered and quickly jumped into the void as the group considered the implications. 'The main thing to remember is that there is no need to panic at the moment. The levels of HB are way below the strength needed to affect our bodies. No matter in what way the particles might affect us.'

The male CNN reporter had stood again and waited with his arms crossed. 'At the moment? Is that what you are scared of, Professor Murray?' Bert looked across at Sam and watched as he sat down again with a thump. He could see his friend was overwhelmed by tiredness and goodness knows what emotions.

Bert waved a forefinger left and right in front of his chest as he spoke for his friend. 'I'm not scared of anything logical. It is important not to deny reality. But stay logical and do not sensationalise this news.'

'So you know why this is happening, right?' The man from CNN was a pain in the arse.

Bert crossed his arms. 'How to describe the indescribable? Well, the Higgs Boson creates a field of virtual particles that pop in and out of existence. In existence, the virtual particles provide mass to others and that slows everything down. Like moving through treacle. But the treacle is getting thicker because of the HB storm and thus must affect other particles and the balance of our universe. That is what we need to analyse as quickly as possible.'

The Director General stepped in. 'No, we can't describe what might happen. It is abnormal but we do aim to find out what might happen. As the DG, I am warning everyone that it is happening and everyone should start to think about the consequences. Increased examination of this HB storm by the world's scientists and governments will help resolve any issues caused by it.'

Bert quickly added above the roar, 'Don't think about why this is happening, leave that to the particle physicists. Think what, when, where, and how. Within minutes of this briefing, of your vital reporting of it, we will have eleven thousand particle physicists looking at the data around the globe. That means for twenty-four hours a day, seven days a week they will find solutions to the issues the HBs will cause. We at CERN will focus on the question why. We will find the answer.'

The Director General motioned for the audience to resume their seats. He waited a few minutes after touching Bert lightly on the shoulder to reassure him he was taking control. 'Ladies and gentlemen, may I remind you of the point of this news conference. I am sorry we cannot give you more information. The basic facts are now online at CERN.ch under "HB storm". I am also sorry, we cannot take questions, as frankly, crazy as it may seem, we have no answers.' He lowered his voice and spoke gravely. 'But, we have a potential problem that affects the whole world, all eight billion people. No one can stand alone on this matter.' The DG expressed every ounce of his conviction. 'Now you know about it. By tomorrow all eight billion will know. At present, there is no solution and there is no answer to an imponderable problem. Now the governments and scientists of the whole world can start to consider the implications and provide that solution.'

★ ★ ★

The reporters had left the chamber within thirty seconds of his final words. Within ten minutes the western world saw the media's initial reactions.

"IS THIS THE END OF THE WORLD? EOTW?"

"THE TRUTH IS OUT THERE – WE HOPE!"

Sam traipsed out of the chamber as he turned on his mobile. Within a minute Briony was on the line. 'Oh Sam, my darling, Sam. Why didn't you tell me? I would have kept it secret.'

'I am sorry, love. The whole thing has been overwhelming and I didn't want to worry you.'

'You are silly, taking onboard all that stress. Promise me you'll never keep anymore secrets.'

'I promise, my love. By the way, how did you find out?'

'It was chaos in the laboratory, everyone's mobiles were dancing on the desks. Twitter, Facebook, Snapchat and Instagram were all howling out the same message, you know. So we put on the TV and there was the breaking news on every single channel we tried.'

Sam was back in the fresh air, he paused and punched his words out. 'You know what will happen now; every TV channel or radio station will find a pet scientist to scare their viewers or listeners. It will be the same madness the world over. Instant decisions, instant "EOTW" conjecture and instant misrepresentation.'

'Don't be angry Sam, not with me. Just come home and give me a hug, OK?'

'That will be the best part of my day. At least the scientists know the issue before the governments and so they can prevent any cover-up.'

'You did it, my Sam discovered... wow! Darling, do you know how much I love you?'

'Proper love, I know. But now we will have the avalanche of theories. A front, a barrier to the shock and denial that everyone will experience, like I have over the last few days. My God, what...' He said his goodbyes and promised to rush home before turning his mobile off, stabbing at the button and leaving the 60 missed calls in a distant router.

★ ★ ★

Having left the building by a discrete rear door, Sam collapsed into the Merc beside Bert. He wanted his friend to reassure him as they hit the rush hour traffic on the autoroute heading eastward along the lake. 'Can we be saved, Bert?

Bert stared through the windscreen at a never ending line of cars. 'Why are you so negative?'

'Because you are always so positive. That makes sense, doesn't it?'

Bert thought about it for a few moments. 'You always were like that.' He patted Sam's arm. 'We make a good team, hey?'

'A good team, Bert, always a good team.'

Bert laughed. 'Six billion Swiss francs invested in CERN and no one can tell us what is going on...?'

Sam's eyes blinked constantly as he turned away to look at the Jura mountains to his left. An Easyjet plane wallowed in the sky on its way to God knows where. 'Yes, Bert, one person can tell us what is going on...God. And we don't have a direct line to him.'

They fell silent and remained silent for the hour it took to drive home.

★ ★ ★

The DG sat in his darkened office at CERN, the exterior window blinds were lowered to cut out the reality of the world, the internal blinds to exclude the scared stares of his staff. But his face was illuminated as he read "The Times" editorial comments on his crisis, an online, instant response, trashed out by a journalist in the thirty minutes post conference.

"There are reputedly seven stages of grief. It must be considered as true, as there has been grief enough, the malaise in Man's history. The stages can follow the same logical sequence, or redistribute themselves in a haphazard manner. And grief has always been disturbing for the equilibrium of humankind's psyche. Grief over a deceased loved one. Grief over the end of the world. Hashtagged, Facebook'd as #EOTW, a depressive and instant abyss created in our so-called social networks that are truly anti-social. Shock and denial is already spreading through the hot-wires of the rumour mill via thousands of media companies and their reporters. But remember, this is not reality. All of them know nothing, absolutely nothing. Exponential hysteria about everything is the rule of the day, today and this week. Any information at the moment is not fact, it is so shallow and uninformed as to amount to nothing. I understand, in my media world, that minimal factual communications is the norm nowadays and now it is the only format that is both absorbed and believed. WhatsApp Instagram and Snapchat give an immediate view on the now, and nobody relies on history and the past as it is too slow and too boring for most. People live their lives in other people's lives and can miss life itself. As nobody knows what is going to happen, it is easier to fabricate the news, or should we say sensationalise the lack of news. As in times of war, everyone is gripped by the experience and the undercut of grief. Life will become a series of emotional expectations for a grieving humankind that has immediately locked itself into the cycle of the seven stages of grief."

Ralph rubbed his eyes and murmured, 'Providing an easy outlet for governments to falsely manage their population's expectations,' he leaned into the screen again.

"The first stage of grief is the denial of reality. A shock so huge that disbelief tempers the pain. But as this shock seeps through all the contrasting cultures on earth, it must lead to excruciating and unbearable pain for all people. The different religions, types of economy or nuclear families must all experience it. Suicidal pain for some and guilt for most, as they finally recognise all those things they should and could have done, but have not.

The third stage of grief is to come, an unleashing of people's anger. The blame will inevitably be directed at the scientists and the governments. A feeling tainted by a "why me" questioning of the inner consciousness and a bargaining with one's God, or one's lesser but more touchable fellow man. An effect, a plea to substitute the self for a loved one.

When all the adrenaline has dispersed from the anger, the depression will set in. Inward reflection and loneliness will come to the fore as we withdraw into ourselves.

Inevitably a calm must return with time, the timing set by EOTW. An inevitable timing providing a focus for the future. An adjustment to reality and requiring an organisation for achieving an acceptable plan on time. Giving us all hope eternal that Man will retain until the moment of his death. It will allow us to reconstruct our plans for life and most importantly all of our family needs.

This is how we humans deal with grief. Eventually, we will accept the facts. Not happily of course, but with an understanding that builds a dream for a future, our future and this will carry all of us through the toughest of times."

Ralph stabbed the off button on his screen and wiped away the tear running down his left cheek.

[2]

Denial of Reality

I T WAS THE first Sunday in June, and it was Father's Day. A good reason for Natalia to invite Sam's family to meet up for a celebratory barbecue and a first opportunity for the men to unwind after the HB announcement. There had been uncertainty for the world's scientists who were postulating what to measure and review. And cognitive dissonance for the rest of humankind – are we changing, am I bothered? But Natalia was bothered. She worried about the extra strain on her fading marriage; she was more worried about her Bert than a science fiction storm. The Bert who had been slipping away from her since his Nobel moment. She could see the new stress and strain taking a further toll on them. His out of world thoughts were slowly minimising her universal family.

She smoothed away her worries and prepared everything for the simple barbecue to be held at Chalet Suvarov. On the terrace above the swimming pool she placed a vase containing wild Lupins on the table, a pretty blue cloth to match the sky. She turned to look at the chalet she loved. A powerful pink statement, imposingly set on a hillock that clung precariously to a Prealp. She liked its history, the way it had absorbed the personalities of its famous visitors and now reflected their glories through the tall oak windows. She yearned to recreate the romance of the Princesses and country makers who had sung in the salon, idled in the Jekyll garden and walked the high pastures and cols 150 years ago. Her guilt tinged her joy, now it was an oil oligarch's asset bought using daddy's small change. A long term investment bolstered by the large plot that also ensured the absence of any neighbours unless bovine. She delighted in the regular chime of the cow bells echoing in the high ceilinged rooms throughout the spring as they continuously grazed nearby. But in summer, they departed for the high alpine pastures, leaving the delicious prairie grass to be scythed and baled by the farmers for winter fodder. Solitary, the pink house sat in the high and bright sun. A place of late rising for proprietors and sleep narcolepsy for growing teenagers. She wandered back along the path to see if anyone else was enjoying the day.

In the grand kitchen, Natalia held a greasy pain au chocolat in her left hand. She pointed it like a gun at her husband. 'The supermarket! You bought this "говно" from that hole, when we have the best boulangeries in the world?' Her distaste was manifest. She marched around the marble island to confront him.

'They're not that bad. The village bakers have taken a three week holiday as normal. You should know what the culture is like here. Family first, business second.'

'Moya Lyubov. Have you learned nothing in twenty years of marriage?' Her green eyes swept him up and drew him in. Her mind permutated his comment into work first, family second and wife third.

'Yes, the goat has learned to love you more.' She saw he was breathing faster, the first time he had been interested in her for months. Natalia came close and coiled herself around him, one calf nestling behind his. Her platinum hair was perfect, her lips red and full. She opened her cream silk dressing gown to reveal her full breasts. 'No.' He was adamant, his body was taught but she could see he wavered.

'Why not? You know you want me.' She caressed his engorged groin with her free hand. 'Let us go back to bed, my big man, or we can do it here?' She enjoyed teasing him.

Bert tilted his head to the left. 'Because.'

She threw the very limp pain au chocolat onto the black worktop. 'Huh, you are working too hard? Or am I too fat?' She placed her face a few centimetres from his. 'What excuse husband?' She shook him hard by the shoulders and ranted on. 'This has been going on…maybe you have the answer "да"? Maybe it is HB poison sterilising my man?' She paused for breath. 'Sure, these particles have polluted your mind many years "да".'

'Calm down, Natalia.' He held her away by the waist, gently squeezing its rolls. 'Listen. HBs are in my head and not in my underpants.'

She could see her bluntness was having some impact. She pushed him away but then changed her tack, closing again she placed her hands flat on his chest and murmured. 'Lyubov, you never even told me about this HB crisis. HBs are like a mistress to you!'

'Oh no, not true'

'True! You came home and you never even mentioned the stupid end of the world.' He was looking at his feet; so she demanded an answer by lightly slapping his bald patch. 'What is important to you, huh?'

He weakly remonstrated with her as he turned away to fill the kettle before switching it on. 'And you never listen to the news, do you Natalia? It was instantly splashed everywhere, on every type of media all across the world.'

'"Нет", not my point.' She tossed her hair. 'You should have woken me when you came home. You never kept secrets from me, and to find out…' She flung her arms in the air and let them drop dramatically to her sides. '"да" with a text from Briony…' She blew a pretty but insolent raspberry with her full lips. He felt the warmth of the air skirt his cheek.

Bert slowly spooned fragrant Darjeeling leaves into their old blue and white teapot. 'I couldn't tell you before the announcement and it didn't seem right to tell you late at night.' He tapped the spoon hard on the china. 'Why not before, you might well ask?' He opened his arms wide with his palms face up and invited an intelligent reply.

'I am your wife "да"!' She shouted from a metre away. 'Wife! Occasional lover. Best friend, sometimes. Remember me?'

He waggled his spoon in her face. 'I repeat, why you might ask? Because I signed a confidentiality agreement to keep CERN's business secret until CERN chooses to publish it.' He started to pour the tea. 'Because it was the most momentous announcement ever made to the world. It was not a night night, sleep tight type of chat. Was it?'

It was far too logical an excuse for her. 'Bert. I am your love and you did not tell me. Why did you not… how can I ever trust you "да"?' Her voice wobbled with artificial emotion. She grabbed a different pain au chocolat from the Denner supermarket bag and stuffed it into her mouth as she stamped around the room. Crumbs fell across the parquet floor. He watched the show; it was part of the fun of being together.

Natalia paraded around the marble island, which was in its usual state of disorder. Her eyes fixed on him, he was the target. Bert grabbed a small plate and chased his wife with it. She waved him away. 'Stop being so exact, Bert. A bit of mess never hurt.'

'But I like being exact.' He noted her sharpness had already lessened. He smiled engagingly as he handed her the plate and she took it.

'That's because you spend all day putting exact things, in exact places, with exact reasons. Life's not like that huh. Humans do not think "exact", dear husband. They…what you say… subconscience dwell on their emotions.' Her arms were raised high and wide. 'On inexact being, feeling.' She still wanted him, she was boiling over with desire. 'Remember them? Remember I am like the rest of humans and not a hard particle?'

Bert nodded his head with mock gravity. 'Subconsciously, like the rest. I agree! And you are my opposite so we attract my dear.' She yawned as he crossed his arms. 'But it's my job, Natalia. Being exact, making things fit. Because anything you can touch or see is in this universe or the seven other universal bubbles that exist.'

'All "говно".'

'Listen, somewhere, there is an exact truth and it is beyond our tiny piece of known space and way beyond the seventy billion miles we know of; and in all probability, a billion times further again. That absolutely demonstrates our inadequate knowledge of us and who we are, that is what I am trying to define.'

She sighed deeply. 'There you go again, big speech, talk talk, try listen listen, Bert. I just want my lover back, not the answer to everything. You have changed since your new experiments, as if…' She slapped her hands against her ample sides and tossed her hair as she changed her tack again. 'Do you really think anyone is bothered about this not likely, end of world?'

'Of course they're bothered, because it is likely and people think so because we have said it is.'

'"Нет", no one is truly bothered, Bert. Because it is not happening. There is nothing you can see. We are all exactly the same, nothing lost and nothing gained.' She smiled to emphasise the superiority of her points.

Bert was relieved, he had always hated an argument with her. He spoke quietly. 'Look at the steam coming out of that kettle. There are constantly more and more molecular vibrations in the phase change. Particles are spreading apart and thus further absorb energy from the heat source. My exact physics mentality is all around you!'

'"говно", get a life, Bert. What matters is now, today. The kettle is boiling for that nice cup of tea you are going to make me, my delicious man. Hot like you.' She couldn't understand his obsession with finding the fifth world, the meaning of life. But she rationalised that an argument had always made their sex better.

Bert started to pour the hot water into the pot. 'But truly it isn't now that matters, is it? What matters are the electrons and protons excited by the electricity used to boil the water. The status of matter before and then after heating. Anyone can understand now. It's not hard to see now, is it?'

'I see now Bert, make my tea!'

'But all those things you can't see, can't touch and can't hear are far more important in my world. Because everyone assumes the status quo and do you know what? It may not be valid one day soon, my dear, and I for one worry about it.'

She caressed his stubble with her buttery hand before pecking him leaving a red lipstick mark. 'Bert, my exact Bert. Where would the world be without you?' She wiggled his right ear. 'You know, I love you nearly everyday, sometimes every hour but you need to let go sometimes.'

He kissed her, a gentle touch on the lips. 'Why don't you love me forever?'

'Because forever is never.' As his hand smoothly slipped upwards and underneath the fold of her gown, the kitchen door creaked open and their daughter entered the room.

★ ★ ★

A frustrated husband marched his tea and pain au chocolat outside and into his garden paradise. His body ached for her but in the last few years he blamed her distractedness brought on by their teenagers' behaviour or her hormonal change for blunting his desire. He loved her on the particle level; he was negative and she was positive and he thought that was all that mattered. He strode purposefully down the path until he was standing in front of the etang. At the pool, he paused and watched the shimmering reflections from the rounded purple beech conflict with the serrated edges of cinquefoil. The fingers of marsh grass dipped languidly into the water. Their thin leaves like wind-blown TV aerials, drowning in the cold refreshing spring.

He started to talk quieter than the breeze. 'If I heard something, then it was when I was relaxed. It wasn't passers-by, they are too faraway and certainly not my boozy imagination at four o'clock in the afternoon.'

'It was a perfectly normal day when you were alone,' she said as a whisper.

'Bollocks'. It had been a favourite word of his for the last weeks. She cackled with laughter. The force of it made Bert abruptly drop to the verdant bank of the pool. The cup and food rolled into the water with two plops.

'So you do hear me, then?'

He spoke as an echo of Her soft voice. 'It's worrying, but hell, anything and everything can be considered as "normal" after the surprise criteria have been "normalised" by humans.'

'So you hear me?'

'Of course I can accept it could be true. But it's not normal, is it? Whatever "normal" is. And so in reality it's just bollocks.'

'What is normal, Bert? The HB storm? Black holes and multiple dimensions? Normal is about conforming to a standard and you do not conform. Normal is also relative, and relative can change in an instant.'

'And Einstein said, "When you are courting a nice girl an hour seems like a second. When you sit on a red-hot cinder a second seems like an hour. That's relative."'

'I agree, I heard him say that.'

Bert considered the options with a frown. Was he completely bonkers? Did other people have discussions with strange voices? Yes but they were all mad. Unlike him, unlike his normal. He stood and walked carefully around the pond shaking his head. He took a minute to mull it over as he kept his head bowed low and his eyes fixed on the giant white flower from whence the voice emanated. Eventually he asked it, 'How can you speak to me?'

'I'm not speaking, Bertie, you are listening.'

'Don't call me Bertie, my mother used to call me that when I was in trouble.' He paused. Had the flower heard his mother if it claimed it had heard Einstein speaking? So he asked her directly, 'Listening to what?'

'*To my essence. Listening to me, Lily!*'

'Define essence.' Bert was sharp with Her. Lily was a girl's name wasn't it?

'*We have been here since time began. Forged in the mud by pressure and heat. Our DNA was yours too. Maybe that is "essence" in your need for a definition? Who truly knows apart from me?*'

He sat again to listen more closely. 'Carry on. You have my attention, despite the impossibility of a lily speaking with me. Of course, you might be a reflection of my thoughts, bouncing off the meniscus.'

'*Clearly not, Bert, as I hear your thoughts but I am not replying to them. However, you may wonder what was the first dust of earth made from? Imagine it, spun in the cyclones of time, as the vortex created space and the universes. Maybe earth was seeded by a comet from a different universe? Who knows? Certainly you don't, despite your search.*'

'Bollocks, how do you expect me to believe any part of that?' He crouched low and as close as possible to the etang. He wanted to see if she moved as she spoke. He was disappointed as there was nothing moving. Not a tremble to disturb the mirrored surface, only his startled reflection.

'*You can't believe anything without proof, can you, Bert? But greater men than you have calculated starts and ends and nobody thought to calculate anything about us plants.*'

'In my view, numbers are always relative but inadequate. Calculations are meaningful or meaningless; five minus minus five is ten and that can't be right. I never had time for numbers. They are a confusion in life. Electrical polarity is slightly clearer, slightly more useful, but particle parity is the only plus and minus that truly counts.'

'Correct, professor. A balance of time and energy, matter and antimatter. You and I are relative to each other and so you are attracted to me. That is why you hear me.'

He started to walk away. He was puzzled because Lily sounded logical. He wasn't imagining it, if She could think so differently to him. He really had gone insane. She stopped him with Her call and he felt compelled to turn and look at Her.

'Remember your waking dream before you discovered the HB storm. We need you, Bert. You are the one. Logical and remorseless. Find the way to secrete yourself below the soil and hide with us. Your intelligence can help all the world to successfully hide and be reborn on The Return. Understand Man's ending and tell the world.'

He turned and strode quickly towards the house. A staccato walk, stop, turn and look at the etang, a shake of the head and a wring of the hands before setting off again. Fuck, he remembered every word he had imagined pre-HB. He stopped and put his hands on his head and stared at the mountains high above him. But she wasn't as logical as he had first thought, as he for one had no intention of an early burial. Bert didn't hear the other plants and trees in his garden as they chattered happily in the background, and Bert heard nothing more from Her, Lily. If he could hear Nature's debate on historical human issues, it would have alarmed him further, it would have driven a normal man insane. Nature laughed at the same pattern of human self destruction that loomed again. The flu after World War One that killed 50 million humans. The death of 6 million Jews in the camps. She debated death with her followers on a new scale as they felt the HB storm brewing. But this event was a billion times worse than anything in humankind's history. As Bert left the garden, Lily hissed, demanding their silence, and the natural world went quiet at Her command.

★ ★ ★

The two families relaxed on the terrace roof of the pool house. Directly in front of them was the lake that resembled a scimitar of burnished steel. Briony looked across at Josh and Liam and decided not to admonish them for having their feet resting on each other's grey wicker chairs. There were more important things in life. The boys were interactively playing "Badlands" on their iPhones, although the only interaction she heard was an occasional grunt. She blew out a long breath and moved her gaze to Allie and Hannah who were silently sharing Facebook updates on their iPad minis. She had befriended her daughter on Facebook to watch her mood, to detect any early fears about the HB storm, but so far all seemed calm and that was a relief. Sam smiled crookedly at her, he and Bert were on Weissbier, a lot of Weissbier. They were addicted to the wheat and barley fermentation that gave it a unique taste. She waved a no with her forefinger but she truly meant yes, drink more and relax. Several large steins had already soothed most of the mens' worries away. Which left her best friend Natalia as her only concern. She could feel the discharge between a negative Natalia and a positive Bert, they were poles apart. They had argued over ketchup on burgers or not; on or none, a constant to and fro, and even the vignoble for the Syrah. It was the worst since their last bad patch in 2012. Briony grabbed the bottle of red Valais wine and poured her friend another glass. It would help them mirror their relaxed husbands' behaviour.

Sam slurred his words as he told the two wives how positive his week had been at CERN. 'The first sample of The Envelope is umm...due here next month,' he hiccuped, 'However, I doubt if we'll be able to test its efficiency. There's too much work, not enough time.'

'No worries pal, take it at face value hey. After all three weeks to find and develop a polymer to deflect HBs is some feat, don't you think?' Bert wasn't negative but equally he wasn't very positive, despite the alcohol.

'There is an obvious answer, mate. The Chinese were developing it before the HB storm, you got it? They needed it for their space exploration, the equivalent to Voyager yeah.' Bert mumbled something under his breath as Sam garbled on. 'It's specialist and lightweight to encase the insides of new space probes.'

Briony encouraged her husband. 'I remember Voyager as a child, isn't it still moving away from earth 30 years after its launch?'

He clung on to her support. '41 years to be precise, but the probe will expire soon because it can't take the impact of many more plasma waves as it closes in on the sun.' He tapped his nose, 'That is why the Chinese are so clever.'

Bert interrupted him, Briony thought he was rude, but that was Bert. 'Where did this Envelope come from exactly?'

Sam turned away from his wife and back to his friend. 'Remember Wang, the director of High Energy Physics in Beijing?'

'Yep, he was a cool guy.'

'He told me that it was developed in a secret facility at the Jiuquan Space Centre.'

'And who was it that tested and proved that it protects humans from HBs?'

'They did, of course! The Chinese scientists at…Jiu…wherever.'

Bert raised his eyebrows. 'I sincerely doubt it. They have a tiny collider in Beijing and there is no way they could create HBs like we managed to. No way!'

Briony smoothly came to Sam's defence. 'Hmm…I am sure they did, Bert. Didn't they, Sam?' Briony was certain there was an answer. She had the wrong concept of the time, money and intelligence to create even five HBs a day, despite years of listening to her husband.

Sam gave Briony the positive reply she required. 'Yeah, of course they did. They had a secret collider facility at Jiuquan since 1958, as long as CERN. Like…amazing'

'Ffur.' Bert wrapped his lips around his stein and sank half of the contents in three large gulps. He burped loudly. 'So secret, that the CIA and MI6 didn't know anything about it?'

'Of course secret, mate. Just like the ground based missile that they used to destroy their own satellite in 2007.'

Briony noted that Sam was happy to believe the unsubstantiated explanation for The Envelope; the whole world had instantly latched onto the concept. It was their potential saviour. Briony was equally irked, 'I remember that on TV. Aren't the Chinese teaming up with the USA to manufacture an anti-missile shield and then to place it near the Russian borders?'

'More red, Briony.' Natalia shakily pushed her glass towards her friend. 'More Russian red, do not trust the shits.'

Sam nodded eagerly to his wife. 'Absolutely, darling! A joint defense system ever since the Russians decided to throw their weight around in Syria.'

'"да"! My father was buying gas rights there. He did not care about the war, only money.'

Bert looked at his wife askance. He returned his gaze to his pal, 'And the Chinese are going to use a combination of Yin, Yang and Fengshui to locate these missiles.'

Allie had been listening closely. She made a timely interruption into the argument by asking her dad a question.

'All my friends on Twitter are asking me to describe this Higgs thingy…Will you tell me what it is again please?'

Bert smiled at her. 'Higgs particles exist for a fraction of a second and make other particles heavy. Too many Higgs and the other particles move slower, like moving through treacle and that changes everything. That is 32 words OK?'

She handed the iPad mini over to him. 'You don't get it, do you, dad. Can you type that in with less than 140 characters? And dad, like er – far more simply?'

Her brother laughed openly at his sister's ignorance, whilst Liam and Hannah politely smiled. Josh teased her wickedly. 'C'mon…sis, your friends won't get it anyway. We're talking about trillions upon trillions of extra HBs hitting our earth.'

'You doik, you think you know everything.' She tossed her hair and looked away.

He slowed his speech. 'More treacle to tread more slowly, more interaction with dark matter, and our dads have no idea what may result.' Josh added, 'And dad, by the way, you used 31 words.'

Hannah leaned forward this time. 'My friends, not just Allie, don't need all the scientific talk, Josh. They just want to know if we can avoid the Deeps, assuming it gets worse, of course.'

'What's the Deeps,' asked Allie.

'Anywhere below the earth, you know, it's just an expression that has appeared across social media,' replied her friend.

Liam crossed his legs, still supported by his friend's chair and kept his head bowed as he commented. 'Look sis, your friends, are all Christians and are searching for Armageddon. The coming of the four horsemen of the Apocalypse!'

'Whoa, hold on there bro.'

'Never mind the horses,' Josh stood up. 'Listen, we have radiation particles hitting us that penetrate everything. Supposing you knock out an electron in our body somewhere, then it may make us mutate and all that stuff. Is that simpler?'

Hannah stood up to face him. 'I do understand, you know. Girls aren't thick! Of course, it's impossible to overstate the importance of our dads's discovery.' She couldn't resist a jibe. 'Maybe boys will be mutated but girls won't as we have different DNA?' She clapped her hands together loudly and once only to signify the end of the discussion. 'Thus leaving us women to rule the world.' She pumped her fist into the air.

Briony cut short the brewing disagreement. In reality there were eight differing views around the table and another eight billion more around the world. 'Hmm, I like treacle on my porridge every morning, so if we have more treacle, does that mean we need to eat more...?' She knew it would be sufficiently boring nonsense to encourage the children back into their electronic worlds. She turned towards the other adults as the teenagers returned to their ether. 'I feel like I'm the muggins round here. We had so little information about anything at their age, we couldn't argue about things like they can now.'

Sam remarked, 'They have instant universal knowledge to hand on a 5G network.'

Natalia chipped in. 'In Russia, we were lucky to have a few textbooks "да". My father sent me here to learn. But now learning is dumber and quicker. I say, better clever with news the day after.'

'Oui, oui, true and dare I say scary,' replied Briony, 'and of course there is an instant emotional reaction to any news, even when it isn't factual. That worries me, especially for our kids.'

'But now we have changed for the better "да"? They show no fear of the HB storm; they share their thoughts with friends and support each other.'

Briony knew that Natalia was right. The children also saw the event "as is" and not as it could be in the future. It was a slight comfort to her as she watched them carry on as normal. Maybe, she hoped, adults could do the same. She turned to watch her friends.

'Natalia, you never learn, do you.' Bert grimaced. 'The kids need to talk about practicalities for god's sake. They share their reactions rather than emotions, but they need to think outside of the box. Literally, that is!' He pointed at the four kids with their current and never ending obsession with electronic boxes.

'Bert is right, girls,' said Sam. 'They have no idea about essentials that may help us through the crisis like reductionism or electron tunnelling.'

'We have,' said the boys in unison without looking up.

'What,' exclaimed Briony.

Liam continued with an explanation, 'Reductionism is a philosophy to solve problems. Break them down into smaller and smaller parts and you eventually solve the overall problem.'

'But Liam.' Hannah was retaliating for the earlier attack on her. 'Reductionism hasn't told us how we understand consciousness. I was only talking to the vicar in Vevey about it last week.' Briony preened her parental pride as her enlightened children argued. 'And neither does it explain romantic love.'

'I concede that, sis. Science can't answer everything but neither can God.'

'God helps, though.' Everyone was surprised by Allie's comment. She looked up. 'I do have some thoughts you know. I'm not just a socialite!'

Her surprised mother asked for everyone: 'What do you mean daughter?'

'Well, my friend at school is a Jehovah's Witness and he's really nice. Like, really cute.'

'And?' Natalia quickly prompted her as she veered off script and into sexual connotations.

'And he says "the great tribulation" will climax at the battle of Armageddon. All of humankind who are not doing God's will are going to be dead meat.' She picked up her plate and scraped some scraps of burger onto the central pile of rubbish.

Hannah moved closer to Allie and put an arm around her. 'We do see that our friends are scared, Auntie Natalia. When I tell them that Jesus Christ will return and reign eternally. Well, they need more than that. It's not good reductionism, is it? But if I then tell them an Antichrist will appear at the end of our world, that really freaks them out.'

Natalia was deeply moved by the girl's spirituality. It also made her feel uncomfortable, inadequate as a mum. 'Girls, if the Devil sails in on the HB storm, then we have truly lost.'

Bert rebuffed her again, 'I certainly wouldn't give up so easily.' Briony saw her friend wince at the harshness behind his words.

Allie was hugging Hannah in return. She gave her cheek a peck before responding to her mum: 'But then Hannah tells us the Bible teaches that Christ will come back to the earth to destroy his enemies. He will make the world a better place and establish peace.' There was a collective but silent "ahhh" around the table. 'It's compassion like that which makes Hannah my best friend.'

Briony could barely speak due to the lump in her throat. 'That is exactly what will happen, children, hmm…so you mustn't worry about anything. That includes our two junior professors.' She looked across at Natalia for reinforcements.

Natalia spoke gently, 'Remember your dads are the most brilliant physicists in the world and are trying to save everyone.' There was silence for a couple of minutes. Then Allie handed her iPad mini to her father once again. 'In Twitter terms, what's tunnelling?' They all laughed.

★ ★ ★

Lily squirmed her rhizomes deeper into the mud of the etang. Their talk of God and the Apocalypse was premature. But she took comfort in the constant communication of the weak faith shared between the humans. Any instant and repeated untruth was non-reversible and to Her advantage.

As Lac Léman flushed pink, Sam and Bert walked away from the group. They strolled towards the forest at the foot of the garden so that they could catch up on each other's thoughts. They paused to watch the magnificence of the life-giving sun disappear below the distant Jura mountains.

'Well, Sam, did you manage to predict how many HBs will be hitting the world at a possible end point?'

'Umm…the best guess is a US centillion. Then there is no life above ground and only mole-like humans below.'

Bert grunted. 'That's enough, then.' They walked on but in total silence. Their faces were rosy from the sun and beer, relaxed although thoughtful. Lily wanted to tell them that the storm would grow stronger than anything they could predict because she felt the metamorphosis better than any man-made detector. She held her piece, she would only speak with Bert. He continued, 'I guess we want the unpredictable to occur; a dramatic reduction in the HB count.' She thought he was a stupid fool, she was planning on his stupidity compared to Her intelligence. 'I've been thinking, Sam.'

Sam gently touched his shoulder. 'Tell me.'

'When a particle of ordinary matter meets its anti-particle, the two disappear in a flash, as their mass is transformed into energy. They annihilate each other, equally. We think equal amounts of matter and antimatter must have been produced at the Big Bang. Or has that always been a wrong assumption by us all?'

'No, you can't say it was wrong. Too many physicists have studied it and the evidence seems incontrovertible.'

Bert continued. 'KK, so why didn't matter and antimatter completely annihilate each other after the birth of the Universe? "Why", is my biggest question. Because I think, if I find the answer to "why", then I can understand the HB storm.'

Sam dragged Bert's shoulder back to stop him walking. 'I never understand how you bounce around inside your mind.' He gripped it tightly. 'It's true in all cases that a particle in one class always has a superpartner in the other class, a "balancing of the books". If you think you can challenge this supersymmetry and unify the three fundamental forces, you will be a true genius, mate.'

'I am a genius, I know that but think, at high energies we have seen evidence of particles moving between our world and some unseen realm.'

'True, we saw particles suddenly disappear into another dimension in the last experiment in April.'

Bert hesitated. They were passing the etang containing the talking lily. Maybe his friend would think he was bonkers if he told him about Her? Maybe she was listening? 'By definition, particles originating from an extra dimension could suddenly appear in our world. That has to be considered too, yes?'

'Blood and sand, are you trying to tell me that the LHC experiments not only bordered other dimensions but also broke into them?'

Bert shrugged his shoulders. 'I don't know, pal. Over the past billion years, nature has already generated as many collisions on Earth as a million of our LHC experiments but the planet still exists.'

'I remember the CERN safety report before we started experimenting,' said Sam. 'There was no basis for any concerns about the consequences of new particles or forms of matter that could possibly be produced by the LHC.'

Bert wouldn't let it go, for a few seconds his eyes searched the etang for any signs of life. He listened intently to the silence. 'The LHC might well have created a microscopic black hole but we calculated the risks of a "killer strangelet" in a catastrophe scenario. The reality is, we never seriously inspected that risk.'

'No, but any holes would quickly disappear. They would decay into the same particles that produced them.' The theories had satisfied Sam at the time, although they had been unproven.

Bert replied slowly and deliberately. 'You must realise, we need to find the illness and not treat the symptoms. But we can't treat the symptoms anyway, can we?' Sam gave him no response.

Briony plunged beneath the surface of the swimming pool; within a few seconds she broke the surface and gasped before disappearing again. The water transposed the alcohol as it washed her eyes, with glittering bands of sunlight imploring

SOMETHING TO TELL YOU

her to remain below. It was too fresh to delay so she kicked hard to reach the cascade wall. Hanging onto the rough concrete with her elbows spread wide she spotted her friend wrapped in a blanket on a lounger. Another glass of red wine was at her lips, made redder by the sunset. Turning away, she saw the gloom of the black mountains opposite were spreading into the lake in a battle with the dwindling light from the west. She sized the sun using her fingers as gun sights, goalposts to target her emotions. She knew what to do. Three strokes took her to the steps and Natalia. Rubbing her hair vigorously with a towel made her hard to understand. 'Thank you girl. It gave me one of those moments in life to be treasured.'

'It is nothing. 21 degrees is madness.'

She dried her legs. 'True but awesome. Are you OK?'

Natalia moved with an effort, clutching her empty glass. 'In a quiet home dwells the devil.'

'Yes, I've heard that Russian expression before. And you also say "there was and there wasn't".' She could see the tears in her friend's eyes.

'What will be will be is not the answer I want. The cold has gone to your head.'

Briony enclosed her arms around her woolly friend and whispered. 'C'mon…keep going.'

'The selfish goat, my super intellectual Pan is mad. Searching, searching, searching.'

'Sam tells me the same. Bert does no real work now as the fifth world has monopolised his time.'

'But I love him, the kids need him.' She convulsed and hid her head in the mohair. Her friend shivered as she held her more tightly. It took the deepening darkness to bring them back to earth.

After Bert had searched the receding pond, they continued back to the pool house and their families. Natalia chided the men on their arrival. 'So, you have been considering life on a particle level. Logical and precise "да".'

'Of course not, Bert and I were remembering the children's words this afternoon. I go to church as I have faith in humankind. So the God particle was created by something, or someone.' Natalia nodded in agreement.

Bert threw his arms in the air. 'And what Sam said is neither logical nor precise, you stupid woman.'

Natalia shouted back. 'There you go again. There are other ways of living life, you know. With emotion, you might try it "да"!'

'I am emotional about stuff like nature,' said Bert defensively, 'especially plants like my marguerites. I cherish and love them every morning by cutting away the dead heads and every night I water the pots. By default I am therefore an emotional man.' He paused and pointed a finger at the etang. 'In fact, I can talk to plants.' Briony laughed as Sam and Bert scraped out two chairs and sat clumsily next to their families. 'I accept all your criticisms, I know I am an awkward sod but someone has to be.'

Bert turned to listen to Liam who was explaining the plot of "Angels and Demons" to Josh, the book by Dan Brown that involved CERN. He loved the book and offered to lend it to Josh. 'I know it's probably not serious enough for you, but it's about the end of the world, like now maybe.' Josh shrugged for Liam to continue. 'The CERN director discovers one of his physicists has been murdered. The dead professor's chest is branded with an ambigram of the word Illuminati.'

Hannah interrupted him. 'What's an ambigram?'

'I have no idea, I hate English. Anyway, they discover that the Illuminati have stolen a canister containing antimatter and they only have twenty four hours to save the world, after which matter and antimatter will join together and cause an explosion a million times worse than a nuclear bomb.'

'Is the book any good?' Asked Josh. He yawned and raised his eyebrows.

'Quite frankly, no. But it's just like our dad's experiment and in one scene the Pope meets with a physicist who believes that antimatter is capable of establishing a link between humanity and God.' Bert put his hand to his mouth and then slowly stroked his cheek with his fingers.

Briony rose from her chair and grabbed her son's arm gently dragging him to his feet. 'An ambigram retains its meaning when viewed from a different direction or perspective. And on that note "leave must we".' Pleasantries were exchanged and the Murrays climbed into Sam's old Toyota Prius. Bert escorted them to the gate and happily watched them glide away down the lane, whilst Lily watched over all their confusion and was equally as content.

★ ★ ★

Natalia sprawled in bed beside her husband, they were on their backs in the dark, rigid and with a large space between them. She quietly asked him a question: 'The news about the HB storm is all via the internet. But that is because everyone absolutely believes it, "да"'

The statement made Bert feel uneasy. 'Well, it works, I guess. The Higgs countdown predictor is coming out soon as an App. It makes it easy and instant so people can see we are below the danger level. Simple and electronic is what people demand.'

Natalia stifled a yawn. 'I imagine that today could be our last day of peace, despite you upsetting me.'

'It can't be that gloomy for you, can it?'

'It will be soon, moya Lyubov. Everyone will feel overwhelmed. Not the children; I think the adults will crumble first.'

He thought carefully before he replied. 'But nothing has changed. That's what you said earlier and most people don't seem bothered.' He knew everything had changed but people were denying there was a problem, they still believed that their lives would last forever. They were all denying the truth and the truth had just dawned and now had no setting.

She turned on her side with her back to him. He struggled to hear her words. 'But that is all for tomorrow and today is today, huh. So when you wake up, look at the words in your father's day card. I know you have not! It was Allie who found it in a shop in Vevey.' She remembered the exact words. '"A father is a person who stands beside you so that you never fall. And quietly moves away when you've learned to stand on your own".'

Bert could only picture the photograph on the front of it. There was a little girl feeding some ducks swimming on a pond. Stood next to her was her father. It was too sad a thought to go to sleep on. 'Well, at least I remember the photo on the front of her card. And I also remember Liam's for Sam. There's a boy standing and trying to fix his moped with parts spread all across the garage floor. Quote. "At this point I always think, what would dad do? On the opposite page was a bunch of expletives".' He waited for an answer but received none. It was a poor attempt to divert her attention.

'Goodnight, Bert. Happy father's day.' She closed her eyes and fell quickly asleep. Her husband remained on his back watching the light slant through the curtain, like a Crusader's sword, poised to exact God's wishes.

[3]

Lies and more Lies

S AM TROD GENTLY between the trollius which lolled
their yellow heads close to the marshy ground, refreshed
by the slow rain in the dark night. He shouted at his chocolate
Labrador to follow him, wondering if it was a stone marten or
a vole she was snuffling after. His voice soaked into the day,
alerting nobody to his thoughts and depression, the questions
in his mind about the HB storm. From the hilltop above Blonay
he could see the Alps in the distance but they were clearer than
any entombment underground, protected by The Envelope.
After that, all remained blurred. Was saviour an impossible
dream? He took a few deep breaths to recover from the slope
whilst looking at the hills misted below. The damp seemed to
be suspended in the air and his worries seeped downwards
to join it. An optical illusion that made humans and animals
pause to consider their surroundings. He turned towards
home with a shrill whistle at the dog. She splashed through the
waters soaking the ski runs leading to the Tennasses swamps,
her tongue bright in the distance. He glanced at his watch; he

had two hours before the meeting so he quickened his pace and whistled again.

The meeting with the DG in his office at CERN was always going to be quick, three weeks into the mayhem and with an unpredictable timeline. Sam spoke quickly, glancing at Bert as each point was made. 'So, in conclusion, Ralph, The Envelope will be available to all countries now the Chinese are ramping up production. The CERN team for coordinating the ideas from scientists worldwide is now complete and the databases set-up, but we need some big-hitters to help us. So anything you can do through the Yanks seems the best bet to me.'

The DG demanded further action. 'Has version two of the HB predictor gone live yet? You know I'm under pressure.'

'Yeah, job done and we have put it out as an App across most formats last Friday night. It's downloadable from any PC and of course available on all mobiles.'

'That's a relief, it's something for people to focus on.'

'Now no one can miss out on the good news as the HB count is pretty stable at the moment.'

Bert made an aside, 'Stability is not guaranteed DG and I for one would keep the Yanks out of our project.'

The DG held his cheeks in his hands with his elbows planted on the leather top of his desk. 'It is not a project. View this as the end of humankind, Bert.' He sat upright and held his hands palm upwards. 'Sorry for being abrupt, it's just the stress. You die if you worry, you die if you don't, so don't worry.'

Bert smiled at him. 'Who came up with that, boss?'

'Me. I said it five seconds ago and at present it makes sense yes?'

Bert responded kindly. 'Don't worry, boss, shit happens. It's just shit.'

Sam wanted to bring the meeting back onto the agenda and so he explained the technique for the HB predictor. 'We are guessing, as Bert says, that the HB storm is not going away. We also know that people are thinking that a slight reduction in the reading on some days, is good news. Whereas the overall trend is crap.' Bert and Ralph waited patiently. 'The Higgs cataclysmic limit is now set at a nominal level designated as level zero. That is the point when humankind must have expedited its saviour. We must be underground, out of our minds on cocaine or something similar as per our usual conversations everyday for the last three weeks.'

Ralph posed the obvious question. 'I will be asked when do you think we will reach zero?'

'Currently our team estimate it as March next year, but quite frankly, who knows.'

The DG waved a biro at him. 'Give me the subtleties as well please.'

Sam continued, 'We have launched the predictor as limit numbers, 5 10 etcetera. Zero stands for critical, be in a bunker with The Envelope protecting you. 100 is now, today, well 95 ish.'

Ralph placed his hands behind his head. 'Above zero we are all OK. That is the new message, yes?'

'Yeah, and the media advisers and the psychiatrists say it's working, people seem to be acting normally.'

Ralph sat back and swept his hands across his greasy grey hair. 'We predict the gradual but not the critical. We say there is no danger yet, but all hospital, Civil defence resources etcetera etcetera.'

'You've clocked it, boss.' Sam was fully behind the rescue programme. But inside, his belly fluttered. 'There really is no panic across the world; I know it's surprising but the experts say because the threat is so great and totally invisible, well everyone is in denial. All the polls suggest that people just need to lean on a solution.'

Bert sighed. 'And that is what you are giving them. The big lie.'

Ralph looked at Bert, who had remained quiet during most of the meeting. 'You have seen that the world governments have concluded we should all go underground and encase ourselves inside The Envelope.'

'Shove it, it's the big lie.'

The DG spoke very precisely, 'They have decided that we must meet all people's basic needs in these bunkers, these sanctuaries. They believe it is fundamentally good to pin people's hopes on the protection offered by The Envelope.'

'Bollocks.' Bert said it very loudly. 'Psychologically yes. Scientifically no, and for sanctuaries read graves.'

Sam hesitated before continuing to tell them about the worldwide myth being spun: 'There will be medical facilities in each bunker and all necessities from education to cremation in the biggest ones. These will be linked in someway to the ancillary ones, but we haven't agreed the mechanism. That is a typical reason why we need more resources, a bigger team.' His face glistened with sweat as he spoke. 'So, umm…the thing is, the world population believe the earth is a barrier to HBs and umm… with The Envelope, it gives them a chance of salvation. They err… believe the combination, that is earth and Envelope err…will slow down the number of particles penetrating their bodies.'

The DG rounded it off, 'And someday, the storm will abate.'

'As I said, it is all bollocks. A fucking fairy tale. And you both know that don't you?' Bert picked up his laptop and walked out, slamming the door behind him.

'Of course we know, Bert.' Ralph shouted after him. 'Simple and abrupt is not what we need!' Ralph turned to Sam with a sigh. 'So Sam, the Chinese plastic and a few hundred metres of soil might help us. If nothing else, it gives people a focus on survival, yes?'

Sam replied softly, 'I might even use the word faith. A faith in surviving.'

'Faith is a good word, Sam. From now on you are heading the science team responsible for our protection and any science requirements to do with The Envelope. I have already spoken to the Yanks as you call them and I'll also send you the key contacts for the worldwide protection teams by email.'

'And what about Bert?'

Ralph sighed. 'Bert is and always will be an enigma. We must give him all the time in the world. If he wants to concentrate on the reason behind all of this mess, then that's OK. Why did we get into it? I have no idea, but Bert may find out.'

'Do you think it was...'

'No, not us. Anyhow, he searches for the impossible as you well know and that leaves you to deal with the possible.' He looked up expectantly. He knew Sam would understand their roles.

'Job done,' said Sam. 'I'll speak with Bert later and make sure he understands and at least compromises.' They shook hands and Sam left. There was no choice, there only was.

★ ★ ★

Sam caught up with Bert an hour later. They faced each other in the shed. 'What's sodding up with you?'

'Nothing. No worries. The Chinese team have a protective envelope and expect to start shipping it worldwide within a month. They don't share the "recipe" and there is no independent testing behind it, because there is no real solution.'

'You have to trust someone, sometimes.'

Bert looked like he was sucking a lemon, 'You have an unbreakable faith, Sam. Faith in God, faith that everything will be alright, but I don't.' He crossed his arms.

'That's OK, you know.'

'Ffur, the predictability of the strength of the storm is getting harder, not easier. You've seen the huge peaks and troughs.'

Sam rammed his arms under his armpits and stamped around the room. 'I grant you that the intensity of the HB storm is uncertain. But why are we so quick with outlining a method for salvation you might well ask?' He opened his arms wide. 'You know the answer. No envelope, no hope. What time have we got? Four months? Six max? How many will die before we go below? That is assuming the theory around level zero is correct.'

Bert stabbed Sam hard in the chest with his forefinger. 'The predictor is wrong, as you well know. You cannot predict something when you have no idea what the effect is on humans. No, pal, believe what you like. No Envelope, no hope, is not the question. The question is, how many will die early because of going below?'

Sam stood his ground and pushed his friend's finger away. 'We have never agreed on everything but frankly, Bert, you always thought you were right.' Sam could smell Bert's garlic breath. He stood his ground. 'But you know what, mate? You can also be wrong!' Sam stormed out and crashed the door on it's hinges, leaving Bert holding his head in his hands. He wandered to the door that remained ajar from the harsh rebound. He closed it slowly on the world which was denying everything.

★ ★ ★

Four hours later, Bert's phone "tring'd" on his desk. The Director General's PA demanded he and Sam must go to the conference room behind the main CERN reception. He asked for the reason but was told to just get there now. Bert collected Sam with barely two words exchanged. In the car he watched his friend turn and scan the passing countryside through the side window. They sat in the conference room and continued their strained silence for a long twenty minutes. The closed vertical blinds covering the half-open windows flapped gently in the light summer breeze. They heard two, maybe three cars pull to a quick standstill outside. It could only be their visitor as CERN reception operated a traffic restricted zone. Two men walked into the room without providing any greeting. Lean, hard and in their early 40s. Dark grey suits, white shirts, blue ties and with jackets partly buttoned to hide their guns and radios. Bert smiled at them as they combed every nook and cranny and received a hard stare in return, the unspoken demand for complete silence. He turned to wink knowingly at Sam, who ignored his irreverence. After two minutes the secret service left and a grotesque enamelled smile fronted a lone man. He had a brown wrinkled face beneath his grey silvered hair. Mitch Donally had been well known to the physicists when he was the US Vice President. It was when he had several months left in office that he had ruled himself out of the Presidential race. His backing for Hillary Clinton as the Democrat candidate had seemed unequivocal. However, it was rumoured that his health, or his age had kept him out of the race that ended with a Trump victory. The truth was his adamant and immoveable views on Iraq, Syria and the Islamic Caliphate had cost him party support. Donally had backed the wrong policy.

'I'm pleased to meet you again, Bert. And this must be Sam.' He shook their hands warmly and pulled up a chair.

'Come straight to the point, sir.' Bert was abrupt but still smiling, whilst Sam was fiddling nervously with his mobile in the great man's presence.

'Of course, we have no time. But you know that most, out of all of us. In fact out of the whole world population, you are the two men who know the worst, don't you?' Donally smiled, encouraging some response.

'It doesn't sit easily with me sir.' Sam spoke hesitatingly. He tried a smile and received one back. 'The responsibility that is.'

Donally reassured him: 'You have no responsibility, son. You are the one we have to thank. Now you can focus on the science alone and leave CCOW to manage the disaster.'

Bert looked blankly at Donally. 'What planet are you on?' Donally's teeth gleamed back across the room. 'Let me guess about this CCOW. You are planning on exterminating everyone, leaving you and the bigwigs to survive, yeah.'

'The planet is the point, Bert.' Donally emphasised the name. He crossed his legs. 'As you obviously don't know from Ralph yet, I am heading up CCOW. The new body, Central Control of the World. I left a meeting of the G20 delegates who have also been elected to it about half an hour ago. We pulled them all into the UN offices in Geneva to guarantee secrecy.'

'Shove secrecy when we made everything very public from day one.'

Sam interrupted his friend. 'Please read waiting until a few things are in place so as not to scare the public, mate.' The T in mate was spat into the air.

Bert had vaguely heard about an idea for CCOW the week before. He had dismissed it as the Yanks trying to control the world as usual and hadn't realised they had other countries' backing. Now he knew they'd succeeded, he was glad that it was Sam's new job to provide the science behind this administrative and palliative saviour. To Bert, prevention was now off limits, but he didn't really care.

Sam painted a picture: 'CCOW will be the entirety, full stop. Everything will be communicated through the organisation and The World Council agrees the strategy, leaving the tactics to CCOW.'

Bert looked straight into Donally's blue eyes. He remembered the YouTube video of The State of The Union address a few years before. Most people commenting, were convinced Donally's eyes were reptilian, pure black and evil. 'So CCOW has been created to tell the lies and keep the world population towing the line, right?'

Bert shivered as the Ex-Vice President pulled the two scientists under his control. 'Correct. Without CCOW we have no world. No one toes the line, everyone loses the plot and bingo, there is no chance of survival for anyone.'

'I get the reasons to lie Donally and the need for a mechanism but...'

The VP's timing was perfect, 'And you know what Bert? Virtually every country has signed up to it. Blatant manipulation to retain control is accepted. And people are going to let us keep them safe and keep them calm because they have no other frigging choice.'

Bert exhaled and clenched his hands tight on the sides of the chair. He spoke calmly. 'That makes it even more unbelievable. Every country agreeing is a world first.' No one filled in the gaps. 'Hey, no worries pal, what's the lie you want telling, Mr. Vice President?'

'It's not a lie, Bert. It is a fact. We want you and Sam to support The Envelope; publicly, globally, vocally, unequivocally at the next media conference being set-up by CERN.'

Sam was the first to reply. 'Why wouldn't we, sir?'

But Bert interjected quickly before Donally could respond: 'Because it doesn't work and we know it. That's why. Nothing can work. It's a placebo.'

Donally shifted his legs and sat with them apart. His forearms rested gently on his quads and he smiled. 'You are a clever man, Bert. A serious man who wants the best for the world. So listen up. We have a plan. 196 countries will be sticking to the same plan. No deviation. No thinking. Just the plan.' He paused whilst they both took in the consequences. 'Let it go.' Donally stood and went to the door. Before opening it, he gave a final order. 'It's your choice, boys. Support The Envelope, support the plan and hope we save the world.' He left quickly, an agent behind the door closed it on the shocked couple.

Sam watched his friend. 'You can do it, you know.'

Bert grunted. 'The ultimate lie. Join us, be happy, go underground and die. Some choice we've been given.' He walked out of the room and left for home in his Merc, leaving Sam to catch the train.

Towards sunset, Bert stood motionless by his flower pots with a green watering can drooped in his hand. The plants had expanded, the tending gave him thinking time. He had started counting the dead heads since the start of the HB storm, up to twenty per plant each evening. He walked away from his task with a single sustained thought: What outside of our universe is causing this?

* * *

Natalia slurped at the thimble of vodka. It was nine o'clock and the kids were at school, Bert at CERN. She was wrapped in her dressing gown and slumped on the sofa in the conservatory. Her feet were balanced precariously on the coffee table, her Ipad on her tummy. The TV was blaring and Phil Collins drifted in from the kitchen radio. She swore as she missed her mouth and precious fluid soaked into the pink flannelette. Her bleary eyes blinked at the TV. It took a minute for the shock to register.

The same banner headline was used across the globe.

- ONE MESSAGE, ONE WORLD -
"A JOINT AND SIMULTANEOUS BROADCAST FROM THE LEADERS OF ALL 196 COUNTRIES OF OUR WORLD."

She looked at RT news on her Ipad. It was the same screamer and then she heard the words, deep and slow from the radio. It suddenly became obvious, every instant communication method used by humankind was about to broadcast the same message, in every language, in every country around the world. The banner repeatedly flashing on screens or the message interrupting broadcasts to be seen and heard as a beacon of hope. The words were an alarm call, a staccato repetition ten minutes prior to the actual speech. "One message, one world."

A declaration of togetherness unknown in human history. She sat inert, her hands clutching the settee, too inebriated to text Briony and assuming her husband and children knew this was happening.

Maybe the weather was changing and the clouds had sped away from humankind. It seemed that the scientists had already abandoned trying to explain to the populace what was actually happening on earth. The media were bored with explanations, that was old news. But today was a day of clear blue skies, seemingly blue everywhere as the Swiss TV channel sped across other nation's screensavers. She knew this clarity was an impossibility unless it was created. The sort of day where the sun flashes off every pool, lake, river and the tiniest drop of water. A miracle light that can dazzle the eyes. A day in paradise that everyone has always welcomed, but not this day. Not on announcement day.

Most countries chose their President, King or Queen to make the speech. Odd ones chose a Premier or even a dictator. All of these trusted personages were sitting or standing in front of a backdrop of the most movingly beautiful place in the country. An iconic place. A place to be remembered. The speech was to be made at eight-thirty, Greenwich Mean Time. It was never going to be a convenient time for all of the countries. As nothing was convenient anymore. She was entranced by the summary screens, the iconic places in the backdrop; she remembered her joy when visiting a few of them with Bert. It made her sob, so she downed another vodka and refilled the crystal thimble ready for the second half of the bottle to be consumed in a blackening scintillation.

Machu Picchu's sun gate adorned the Peruvian President. The symbolism of the sun and the ancient Inca culture sat well on his shoulders, the ancient city lay below his waist. She thought it ironic that the ultimate death of the Inca culture had been ignored. Xi Jinping sat on a Han dynasty "ta", embroidered with seven red and gold dragons to symbolise togetherness. The Great Wall of China snaked its way upwards and into the distance behind him. The camera angle was from way above the President, to accentuate man's creation that was visible from space. The USA remained traditional with The Oval Office hosting their President but the British had declared their insularity with a live photograph from a satellite high above the British Isles. None of the leaders had considered the images created by their media consultants. Significance was for their teams to consider as the leaders nervously waited to give the greatest speech of their lives. They gave an odd cough, took a drink of water or shook their papers, worried in case the mirrored teleprompter failed. At exactly nine thirty, Swiss time, on Monday June 13th 2018, they began. Her Ipad screen faded from the multiple images and concentrated on Putin sat in Red Square. She felt comforted watching Russian TV, safe at home.

The same fanfare gently swelled louder and louder before collapsing into their opening words. Richard Strauss had created the music called "Also Sprach Zarathustra" after Nietzsche had written the book depicting creation and destruction, eternal recurrence. But the world heard the tune from Kubrick's 1968 movie, "2001: A Space Odyssey". It was the only neutral, non-religious track that had appealed to all the leaders. She thought it was remarkable that they had agreed the music. Everyone recognised the tones and the symbolism from the first notes. The cadence made Natalia's heart slow and her thoughts deepen.

Putin spoke, 'this day is a good day.' The pauses were orchestrated with the french version on the TV. 'I want to talk to you personally, with each one of you, my people. I want to explain our response, the world's response to the Higgs Boson storm.' The cameras zoomed into the leader's eyes, strong, unflinching and resolute. She hated Putin and all he had done to her Russia and so she looked away, disgusted by him. 'My people. I speak in our language but share a universal message around our world. A day may come when the courage of humankind fails, when we forsake each other as human beings…but not this day.' Canned applause augmented that of the cronies stood nearby. She had started watching again, her eyes narrowed. 'We ask you to unite and remember your humanity in this inhuman crisis. We ask you to protect and provide for each other in the coming months as we determine the outcome of the HB storm. We ask you to seek your personal courage from deep within and engender hope, and love, and calm, as we face the same enemy.' Subliminal images flashed invisibly across all types of screen. Innocent young children, people praying, lovers arm in arm. 'No science can stop the ending. No prayers will prevent the truth. The human race faces extinction…but not this day. Not ever.' A roar of approval swept the airwaves, the leaders beckoned for silence in unison, coordinated between the 48th and 53rd seconds of their speeches. 'Praise our civil defenders, the local authorities working with the government. Our armed forces, firemen, medical staff and police. You know there are too few but you must now help them to prepare our country for whatever the storm throws against us. We will create places to shelter and avoid this curse of nature, until nature welcomes the human race back on to the face of the earth.' More loud cheering. 'Our scientists have joined together in a clarity never witnessed by humankind.

They have set about denying nature and promise us a future. The material we now call The Envelope, will be distributed to all our new underground bunkers. The HB storm cannot penetrate it. I tell you now, that I, and all the leaders of our world, have faith in The Envelope.' Pictures of The Envelope being manufactured were shown behind the leaders. 'We hope eight billion people will share our faith and calmly enter the Deeps during the two weeks before the HB storm reaches baseline zero.' 196 pairs of hands were clasped together and shaken slowly upwards and then downwards. 'It is a marvel of the human race that we can create enough bunkers for us all. It is a marvel of the human race that we can stock all the bunkers with food and water to last many, many years. Nine months is enough to create Man and nine months is enough to save Mankind in the Deeps.' The leaders used the slang for the bunkers that had been bandied about by the media, the fake news pushed out over the last few weeks. A common connection with their people. 'Wait patiently for our new lives. Have courage, plan for The Return. We must all wait patiently with hope and love, in strength as one.' Putin leaned forward and confidentially spoke to each viewer. 'It is time for the selflessness of giving, of sharing, this is the greatest antidote we have against this onslaught…that is you and me. That is us!'

Natalia picked up the bottle and swigged mouthful after mouthful, spilling it down her chin. Her dressing gown was now a deep mottled pink. Her eyes were wide as she watched pictures of the Moscovites listening to Putin, watching a giant screen. They were clinging to those nearest to them. Office workers were arm in arm, families clasped in tight hugs, strangers placed a hand on the back of those in front of them. Putin began again, he shouted out, 'The faith of all religions are combined for the first time. Nothing…nothing! Will tear us apart. We the human race refuse to be beaten by a natural phenomenon.' The wild emotion spread around Red Square, a common will to live, to be. He dropped his voice to give gravity and hope. He waved his right forefinger. 'All the people, in all the countries will be stronger in the end. We are part of the universe and we will remain so!' The national anthem of each country was dubbed over the final frames of the leaders. RT segued across the global TV networks. Natalia saw that some leaders held their hands on their hearts. Others saluted. But the most poignant gesture for her was that of prayer appropriate to their God.

Natalia staggered across the room and thumbed the TV remote to off before collapsing on the floor in a heap. She thought of Bert and knew he would criticise the message. Natalia whispered into the dust. 'I love you Bert, I love you so much but please let up on me now.' She knew it was a vain hope, he was slipping away from her but she also knew he still loved her and always would. The thought of her children's emotions whilst listening to the message never came to her. She had passed out in a pool of vomit.

★ ★ ★

The day after the communiqué, The Message, CCOW commenced formal operations. Sam had created a summary of first actions for Ralph, Bert and his senior managers.

"Every country will have a link into CCOW headquarters via The Grid. G20 countries alone will participate in the central facility that will be based in the USA. But each country will have a new civil protection arm, PPS – Population Protection

Services -, an agglomeration of all local civil services with a single objective. To create and populate the bunkers. These vital building blocks will be in place within one week. They will then be grown exponentially to an assumed full service within the following month.

The High Point Facility under Mount Weather in Virginia, USA, has been chosen as the best possible HQ for CCOW. Other places could match it in terms of security, size and history. However, the proven ability to track manmade and natural disasters, plus the Americans' communications networks and vast storage on Cray computers helped in the final choice. Up to 2000 employees will be based there and most of those chosen will be single. The Envelope will be fixed to its interior by the start of July. I will visit there next month, work permitting. Please find attached below a sample format for CCOW's first briefings to Mankind."

★ ★ ★

CCOW – CENTRAL CONTROL OF THE WORLD
Briefing
All polymer plants in China have now commenced the changeover to manufacturing The Envelope. On time and to plan. USA and European plants will follow suit during August. Full supply for all currently known bunkers will be ready before the middle of October. Factories manufacturing wallpaper paste have been given a new recipe of starch and methylcellulose including a Ciba-Geigy epoxy resin. This paste is the perfect glue for fixing The Envelope to all internal bunker surfaces.

A minor inconvenience. Green light

Relatively few difficulties should occur with maintaining supplies of plastic wrappings for our food, but manufacture of plastic bags, and cling film will soon cease. Please re-utilise your existing supplies and follow the "airtight" campaign. Thank you for your continued abstinence from panic buying and over stocking.

A moderate inconvenience. Amber light

Nothing to report.

A major inconvenience. Red light

Remote areas of China are not responding to The Message. The army is reinforcing the local police to guarantee stability ensuring zero impact on supplying The Envelope.

General news

Japan is recommissioning three nuclear power stations that were closed after the Fukushima disaster in March 2011. They are adding automated surveillance systems and are confident of providing a consistent supply of electricity to all of their bunkers by November.

The United Kingdom is struggling to find large enough bunkers for centralised medical centres. They have suggested a new method for managing medical care and are sharing this with other countries via CCOW. This involves the development of HB buster vehicles based on articulated lorries. The lorries will be automatically guided between bunkers, enabling essential and highly technical medical equipment to be shared as required. BMW are actively working with the UK government to fit the lorries with their "Vision Zero" system, which has been extensively tested with Baidu their technology partner, both in

Europe and in China. We think other countries will follow this approach.

The certificates of fidelity will be issued by every government on September 1st. This will protect every person's assets, whether home values, bank balances, or stocks and share prices. Fidelity teams from local tax inspection offices will agree the status quo with each person and every business; then they will issue a guaranteed value certificate based on the asset value dated 11th June this year, pre The Message.

We can therefore reassure everyone, across country and social boundaries, that they cannot lose out by going into the Deeps and all will be reinstated after The Return. A decree to this effect was codified by The World Council yesterday.

Welcome to the CCOW Facebook, Twitter, WhatsApp and website. Now you can nominate the top five "indispensables" that you want in your temporary life underground.

Voting closes on the 11th of August. So vote now. Is it fresh coffee you want or a jacuzzi? Have fun with the "indispensables" App.

HB Predictor today
Great news. The predictor is still at 98 and has been holding steady over the last three days.

"Remember – without "ethical culture", there is no salvation for humanity."

Einstein

"The great secret of morals is love."

Shelley

Sam added a footnote. The tone has been set. A stop – go centralised assessment will be updated on the CCOW website every hour and shared around the world by the media. This glut of information will keep the media occupied, whilst governmental staff will share realities through an encrypted website and messaging service called CCOWsecure.

To Ralph and Bert alone, he added a further note. Based on our last conversation, the truth will only be transferred by secure telephone links between the head of CCOW and the nominated politician in each country's inner cabinet. CCOW will function to make the world stable and safe and give confidence to humankind that there will be a future.

★ ★ ★

The June afternoon buzzed through a shimmer of heat, a good time to walk in the shade of the trees. Bert and Natalia strolled in silence before he left for CERN and his impossible dreaming. Bert was impatient to depart, working strange hours suited his mood. But she held him back, gripping his arm so tightly, that he wobbled as they walked. He guessed she wanted to declare peace, at least for the children's sake and waited on edge for her apology. That is how he saw the circumstances, it was about her bad behaviour and her lack of support for him. He jolted inside.

'Life now is where you are. There are no cultures, no countries, no me, just us.'

Bert responded to Her. 'Humans are the prime animals. If we cease to exist, we leave a poorer world. A world bereft of humanity has no thought, word or deed. No ideas, no love and no emotions.'

Natalia quizzed his perfect silence. 'You seem quiet, is it me?'

'Sorry, I was just thinking too much as usual.' He grabbed and squeezed her hand. 'Can you hear any grasshoppers yet?' As she listened, so did he.

'Are you bored with us, Bert? Is it all too mundane, living that is?'

'There is no alternative to living one's life.' His thought was adamant and silent.

She kissed his cheek. 'I always liked your love of nature, it encourages me outside.' Three large buzzards hung in the blue sky above them. They were gently circling above the border between the forest and prairie, where shrews and mice innocently played with no fear. A strident "peea-ay" of a buzzard drew the humans' attention. It resembled a cat but held a threat that hung in the still air.

'So what makes you think that, then?'

Bert ignored Her and concentrated on his wife. They stood on the edge of the hill and watched the white sails of the yachts heading towards the mouth of The Rhone. Their bows ploughed into a disturbance of white grey sediment dumping into the lake. The spoils of the river passing through the green valley sliced across The Alps and on the way to the French plains.

Lily was persistent whilst he was near. *'You can't stay in your own home. She will never stay. She will go into a bunker. Think Bert, if there is no wasteful and unfocussed spread of labour and assets the concentration on creating the Deeps must succeed. It must be a concentrated effort for you and she to survive together.'*

He shrugged before replying. He had never believed in forever togetherness. 'People will feel what? Claustrophobic, scared of losing their possessions, needing to know their extended family is safe elsewhere?'

'Why did you just shrug your shoulders? Is it me?'

'Oh, it was nothing. Just the thought of going to work.' He kissed her gently on her hair, the walk had made their peace without an apology. He guessed that Lily must feel their weakness and wondered why She preyed on it. 'On which note, I have to go, my dear.' They turned to walk back to the chalet. As they passed the etang he stared at Her. 'Impossible,' he thought or did he say it out loud? 'No, it is impossible and I am imagining all of this.'

★ ★ ★

Sam watched Bert stroll through his domain. Bert stared straight ahead, avoiding eye contact with his old team as they were now considered deserters; seconded off Bert to work on catastrophe prevention with Sam. Bert stopped by Sam and sat on his desk. He started to flick the elastic bands still dotted around the surface since the HB discovery. 'Any news from ALMA? The largest astronomical telescope in the world must have found something for fuck's sake.'

Sam was certain. 'I spoke to Quintana yesterday. He has nothing for us.'

'A billion dollars spent and they've got nothing?'

'There are no detectable temperature changes in any stars out to seventy million light years. So Quintana says that any disturbance causing the HB storm must be beyond umm... that distance.'

Bert stood. 'Ffur, I guess it's not your problem, really. You have my whole team but no one is looking for the truth.'

Sam replied with fists clenched on the desktop, 'Focus, Bert. You have to frigging focus on now, what we can do for humankind. Now is the issue, not what might be the cause x light years ago.'

Bert chose to ignore his friend. 'Millimetre and "sub mill" waves are absorbed or distorted by water vapour, correct? So that means ALMA hasn't detected water and by default any form of life. The HB storm hasn't affected structures in this universe. Or more precisely, not structures, life forms.'

Sam was amazed. 'You believe in life out there? That's a first, you always said we were the only ones.'

'I didn't say that, pal.' Bert pushed himself off the side of the desk and headed for the shed.

'You can help us formulate a second sub-envelope if you want, mate? Come and work with the proles, yeah?'

★ ★ ★

Bert didn't deviate, he was looking forward to listening to the Brahms piano concerto no.1, played by Malcuzyinski. He had played the CD at home and marvelled at the emotions in his breast. Feelings carried by the same sound waves that had reverberated around the salon when the pianist had lived in his chalet. A piano piece affected by Brahms's friend, the legendary Schumann, who had attempted suicide. Would any intense friendships lead to suicides by the fear of the HB storm? He pictured himself and Sam in a pact and dismissed the idea.

Bert firmly shut the door and placed the headphones over his ears. He shut his eyes and slumped into his battered chair. Cutting his thoughts adrift he let his subconscious work, his eyelids flickered and his mind wandered. 3.8 billion years ago there was a hot dense point, a billionth of the size of a nuclear particle. Since then it has expanded. It inflated in 0.1 milliseconds and probably dark matter formed making up 24% of this universe. But when was the dark energy created that represents 71%? This unknown entity that caused the last expansion of the cosmos. What catalyst gave such an acceleration that managed to overcome gravity and continues to reduce the numbers of new stars and galaxies forming.

He started and nearly fell from the chair. Increasing the volume of his music, he let himself drift away again. Dark energy is an unknown energy field, a property of space, but how will it all end? The big crunch, taking the universe back into a point again? Or a big rip that separates it further and sends it into oblivion? Maybe we have infinite expansion? I doubt that. However, the uncertainty principle means we can't truly know, we can only theorise. We can see seventy billion light years outwards to the furthest observable edge of our universe. But it is too little and too late. Because we need to know what is beyond that. Surely the HB storm must be coming from there, from beyond. His last thoughts were made as he drifted into a light sleep. He pictured Adam and Eve with God and the Devil but the face of Adam was Sam's and Eve was Briony. The worrying visage was that of God. A perfect reflection of himself.

★ ★ ★

Briony looked out of her office window and saw half the lab technicians huddled around a screen. Swivelling herself out of her chair she crept up behind them. 'I understand that Jack's double-decker KitKat is a big hit with my staff but I also need your experimental results for the defoaming agent in the new Nescafe.' No one turned around or spoke to the boss. She peered over the top of Jack's shoulder and read his screen. 'Oh my God.' Her hand covered her mouth as she read down the CCOW briefing with the others in total silence.

CCOW – Central Control Of the World
Briefing

Twitter campaign update -AHB Against Higgs Boson. Our strength is amazing when pulling together. Thank you! Three billion retweets have been made over the last two days.

Centres for euthanasia will immediately be created in every country. Each country is formulating the best legal process to make this alternative available for those who want it. We understand some of us cannot manage the short time below ground or cannot be brave like the majority. The only debate is on how to process the numbers of people wanting to use "the sorting", as we close in on Deeps Day. It is impossible to set a new world law that covers different countries' religious and cultural beliefs about death. Therefore, the decision has been made to let people die in their own homes with help from a doctor, friends and family. The key criteria of the process will ensure that there is no chance of subterfuge or collusion and thus prevent murder for financial gain or pure hate and revenge.

Practical actions agreed at yesterday's World Council.

A free convertible currency, called the supra-national currency, SNC for short, was valued against all other currencies at yesterday's levels. This valuation is now fixed until The Return and therefore everyone can safely and fairly move between countries to be with family and friends. You will not lose out.

The asset values of individuals and businesses were frozen as per plan and with few disputes. Tax agencies in most countries report less than 5% in dispute. Particular countries such as Greece and Switzerland have a higher dispute rate. Leaders expressed their disappointment at the "hiding" of key assets in certain countries.

All last testaments will be fixed and cannot be changed after October 1st. Make your will now.

The freeze of world stock market rates and all shares in all countries was effected last Monday. This has now stopped the turbulence in the financial markets and brought stability to all peoples and businesses across our world.

Briony placed a hand on his shoulder. 'Wait Jack, stop scrolling down please.' She turned to her team. 'Listen, I'm sorry for being so flippant, I just didn't know OK. Please take half an hour for yourselves to absorb all this.' They all stood motionless for a few seconds before moving away, leaving Jack and Briony alone. 'We've known each other a long time, my friend. Do you want to read this together?' She could see his eyes were glistening behind his glasses as he silently turned back to the screen. Briony crouched beside him with one hand on his arm as they read the remainder of the CCOW briefing.

A minor inconvenience. Green light

People over 60 years old are worried that they will not be allowed into the bunkers. CCOW with the backing of The World Council has categorically stated that this is a vicious and nasty rumour.

A moderate inconvenience. Amber light

Gold reserves will be revalued over the next two months. The extraordinary increase in gold bullion values is normal in times of uncertainty. Three observers from three independent countries will visit individual countries reserves and verify the weight and carat of all that country's reserves. The triple triangulation i.e. by the three allocated judges, will be set using a random lottery to be held on the CCOW TV channel on August 1st. All gold revaluations will be complete by December 15th. The final valuations will be published by CCOW for all the financial experts in every country to sign off as a true figure. Clarity is our watchword. Fairness is free.

A major inconvenience. Red light
Nothing to report. All is going really well. We will succeed.

HB Predictor today
Remember, the Higgs Boson limit of zero is the point when we must all be underground. This is currently estimated as March 2019.

Today is a good day. The HB is level 97.5 and has been steady for a few days.

Your questions answered
Am I ill?
Of course in a way, we are all ill. Attacked by something so small and invisible that we cannot measure how ill we are. But we have a choice to go down into the bunkers or not. Why wouldn't you? Remember, the HB danger level is a long time away. We have months to prepare. When the predictor reaches zero, we must be underground and protected by The Envelope. Bunkers give us survival, no bunker means an undignified and unpredictable death. We know nothing more as yet but our scientists are working hard to give CCOW the answers for you. But when people are ill,

they see things differently – the clarity of the stars, the different shape of the trees, the song of the birds and the ever changing sky. That is what you must also hold onto, the beauty of nature now, as we must appreciate what we have. Safe shelter is coming.

What about my house?

Of course your property will be protected. Your possessions will remain in your home and remain safe. When the time comes, close up your home, seal all windows and doors with tape. The army will patrol all areas as the majority of us go below and they will be the last to enter the bunkers.

Is my town still safe?

What factors will stop everyone tearing each other apart? "Dog eat dog" is an idiom found in many languages. In Spanish: "mundo de fieras". In French: "L'homme est un loup pour l'homme." What will keep the majority of peoples on the straight and narrow? Our humanity, that is what! We are not animals. We have our combined intelligence working with our hope. That gives us a clever strength to succeed. Only working together in a common cause gives this certain answer. We are asking you, each one of you, for an impossibility. So that we all can achieve the impossible. If we do not pull together we will all die. If we do, we can all live.

We are protecting all people, in all civilisations from the heat of the Sahara desert to the ice numbing wastes of Greenland.

Do I know everything?

Each country has a single control centre utilising the existing strategic centres for major disaster management. All events are controlled and integrated through CCOW and therefore everyone benefits from the brightest ideas and also in their implementation across the world. The joint actions agreed by all 196 countries of our world is impressing every person in every country and across cultural divides. We work as one.

How long will we hibernate for?
No one can tell. The storm may dissipate as quickly as it arrived.

How much food and water can we store in the bunkers?
The maximum possible that we can stock in the time we have. Nothing will be left outside of the bunkers, so each of you needs to be inside one. Our aim is for two years food, water and medical supplies as a minimum. We believe the HB storm will fade and die well before we face any shortages.

What happens if the HB storm has not ended after two years?
We leave the bunkers and take our chances. We go home. Remember, we have no knowledge of what destruction the particle shower will cause at that time, if it ever strengthens. As quickly as it has appeared, it could disappear. The impact on our bodies is still unknown. Maybe after two years there will be no impact as we will have mutated to live with the storm. A genetic change may have occurred within us. Maybe the structure and nature of the HBs will have changed and interacted with some other particle. We are prepared for anything.

QUOTES FROM OUR GREAT LEADERS
The Emperor of Japan
   "We have exponential technological insights but we have no comparable change in our thought processes. We are much more than mammals but we do react to basic needs. This is an

emotional reaction, so we will address those basic needs and retain control of our emotions."

The President of Peru

"Most religions predict the end of the world and face it with strength. We learned much from our Inca ancestors who believed in reincarnation. All the main religious leaders met in the UN headquarters in New York and all categorically agreed this is not the end. They agreed we must work together and with respect, hand in hand and lift up our faces to our God. All religions with all peoples as brother and sister to make the great defence strong."

The President of the United States of America

"The great defence – is it a good word? No, it is not good… it is great! The world religions all have different interpretations of humankind's existence. The reason why we are here. Different starts and different endings. But we all agree that we must take a practical and scientific approach to the oncoming storm. To shelter and ensure survival of the human race. Each person will rightly take comfort in their religious beliefs. We never forget our Gods, we use our faith as strength to achieve the impossible and the impossible is possible."

The Chancellor of Germany

"I heard an old man say the world is doomed. So I took him by the hand and led him outside to watch the sunset. I said to him: Trust the young, my friend. Trust in their energy and enthusiasm to save us all. No one, no matter what age, will be left out of the bunkers. Remember the new creed being adopted

by all the people of our world is to have faith in us. The new faith, us against the Higgs Boson will always be our faith for each other. Have faith and you will see the sunrise again."

Jack rolled back his chair and looked up to face her, 'What do you think boss?'

'I think, I didn't really think if that makes sense.' She sighed and stood up to walk away. 'Please go and tell the others to take an early lunch and not to come back until two o'clock.' She turned towards her office, the weight on her chest had squeezed the oxygen from her and she slowly made her way back to collapse in her chair. Between each deep breath she murmured Oh Lord hear my prayer. She prayed for her children, she imagined the stress Sam must be feeling, god how she loved him, how would they cope without each other. She resolved to look after them all, no matter what happened.

★ ★ ★

As the sun set, a red flattening of the light enhanced every detail in the valley below Bert. He sat hand in hand with Natalia on the first floor balcony. His day of thought had not spared his emotions. It was an unusual day for him, a once in a lifetime event. A day of sentiments rather than serious thought about the HB storm. For three weeks he had slowly cut himself off from the day to day experiment on colliding matter and antimatter; he made sure detectors were closed down correctly, files closed with summary actions recorded. He had been set lose to imagine his way to the cause of the storm and that was what he did best. Thinking outside of the box, drawing on theories and scribbling endlessly on the six whiteboards in the shed.

But now was a moment of solace, CCOW had cracked peoples hearts by telling them the truth. He looked across the prairie and rejoiced in the early summer flowers. Pink lychnis were held high on grey scaffolding stems. Much lower were blue gentian that crept from the edge of the rocky outcrops on the south side of the garden. Astonishing blues, made bluer in the redness of the setting sun, caressed by greener greens. 'Can we make up at last, Natalia? I know this year was hard for you. I know what I am and what I do and I'm sorry.' He squeezed her hand.

'Huh, maybe. But my man, the last six years have been hard. To the devil is an old expression in Russia "да". You know it, and you know the pressures.' She lifted her head and stared at him. 'I am only human.'

Bert smiled. 'Now or never?'

She never resisted for too long. 'Now.' She leaned into him and he held her tight. His arm cradled her neck and helped incline her face towards his. 'I am scared for us. The family. I want to protect us all and I cannot see how.'

His voice cracked. 'I'm scared too…but just know that I love you and will always love you. That's all that matters.' He pulled her off the chair and led her through the bedroom door. As he lowered her gently onto the bed he kissed her right ear. 'Trust me.'

Before they slept, she slipped her hand into his. They were lying on their tummies, face to face in the moonlight that slanted through the tall window. 'I hope I do not die at night.' A sigh whispered across his face.

'Why, my dear?'

'It seems wrong dying in the dark of the night. The day is always happier for me. As if light enhances something deep within my psyche.'

Bert was inexact with his answer. It was still uncomfortable to say it on a strange day of emotions. 'Maybe the light touches your soul, touches everyone's soul. We seem to have the same narcosis across the world.'

'But it is good, is it not, moya lyubov? The way everyone is getting on with their lives and starting to create a new future for us all.'

He stroked her hair with a languid hand. His eyes closed and his breathing slowed. 'The night is unhappy, that's why we go to sleep. We can dream all the bad things into oblivion.' One eye opened, 'define getting on.'

She murmured, 'Happy and unhappy. Day versus night.' She snuggled closer. 'I remember my priest in Moscow, like it was yesterday, although I was only eight years old. The Orthodox view of creation comprised the living and the dead, the visible and the invisible. A whole that was not divisible and an effect on one had an effect on all. God was not greater than Evil and Evil no less than God. Satan, Lucifer, was once a good angel, the light-bearer. Even likened to the morning star.'

Bert was too exhausted to listen. 'Too serious, night night.' He squirmed closer and kissed her sleepily before collapsing into his first deep and profound sleep for a month.

She turned away from him but he shared her dream. They were dreaming of the balances in life, a giant set of scales where she ran along the beam towards him and he tipped further away from her. He tried to run to her but the beam was too steep and he slipped backwards. A shared beam tipping them one way and then the other.

[4]

Pain and Guilt

B RIONY SIPPED HER café. Bigger than an espresso, fresh from the Nespresso machine and always black. 'I do love it here, Sam, I mean everything about it. The relaxed culture, the way it feels almost Mediterranean. But counterpoised by the Swiss exactness for life.' She turned to her left and looked upwards to admire the glossy black wood and glass creation that was their Huf Haus. A series of planes and angles to reflect the magnificence of the view. The modest house in Blonay felt like home but she knew the emotional ties could be rescinded at any time. They had rented it for nearly nine years as it was tax efficient and stress free with their busy lives. Ironically, now it was theirs for life, or at least as long as they lived. CCOW had decreed that variations to home contracts would not be allowed until The Return. She heard the funicular train from Les Pléiades trundle slowly past, rattling its way to Vevey; the usual route for Briony to go to work at the Nestlé HQ and Sam for his mainline connection to Geneva. It was convenient for their work and convenient for their children to go to the local

International school. It gave them all more time to be together, which is exactly what the family desired. She dwelt on the thought of her family, full of love, who respected each other as they respected everyone else, crisis or no crisis.

The adults sat bathed in the early morning sun. The smell of fresh croissants wafted from the table, an edible delight bought five minutes earlier from the local bakers and never a supermarket. 'Everything is so luminescent, an elemental mixture of lake and sky. So pretty. I imagine heaven must be like this.'

'But what, Briony? You live in paradise but…'

'Hmm…well, we have two lovely children but I always wanted more. You know that, don't you?'

'Yeah, I clocked that years ago and then our jobs got in the way didn't they?'

She just shrugged. Her face had lost a smidgin of her early morning happiness. 'You have made my life complete. Remember, you are my proper love.'

Sam's phone bleeped before he could reply. It indicated an email from work. He touched the screen and slid the words into view. His cupped hand shaded the screen.

'Oh hell.' He dropped the iPhone with a clatter onto the teak table.

His wife quickly leaned across and placed a hand tenderly on his left shoulder. 'What's wrong, darling?'

'The predictor is wrong. At least I hope so. The overnight results have just been analysed by Jeffries.'

'What's the level?' She demanded an answer.

He couldn't look at her. 'I can't tell you, but I need to go.'

'Sam,' she demanded, 'I'm your wife. You know I can keep this to myself.'

'It's dropped from 98 to 80.'

She saw his gasp for breath and stepped across to hug him tightly. She hid her tears in his shoulder. A slow minute passed before they were calmer, she whispered into his ear, 'I would have called a girl Jennifer and a boy Jonathan.' She hoped he wouldn't see she had been crying, she didn't want to burden him further.

'And I would have loved our third and fourth child as much as I love you and the kids. Proper love that is.' He kissed her on her lips and walked quickly inside without looking back.

She sat down hard. The view was forgotten and so was the imagined past as she stared at a solitary red rose bush in the sparse garden. Sam had bought it for her as an anniversary present when they had moved into the house. Her heart was thumping, life surged between chaos and calm, scary and relaxed, but she gradually calmed herself. She had the same family, the same home and was doing the same job without any signs of illness in any of them. She sat quietly until she heard the door slam behind Sam and then waited ten more minutes before going to gently wake the children. They deserved a lie in. All thoughts about her day at the laboratory seemed unimportant as she carried two glasses of fresh orange juice upstairs to her babies.

Briony knew Sam would stop at the pharmacy in the road next to Blonay train station. Her friend from her children's school had told her what he had been collecting two weeks ago. The Nefazodone was easy to find in the bedside table and this morning he was out of pills when she had secretly checked. Although it was only a fortnight since he had started taking the anti-depressant, she could see the benefits for Sam already and respected his secret. He was a proud man and would have felt ashamed to admit his need for help. She was universally bonded to her man and would do everything to help him.

★ ★ ★

Bert walked up to the edge of the etang and stared hard at Her. The shadows of the trees across the still water were already shortening. A bright white sun shone from high above the sharp points of Rochers de Naye. 'Why are you talking to me, Lily?' She was slow to reply. The silence renewed his doubts. Did she exist after all? Maybe he really was bonkers.

'*Because you are the closest any human has come to understanding the true significance of matter. About what makes up life.*'

He took it as a compliment and nodded slowly as he chewed his bottom lip. 'And your point is?'

'*Your experiments on matter and antimatter.*'

'Are you confusing the meaning of life and my desire to answer fundamental physics questions?'

'*If you want to call it that, Bert. Just physics.*'

Bert folded his arms and turned to squint at the sun, examining the scree. He took his time before returning to confront her. He blinked to remove the small black clouds floating within his retinas.

She spoke immediately. '*The meaning of life is a quaint little phrase, isn't it?*' She sighed and he thought her leaves contracted downwards a millimetre or so. '*We have always spoken with you, over many millennia. Empedocles and his elements in 430 BC, Democritus and the soul. There have been many clever people but none of them touched the reality like you.*'

Bert cut across Her. 'Philosophy always failed Man, didn't it, Lily? Maybe you don't agree. From Descartes to Nietzsche, a belief in vitalism, that life is non-material.' He looked up again at the beautiful blue sky. There were no clouds and it was predicted to hit 33 degrees. 'How can something so perfect be killing us?'

'Are you living or existing, Bert?'

'I am always living, every breath of my life I intend living. Existing means nothing to me. I exist in a world and I have always wanted to know why. Then I will fully live.'

'Nymphaeaceae also live. We ignore the sludge at the bottom of humankind's ponds and lakes; instead we absorb the detritus of your inadequacies.'

'I'm not impressed by your analogies. We cope with our own mess.'

'You never cope. You always fail and are failing again. You need to tunnel and flee. Run away from your mistakes.'

'An early burial isn't the answer. It's a coward's way out.' He said what she wanted but thought about his friends. For a moment he seriously considered joining them in the Deeps.

'You are cowards. All of you! Call me what you wish, Bert; Lily or Lotus. The name doesn't matter, not the name, as my true name is lost in time.'

'Lily is your name. I am talking to Lily.'

'You are talking to an angiosperm. I am micro-metres small, 1.8μm for each of my pollen. Whether something is smaller than you or bigger than you, only constituency will matter in the face of the HB storm. But I know we will die last. Flee with your family. Time is running out.'

He walked away from Her. She was right about humankind and she truly was talking to him. He recognised that truth despite its absurdity. But she couldn't understand his thoughts about the Deeps, that much was certain. His family and friends would go into the Deeps, he knew their weaknesses. He clearly saw the Lowest Common Denominator in everyone but she did not. He would never go into the Deeps and be brought down to Mankind's level. It was time to think, time to be in CERN and bounce an idea off Sam.

★ ★ ★

Natalia grabbed the vodka bottle from behind the radiator cover as soon as the roar of the Merc had subsided. The booze helped her think more clearly as she flicked through the latest briefing on her Ipad. The alcohol and CCOW briefings were now a drug for her, to be administered three times a day, subject to scrutiny from her kids, as Bert didn't notice anything now.

CCOW – CENTRAL CONTROL OF THE WORLD
Briefing
The World Council has debated the current unrest in a small part of the population. All its leaders have been appalled by the ignorance shown by drunks and drug users. The people who have fallen so low in our societies that they don't care anymore. They do not share the vision of the majority, the world's population. Of food, water and shelter, the narcotic driving forces to guarantee our safety.

The Council has therefore agreed new rules for strict enforcement of the law to deter those who do not adhere to The Message.

Minor offences such as stealing will be punished by immediate imprisonment without trial. These prisoners will not be left on the surface but do lose all rights of appeal. Prison warders and the army will be the last to enter the bunkers. Prisoners will be escorted into the Deeps at the last possible moment and are not guaranteed to be united with their families.

SOMETHING TO TELL YOU

Major offences such as hoarding, buying and selling items on the black market and the general offence of disturbing our working harmony will also be punished without trial. Death will be administered by lethal injection by a prison or an army doctor.

Looting, rioting and murder will result in death by public execution. Firing squads will be provided by the army, and public squares will be used in each major town and city to stage the executions. They will be held on a once per week basis and will act as a warning to all. Fridays, Saturdays and Sundays will not be used as execution days out of deference to the majority of the world's religions.

She tossed the Ipad onto the sofa and wandered to the window. She thought of the people in Montreux below. Kill them, she thought. Her palms rested on the pane, her forehead banged forward. Kill everyone who doesn't commit, just fucking kill them to fucking save my fucking family. Her fists clenched and she smacked the window hard, the smudges shook in front of her before she returned to look at the briefing again.

A minor inconvenience. Green light
The existing law enforcement agencies and judges will undertake all sentencing for the three levels of atonement stated above. This will ensure absolute truth and fairness.

A moderate inconvenience. Amber light
We do not expect to need more than the existing levels of enforcers as trials will be fast tracked at one hour per accused, maximum. There will be no method of appeal. Army captains will be trained to adjudicate in any excess cases, if and when required.

A major inconvenience. Red light
Please do not attend the firing squad events, unless of course you want to show support for the genuine people who want to maintain an honest life until we move together into the Deeps.

HB Predictor today
CERN have experienced a severe technical failure. Several cables have burnt out on the HB experiment that provides the core data on the hourly strength of the storm. Three people died trying to fight the ensuing helium fire. Despite this disaster, we will bring you the latest results as soon as it is back online. This may take a few weeks to resolve.

"Compulsion precedes morality, indeed morality itself is compulsion for a time, to which one submits for the avoidance of pain."

Nietzsche

"The law is the witness and external deposit of our moral life. Its history is the history of the moral development of the race."

Oliver Wendell Holmes

She kissed the bottle, one gulp, two then three and four before gagging and flopping sideways onto the cushions. She had always liked Nietzsche, he was always right in her opinion. She mumbled all that she could remember. God is dead. God remains dead. And we have killed him. How shall we comfort ourselves, the murderers of all murderers?

★ ★ ★

Briony had always insisted on her children sharing their "E lives". She had insisted there must be no secrets in their household and promised not to judge her kids; she promised not to constantly pry, but now she felt the need. It was a good time for their mum to know how they felt and that was how she justified her "E-dropping". She was sat in the Néstle laboratory, her phone in hand, fascinated by the morning "E regurgitation".

Allie sent a Facebook message to Hannah as soon as she woke up. She shared a room with another girl in the school boarding house called Le Cerf in the village of Villars. It was a pretty place, an old pine clad hotel, close to Aiglon school and as good as having her own apartment. 'I just got this new app off my friend Izzy who is really HB anal. Check it out. It makes fun of any drop in the HB predictor score. Like, it's still 98, bothered. You input a low score and lol. OMG I have to go to school. Love. x'

Hannah replied immediately, within five seconds. 'Thanks Allie. Let's get together next Friday night when you're home. We can hang out on the promenade in Montreux. OK?'

'OK, have a great week, nothing really changes so we're gonna be fine. Love Allie. x'

Coincidentally, Josh sent Liam a message at almost the same moment. Briony watched the conversation unfold, it was wake up, I am a teenager time. She thought that Liam must be biking to school when he received and read it, probably riding with no hands on the handlebars as usual. 'My stupid sister got this app off her mate. What a load of rubbish. P.s. did you read CCOW's latest? F..k me.'

Liam had left his bike in the bike shed and was sauntering towards the main entrance to Haut Lac school as he replied two thumbed. 'Yeah, saw CCOW, I think it's a good idea. Shock nutters into staying sane! But clashes with my beliefs I guess. Fuck it. Kill em if they step out of line.'

Josh immediately texted back. 'Yeah fuck em. Imagine the scum of the earth in your bunker. P.s. any ideas on which will be your bunker, mate? Better be the same as ours.'

Briony carefully placed her mobile leaning against her workstation. She didn't want to know really, but then she picked it up again. Maybe the boys were right and she was too soft.

Liam replied in an instant. 'My dad says he can arrange that. But he says we must avoid the hydroelectric tunnels above Montreuxas it will be noisy. Are you worried?'

The reply from Josh came about an hour later. 'Honestly, I'm scared to death. It will be fine with wifi and stuff but my dad's really against going below.'

'Just got to do it Josh. We'll all help each other. My dad was telling me about the bunker at Denver airport in the USA. CCOW have really made stuff happen, so we'll all be OK.'

'Don't want to think about it L. See you at the weekend in Vevey. We can all meet in Starbucks.'

★ ★ ★

Sam and Bert were in the shed. Sam had forestalled his friend by marching in on him as soon as Bert arrived for the day. Bert's feet were on his desk as usual and Sam was leaning against the window after quietly telling him the latest HB predictor count. 'Why mate? Come on, give us clue.'

Bert opened his arms wide. 'Not why, when is the question. You knew that could happen. The only why is you denying it.'

'I'm not denying it. But when I clocked 98 down to 80, you have got to admit that is crap.'

'Bollocks, you mean scary not crap. After everything we've been through, you refuse to use science as your psyche.'

Sam remonstrated, 'For goodness sake, you sit here theorising, whilst I take endless telephone calls, manage my team and spend hours on emails and reports from around the world. And you, you jammy bastard, you just sit and think!'

Bert shrugged his shoulders. 'It was your choice, mate, not mine, yours. All I can say is chill, KK.'

Sam sighed as he twisted around and placed the opposite shoulder on the window to ease his aching back. 'Hell, I feel unbalanced but I am still objective if that is what you are getting at. Denver airport was my biggest shock yesterday.'

'What's that got to do with the crisis?'

'It's the USA's main bunker and has always been there but a big secret. Like umm…, truly no one knew anything about it.'

Bert was non committal. 'I flew in there once for a convention. They said the airport covers 130 square kilometres with an underground automated baggage system that lost my luggage. As there was no sign of a bunker anywhere, what do you mean?'

'I mean Denver is the largest international airport in the USA and the third largest in the world. They built a huge network of tunnels underneath it, which included the automated baggage system but they were always going to close that down, apparently. They built five extra buildings that they called a mistake, and spent three times more than the budget. All funded centrally and secretly by the US government.'

'So the shock is how they kept it a secret?'

'No, Bert, the real shock is how they linked it years ago to the North American Aerospace Defence Command under Cheyenne Mountain. And to Peterson, where they have the

United States Space Command, Air Defence Mission, United States Northern Command and dozens of other major business headquarters.'

Bert blew a large raspberry, 'Ffur, so it was super secret as well as clever, then?'

'All of that. But what really hacked me off is the list of chosen internees in this secret frigging bunker. The favouritism that has been applied.'

'I get it. So come on, who has paid to enter this giant grave?' Bert was smiling at Sam's worried face.

Sam intoned a few dozen names. 'Tom Cruise, Oprah Winfrey, Norman Schwarzkopf, Lord and Lady Muck and numerous others who already own transit houses nearby.'

Bert shrugged his shoulders. 'It doesn't matter. Buying your future will still be subject to the LCD.'

'We are just proles, mate…hold on, what do you mean?' Sam stepped away from the window and took a seat.

'LCD – the Lowest Common Denominator. It works like this. Picture in your own family the one person who is always last to be ready to go out.'

'Liam.'

'Well, everything revolves around the LCD, which in your case is Liam. So you know the maths, the LCD is the fraction that is the lowest calculable. It was Edward Kennedy who said ."The press can resist the standard of the lowest common denominator, the rationalisation that all news is fit to print that has appeared anywhere else". But no one resists the LCD.'

'I haven't got a sodding clue where you're coming from, Bert.'

'My point is. Twenty percent of people will cause issues with your bunker plans. They will not like what is proposed before they go in nor when they are on the inside. That is 1.4 billion of the world population. Think about it. It takes a terrorist group of a few hundred people to change a country's government. So how do you control that volcano of emotion, then?'

'CCOW will control it. It's a psychological war. Plus people want salvation. The planning for the bunkers is nearly complete in every country. Old salt mines, government underground facilities, road tunnels are being blocked up. The doing has started, thank God.'

'Sam, if the predictor reading plummets like this every week, you are stuffed. The LCD will revolt and everyone will exist at their primeval level.'

Sam stood to leave in a huff. 'Yeah, but you don't believe in running to safety anyway, so you should stop criticising.'

Bert was still interested enough to ask. 'So what are you going to tell CCOW about the predictor?'

Sam said, 'I have already had two chats with your best mate Donally. I said the true figure was now 80 and we have no explanation for it, but it is true as far as we know.'

Bert's mouth was set in a grimace. Sam saw the rigid face and waited for the explosion, 'What did he say?'

'He said that based on my earlier phone call at 7am this morning, he had already bought us some time.'

'I saw the CCOW lie,' seethed Bert as he dropped his feet to the floor with a giant thump.

Sam shifted uncomfortably on his feet at the word lie. He guessed his friend knew he was actively involved in white lies to keep people calm. But that was his job, to keep the peace. Sam asked the only question applicable to Bert: 'So how's your research going? Any clues to the cause?'

'Research or guesswork? You know the answer to that.' Bert paused, and saw the anguish in his friend's face. 'Look, my question is: Where does the entropy go to, or come from in my meltdown situation? I believe it must be from a parallel universe. I discussed it with Josh the other day. He's a good boy, Sam.'

'Because he thinks like you, you mean?'

'Like me, yes, but slightly differently in that he listens, whereas I don't.' Bert outlined the conversation he had had with Josh. 'I told him what I had been researching about the HBs. Whenever the entropy of a system appears to decrease, there is always a corresponding increase in the environment in terms of heat or waste, as you well know, yeah.'

'So your boy is clever and took it all in. Why are you telling me basic physics Bert?'

'Because he asked me to define entropy.'

'Bert, it is the measure of the amount of disorder. I bet you used the bookcase analogy. Books neatly arranged in size order versus haphazardly. Move a book in the ordered situation and you notice it but move one in the latter and you don't.'

'That's my point, Sam.'

Sam opened the door. 'You have lost the plot, mate. Why are you pursuing this line when the world is falling apart?'

Bert looked up at him. 'Do you remember us talking at Uni about Hugh Everett? He said, that parallel universes exist and they might branch off from ours. So we have been looking outwards for them. Into an ordered universe. And we have not seen a book move in our universal library.'

Sam remembered. "The Many-Worlds theory" had attempted to answer why quantum matter behaves erratically. 'So what?'

'Think about it, Sam. The quantum level is the smallest one science has detected so far but it may not be small enough.

There may be something even smaller. What if we are looking outwards for the multiverses, when we should be looking inwards? Positively staring at something currently too small to see and in our past.'

Sam walked out of the door without a response, there was too much to do to waste time on theories. He slammed the door shut to isolate Bert's madness from his team. Jesus wept he thought and then regretted the profanity immediately. His mate would be re-formulating his latest theory, "the too small to see derivation". Sam knew his fellow scientists would laugh at Bert's concept, as it was based on the idea of the original Big Bang particle, the holy grail for a particle physicist. What a stupid use of valuable time.

★ ★ ★

Briony marched into the supermarket near the office in Vevey. It was lunchtime and a few minutes after noon. The inhabitants of the Swiss Riviera always stopped for lunch; even the car parking was free to make it easy to lunch in town. So the supermarket visit was a ritual which she had started many years before, a small English rebellion before acceptance of her new Swiss life. It still bemused her that nobody ate a sandwich sat at their desk, and she knew it was considered anti-social, but still, she was English. On her way to the shop she enjoyed walking by the lake. Today she noticed the lack of flowers in the beds for the first time ever. The workers from the commune were too busy coping with the HB emergency, so filling the flower beds were a luxury of history.

As she shopped, she noticed a second difference. There were small groups of regular shoppers who recognised a friendly face. It seemed they wanted to talk, to discuss the latest CCOW news bulletin, the state of their canton and nation. There were no smiles but equally she saw there was no anger. She dawdled past a group of old women and overheard their topic of conversation.

One in a red blouse said, 'They used to shoot people in Germany for doing no good and in the countries they occupied.'

A white blouse rapidly backed her up: 'It stopped people stepping out of line; they were scared by the harsh penalty. That's the way to do it in my view.'

Red blouse was sucking on her dentures. 'Keep all the youngsters in line. It will make sure the bad uns don't hurt us now, nor in the Deeps.' The rest of the group of five women grunted in unison as Briony sidled a little further, seemingly searching for canned tomatoes. 'They say we will be given our own rooms but anyone less than 30 will have to share.'

White blouse waved her walking stick. 'A good job too.' Briony smiled to herself as she heard the reply. 'Mind, we can watch a bit of TV together, maybe over a glass of cognac each night.' The group were happy with their lot.

She rounded the gondola end and that was when she spotted Natalia. Walking up behind, she saw her friend was swaying slightly as she clung to a shopping trolley. Briony touched her on her shoulder, not knowing where to begin. 'Hello, girl. Isn't it amazing that there's no panic buying? Or am I the muggins around here?' There was no reply, only a vacant look. She tried again. 'There would be no point I guess, risking an exquisite death.' Briony could see her friend was a little unfocussed. She leaned closer and looped her arm through Natalia's. 'Are you alright, my love?' She leaned even closer but couldn't smell any booze.

'I am fine. I was in Montreux earlier and the exotic flowers were gone. I expect the HB storm made all the petals fall off. "говно"' She lurched slightly and Briony grabbed her other arm to help steady her.

'No, girl, the commune are busy building a bunker under the Rochers de Naye. It's an offshoot to that tunnel that leads to the restaurant terrace hanging off the cliff face.'

Natalia swayed. 'Huh, I love the flowers in the mountains but the commune have not planted the water avens yet.' She was talking slowly and the commune had never planted natural mountain species.

Briony tried to bring her back to reality: 'Are the kids OK?'

'Visiting is good but home is better.'

'Hmm…what?'

'Russian "говно"'

Briony spelt her words out, nodding to each one 'Are the kids OK?'

'"да" OK. After barbecue, seemed relaxed. What you say… talking with each other. They share things with me not much,' she shrugged, 'electronic…lally at least.'

'Yes, teenagers hey, avoiding mum and dad.' Briony smiled at her friend. She said it gently, 'Have you been drinking, by any chance?'

Natalia hung her head in shame and came clean. '"да" much since breakfast.'

Briony pulled her closer and gave her a giant hug. 'Why, my love?'

'It is Bert, the devil today and God tomorrow. I do not understand. He is not with us anymore…' She started to sob on her friend's shoulder making the words lumpy 'In a year… we have been "us"…one night…it is as if he is lost.' The group of old ladies were watching the pair from a distance, so Briony pulled her friend behind a rack of crisps. Ironic, she thought, they would go well with the booze. Natalia sniffed. 'Do not tell Sam, he will tell the goat?'

'Of course not, just promise that you will keep talking to me. I mean it. Friends for life and all that!'

'I promise, thank you.' Natalia pulled herself clear.

'What were you drinking?'

'Huh, Russian vodka, of course. I just came to buy more.'

She laughed, 'I can understand the vodka, you being a Muscovite, but you need to stop, OK?' Briony willed her to say yes.

'He cannot smell it.' Natalia was smiling in triumph.

'Yes, I know that. The lack of smell confused me.' Briony paused, she could see the tears welling up in her friend's eyes again. 'But you need to stop, OK?'

Natalia sobbed her reply. 'I am only human, I told him that.' She shuddered. 'And my husband is inhuman.' She cried, the tears pouring down her cheeks. 'He thinks he is a God and that is worse than inhuman.' Briony had watched the married pair for years and had seen Bert's arrogance and selfish behaviour. But she thought despite the outward tensions, they were a solid couple. Natalia and Bert loved each other for their faults. They were diametrically opposed in every way. That was the attraction. She escorted Natalia out of the store and left the vodka and her own shopping basket on top of a pallet of beer near the exit. As Briony turned to look back at the stash, she could see the old ladies were now watching them leave before restarting their gossip. She reasoned it would be a new subject.

★ ★ ★

Briony guided her friend to the nearest coffee shop and thoughtfully placed her in a dark corner to protect her eyes and her identity.

'Come on then, I've seen your steady decline… again. So you say it's Bert's uniqueness this time? Or like last time, is it his male chauvinist – I am right all of the time attitude?'

She watched Natalia heave a giant sigh of relief. 'I think, I know, I…we have to live separate, "да" separate.' She thumped her elbows onto the formica top and gripped her cheeks. 'Huh, I knew that last year but could not face the thought, "нет".'

Briony leaned across to gently pull her friends hands down to the table. 'Then along came the HBs and you feel guilty if you leave him, blah blah blah. Being a good wife, and what about the children blah.'

Natalia grinned at her. 'So you are Russian, blunt, so to the point.' But the moment was lost. They turned as one to the TV screen further down the bar, the waitress had turned up the volume and the feature stopped all conversations in the cafe.

CCOW – CENTRAL CONTROL OF THE WORLD

Briefing

The importance of good communications in all the bunkers will ensure you can have great entertainment every day. This has received a massive boost. Wilocity, an American/Israeli company, specialise in the fastest wifi chips on earth. They have agreed to provide every bunker in the world with their latest beta-test wifi chips, which are being built into new earth-penetrating Netgear routers. The super high frequency was first introduced in 2014 and the latest version allows unlimited wireless transfers. But there will be a small limitation on interactive gaming and movie streaming between bunkers. We just cannot solve this technical issue in time. However, expect the fastest performance to meet all your needs in your bunker, giving 24-7 fun for all the family.

'At least our kids will be happy, Natalia.' A sour-faced old crone turned to hush them.

Simply put and to stop all the rumours circulating. There is no rationing of drugs. Doctors are not allowing old sick people to die. Please ignore these stupid rumours and keep looking at the CCOW broadcasts for the truth.

HB loan certificates, or the so called storm bonds, were introduced last week. These will allow your government to borrow money from other governments. They are the only method for capital transfers allowed until The Return. Great news! They are proving to be a huge success as the populations of the richer countries are buying them in their billions. This will allow the poorer Third World countries to effectively borrow money immediately and fund their bunkers.

A minor inconvenience. Green light

The use of mobile telephones to talk to friends and family in other bunkers cannot be guaranteed at present. Experiments are showing us the difficulties of supporting and networking 5G telephony. However, we expect this issue to be resolved shortly. You can of course use wifi to Facetime, Hangout and Skype.

A moderate inconvenience. Amber light

We understand that some countries are running low on stocks of paracetamol. This is because one constituent in the manufacture of this drug has been used extensively to make The Envelope paste. Please be assured that every country will have a surplus of this fundamental painkiller by March 2019 when we enter the Deeps.

A major inconvenience. Red light
Please understand that the scientists have assured us that the HB predictor level has not changed much since last week. We apologise for the lack of data due to the catastrophic fire. Our thoughts are with those who perished and their families.

HB Predictor today
We are still awaiting new parts. It is not like a car as items have to be specially manufactured. The fire was severe and it may take a few weeks to repair.

Briony whispered to her friend behind a cupped hand. 'I'm not sure that's true.'

'Why?'

'Hmm…,' she hesitated, just because.' It was better to keep quiet and listen, Natalia was the wrong person to share secrets with at present.

"Adversity has ever been considered the state in which a man most easily becomes acquainted with himself, then, especially, being free from flatterers."

Samuel Johnson

"There is no time to pass new laws and debate the facts in parliaments, we must just do it. No time to think, nor to procrastinate. Just Do It!"

President Trump

Your questions and answers from the App – stormbrain

Can we stay in our houses?
*It is not possible to "envelope" individual houses because there
is too much work to ensure all people can be safely protected.
Plus everyone does not have a basement with the added safety of
surrounding soil. However, by pooling our resources together, we
can protect everyone. It also means that all essential services can
be located safely in bunkers adjacent to you, the people. Imagine
sitting at home and needing surgery but not being able to go to a
hospital. We are in this together and we will make it work.*

Has anyone been killed yet by a firing squad?
*No, nowhere in the world. Minor disturbances have of course
occurred but the world was never a quiet place, was it?*

Has food been rationed anywhere?
*Remarkably it has not. That is great news for all. Yes,
governments have commandeered some stocks of tinned and
also dried food. Maybe they will commandeer more, but only
when the HB predictor level reaches 50 or less. Many people have
told us on the stormbrain comments page that they are missing
dried spaghetti and rice. But all supplies of essential foods
have remained constant. In addition, we have no shortages of
electricity so everything is operating normally. This applies to
every country in the world.*

*Congratulations to you all on being so calm, so thoughtful
and giving.*
We are working together and that is outstanding news.
A world first, well done all.

FOCUSSING AND RESOLVING OUR ISSUES TO SAVE MANKIND.
THIS HAS BEEN NAMED BY THE WORLD COUNCIL AS:
"CONVERGENCE".

Briony rubbed the top of her friend's arm, 'Aren't CCOW doing well Natalia? It seems life goes on as normal, and what a miracle that is, isn't it?'

Her friend was staring at the ceiling with a cold coffee in front of her. 'I am so tired, you cannot believe how tired I feel.'

'And I can see you're depressed. You should confide in me more.'

'I know and I know I can trust you. I think it could be the menopause. I am tired, down and fat. No wonder Bert does not want sex.'

'That is crap, girl. Make a doctor's appointment, won't you.' Natalia's chin wobbled but she couldn't reply. 'Just do it, OK.' Briony reached a hand across the table again and didn't let go until the tears had dried up.

★ ★ ★

Natalia and Bert retired to the salon together that evening at her insistence. They both knew they had unfinished business. It was hot and humid outside but the salon lay in the shade of the wisteria, and therefore was cooler and more comfortable. She deliberately sat opposite him in her armchair, remembering their past and planning to tell him about their separate futures. Bert sat rigid and upright in front of her, watching her quietly. She knew she was slurring her words but she didn't care anymore. She was determined to tell him about what they had forfeited during their married life but it was all a bit vague in her head. On impulse she blurted out, 'I wish my father had been proud of me.'

'What do you mean?'

'I wasted his money. I was sent to the best schools and I did nothing to make Count Suvarov proud.'

'You have never admitted that in twenty years. Were you so bad at school?'

'I did not try at anything. I did not want to be there.'

'Because?'

'Because I knew my daddy was worth five billion dollars. Because I knew I could have anything I wanted without effort.'

'Is that why you don't see him much?'

'That is part of the reason "да". But I cannot face him, he challenges me to be better, even now.'

Bert shuffled around on the settee, 'I can't believe that, you never told me until now.'

'"Нет", I could not tell, I would be…what you say…admit to fail, but you, you are a huge success.'

Bert asked gently. 'What is the other part of the reason?'

'The twenty years old model bitch that he dumped my mother for.'

Bert stretched his legs along the sofa cushion. 'You said that years ago my dear. Remember, people are like particles, they attract and repel. Like you and me.'

She missed the opening as she slumped further into the seat squab, weighed down by vodka. 'The bitch smelt rubles.'

'Well, maybe, but that isn't what I meant. You must have met people whom you speak to for the first time and instantly dislike them. Instantly, without any reasons.'

'I loved Briony and Sam the first time.'

'Precisely, it's particle physics.'

'Briony, I love because she is a clever chemist. She loves her husband. They had no sex until married. "говно" I say.'

'My point is; there is no obvious reason. You just don't like someone as soon as you meet them, or you love them instantly. Like you and I.'

Natalia vehemently disagreed. Her words weren't coherent. Half an hour earlier she had repeatedly sunk shots of vodka until she had felt sick. The consequences were growing exponentially. 'No, no, no, it is emotions and thoughts, not particles and attraction.' She carried on in a rant but he wasn't listening anymore.

After a few minutes he interrupted her. She jerked to face him. 'Natalia, shut up and listen for a change. It's not circumstances that make and break relationships.' He paused so that she could understand the hidden implications. 'It's not your weight, your hair loss or your acne. It's simply choices.' He stood up and walked to the door.

She turned on him. 'Bert, that is the problem. You, your stress, how you want to save the world…you see nothing day to day.'

He had one last point to make. 'I see everything day to day. Have another drink, why don't you? It makes it worse, you know.'

Natalia blustered. 'What do you mean?'

'Maybe you didn't realise how badly you're slurring your words. Maybe you don't care anymore.' He walked out and returned from the kitchen with the empty vodka bottle that she had so carefully hidden away. 'Gone native Russian, have we? All hope lost in a bottle?' He let the bottle crash to the floor. This time he walked out and slammed the door behind him. Natalia sat and silently sobbed. After a few minutes she curled into a foetus and closed her eyes to sleep.

At midnight, she hadn't moved. The window was open and she heard the church bells toll, twelve slow rings that echoed up the valley. She stayed still, listening for Bert moving around but she heard nothing. Natalia unfolded her stiff body and slowly hobbled towards the window. Looking out she saw the tilleul tree growing out of the small roundabout behind the chalet. The moonlight flattened and shortened the shadow of the tree, giving an eerie sense of evil. It was quiet and seemingly not disturbed, but she felt it was brooding. A silly thought, brought on by the booze and emotions.

★ ★ ★

A few kilometres away, in an exact opposite of space and time, Briony rested her breasts on Sam's hairy chest. They were both sweating in the heat after their violent love making.

'We weren't too noisy, were we, darling?' She giggled.

'No, my love, we weren't.' He emphasised the "we". She slapped him on his shoulder and giggled again.

'I went into the supermarket as usual today and Natalia was there.' He murmured something unintelligible. 'She was drunk.'

'Oh dear. Do you want me to talk to Bert?'

'No, exactly the opposite. She said Bert was unbelievably negative and insular. That he was the cause of her drinking.'

'He usually is negative!'

'No, worse than normal. Hmm…lost in space is a good way of putting it.'

'Tell me about it.'

'He had said to her, think of all the people you have met in your life, including your family and put them in a hole. A cold dark place, with no space, no entertainment, bad food and poor facilities.' She remembered Natalia's words exactly. 'Think of the things those people said to you during your lifetime. The things they did to you and multiply it a thousand fold to hatred. Can you survive that? It will fry your brain and erode all your humanity.' Sam remained quiet but breathed slightly faster. 'We can be better than that, can't we, darling?'

Her husband responded quietly. 'Have no fear, we will be better than that, my love. Bert can be so cruel sometimes.'

'I love you so much, my darling. Don't let anything tear us apart, will you?'

She turned on her back and was tempted to turn on the sidelight to look at her love. She decided to maintain the moment and left it off. 'You know, I saw real pain in the faces of people at the supermarket today. I hadn't noticed it before. And then at work as well. People appear to feel guilty. They are acting worried but are not actually worried, if that makes sense?'

'Meaning what, love?'

'Hmm…I guess they feel that they can't do anything for their families. So they are worried but know and trust the government to solve all their problems.'

He thought out loud: 'Implying the world is becoming even more selfish?'

She replied thoughtfully. 'Self-centred?'

'Listen, darling, it is a natural progression of their grief and also an easy cop out. They don't know what to do and so they take onboard the guilt. The responsibility is horrific. A vicious circle of more mental pain as the guilt increases.' She heard his anxiety for the first time and turned on her side and threw her bare leg across his.

'You have stopped talking about work, you know.' Briony pulled the hairs on his chest.

Sam turned towards her. 'That's not strictly true. I can't talk about what is really happening in this world and in fact in any other world.' He sighed deeply. 'It's too hard to contemplate. Maybe we should concentrate on now.'

She tightened her grip and pushed her body onto him. Their sweat warmed up, 'Tell me. Ramble a bit, I don't mind.'

After a short pause, he spoke gently without pause. 'We are insignificant, a mountain of flesh, billions of particles being destroyed by one. I am seeing and hearing things that make life unbelievable. You can't believe any fact on the internet. It's a world wide conglomeration of lies and all controlled by CCOW. You can't even reserve a car parking spot in Geneva airport, without someone selling you Convergence.' She asked no questions, she trusted him implicitly. 'The mobile morons are convincing themselves that they have to use their phones for all their waking life to listen to CCOW. And believing everything that is broadcast.'

'I don't. I only listen or watch when it is rammed down my throat.'

'I clocked that, but you are an exception and maybe that's because you're on the inside track?' She grunted. 'Look my love, there is a real news blackout and CCOW orchestration in everything we see. I can't say more, you know.'

She stirred. 'But it is all about the good in people and meeting their emotional needs. I only see the positive spin on everything. Whether we are brainwashed or not, it feels positive, despite the lie on the level of HBs.'

Sam kissed her. 'That's the trouble. Bert is seeing only the negative spin.'

'What about you?' She had felt compelled to ask.

'I love you so much, my darling. Don't let anything tear us apart, will you?'

'Very subtle and...'

He made light of it all. 'It puts a different spin on global warming and carbon dioxide, doesn't it? They aren't so important after all now.'

She pressed him further, his voice had risen an octave, 'Tell me how you feel, Sam.'

Sam sighed deeply and took a few deep breaths. 'This all feels like grief, that none of us have ever experienced in our lives. But we have no time to grieve for our old lives, they are ending. We have no time to panic about the coming storm because we cannot do anything alone. We all need each other.' He thought about it and she stayed silent to help him. She thought his words were purging the detritus out of their lives. 'Alone, no one would survive. With each other; well, we will be safe, secure. Able to become strong again and resume our normalities.'

'What a funny new word, as if anything will be normal again. And a great speech, husband, but I've noticed you're not sharing your feelings anymore.' He grunted in agreement. 'Jean-Jacques Rousseau lived here, you know. He defined civilisation as when people build fences. We are all a product of a fenced in lack of freedom before HB but now, I don't know. Is our unnatural way of life such that going into the Deeps is no worse, no less natural?'

He sat up and turned his legs over the side of the bed, ready to go to the toilet. Before he rose he said one last thing, 'It is faith that pulls the world together to meet a common cause. There is goodness in people and we can work together.'

'And that is why we have always been practising Christians.'

'Yes but Bert disputes my faith in people. He only has faith in science and that is a misplaced trust.' He left the bedroom, leaving her to dwell on his words. She wondered how deep a rift was developing between the two best friends. It seemed the HB storm was tearing her world apart but the country was OK. There was the same attitude in the country that must have been shown in World War Two. It seemed to her that all countries were showing grit and resilience in the face of hardship, but maybe Sam knew better. The TV news tonight had reported many countries were planning great national outpourings, celebrating life and solidarity against the HB storm. The BBC said that HB street parties and local fetes were planned worldwide, with parties in Tiananmen and Times Square, "together forever " nights in the Jordanian desert and floating on rafts on top of the Andes at Lake Titicaca. It was anticipated that there would be huge crowds in major city centres. Banners, solidarity, a will to work together and survive. That was her dream and her husband's crusade and so she felt comfortable on a loving summer's night, her legs drawn up and hugged to her chin.

Sam collapsed back on the bed. 'I always wanted to surf a giant wave in Hawaii but I guess I won't now.'

She stretched her legs flat and leaned back on to her elbows, 'What else did you want to do, my love?'

'I wanted to land on the moon. I think my time has passed on that one too.'

'No, silly. We have all the time in the world.' She pulled him down to her. They desired each other more than ever.

★ ★ ★

Lily started to talk to him again that night as he faced the tilleul tree. He was standing on the first floor balcony, on his left were the bright pearls of Montreux way below.

'We are the birth flower this month and many humans celebrate us. Why do you do that, human?

Bert turned a full three hundred and sixty degrees, searching for the emanation. He tried to triangulate Her position by responding to Her question. Now he knew She wasn't tied to the pond, She was everywhere She wanted to be. He spoke quietly into the air, a breathless answer. 'Monet made you famous.' The bells on Montreux's oldest church tolled again. A dull pleasant monotone that carried across the still night and made the owls screech in the trees above the chalet. He nervously searched the darkness, pacing backwards and forwards along the balcony. He tried again. 'The American Indians ground you up to make flour.' There was still no response. 'In Greek mythology the inhabitants of an island ate you to forget their woes. The lotus-eaters used you as a drug, so that they could sleep peacefully in apathy.'

'All I can see are these same humans who mistreated us are going to die. Do you see the beauty of the lake, the mountains and the sky anymore or solely death invisibly pouring from the blackness of space?'

He deigned to answer at first and let her stew for a minute. 'And I see us, humankind, dwarfed by many universes with no concept of space and no concept of you, Lily.'

'You see nothing, because you have no hope, Bert. But all others, including your family and friends, have hope, and that is what gives them their inner strength. A focus on something

within nothing that will never end, and it gives them the strength to go on.'

He stayed quiet and still, afraid that talking out loud might mean he would be heard by his wife inside. Heard and judged as mad. He chuckled to himself, his tummy muscles tight and painful.

'*We can disperse and survive in terrible conditions and you can learn from us. Be with us, have strength to go on, Bert. I can save you.'*

Bert gripped the rounded edge of the balustrade. His nails dug into the soft tar pine as he whispered, 'Listen to me Lily, I don't believe in hope, as hope has a nothingness about it. And I certainly don't believe in any God, or any form of faith.' He waved his hands towards the village of Caux set high above him. 'Not Rosicrucian as based up there. Not Coptic, Buddhist, Hindu, Christian or any of the religions and their supreme beings.

'*So what do you believe in?'*

'I believe in matter and antimatter. Matter made this universe and is my God.'

'*So you show no human emotion and no human weakness or frailty? You are the purist of souls. Is that right?'*

He tipped his head to the heavens and laughed at her rhetorical question. 'I don't believe in climate change, in the jet streams permanently moving their position. Nor in ecology and alternative energy, they are not facts, only beliefs. A change of state caused by something in the world, a symbiosis.' He ran on, drunk with the thought of losing his wife. 'I do believe in emotion, Lily. Not a chemical chafe in the brain, nor a response to love or beauty, but a particle change. A differentiation in the particle entropy inside of us and in super symmetry with a soul mate.'

'But you are dying. Can't you feel it, human? It is your ending as the emotional species and so you should be with your soul mate then!'

'Rubbish. The end of the earth and my demise is because the amount of Higgs Boson particles is increasing above the norm. It has no impact on our emotions. The effect is simple and misunderstood; the creation of new particles that will break our stability and kill us. But it will never change my emotions. Me, my emotions, my love, my purity of goodness.'

'How is that possible for a scientist?'

The time felt right to debate with Her. She was encouraging his thoughts and he wanted to draw Her in and understand Her. 'Many particles with mass will have their mass super augmented and the smallest, like neutrinos, therefore become dangerous for the first time. They won't simply penetrate everything, leaving behind equilibrium. They will destroy because there are other particles smaller than the neutrino and smaller again and we have no idea what else. A change is happening, so as big lumps of meat we are dead.' He thought about the changes to humankind, 'But tiny animals like ants, flowers and of course the lilies. They may survive longer or at least until the point of complete elemental decay.' A tear ran down his right cheek. 'Human behaviour will certainly evolve faster now. There will be a change in psyche, but not for long. It is the crescendo of our existence. The governments will control us and everything else. You are right. We are doomed. But we deserve it.'

Lily wasn't in the mood for weak human emotions. *'So you think of the world in its fundamental state?'*

'Of course! What else is there? Matter and antimatter battling for supremacy as particles in many forms, probably more than we recognise.'

'*So you have a missing ingredient x, is that correct, Bert?*'

'X, y and z, and maybe more? We cannot foresee these particles and we cannot predict the spread of them through the seven known universes.

'*So you know nothing?*'

Bert collapsed on his knees and leaned his head forward to touch the balcony. 'I know everything, and everything tells me that we are lost.'

★ ★ ★

The next morning CERN held their second conference since announcing the crisis. The assembled media wanted answers from the greatest scientists on earth, the men who had brought this issue to the world. Bert, Sam and Ralph were in the ante-room of the UN Council Chamber. A silent Ralph was looking out of a tall window that magnified the brown grass of Ariana Park. Sam sat on a formica topped table kicking his legs backwards and forwards. He looked across at Bert who had his feet on the same table and lay back in his tilted chair with his eyes closed. He envied his friend's mindset. Sam felt compelled to fill the void: 'How are your family coping, Ralph?'

The DG jerked his gaze away from the view. 'I am afraid they aren't coping at all, Sam. They are scared. How about yours?'

'Strangely, they seem quite relaxed at the moment.' He added, after a pause, 'I believe they're relying on our church and supporting each other and their friends.'

Bert's eyes remained closed as he spoke: 'That's because you are their saviour, the Jesus of CERN.'

The DG gave Sam a knowing look before rolling his eyes towards the ceiling. Sam continued, 'What are you going to do, Ralph? I mean, when the time comes.'

Ralph sat in a vacant chair next to Bert. He scraped it noisily across the granite floor to move closer to Sam. 'We have a small farm in Provence and some wine cellars that interlink beneath the house and outbuildings. So I am going to get hold of some Envelope, make the cellars safe, and go below as a family.'

Sam was incensed. 'Surely that's obscene, especially in your position?' Ralph hung his head and didn't answer.

Bert opened his eyes and let his seat topple forward with a crash. Taking his legs off the table he applauded Ralph. 'Good for you, at least it's a humanistic and caring plan.' He turned to his friend. 'Why shouldn't he, Sam? Don't you wonder how many other people are playing a different game to the one you want?'

Sam whined his reply as he too had a plan to keep his and Bert's families together in the same bunker. 'It doesn't seem moral, that's all.'

'Moral? It's dog eat dog, pal. There are millions of subtexts beyond our comprehension. Power, sex and money makes the world spin round.'

Sam was about to reply and deny Bert's theme that the world was rotting away from the inside as well as from outer space but an aide opened the door.

'We are ready gentlemen.' They sidled out to face the press, Sam went last.

The briefing was brief at twenty minutes. Only Ralph and Sam were scripted to speak, leaving Bert to yawn, cough and gaze at the heavenly roof, where José Sert had painted five muscled and half naked men gripping each other's wrists and hands. The alarming giants spanned the room like rafters, a symbol of solidarity between the five continents and depicting international brotherhood. As he considered heaven, the media considered Bert, wondering when he might speak. Sam glanced at his friend, worried about what he might say. Bert had always been newsworthy compared to him; Sam remembered the first announcement and his loss of control. What a bastard Bert could be. Sam grew more apprehensive as the open questioning came closer. He listened to the CERN bosses confirming the HB storm was still happening, that it wasn't as bad as first feared, that the world had more time than previously thought. His stomach tightened and he felt nauseous. The end came and the DG stated there was a mere five minutes for questions.

CNN: 'What has happened to the predictor and how long before you have it working again?'

Sam took the question and blurted out the prepared answer. 'The time taken to make repairs, and then recalibrate it, is solely dependent on an elite but very small team of scientists. Therefore, we must take our time, be safe, and then make multiple tests to make it accurate.' He felt better immediately.

CNN: 'So why is the project sealed off for all access, including by your own scientists? There are guards stationed everywhere.'

Sam calmly replied, 'You must understand that this is a complex instrument. The team are working on the process for repairs in their offices on the campus or at manufacturers and do not need constant access to the detector. The damage has been analysed at site and then was announced by CCOW. Now we will fix it as soon as possible.' He felt even better.

The BBC: 'Professor Murray, what level do you think the predictor count would be now if it was working?'

Shit, he said it under his breath and completely locked up inside. It was Ralph who stepped in and gave the direct lie. Sam was sweating and breathing heavily by his side. 'The level may have gone down. We think it has a little, but of course that is based on a calculation, partly the law of the iterated logarithm and of course it is totally empirical.'

The BBC: 'Excluding the nonsense in your reply, with respect sir; could it go up again?'

Ralph was happy to comment further through his tight smile. 'Of course it can go up! It cycles in peaks and troughs, hour by hour. Frankly, anything is possible but we hope it will improve.' Bert squirmed in his seat. 'Please remember this, everyone! Next week it could go down and the week after it may pop back up again. Also remember that nothing changes if we go underground, we still have our families, health and healthcare, education, law and order and even our dearest pleasures.' A few of the journalists present sarcastically clapped a few times. One cheered bravo. Sam relaxed again, his crisis over.

The sarcastic applause had discouraged Sam from adding anything further, but he wanted to say a few words, to be seen as in control: 'We are happily working together as hard as possible and, to echo CCOW and The World Council, we will win!' At that point most of the media present focussed directly on Bert, as they could see he was uncomfortable. His eyes searched the room and he grasped the arms of his seat. The man who had never failed hadn't said a word.

Al Jazeera: 'Professor Leinster, why have we got the storm? Two months ago, you said you would find the answer and I am sure it is the question we all want answered.' The reporter held her hands up in supplication.

Bert stood up, his hands in his pockets. 'I will and I won't find the answer. I didn't say how long it would take. Maybe we'll all be dead by then.' He sat down, a deflation felt by all the journalists. The first sign of any negativity from a top CERN representative.

Al Jazeera: She was shocked by his reply and her voice broke as she asked, 'Have you found nothing at all? Come on Leinster, what do you mean? You never talk in riddles.'

Bert shrugged his shoulders. 'I do this job because there is no answer, just a never ending search. That is the logic. You ask your questions because you think there is an answer to everything. An emotional and emotive one that answers the meaning of life when we might be dead. It's pure bullshit.'

There was an uproar as most of the journalists shouted out a query, determined to ask Bert the next question.

Al Jazeera held the floor: 'Why do you think we are going to die?'

Ralph stood up and waved for calm. 'Please, ladies and gentlemen, do not be distracted by the independent wit of my esteemed colleague.' He motioned to the lady from Al Jazeera to continue her questioning. As the audience shouted loudly again, he pointed to her alone above the clamour.

Al Jazeera: 'I must ask again: Have you discovered a dire, a fatal reason behind the HB storm, Professor Leinster?'

'No, we have found nothing. The storm could go on for decades or end in five minutes time.' There was uproar once again. Bert shouted but few heard him. 'You think we are only as good as each other...whether it's laying concrete or brain surgery. You think that we depend on each other.' He was going to out the lie about the predictor and postulate the storm would never end, until he glanced to his left and saw Sam's contorted face. His best friend's eyes pleaded with him. Sam's head moved imperceptibly from side to side so that a camera wouldn't notice. Behind a cupped hand, he finally gave a silent please towards his best friend. Years of love and friendship went into the mouthed word.

Bert turned to stare into the live camera, he paused and watched the red LED blinking at him. 'Listen.' The room quietened immediately. 'The HB storm started instantly and so it is conceivable that it may end instantly.'

The journalists heaved a sigh of relief, giving Ralph the perfect moment to dismiss the audience. The three scientists walked back to the ante-room and locked themselves in. Ralph and Sam paced around the table and Bert sat defiantly with his arms crossed. After a few minutes, Ralph spoke quietly to Bert: 'You don't need to come to anymore briefings, Bert.' Bert was surprised that his boss then smiled at him. 'It's OK, you know.'

Bert understood the end of a relationship. 'KK, I do comprehend that I live in an unreal life. Really I do, Ralph. But you know what, I couldn't have come to any more of these. I truly don't understand how you two can live the lie.'

Only Ralph answered: 'Because the lie is all we have.' Bert stood and walked to the door. He turned back and said goodbye as he unlocked and opened it. Then he quietly closed the door and drove back to the shed, leaving the others to work on the escape from the most inexplicable event on earth. Its end.

★ ★ ★

The phone had been hanging in her hand for ages, it seemed like ages to Natalia but the clock denied it. She watched the TV, the announcer cut through her hangover as she reached for a tissue to dry her eyes.

CCOW – Central Control Of the World
Briefing
Today we have launched the basics campaign.

Our promise is safety and security to meet all your basic needs. The World Council promises this and it will never break its promise.

> » *We pledge shelter in the bunkers for everyone. All races, creeds, religions and ages.*
> » *We pledge food and water, sanitary systems, light and heat and healthcare for a minimum of two years underground.*
> » *We pledge that the education of children will continue.*
> » *We pledge to keep families together. Happy and strong.*
> » *We pledge to keep you safe and secure by bolstering your police and armed forces.*
> » *We pledge to entertain you with wifi and TV channels and also give you opportunities to remain fit.*

You can find more details applicable to your country on http://thebasicsnow.org

A minor inconvenience. Green light
All meat and fish products served in the Deeps will be frozen, tinned or dried.

A moderate inconvenience. Amber light
We understand that your health and fitness is paramount and therefore as you enter your bunker, older people will be given the opportunity for health checks by local doctors. The age limit will vary by country depending on local demographics and health

care standards. It is highly likely that older people will want this, in order to establish a benchmark for their health and fitness and receive any preventative treatment before entering the Deeps.

A major inconvenience. Red light
Please understand that we cannot let your pets join you in the Deeps. You know that this cannot work. The mix of animals and humans is not possible in enclosed spaces, that is why we are not taking any livestock underground.

Your local council will be aiding you all the way. There are already clear instructions on how to leave your pets roaming on the surface that links into the independence for all livestock at Convergence. This will ensure they all have the best chance of surviving the HB storm. Free facilities to "put them to sleep" will be offered if required.

Natalia hit redial one, the screen read dad mobile. She breathed slowly through her mouth, there was no response, she took more deep breaths and then he picked up. She could hear tinny reverberations of distant voices outside the shed. 'We have got to talk, Bert. For the children's sake.'

'It's a bad time. I'm watching the CCOW briefing.'

'Do not be hard on me, Bert. I am having a bad time, OK.' She listened to the tone of his voice for a sign. For a truce.

'I get it, but what do you think?'

'I think we have to separate.'

'Yeah, we have known that a long time, my dear. But what I need to know is what do you think of the briefing.'

'I think it gives me every reason to take the children into the Deeps, but we cannot wait for you. We cannot live together until March, you know that, "да".'

'We can talk later. There is no argument about us, I get it. But don't go into the Deeps, please trust me on this. It will be a horrific slow death mangled by a million people who can never be friends.'

'You are wrong for once, moya lyubov. You have lost it, I heard you talking to yourself in the middle of the night.' He didn't reply so she gently pressed the disconnect button and turned back to the TV.

HB Predictor today

CERN say it is still at a high reading. So this was good news from their media conference held earlier today.

"In the middle of difficulty lies opportunity."

Albert Einstein.

Scientific briefing

The Higgs Boson particle is like an ephemeral being that invisibly glues our world together, or should we say our universe. HB particles are highly unstable and immediately decay. When you try and measure something that exists so briefly, it is already nothing. The other clear idea to place in your mind is that particles all spin like a top; but Higgs is the first "spin less" particle and is a new type of matter. Very different to what we have known before. That makes it hard to understand what is happening now.

There are many thoughts, for example. Cosmologically, what made the Big Bang – the start of our universe? If you have enough Higgs Boson, let us say the size of a grain of wheat, then it could have put the "bang" into the Big Bang. But we don't know, we can only surmise and experiment.

Scientists always fall back on one idea, which is that of "tagged symmetry". That means a unified whole, one thing, with a single type of interaction or force. Be it the symmetry of your face or a steel sphere. It can be explained by simple equations but if symmetry goes wrong, like now, what happens? Fundamentally, life is symmetrical in every way. We all know that. All computers work on a basis of on or off, zero or one. Now our lives revolve around zero and one, maybe God was zero and The Devil was one. Symmetry thus applied from the start of "us". Another thought: maybe symmetry doesn't apply in the case of the Higgs Boson storm. We do not know.

Remember, make the most of now by helping others and working hard to create the Deeps. All things are transitory – here today, gone tomorrow. In truth and in time, all of this, all of now, goes way beyond anything we see and do.

Do Tweet your thoughts. #intruthandintime and share them with the world.

Natalia started to Tweet immediately after hanging up on Bert.

#intruthandintime husbands who are bastards should stay on the surface.

She hit send and immediately regretted it. But she looked at the response to the CCOW Tweet many times in the following 24 hours. Out of 100 million Tweets concerning #intruthandintime, only a few castigated their husbands or partners. Three were direct replies offering to have sex with her. She also noticed that no one Tweeted about anything serious and important. Most comments were centred on an owner's love of their cat or dog, allowing them to be put to sleep or to roam, that was the sole question puzzling humankind.

* * *

Liam texted Josh: 'What planet is your dad on?'

Josh replied, 'Somewhere beyond our universe I think. He and mum had a fight again. Big one. So he's spaced out I guess.'

Liam replied, 'Did he really imply we are all going to die?'

The response was instant. 'My dad would never let us die. If anyone can save us, it's my dad.'

'And mine Josh. And mine. We are in CERN in ten minutes. First trip – Fab.'

* * *

Sam had never shown his family where he worked and so Briony asked him outright if they could all go. She felt it was about time they saw the LHC as the visit would be an antidote to their HB trauma. He had already told them that the predictor area was off-limits during repairs. But Briony didn't care, her objective was for her kids to see their dad's place of sacrifice. As they drove to CERN Sam had explained that all the particle physicists were looking at the data generated up to the May announcement but it was pointless generating anymore. The equivalent of four million memory sticks of data had been created and that helped Briony see his point. Dad had told them that even with The Grid and 170 collaborating data centres, plus thousands of scientists, there was too much data and now there was no time. Briony told him that it was OK, he was a huge success and could do no more, and the kids listened and that made her happy.

Sam's voice boomed around them. 'In space, no one can hear you scream.'

'Very funny, darling,' Briony turned to the kids, 'Alien, 1979, but quiet, yes spookily quiet.'

They were stood outside the lift that would take them underground. Around their necks were lanyards holding a blue steel canister 2 cms long. It was their access token to trigger the biometric scanners and gain entry. Each of them took it in turns to enter the first set of concertina doors, which immediately closed behind them with a hydraulic swish. One step forward, recognition from the eye scanner, then the second set of doors smoothly opened. As well as the tokens, they had been given small radiation badges pinned to their lapels and yellow plastic safety helmets.

Sam warned them, 'We're going down to where it's pressurised, so if we hear a loud alarm, that is a warning wail of three seconds high pitched and ten seconds low pitched, then we must walk up the steps to make sure we slowly depressurise and don't get the bends. Got it?' They nodded excitedly. 'Then let's go down.'

At the bottom of the deep shaft, he guided them the few hundred metres towards the heart of the LHC. Firstly, they passed the old machinery that had been shunted to one side, its millions of wires exposed for all to see. Obsolete technology and now dead and useless but not worth removing. And then Briony gasped. The green gantries, tall stairs and giant yellow cranes paled into insignificance as they marvelled at the cathedral size of the newest cavern. There were yellow sodium nebulas spread across the roof and a wall of noise from hanging gas systems, cooling fans and hydraulic pumps that maintained the system in its redundancy.

He gave a commentary as they walked. 'The hoists above the LHC allowed us to build it and we use them now to move pieces for repairs. Of course one day we may remove the whole thing but that would be expensive.'

Briony was looking upwards and didn't see his face as she asked an innocent question: 'Is the HB predictor in the other experiment close to being fixed yet?'

'No, nowhere near ready. By the way, don't worry it's 4 kms away. We were putting 11,000 amps through the magnet cables and a bad joint caused a meltdown and helium fire. So it's down the pan, love.' He was describing a true event, a quench, but in 2008 instead of two weeks before. 'What you have to realise is that we are controlling billions of atomic particles as we accelerate them. One million atoms can fit across the breadth of a human hair and an atom is made up of many particles like quarks and electrons.'

'Dad!' It was Hannah who protested. 'You said a non-scientific trip!'

'OK. Well, the giant blocks of steel are used to remove the halo created around the thin beam of accelerated particles. A bit like cutting out all the colours in a rainbow to leave red alone. The ring around which they are accelerated is twenty seven kilometres long but it isn't circular.'

'How come?' Hannah was impressed.

'We are in the LHC experiment that sits on one of eight straight sections. All experiments must be on straight sections. These are joined by eight curved sections, with eight points of access to the surface.'

Liam asked his dad a question: 'Is it like a laser, then? Can you slice through the earth and blow Iran apart?' They all laughed uneasily.

Sam answered him: 'No, son, we control the power and the particle make-up of the beam and of course the acceleration. So we are always in control. But after sixteen hours we must dump the highly charged particle beam into the tangential tunnels.'

'Like put the brake on?' It was Liam again.

'Not quite. We can't afford to slow the particles electronically so we plunge them into the earth. A diversion into a tunnel directed by the super-cooled magnets.'

Hannah asked the question that was on Briony's mind too. 'Did you and Bert start the HB storm, dad?'

'No, love, we can't have done. The maths doesn't work.'

'Good,' said Hannah, 'I've told all my friends that it was a lie on Twitter.'

Her dad put his arm around her shoulder. 'Don't believe everything you hear and see from now on. Just trust your mum and I, as there are so many rumours and lies. The fact is, even I can't believe some of it.' He pointed out the vertex detector, the Cherenkov counter and the calorimeter that measured energy. 'There must be no one underground as the collider accelerates the particles as it is too dangerous. The compressed particle beams are released into the torus and we compress them using magnets from something that is sausage size down to a 1 mm thin stream that enters the detectors. Out of ten million proton collisions per second, the trigger selects the interesting events...' His daughter looked accusingly at him. 'OK, back to practicality. It is impossible to react to the HB storm by creating new experiments, as we barely muddle along with a twenty-year lead time for any programme development.'

Briony queried, 'How do you measure the velocity of the particles?'

'Velocity is measured in the Cherenkov detector. We have teams of people integrated by computers in many locations but we only see "now" for an instant. We analyse the particle trajectories and detect a snapshot of the collisions.'

'That's all unbelievable.' Hannah was bewildered.

'Cutting edge, not unbelievable. We believe we have an understanding of what really happened one billionth of a second after Big Bang an amazing fourteen billion years ago. At 0.001 seconds we had protons and neutrons. One billion years ago, we had matter and antimatter in equal proportions but of course there is an imbalance now, which is a big question, why?'

He looked at his daughter, 'But dad, that's all ages ago and not simple!'

'So...at 380,000 years ago we had atoms for the first time, that's simple. However, the real issue is the human mind can only cope with looking at now. And now, well we only perceive matter. That is why we started the new matter and antimatter experiment. It was designed so we could see what happened to the antimatter. Our doppelgänger.'

Hannah said it again, 'So, as I said, it is unbelievable to understand the science you have used, dad, and impossible to understand what makes up our universe.'

'Yes and no. Ask your Uncle Bert. He is the one who has the answers but he's just not telling.' Briony asked Sam what he meant by his comment. 'Bert is and always was a loner. He is languishing in his thoughts as usual and not giving any other scientist a look at his theories. So we can't help him to develop those thoughts.'

They turned to leave the chamber with an afterthought from Briony: 'It would be a comfort to all if Bert enlightened the world. Gave us an explanation.'

Hannah put her hand on her mum's shoulder as they walked. 'I think our God is the only true comfort, mum.'

Briony was confused. 'Why do you need to mention that, love? All of us in our family have total faith, don't we?'

Hannah replied uncertainly, 'Well, at school we have been studying Christian eschatology.'

Her mum was so proud of her even knowing the word but she felt compelled to add some facts for the benefit of Sam and Liam. 'Eschatology, from the Greek, meaning last and discourse, a study of "end things". They looked at her blankly. 'Look boys, it's applicable in the HB crisis. Whether the end of an individual life, the end of the age, the end of the world and in finality the nature of the Kingdom of God.'

'I'm impressed, mum, we spent a three hour lesson on it,' said Hannah.

Briony smiled at her. 'Is the school studying the destiny of humankind because of the HB storm?'

'Yeah, they think it will help us all. Knowing and thinking about stuff. Death and the afterlife, Heaven and Hell, the Second Coming of Jesus, the Resurrection of the Dead, The End of the World and the Last Judgement.'

Sam interrupted his daughter as they ascended in the lift: 'And of course, the New Heaven and New Earth to come after The End?'

'Very funny, dad. Ascending in the lift to heaven. Funny daddy. We are not going all the way up to heaven, are we?'

'I hope not, love, we have to have supper first! But The End will come at an unexpected time and people won't expect it. There are many passages in the Bible about it, but nothing specific really.' He quoted from memory: 'Of that day and hour no one knows; no, not even the angels of heaven, but My Father only. But as the days of Noah were, so also will the coming of the Son of Man be. For as in the days before the flood, they were eating and drinking, marrying and giving in marriage, until the day that Noah entered the ark, until the flood came and took them all away, so also will the coming of the Son of Man be. Matthew 24:36-39.'

Liam chimed in, 'Nice one, dad. Can we concentrate on the eating and drinking please as I'm starving?' The family glowed with happiness as they exited the LHC building. Walking to their car they were quiet, soul searching in the depths of the earth.

Sam broke their silence. 'When Professor Jackson took me on my first trip below, on my first day here, he gave me these words of wisdom. "This is a place made light by man's ingenuity. A place made dark, as dark as the start of time, once the lights are turned off behind Man. Only work in the light, Sam."'

★ ★ ★

A few days after the trip to CERN, Briony used her mobile to call Natalia. 'How are you?'

'Fine.'

'A woman's fine or a man's fine?'

Natalia sighed. '"ровно", life is hell.'

'Is Bert still off the plot?'

'He has disappeared into a different world. As if he has gone mad.' She sighed heavily again. 'He said we can separate, but I love him so much and his...what you say...mental absence hurts.'

Briony could hear her start to cry. 'Look, our men have got so many questions and queries in their heads that they can't possibly be acting normally. Imagine the stress they are under. And remember what I said; we are the strong ones in the family.'

'"да", I understand, but I do not have your... your assertiveness.'

'Listen girl, you have been closeted away from the real world for years. Now you have to learn to be an independent woman again. Society has changed, love.'

'That is all true, with daddy's money and no real work, I am not exactly a feminist.'

'And remember your husband, your relationship has also formed your mindset.'

'"да", "да", but I must try to support Bert and then cope myself. I feel responsible for saving him, god knows.' Briony was laughing. 'Why do you laugh at me?'

'Not you, silly. Supporting a husband acting strangely is normal!' Natalia started to chuckle, deep from within her breast. 'Do husbands tell us everything? I don't think so! So nothing has changed really, has it, Natalia?'

Natalia stayed silent for a few heartbeats. She said softly. 'Nothing apart from my husband.'

'So how about you and Allie meeting up with Hannah and I? We can go into Vevey on Saturday for a girlie shopping trip.'

'That will be lovely, see you then. Bye.' Natalia drifted off the line, leaving her friend to tap the top of her desk.

★ ★ ★

Hannah sent a text to Josh. It was the mid-morning break at school. 'OMG, cancelled white water rafting trip Auvergne. Say HB prep comes first.'

Josh instantly replied. 'Rafting, not that important really.'

Hannah texted him back. 'Yes it is. The hunk is going. All us girls imagine him in his bathers!!!!!' It made Josh laugh for the first time in weeks. He was sat alone in a study room, the lights were off. He had heard his parents angry exchanges the previous night and covered his head with a pillow. Someone knocked on the door.

'Go away,' he shouted louder than normal. Searching the darkened room gave him zero comfort and so he decided to contact Liam. This time it was on Facebook messenger. 'Can't believe all games development been stopped. IT people working on important questions to do with Higgs.'

Liam was at home in Blonay and lying on his bed. The TV was tuned to a car programme, his laptop was being used to surf the net and his mobile was for communication with his mates. 'Lol – will close down the mobile network next?'

'Never,' came the reply.

'Cause?' asked Liam.

'Cause it's a way of controlling us. They see everything we say. They know where we are.'

'Flip me, didn't think of that.'

Josh was always more thoughtful than Liam. He put time into his texts. He remembered half heard conversations between his mum and dad. 'CCOW knows everything and so controls everything.'

Liam gave up. 'May as well be a zombie then.'

'C'mon…Liam, you already are.'

★ ★ ★

The market square in central Vevey was buzzing as Natalia and Allie parked illegally in a disabled space. Allie reminded her of the last 140 franc fine just a month before but Natalia was not for budging. She wasn't prepared to queue and wait for a vacant spot. It was a T-shirt and shorts day. A perfect day to browse the temporary stalls set-up near the pontoon where the steam paddle ship called each half an hour. Natalia craned her head to search for her friend under the covered part of the market with its gigantic clock. A few hundred people were queuing at the various stalls to pay a twenty franc deposit on a glass. As she drew closer, she saw that each one was etched with the words "Marche Folklorique 2018." The purchasers were then proceeding to sample the dozens of local Lavaux wines for "free", providing they used the glass. But the tasting had become a binge, partly because they could have as much as they wanted. Partly because the shadow of the HB storm lurked and merged with the shade. Most people were topping up their glasses and then sitting on the steps outside the market to enjoy the sun and vista. It was a taste of paradise. Gruyère cheese and ham bought from the stalls, a variety of fresh baked breads, copious amounts of wine and fun with friends. She waved frantically at Briony and hugged her tightly before they purchased their wine glasses. The two daughters disappeared towards Starbucks, leaving the women to chat, green-yellow Chasselas wine glinting in the sunshine as they cheered each other up. The sun warmed her heart as they sat. Nothing really mattered, her friends and family were all happy and healthy and the HB threat paled into their alcoholic breaths.

Natalia was telling Briony about the latest rumour she had read on Google plus. 'Did you hear that we can buy a chemical to improve our chances?'

'Do you mean a chemical or a drug? In fact, just tell me what it is.'

She was vague; Natalia was always vague on details. 'I do not know but we are all taking echinacea and garlic pills, apart from Bert of course.'

Briony sampled her wine. Her eyes closed momentarily to avoid the brightness as she tipped her head back. 'Why are you taking those?'

'They boost the immune system. So, our bodies can fight the HBs.'

Briony answered sensitively: 'Well, I think that's a great idea.' As a chemist she was thinking it was a crutch, another drug to prop up her friend. 'How was Bert last night?'

'Huh, he did not come and sit with me. No further conversations. We have to do something.'

Briony came straight to the point. 'Are you still in separate bedrooms?'

'Still, he has locked himself away. Sometimes I think he is mad, listening to voices.'

'Don't be daft. I told you it's just stress.'

'Is Sam behaving badly?' Natalia knew the answer and Briony didn't need to respond to her question. Briony shook her head slightly. 'You and I have no time to meet and chat but in fact we have all the time in the world.' Natalia kept her head lowered so those sat nearby couldn't see her distress. She leaned into Briony.

Briony twisted and stood up, she reached out to her friend with both hands and pulled her to her feet and dried her eyes with a tissue. 'Come on, it's time to move. Quiet now, love, the girls are coming.' Allie and Hannah bounced up to their mums with two large shopping bags each.

Hannah spoke first: 'Isn't the atmosphere amazing today? Everyone seems even friendlier than usual, and that takes some beating!' The mums beamed.

Allie spoke to her mum: 'On a day like this, I can't understand why are we going underground? I mean, I know it is to avoid the HBs but seriously, is it that dangerous mummy?'

Natalia answered slowly. 'Did you ask your daddy to explain?'

She crossed her arms and pouted, 'Yes, but he didn't want to chat. He said he was too busy.'

Hannah asked Briony the same question. 'So why are we going underground, mum?'

She responded positively. 'Look. Your dad, me, and Auntie Natalia support and believe the actions recommended by CCOW. The approach is totally logical.'

Hannah then turned to her Auntie Natalia. 'Uncle Bert knows everything, doesn't he? So has he told you why are we going underground? Why not put The Envelope in large nice hotels above ground?'

Natalia gave her a less positive reply: 'Well, the soil also gives protection "да".' She put her arm around Hannah. 'And Uncle Bert has lots of thoughts in his head and…huh…'

Hannah repeated. 'And hmm…why does he disagree with The Deeps?'

Natalia answered honestly. 'He is not telling anyone why Hannah, not me, not even your dad.'

'Nothing, not even because of the stench from the toilets?'

'Not even because of missing his garden.'

Hannah was satisfied with the light-hearted answer and nodded to her Auntie. As they walked towards their cars, Natalia thought further about the girl's innocent questions. She spoke to Briony as the girls walked in front and out of earshot. 'Why are we going into the Deeps?' Briony just shook her head and Natalia's unspoken doubts were lost in the busyness and lost love for her husband as she sedately drove her daughter home.

★ ★ ★

Josh and Liam were high on the ridge of Rochers de Naye whilst the girls were shopping. The lazy race was on as they skimmed across the gravel on their mountain bikes towards home. It was all downhill as they had taken the funicular to the top. Their jerseys absorbed the wind, cooling each boy as he fought to remain in the lead. Liam pulled alongside Josh as the track levelled out and for a few minutes they coasted along, calming their adrenaline pumped hearts. 'What do you know about radiation?'

'Why do you ask now?' Josh stopped pedalling and let his bike slow to a standstill.

'Because I am fucking scared to death, mate.'

Josh leant on his handlebars and slowly unclipped his helmet. 'There's no need to be scared Liam. Our dads aren't scared are they?'

'Yeah but, I don't think they tell us the whole truth, they're dads aren't they.'

Josh considered for a while, he knew more science than Liam and his dad always told him the truth. 'You know, microwaves, radios, and even bananas expose us to radiation. The type of radiation and length of exposure determines the damage to us.'

'Bananas?'

Josh laughed. 'Really mate.'

'So I shouldn't worry about HBs but should stop eating bananas.'

'Yeah right doik.' Josh looked at his friend's long face. 'Look. Radiation is ionising, or non-ionising. "Non" is less harmful as it has less energy. "Non" can cause molecules to move in an atom but it cannot remove electrons, light is a good example.'

'I get that.'

'It doesn't hurt us, right. My dad thinks the HB storm might remove particles inside us, like ionising radiation but he doesn't really know.'

Liam searched for a positive notion, 'But they use radiation for good stuff like to kill cancer.'

'Sure, but it can also kill normal cells in our bodies and that is shit, like the HBs.'

Liam pushed off and started pedalling again with Josh following a metre behind. He turned slightly. 'My mum says they irradiate orange juice. She says it's ionising – the bad stuff but it increases the shelf life. She says there was a great debate in the 1980s. She says it was all really scary then but now everyone thinks it's normal. What do you think?'

'I think you need to stop thinking. Look. HBs are different and we are all in the same shit.'

'But your dad doesn't agree with mine. My mum says they argue a lot now.'

'I know my dad says we can't understand the storm by thinking historically but he doesn't say as much to me now.' He pulled ahead of Liam and scattered gravel onto the grass. He accelerated, his voice was caught on the wind and faded away. 'Think positive, my daft mum keeps stuffing echinacea and garlic down us! What shit, hey.'

Liam shouted as he spurted to catch up. 'Has your dad really lost the plot?'

Liam heard a breathless, 'Who says so?'

'Auntie Natalia to my mum.'

Josh slowed again to make it easier to reply, 'I dunno. Dad is usually right but maybe he's a bit weird at the moment. He's keeping out the way. Thinking, he said to me.'

'Huh, my mum and dad are so loving it makes me want to vomit.'

Josh was serious, 'So long as we all don't start to vomit then we have no radiation sickness. But I feel the same as normal – do you?'

'Yeah, fuck it, I am really good. Shall we swim later? Take a portable BBQ to the beach?'

'Yeah, I'll ask some girls I know to come down. You bring the BBQ. And don't worry, Liam. Life is a guess now, let's just have fun.' The bikes speeded up as they hit a steep descent and Liam's worries flew away in the slipstream.

★ ★ ★

Bert thought that FaceTime was a wonderful leveller. Face to face, with no hiding places. He was speaking to his elder brother, Matthew, who had pestered him about protection from HBs the month before. So he was feeling guilty and boiled. It was the end of July and too hot for the apricot pickers in the Valais as the harvest went into full swing. Dozens of small stalls opened along every major roadside to sell the farm produce directly to the public. A final binge on the sweetest fruit for many seasons. A trickle of sweat ran down Bert's hairline and dripped onto his screen. He sat with his laptop on his knee. In front of him was a mirage where the lake used to be, a moving image, shimmering silver and reflected onto the mountains and skies to create a clouded mirror without end.

Bert looked at the tiny camera above his screen. 'So I was wondering if you wanted to come and share the same bunker?'

Matthew was brusque. 'You think you have paradise there, don't you? All those nice safe tunnels.'

'There's no need to be bitter; we want to help you.'

'I was reading about your paradise on the internet, Bert. A 1963 law made all Swiss households build a nuclear bunker or contribute to fabricate the local community one. It said the country still has over 270,000 bunkers and that they are capable of accommodating the entire Swiss population. You jammy bastard, I bet you still have yours, don't you?'

'No, bro. We made it into a wine cellar.' Bert watched his beer drinking brother grimace in distaste. 'But that isn't the point, is it? No one is using their own bunkers, we are all going into the huge communal ones. No different to anyone else in any country.'

'What about the poor, Bert?'

Bert tried again: 'My point is, I think we can help you more if you are here.'

'You and your money, you mean. It won't save you now, you know. Not even Natalia's billions can help. And come to think about it, what about my wife and her mum and dad. Where are you drawing the frigging line?'

'Bro. I know billions won't help. Nothing will help in my opinion but you can be here and try to even up the odds, yeah.' He groaned inside, he was only providing comforting thoughts, in reality it would be a waste of time. 'But do the poor think about you? Tell me, are they thinking about you?'

'We are all in this together, Bert. You can't buy your way out of this one, pal.'

Bert wondered for the fifth time why he was bothering. A strange sense of duty, of doing the right thing. If he believed in The Envelope he would be trying harder with his brother. 'Come on over. Please ignore the wealth and take advantage of us. Please, I want to help you. We'll fly you and yours over and put you up, and the in-laws. We can arrange it, we can make life easier for you.'

'Can't, hate planes.' His brother was stubborn and had always been jealous of his younger brother's high income. He also positively despised Natalia's wealth and called it blood money, wrestled from the heart of peasant Russia.

Bert finally lost it. 'Well, fucking drive, then.'

'It's impossible to get petrol here. When you can, it's treble the cost compared to three months ago. We can't hoard it, on threat of death...' His brother would continue with the impossibilities all day if left to it.

'Look, we will pay for everything. Jack in your job and come to us for an extended holiday.' He felt like saying, before we all die but refrained.

Matthew was staring at the screen with his arms crossed. 'Anyway, what gives you the idea that you can save us? Seems like the press don't love you anymore.'

'Sod the press. They make it up as they go along. As for CCOW...' He let the truth hang.

'Next thing you'll be telling us, you are talking to the President of the United States, as if he can advise us what to do.' Bert kept an uncomfortable silence, after all Donally wasn't the President. His brother was laughing at him, at Bert's confidence and power. 'What about Natalia's family? What are they doing?'

Bert squirmed. His brother always found a weakness. He was caustic in his reply: 'I believe daddy has bought a mine in

Siberia and is kitting it out for all of us. I could go, it will be the best of all the Deeps. But it would be a pointless journey.'

'So are Natalia and the kids staying with you or going to Siberia?'

'I don't know, bro.'

'Not very happy with her hey? Is that right, Bert? Power and money but a lack of love. You have it all except peace of mind, don't you? Whereas we have no choice. We have to work together for anyone to survive.' It was Bert's turn to laugh at his brother's naivety. Matthew instantly became serious, 'You think the human race is so devoid of goodness and emotional bonding that we can't do it?'

Bert was shaking his head at his own image. 'No, I think you paint an impossible dream that will become a nightmare.'

'Go and stuff your help, Bert. You are the dreamer who needs help.' The angry screen face changed to a disconnected banner.

Bert went to find Natalia who was preparing a salad in the kitchen. They rarely spoke now. 'I Face-timed Matthew a few minutes ago. I thought he would want to be with the rest of the family now.'

She kept her back towards him. 'Family, you say?'

'Yes, family, Natalia. Even if you all go into the bunker and I stay out. Family forever.'

'What did he say?'

'He rejected the idea and finally ridiculed us about money as usual. It left a nasty taste.'

She turned towards him. He could hear the emotion in her voice but he wouldn't close and give her a hug. 'Money never mattered between us, did it?'

His reply was honest. 'Never.'

'So what has changed now?'

'I can't explain us and I can't explain the HB storm. All I know is that we are being pushed apart.'

Natalia turned away and walked out of the double doors towards the veranda. Bert failed to follow her.

★ ★ ★

Sam read the lies alone, he slowly clicked the down button. He thought about telling Briony the truth, the whole truth. His body shivered on the hot day and he gagged into the wastebin at the side of his chair.

CCOW – Central Control Of the World

Briefing

Today is TGD, The Great Defence learning day. #TGDLEARNING.

Each country will immediately start free community lessons that will be made available every day, 24 hours a day, seven days a week. Learning sessions will be given in local communities by experts on dealing with the psychological issues, the shock involved with the HB storm. Most developed countries will have a dedicated TV channel with the latest updates supplemented by social media sites and an App called TGD – The Great Defence.

TGD for less developed countries will use all means available to help people understand our future. Starting with what happens now as we leave behind the pain and guilt and become angry with the inevitable.

Remember, the changes caused by the HB storm are no one's fault.

There is no need to vent your anger. Accept the inevitable.

A minor inconvenience. Green light
The TGD App is not available on Apple's operating systems for at least another three weeks.

A moderate inconvenience. Amber light
We cannot give 24 hour coverage for lessons in more rural areas.

A major inconvenience. Red light
There are no major inconveniences.

HB Predictor today
CERN confirmed that the level remains the same.
    Stay calm, we have plenty of time to understand ourselves and our needs for The Great Defence.

"Guilt has very quick ears to an accusation."

Henry Fielding.

"We all feel the urge to condemn ourselves out of guilt, to blame others for our misfortunes and to fantasise about total disaster."

Deepak Chopra.

> "I hate all pain,
> Given or received; we have enough within us
> The meanest vassal as the loftiest monarch,
> Not to add to each other's natural burden
> Of mortal misery."

Lord Byron

Sam puked again. If he told her they were all going to die, what would she say? It's OK darling, let's not tell the children, we have no choice but to go into the Deeps. It's OK darling, we will live in hell with no food, safety and security and let the HBs fry us in our kitchen. It's OK darling, you make the decision as I trust you for ever. You know I can't live without you as you are my sun and moon. He leaned towards the floor and vomited a second time, his mind went blank as he fought for air, then he vomited again until his guts hurt so much he nearly passed out.

[5]

Anger and the Bargain

AUGUST IN MONTREUX arrived with the gentians, blue and bruised in the mountain pastures. The colour seeped to the washed azure lake where the Riviera engulfed coach loads of Japanese tourists, equally bruised from a fast bounce across Europe. The heights were a harmony of natural greens and the lows a conflict of man-made hues. Bright beds of canna and hibiscus would not be remembered by the tourists in the HB summer. They were distracted from nature by the brown earth and grey concrete which saddened the promenade.

Natalia was looking at her Porsche Cayenne parked illegally in front of the Hotel Splendid. A traffic warden was slapping a ticket on the windscreen for the third time that week. She saw Briony alight with a bump and a run from the electric tram that had brought her from Vevey. Whilst Natalia contemplated the wide perspectives of the horizon, her friend looked up at its narrow and arched reflection in the hotel's windows. They wore white and green striped blinds, blinking at the expansive beauty before them. Briony zigzagged across the busy road determined to cheer up her friend.

It was a bright and lively spot to meet, with a new chef specialising in Thai haute cuisine. They chatted over the green curry and Tom Yum seafood, suitably served with a 2012 Riesling from nearby Alsace. To their right they could see vines bursting with fruit, lines of infantry marching towards Lac Léman. There were dozens of small domains thrust into any tiny terrace giving ripe ordonnance to be blended en masse in October. Loaded by a caring set of vignerons that reflected the generous and open culture, as much Italian and French as Swiss.

'I went to see the doctor,' Natalia wanted her friend to know.

'And?'

'Well, it is not the menopause.'

'And?'

'He asked me if I had any stress in my life, so I said no.'

'But you told him about the hair loss and acne, right?'

'I told him about my depression and fatigue.'

'Just tell me what's wrong with you, girl.'

'He said my adrenal gland is…what you say… dysfunctional. Rest, eat the right foods, avoid stress and take DHEA. I do not know this.'

'None of which you will do, will you.' Natalia smiled back. Briony leaned forward and talked quietly. 'Bert is your stress and you damn well know it.'

'"Ровно", of course but why tell a doctor?'

'Sometimes, I just want to give up on you.'

'My friend, you should try living with a God-like, superior person who exists above our mundane life.'

'Of course it's crap, Natalia, you know, I'm not always a chemist, I am also a scared mother and wife; plain old me, multi-tasking the kids and husband, faults and all.' She looked around to see if anyone was eavesdropping. 'My advice is to think very clearly about Bert, take the pain.'

'I know all this is hard for our men, but with Bert, there is something else.' She leaned back from her food and stopped eating. 'What, I do not know.'

Briony took a sip of her wine. 'I remember when Sam and I backpacked in Tibet one summer after Uni. We both believed in the seven chakras of the body, the Hindu points of energy or the great mysteries.'

'What is that?' Natalia asked politely as she toyed with her food and glanced about her.

'We spent hours sitting with our hands on our knees. Focussing our minds on one of the seven chakra positions.'

'And?'

'For example, the third eye on the forehead or the sacral chakra in the groin.'

Natalia laughed, 'You focussed on your vagina?'

'It worked! It gave us a sense of well-being and sexual pleasure. It improved how we accepted others.'

'So you had great sex, then.' She started to pick at her food again after taking two slugs of wine. Briony placed a hand on Natalia's glass for a moment. A gesture hidden from any casual acquaintances who might be passing.

'Of course it worked, we were young! But listen. Positively thinking through the third eye gives you a focus on the big picture.'

Natalia rolled her eyes at her friend. 'So what happened to your beliefs?'

'I guess we never truly believed. Hmm…strangely enough, our husbands have proved that energy and body are linked in every way.' She sighed a very long sigh. 'Funny that…anyhow, we believed and then got a career and disbelieved.' She held Natalia's hand, 'Maybe you must believe again. Believe in you and Bert.'

Her friend pushed her plate away, 'I have my Russian Orthodox beliefs. Once in, always in. That is my strength.'

'And not drinking vodka of course.'

Natalia replied coyly, 'Without effort, you won't pull a fish out of a pond "да".'

'As I said, no vodka, love.'

'The past is not enough and I am unwillingly in the future.'

Briony nodded, 'In the future nothing can be the same, even a religion.'

Natalia stuttered a heartfelt promise: 'True, but I will never drink alcohol again, if only my family can be as one in the Deeps. No Bert, is despair for us all.'

'Lighten up, girl.'

'I want my man to love me like he did in Stockholm. He has been my only world for twenty years.'

Briony reached across again and held her friend's forearm. 'It doesn't work like that. It doesn't for any couple. Firstly, don' t worship him. Secondly, you can't bargain like that, life isn't based on a scale of rights and wrongs.' She slid her hand away and grabbed her own glass.

Natalia answered as Briony gulped. 'It never changed for us; until the world changed in May. It is the government's fault.' Her voice rose. 'They have got it wrong, "да"? They have sucked the life out of moya lyubov.'

'Shh, calm down, Sam says that CERN, CCOW and the

world governments have got their tactics and response just right. I trust him.'

Natalia rested her arms on the table and yawned. 'Sorry, I am so tired. You reassure me but Bert, huh, he is so negative.'

Briony spoke gently. 'Don't give up all hope, support him.'

'But he wants none of the food I prepare, no sex, no conversation, he is a shit.'

Natalia rubbed her eyes as Briony made her an offer: 'Come and stay with us. We can support Allie and Josh, the two families together.'

'Why now? We have eight months before the Deeps.'

'Because you are hesitating, girl. That's why.'

Natalia looked at her, her eyes were narrowed as she brushed back a stray hair off her forehead. 'Huh, maybe you are hiding something? Maybe Sam tells you things?'

'Maybe, maybe, life is all one big maybe but it will be fun; all of us against the Higgs Boson. And if the level pops upwards, well, we will have had a short holiday together, some respite for you.'

Natalia promised to consider it. The children had been taken out of Aiglon College, it was a time to be at home now. The cost, time and distance seemed irresponsible for the next term and the transfer to the Haut Lac school to be with their best friends had been agreed. The two adults quietly stared out of the window and watched the paddle steamer slide across the water and close on the landing stage beneath them. The pontoon was a modern galvanised monstrosity capped with arched glass. The white steamboat named Vevey was narrow with three decks, a dull yellow funnel and two masts. Sat beneath a stained awning were a crowd of tourists who were determined to make the most of the summer. As Natalia gazed down, she felt the demeanour of the people walking along the promenade. Maybe it was in her imagination, but the crowds seemed jealous, resentful of her in the smart restaurant. She was drawn to a loud noise from the pontoon. The tourists alighting off the boat had entered into a push and shove argument with those over anxious to get onboard. Each tribal group was blaming the other and ignoring the instructions of the crew. Pushes become hits and hits grapples, as a handful of mainly women started viciously kicking one another, gouging faces and pulling hair.

The friends watched in silence for a few minutes. Cries and shouts were clear and strident through the open windows of the veranda. It was Natalia who voiced their concerns. 'Are people really going to work together in the Deeps?'

And it was Briony who gave her hope. 'They can and will. People are capable of the greatest and worst things in life but I seriously believe our greatest times are still to come.'

'Really?'

'Yes really, love; really.' She turned to look out of the window again, to view the chaos above ground.

★ ★ ★

Bert admired the refracted beauty of the water drops on the Merc's windscreen before he wiped them away with his chamois. The shine revealed two circling buzzards hunting above the forest. He was thinking about his family going below. He rationalised the choices – death in the Deeps after terrible trauma trying to co-exist with people you naturally hate. Or death above, simultaneous and symmetrical, but lonelier, alone. But he felt alone now, even when is family were with him. Devoid from reality as he searched for the truth.

'Are you tired and ill, Bert?'

So she couldn't read his mind. He rubbed faster, looking for her reflection. 'No, no one is feeling ill yet and tiredness is an untruth as there are twenty-four hours in a day, to think, to work, to love.'

'So it's love that disturbs your psyche? Love following love. To the ends of the earth?'

'Yes, I love my wife, my family and my best friends.'

'Follow her, then. Go below with her, your ultimate love.'

He reacted carefully. 'It seems strange that music has become more tuneful and the mountains are more beautiful. It all seems illogical.' He loved Natalia, like he had their first days in Stockholm. The thought gave him a clarity on his introspection. He looked at his reflection and knew what he had to do.

'Were you thinking of things you love yet again? The logical Professor of physics mired in inexactitude?'

'We all need love; without love there would be no us, no human race.'

'Without The Envelope, your flesh will reanimate. Our seeds and spores will still be here, tiny but significant. Of course we will die, but much more slowly. Our leaves will wither and shrivel to fall on the water. But we will be untouched by the storm. Distorted by the universal change but not dead.'

'So you say, Lily. But where is your love?'

'I love my host. The legions love me. We are one. Our simplicity will save us but your complexity will kill you.'

'Lily, we are not dead yet and you misjudge our strengths. Our ability to use our love to survive. No matter what.' He went back to flogging the car with his leather; concentrating on his family and mourning their future, completely shutting out Lily. He would return to analyse her later. He was worried that now she could access him at any time.

★ ★ ★

Briony had hated the meeting with the manufacturing directors, her head was spinning as she crashed through her office door and collapsed into her chair. She glanced at her note pad. 1. Reduce the sugar in KitKats. (pointless?) 2. Add filler to baby milk powder. 3. Ice cream production suspended. She stopped reading, tomorrow was another day, or so she hoped. She flicked the cursor on her screen to cover the HB bookmarks and clicking through she scanned the latest stories. The CCOW counterfeit sites had proliferated over the angry month of August. She could see it was an easy way to swipe at the bureaucracies controlling world events and hence a period of indiscipline was fuelled and burned by the internet. But she couldn't understand why so few people were rebelling against the party line. It was clear from her own selection of websites that at no disruptive organisation managed to survive more than a few days before mysterious technical issues stopped their every communication. An occasional blog by a doughty individual would survive a little longer; anything up to a week. But Wikileaks suggested that all bloggers soon became bogged down in ISP or blogging payment issues. A pain in the pocket stopped most individuals. The truth of the information she did see was remarkable if short-lived. Some evenings she verified items with Sam, on most occasions he wouldn't comment, just admit yes with a staunch maybe, or give a derisive no with a snort.

The need to communicate a perceived and accepted truth took precedence in any culture and any country. Israel and

Switzerland reportedly had fantastic underground facilities; each had developed them over many years. Israel to safeguard the security of their people from the Iranians and Palestinians and Switzerland to safeguard the possessions of other countries, rich individuals, and Swiss gold. Japanese blogs consistently reported their government was allowing many small bunkers to be constructed but no one understood why. She remembered the pod hotels in Tokyo which might explain the mindset. Occasional news from Africa referred to scrapes in the earth as the only bunkers available. They had wooden roofs, no facilities and could at best be called a shelter. But she knew there were never going to be enough shelters, never mind the deep bunkers expected to guarantee safety.

Many an instant blog reported the violent protests against the Chinese government, these blogs disappeared the quickest. The action was mostly based in Tiananmen Square, Beijing and reflected the worst uprisings of the students in 1989. She understood the root cause, it was simple. Many Chinese believed sharing The Envelope was a mistake. Most doubted the government's ability to safeguard its 1.5 billion people. Most believed entrepreneurs on the state council were more capitalist than the western capitalists. She decided that people must be jealous of phantom wealth stashed away for The Return.

Throughout August, bloggers in South Africa reported continual upheaval in the poor black townships. The root cause was still the distrust of the whites. Most blacks believed there would not be enough bunkers and all the whites would be given privileged access. President Jacob Zuma, evoking the spirit of Mandela, gave many local speeches. They followed the same line. 'We did not come through our struggles against apartheid for nothing. Our wealth, the greatest of any country, with precious diamonds, gold and platinum, is now lost in the bewilderment of all nations. So now we will use the old mines that created our wealth to house our people.' But Briony thought that any bribe was as good as any other, from whites or blacks. Only the amount mattered and it was mostly the whites who could afford the biggest bribes and guarantee a place in the Deeps. She could see that nothing had changed since her visit to the new Nestlé site to set up the Cheerios production line. She had hated seeing the poverty alongside the new high-rise offices.

Her last port of call was Twitter. She felt that the comments on Twitter held a tinge of irony mixed with depression. #EOTW End Of The World was always trending but mysteriously new trends were short-lived. The top hashtags were #supportCCOW #the greatdefence #notinnedtuna #predictorenglishpremierleague. She laughed at some of the Tweets as she thought of Bert and his stigma about the LCD. The Lowest Common Denominator was applied and the world continued to spin with an undetectable wobble. She pressed the PC off button and slowly walked to the station, dragging her feet and with shoulders slumped.

★ ★ ★

The video bridge between Mitch Donally in Mount Weather, USA, and Sam in the LHC was almost instantaneous. It meant that communications were as factual as when they had been face to face that day at CERN. Sam squinted and leaned into his screen, tiredness was taking its toll on him.

Mitch was demanding an explanation. 'All I want, Sam, is a realistic status report on the power of the HB storm and an anticipated date when we must all be safely underground. Can you tell me that now? I need it, Sam.'

Sam hesitated a moment only, anymore and Donally would snap. 'It is almost impossible to say, sir. The huge influx of particles wasn't predictable and now that it has tailed off we may have a long period of calm. But as I have said many times, it is unpredictable.'

'What does Bert say?'

Sam hesitated. 'Bert says he is happy to keep monitoring the storm until the end.'

Donally was shocked. 'He's not going below with his family?'

'No sir, he has made his decision and he won't change it. He is adamant we are wrong. But it means we can set up his house to become a satellite monitor to the HB detector, with a direct link to CCOW.'

'Do it. Whatever he needs, the stupid fuck. Generators, fuel for his car, oil for heating and any satellite comms to make it a secure link to CCOW.' Donally leaned into his camera making Sam sit back. 'Back to my question, Sam. Is it still the end of March 2019 for Convergence?' Sam shuffled in his chair, scratched his shock of grey hair and still didn't answer. 'Come on, man. The world can't wait for a ditherer.'

'I don't know, sir. Really...'

Donally cut him short. 'OK, I am going to brief it as mid-December. It's better to take the shit now, whilst everyone seems so angry.' He didn't ask for any clarification or agreement, he just assumed. 'Let me know if anything changes and I mean the slightest change.' Donally cut the link and turned to his aide. 'You heard. Get the team communicating with the government representatives about the age limit. There's no time for anyone to complete enough bunkers. But as agreed, only discussions by secure telephone lines. Nothing in writing. OK?'

The aide had worked with Obama for many years and accepted the responsibility without demure. 'Each country will have to vary the age, sir. Ours is calculated at 54 years-old. China was looking at 27 years.'

Donally grunted. 'I gather people are talking about the "The Shanghai complex". What the hell is that?'

'It's being used to describe a syndrome for a fear of the Deeps. It's an allusion to the vast bunker for two hundred thousand people set below the city in China. The bunker is highly sophisticated and linked by tunnels to key establishment headquarters.'

'People haven't got a clue, have they?' Donally was slowly shaking his head. 'Just make sure all satellite CCOW offices understand they must only focus on the very basics for survival. Time is running out.'

The aide left Donally alone. Mitch opened his left hand drawer and pulled out a bottle of Jack Daniels and a tumbler. Half filling it, he took a slug before leaning back in his chair and closing his eyes. He thought about the eight billion people who could all die. He telephoned his wife to sound off. She knew when to listen which was most days now. 'Charlene, have you heard from your friends about "The Shanghai Complex"?'

'Of course, haven't you?'

He didn't hesitate, 'Terrorism, nuclear accidents, I guess everyone is in need of a symbolic safe haven?' He drank deeply. 'The real reason must be primeval. We sheltered in caves because there was nothing else.'

'Mitch, we agreed to protect ourselves and the family. We will not be the little people clinging to safety in a hole for twenty-four hours a day, seven days a week. No sunlight, no fresh air or fresh food. No space to absorb their passions.'

'Yes but I do have a conscience as well as a duty and I can't imagine how bad it will be.'

She spoke sweetly. 'And that's why you need a cull darling. To make it better for those of us remaining.'

He signed off and splashed another tumbler. There was one last effort before bed. He clicked on the draft CCOW briefing and quickly read down it.

CCOW – Central Control Of the World

Briefing

The HB predictor is back online and reads 58. We understand this will be a shock to most of you, but no one is responsible, and no one is to blame. It is not the responsibility of CERN, CCOW or your government. The HB storm is a phenomenon that is unpredictable in its nature. We all knew that. As the eminent Professor Leinster said a few weeks ago, "The HB storm started instantly and so it is conceivable that it may end instantly."

At present, we anticipate going into our bunkers in the middle of December. This is easily achieved and we can still safeguard all of you. Trust and support your leaders and the specialist bunker teams. Your local tradesmen are working hard for you. They are making us safe, so please support and thank them.

News! We now have the escape teams. Those trained army personnel to drive the Specialist Transfer Vehicles developed by the UK. Unfortunately automation cannot be proven to consistently work so we need these drivers. After Deeps Day, these STVs will go to key places such as hospitals to retrieve equipment or to warehouses for any remaining food that is left outside of the bunkers. That means we can visit any place to retrieve the basics for a normal day to day life and for much longer a period. He didn't want to relate anything to time. *More STVs are being built every day.*

Help us! "Your World CV" is now available on our website. Complete the form and see how your skills can help in your area. We have upgraded The Grid to increase the computer power available to gather all your data. Do please give us all your key information. Are you a first-aider? Were you a plumber or an electrician before your current career? You understand the needs. A skill you have may help the rest of the people in your bunker. Complete this simple list now.

Action! Svalbard Global Seed Vault is located in the remote Arctic of Norway, only eight hundred miles from the North Pole. Funded by the Bill and Melinda Gates Foundation, a joint world effort has actively preserved seeds for humanity. The equivalent of Noah's Ark. There are many places like this but you may not have heard of them. We are still actively increasing their numbers to provide enough seeds to regrow our world on The Return. The World Genetic Resource Group together with The Global Crop Diversity Trust are building larger versions of Svalbard. These are located in Alaska at Prudhoe Bay, utilising the existing oil facilities. Also in Russia at Timan Pechora, which is close to the Trans-Antarctic mountains where natural caverns have been found in the edge of The Ross Ice Shelf. All of the facilities have been under construction and/or started stocking seeds since the crisis began in late May. Google, Apple and Exxon are kindly funding these construction projects to make them bigger and better than the original. It is expected they can be completed

*within the new timescales, as many of our resources have
been pooled together for The Great Defence.*

A minor inconvenience. Green light
*"Your World CV" is essential for all to complete. The local
administrators will be progressing this with you all as it also
gives them a cross-check on age, gender and relationships. This
will allow them to locate and sort everyone correctly.*

A moderate inconvenience. Amber light
*We are working hard on the design for the STVs by incorporating
The Envelope sandwiched into all the vehicles windows. We may
have to use existing trucks and seal them from the HB storm by
glueing The Envelope inside the cabs.*

A major inconvenience. Red light
*We anticipate storing all the main seeds essential for human life.
Cereals, fruits and most food sources will be stored. However, other
less significant species may be lost. This includes many flowers.*

HB Predictor today
CERN said 58 but don't worry, don't panic.

*"Don't Panic is a phrase on the cover of The Hitchhiker's
Guide to the Galaxy."*

Douglas Adams

Donally replied to the email by typing – approved, but see
strikethrough. On the yellow pad in front of him, he made
notes for the morrow.

Key is the provision of light and the impact on the nervous and endocrine systems. As soon as the health balance and the physiological regulation goes wrong, then everyone will mentally fall apart.

He slugged half the tumbler down, his throat was dry. Then he leaned forward and wrote a second note for his next meeting with the heads of government.

Cull hard and cull now? Why wait? Only wait whilst all is calm. Cull creates chaos?

His final thoughts were a statement of fact. The note read.

Don't think bunkers, not bunker mentality. Push shelter and temporary reprieve; assume we will all come out again. His second part of the note read: Armed forces training to run bunkers like prisons.

His last inch of Jack Daniels was drunk with a prayer to the empty room. 'God help all of us. God give me strength to make this happen.'

★ ★ ★

Sam sat in the quiet of the shed away from his team and closed off the HB crisis to think. After a few moments he telephoned Bert who hadn't turned up all day. 'Are you at home, mate?'

'Sure am.'

'Doing anything special.'

'Thinking.'

'I think, Bert, that we think too much, so how about we meet in Montreux in an hour and I rent a powerboat off that company by the casino?'

There was no hesitation. 'See you there.'

Sam remembered the heavenly summer days when the kids were young and both families enjoyed a boating picnic with each other. He hoped to recreate the bonhomie as he walked towards the pontoon. Bert was already sat in the driver's seat of the Chaparral with the exhaust gurgling low in the water.

Sam accosted Bert. 'Are you OK to drive? Frankly, you look like shit, mate.'

'I feel bad but it has nothing to do with HBs.'

Sam eased his way onboard and cast off. Bert hit the lever with the palm of his hand and the boat smoothed its way towards the Chateau de Chillon. Sam had wanted to bollock his friend, it was his prime motivation to meet but looking at him, he felt sorry for Bert. 'I know it's tough at home. You know, if there is anything I can do to help...'

'Take them, take them and shelter them from me.' Bert turned to stare at him, his eyes were grey and sunken but then the phantom shattered as the boat lurched.

Sam was shocked at the ferocity of Bert's plea. 'Why?'

'Because I'm not safe to be around and they need normality.'

'You know I'll do that, Bert, but won't you reconsider? I have places reserved for both families in the Bex salt mines.'

Bert didn't need to reconsider, as he was right. 'Just take care of them for me, KK?'

'OK. But how are you feeling umm...mentally?'

'Seeing the lies upsets me the most.' Bert raised a quizzical eyebrow at his friend.

Sam thought about withholding information but instantly decided against it. 'It's far worse than you hear and see. There are subliminal TV adverts now. They say life is worth living, join together and work together. It was in response to the riots.'

Bert laughed and accelerated to maximum speed, throwing Sam back into the bucket seat. 'I expected as much. Next you will be saying they have put a happiness drug in the drinking water!'

Sam grasped the gunwale and spoke hesitantly, 'Sorry, mate, there are four drugs in the mix at present. Dopamine, oxytocin, serotonin and endorphins.'

From laughter, Bert reverted in a second to outright anger. 'Fuck me. Tell me what for.'

'Dopamine is the usual one for happy feelings. Oxytocin is the cuddle drug to make you love your fellow man. Serotonin is to put you in a good mood and the endorphins to mask pain and discomfort. And the formula has been applied everywhere across the civilised world.'

Bert put the boat's port side towards the approaching steamboat to let the captain know he had been seen. He snorted down his nose in disgust. 'All bases covered, then. What about some psycho babble or are they leaving that to the religious leaders? I saw the Pope speaking last night; what a load of bollocks.'

Sam was compliant. 'I accept they bend the truth, even my lot.'

But Bert angrily interrupted him: 'It's all lies and you know it, Sam!'

'No, lies is the wrong word. You don't understand the deeper reasoning, the politics. The psychological control of populations is complex. It's immense and unbelievable to me as well. But it is working!'

Bert had been away from any form of reality for months. 'You are joking, aren't you?' But his friend had denied most of the terrible lies because of his own weakness. Bert wondered if his friend's faith in God had got in the way of true thought. He eased the throttle and let the hull settle and stop in the smooth waters under the walls of Chillon. The secondary wave lifted the stern and travelled along the hull making them nod in unison. Taking his hands off the wooden wheel he turned ninety degrees to confront his friend. 'Working? Really?'

'Look, mate, it's not always working in every country, but it is in most and you know, I don't know what else we can do.'

Bert searched the walls for cracks, 'Will you tell Briony any of the truths?'

'No. No way. And you? Will you tell Natalia?'

'Don't be daft, pal.'

After a few seconds' pause, Bert turned off the engine, 'Do you know what God is, Sam?' His friend waited for an onslaught. 'God is a figment of your imagination, a nothingness that weak humans believe in as a crutch to their feeble minds.'

Sam knew his friend was only trying to rile him, but this was different from before, Bert wasn't joking. 'Remember Uni when Professor Sims said, "A gestaltism theory of the mind states that our ability to acquire meaningful perceptions in an apparently chaotic world is based on one preconception."' He pointed his finger at his friend. 'You laughed then and got thrown out of the lecture because of your bloodymindedness.'

Bert retaliated. 'So how are you, CCOW or even your God going to control the madness? What psychologist stopped caged rats eating their own bodies, whilst still alive, hey?'

'It was Einstein who said, "The more I study science, the more I believe in God."' The boat rocked gently, the lap of waters carried beneath the hull and edged towards the chateau's algae green foundations.

'Yeah, yeah. What people say is not as useful as what they do, Sam. Go and play with the devil called CCOW and come and see me when you want to exorcise him.' Bert pondered the HB crisis in silence. They bobbed for many minutes, Bert touched his arm. 'I'm sorry mate, I know you came to make up with me or bollock me and I truly mean what I say about my family because I trust you.'

Sam had a lump in his throat, it was hard to reply. 'Put two people together and you have chaos as there is no symmetry between people, only conflict. The food they want, the time they go to the toilet and their standards. Higher emotions will not prevail but there's no need to amplify my pain, Bert.'

Bert turned the key and the engine growled. 'I for one am not going into a bunker as no one can and no one will agree. People need each other to survive at present but after three months below, they will kill each other to live.' The gurgle of the exhaust became a defiant roar as they headed back to towards Montreux.

★ ★ ★

It was early evening, but the sun was still high over Lausanne, the large city lying murky beneath its summer pollution. Sam and Briony chatted quietly on the balcony that led into their first floor bedroom. The children were out with friends at the beach and so they could talk freely.

Briony was probing him about the latest research. 'Did you ever make any tests on The Envelope to see if it degrades over time?'

Sam kept any doubts to himself. 'There has been no time. Too many of our team are tied up with the science of survival.'

'I can understand that darling. Nestlé have stopped production of some confectionery lines because production has been given over to making formula. But surely someone is looking backwards for answers, something to guide us?'

Sam cleared his throat and looked her in the eye. 'Life has become political rather than scientific.'

She was quick to respond. 'What do you mean?'

'Well, the Predictor level has been low for weeks, but CCOW wouldn't tell anyone, so as not to induce panic.'

'Is that what you've been worrying about, darling?'

'That was one worry, but it was a good decision as everyone seemed so angry about life. Keeping everyone calm was sensible and now people seem less angry.'

'But?' She knew him too well.

'No matter what we do, we cannot predict the intensity and effect of the HB storm.'

Briony picked up her iPad and googled Higgs Boson to see the latest trending news. 'So when do you think we'll go below?' She carried on glancing down the results. The first few "hits" provided reassurances, platitudes, positives to dwell upon. Her husband remained quiet. 'Sam, I asked you a question.'

'Sorry, love,' he drew a large breath, 'I think we may be in the bunkers even earlier than the middle of December.'

'Fuck me.'

'I didn't want to say, you know.'

'You hesitated, or are you hiding something else?'

Agreeing and believing with the authority above him was easiest in his depressed state. 'No, love, it's just such a huge thing. Such a stressful time.' He stood and walked to the railings to relish the view. 'I saw Bert this afternoon.'

She sat and stared at his back without responding. It had been such a beautiful summer for the children. They didn't have the same worries compared to at the start of the storm. Life had been full of fun and friends.

'How's Bert doing?'

'We had a chat on a speedboat, I thought it would help break the tension. Old memories and all that.'

'And my question remains the same, Sam.'

'I don't know him anymore, I can't read his thoughts and emotions like I used to. So I guess the answer is he is doing sod all but he wants us to look after his family.'

'And my answer remains the same. I've asked Natalia to come here but she has to make the decision, not us and not Bert.' She decided to be positive and change the subject. She opened an article on the HB particle. 'Your friend Professor Higgs has had a pop at Richard Dawkins again. I say good on him as I can't stand the ungodly man.' She read the headline out loud. '"Higgs reiterates that Dawkins is an embarrassing fundamentalist." He should have said arsehole.'

Sam wearily replied. 'You know you don't mean that. It's not like you.'

'But it's interesting, raking over old coals. "Dawkins is a fundamentalist, decrying that this crisis could be part of God's judgement and also saying God will never provide a solution."'

'Good on Peter.' It made Sam smile. 'Bert is a fundamentalist of course and an atheist...I think? But sometimes he listens to me when I advocate faith and then I wonder what he really believes in.'

'Well, maybe Bert is changing his mind since the storm.'

'He thinks science can be the new religion. Do we believe in the wrong thing do you think, the emotional rather than the practical, is Bert right?'

She laughed. 'C'mon… and is he still your best friend?'

'Always. I love him like a brother and like a brother he can be a pain in the arse.'

She told him more about her chats with Natalia. 'She has to temporarily leave him and we have to help her finalise it. For both their sakes and of course their children.'

He asked the obvious: 'Why on a temporary basis?'

'Because she's drinking as she is scared of the crisis. Because she can't communicate with him anymore and of course to protect the children.'

'My question was why temporary?'

'Because she loves him and wants him to be with the family in the Deeps. So she is holding onto that thought. That they will be together again. Without it, she would be in a bigger mess.'

They both stayed silent and admired the view. The sky was reddening as the light penetrated through the dust and pollution. After a few minutes, Sam stood up and walked across to his wife. Taking her hand he pulled her close to him and kissed her hard. 'Come inside. No children. No boundaries.'

'And?' She was playing coy.

'And I love you until the end of the universe.'

She kissed him tenderly and ruffled his hair. 'As if I didn't know.'

★ ★ ★

Lily's voice came to Bert through the speakers of his Merc as he raced along the autoroute. He had been to CERN out of hours to avoid his old team. All he wanted was a photo of his latest whiteboard jottings and now he wanted to be at home, to hug his children. 300W driven through twelve speakers and a sub-woofer made Lily's voice strong and God-like. She was unlike the small and timid plant of his garden.

'Nature is the exact opposite but equal to humanity. Black versus white, light versus dark and of course good versus evil. The sweet and sour of life.'

'That's impossible. How the hell can you talk to me here?'

'Buy some time to think, Bert. Be healthy as you look awful.'

He increased his speed to nearly double the 120 kph limit, still way off the Merc's top speed. He wanted to understand why She was asking him to buy time? But he remained quiet, he needed more information.

'The Deeps will have food, water and power. You can't survive without them.'

'I agree, but CERN and CCOW are ensuring I can live alone above ground for as long as I can live.' He heard the annoyance in Her voice for the first time.

'A defined death, is that what you want? The last phenomenon in our physical world, a death that collectively eradicates all plants and animals. Are you trying to personally compete with all the species at your death? What an ego you have, Bert. What a stupid, crazy ego.'

'Death is nothing. It is beyond my knowledge but surmountable, of that I am sure.'

'Do you see nature debating the cause of the HB storm? You are a fool for doing so. Nature reacts to circumstances, it does not make choices, has no emotions and cares for nothing.' She was urgent in her questioning. *'What do you believe in? The landscape and products of the earth, as opposed to human nature and human creations?'*

SOMETHING TO TELL YOU

'Is that what we have disturbed, Lily? Nature and the symmetry of everything within it?'

'*We think about nature on a local basis – soil, plants, animals – and never on a universal model. Never a symmetrical model with humans balanced against us.*'

Bert rotated the volume button to zero. It didn't help, she blew over it.

'*Yes, you bleed over protecting eco-systems and the environment but not enough. Nature will always change. It will die if necessary but if you think you can influence nature, you are truly a fool!*'

★ ★ ★

Later that evening, Bert was also sat on his veranda, admiring a red rash that spread across the lake, merging air and water but without any steam. Bert sat alone and lonely until Josh walked out of the salon door to join him.

'How're you doing, dad?'

He turned to his boy. 'Don't give your mum a hard time. She's doing what she thinks is right for the family by moving out.'

'But how are you really doing, dad?'

'I'll miss you all.' It was an open and honest answer.

Josh parked himself on the arm of his dad's chair. 'I know that, I really do. But you agree with us living at Uncle Sam's house and you don't agree about us going into the Deeps, do you?'

Bert smiled at his boy. 'No, but it seems like I am the only person in the world with that view.'

'What shall I do?'

'I don't know, son.'

'You know everything, you are my dad.'

'I think that whatever we do, we have no chance.' It was brutally honest but he was talking to a junior version of himself. Honesty was always accepted in their house. Logic was only shared with his son.

'I love you, dad.' Josh leaned close and hugged him tightly. 'You know I share your views but, well you know dad.'

'And I love you, Josh. Be there for her. Be strong as if you were me.'

★ ★ ★

Bert heaved himself off the veranda and used the last remnants of the sun to cajole his marguerites to grow faster. He talked to them, leaning close and bending the leaves with his breath. He counted the heads as he individually pinched them between his thumb and forefinger. The number came to 58. On stepping back to admire them, he could see the bushes were still expanding. The growth was exponential as if the plant knew there was little time left to seed and die. He turned to sit on the steps of the chalet, caressing the approaching darkness and asking for it to hide him. His emotions were fragile, fluff held within the nature of the view. He could see lights scurrying along the opposite shore of the dark lake. Human ants, and over the national border, so a French species of ant, travelling home to the love and comfort of their families. Then a late meal that would last for three hours, drinking beautiful wine, with a beautiful wife. To be followed by mad, passionate love as a sign of giving. His breath was laboured, his chest tight as he looked towards the village of Glion, a kilometre across the valley. A raised bed of manmade stars and planets that shone through the odd gap in the darkened trees. Above the village hung the real stars, insignificant compared to the street lighting. The stars set in a universe he craved to understand.

His thoughts were slow tonight. Stress, fatigue, and emotion all played their part. He closed his eyes to forget reality and dream his thoughts. His quiet voice carried into the prairie and disappeared into the valley below. It was a private conversation between physical Bert and his soul. 'I had always felt, sat here on my steps, that I was in a battle with nature and of course nature always seems to win. But that was on a minuscule scale, the fight to keep the garden neat, a waste of time. Spraying endless chemicals on creatures with no defence, I gave up, it wasn't fair. The little battles, none of which I ever won. On a tiny scale and insignificant compared to life and death. But this battle is so big that I can't even contemplate it. The recycling of humankind, the bites of the HBs.'

He stood, his bottom was numb, and walked up the stairs to the veranda to find a comfortable armchair again. His madness spun through his brain. 'Why, if we're awash in neutrinos that harm no one, do we suddenly have a storm of Higgs that harms everyone? Neutrinos come from all directions: From the Big Bang that began the universe, from exploding stars and, most of all, from the sun. They come straight through the earth at nearly the speed of light, all the time, day and night, and in enormous numbers. If 100 trillion neutrinos pass through our bodies every second without any harm, what is it that is aiding the HBs to kill us?' He sighed and put his hands behind his head. Closing his eyes, he wandered further, deep inside himself. 'But that is the problem. What are the HBs conflicting with? Are they pure or contaminated particles with a different spin or charge or...' It took a few minutes before he awoke from his doze. His dreams full of nothing neutrinos and everything HBs. The ghosts of the house moved across the tall windows behind him, invisible like the particles but with the same malice and intent. Reflectors of any light, refractors of human emotions. He turned suddenly, spooked by a shadow to his left. It was just a reflection on a myriad of silicates, old glass, imperfect glass that reflected light and emotions in many different directions. 'Reflections are particles, aren't they?' He thought longer. 'Yes and the sum of the light makes our lives alive.'

Natalia walked up the steps from the garden. He heard a soft footfall as he wasn't sleeping. Bert opened his eyes and spoke first. 'It's been a long time.'

Natalia was mellow after her nocturnal walk around the estate. 'Too long.' She sat by him. 'I need to get away. You know why...'

Bert snorted, 'Because I have another woman.'

'"Het". I would know. And you love me.' She was always right.

A last train headed down the hill towards Montreux. The gold carriages intermittently gleamed in the street lights as the Golden Pass locomotive squealed its way around the corner below them. It was the witching hour and the shadows and stars moved and merged.

He started to explain. 'I am hearing things.' He felt confused and embarrassed. 'I am talking to a plant, a lily that lives in the etang.'

'No, you are not.'

'About the HB crisis.'

Natalia didn't laugh. 'It must be stress, an end of the world affliction.'

'But I can hear Her and the conversation feels real. She talked to me in the car today.' He paused to emphasise his words. 'I am logical and serious. I know it can't be real but it feels that way.'

'Rubbish, you must be talking to your…what you say… alter ego, a reflection of your tired mind. Think about it, Bert, you are exhausted.'

He did think for a minute before replying. He looked into her moonlit eyes and loved her so much he dared not tell her. 'I don't think so. I feel sane, I am tired, I agree. I think sane, so I am sane.' He waited a further minute before whispering. 'Aren't I?'

She shuffled deeper into her chair. 'I do not know anymore. You act strangely but we are all acting strangely. I thought bad times would bring out the good in people but…'

He sat upright, grasping the arms of his seat. 'Ffur, but nothing. I am amazed that people are working to a common goal. Amazed!'

'They are scared. There is no alternative; give them one and then the divisions would split the world apart.' She tried to engage him, face to face, but he hung his head in shame. 'Stop the imagined conversations with plants, Bert.'

He thought about the HB storm. If he had the answer, if he found it soon, should he tell? He angrily answered. 'I am a fucking physicist specialising in fucking Higgs Boson particles. Why would I lie about talking to a fucking plant, to you, my wife, of all people?'

'Bert, you believe that a lily is talking to you. You are not lying, "да". You have no concept of truth anymore.'

'Look, Natalia, I am not the scientist lying here. Listen, please listen to me and don't go into the Deeps. The Envelope can't work. The facilities cannot be provided. There is no four star hotel waiting. Just a cramped dirty hole to be shared with thousands of scared people.'

'Is everyone wrong, apart from mad Bert?'

He closed his eyes to think. Maybe she's right. Out loud he agreed she should leave. He knew the lies about the predictor plummeting and the rest from Sam. CCOW, CERN, the governments were lying constantly but maybe, just maybe, they would save half the population. He didn't tell her his thoughts. He hoped he was wrong and everyone would live, the storm would dissipate.

Bert spoke quietly: 'I thought you might be the only one to understand me.'

'"Het", Lyubov. My man has gone somewhere so deep inside his mind that he is not my peasant anymore.'

He watched a tear drop, a single love-filled drop escape and slowly run to the corner of her beautiful lips. 'I am still me, I am not insane. I will find the reason for all this.'

She pulled his tightly gripped hand off the wicker arm and dragged him to her. 'Come inside, make love and be yourself. For me. Can you do that?' He kissed her hard and she led him upstairs to the bedroom. The finality seemed appropriate. The loss enormous.

★ ★ ★

The women were eating lunch in Vevey, one of many essential supportive lunches. Natalia was treating her friend to the menu dégustation in the Michelin star restaurant at the Grand Hotel du Lac. Briony felt scruffy in the ornate Victorian setting. Her old black work suit clashed with the lightness of the room and gorgeous chintz fabrics. Their food was even more astonishing than the setting which induced a relaxed chat. Planning the transfer of the Leinsters to the Murray household came easily. By the time they had eaten the cod superposition, followed by perch filets from the lake, they had resolved the sleeping arrangements and the date for moving in.

Briony was looking for reassurances after Sam's uncertain tone the previous day. 'What do you think it will it be like, when CCOW announce Convergence?'

'Everyone will quietly follow each other into the Deeps. Agreed?'

'I'm not certain, but I hope so. It's just that human nature can circumvent logic sometimes.'

'"Het", not nature or logic. There is nothing else. We will accept, as it gives us hope.'

'Hmm, part of our grieving for this life we lead.' Natalia remained quiet and fiddled with her glass. Briony could see Natalia's point but she felt troubled. The small negative points half indicated by her husband in the prior three months made her question her commitment to the Deeps. She spun her spoon with her forefinger, attempting to make a full 720 degrees. She spoke slowly after a long stare at the mountains beyond the tall window. 'I believe people will stay working together. I mean, it has been remarkable so far. But until we are safe...well, we shall see.'

Natalia was more positive. 'It is all good. CCOW fixed the assets, they fixed the law and order, the bunkers and tell us the truth "да". That is success against all the odds?'

'True, a triumph over humanity's divisions.' They were drinking New Zealand Cloudy Bay wine. Natalia had already drunk three glasses, which helped her positivity. Briony took a small sip from her crystal glass. It was excellent, a gold medal wine, fragrant and full bodied. 'Really, I do agree, but the truth is sometimes lost.'

'What example huh?'

'Hmm…let me think. In all my debates with Sam concerning going below, they've revolved around what other countries are doing.'

'Why?'

'To compare…to make sure the Swiss get it right. I hasten to add he doesn't tell me much but…'

'What countries? Trust me.'

'As an example, Sam says in North Korea, it's as if nobody really thinks and the leadership is going through the motions.'

'You went with Nestlé for new business there, so you know?'

'That's my issue, I don't. It was the country in the axis of evil and now it's reconciled with the South and the Yanks. I know they won't have problems controlling the people but neither will the Swiss or Germans, which are true democracies. It upsets me when Sam says he believes the Korean people will be squandered and only a small percentage of the leadership will survive.'

Natalia laughed. 'The Swiss will definitely control us. One of the great film director's from my Russia, called Nikita Mikhalkov, he said that Switzerland resembled a hospice. One big hospice for all of us to exactly follow our government's bidding.'

'That is a little unfair, n'est pas?'

'No, here will be like Russia. The rich have everything and the poor will be shot. Although, there are no poor.' She meant it as a joke.

'That's sad because it's probably true.'

'We say, there was and there was not.' She sank a fourth glass of wine and waved to the waiter for another bottle.

Briony tutted: 'Steady on, girl. There will be no place to hide and get pissed with us.'

Natalia rolled her eyes at her friend. 'No little tipple at home? I think not.' Briony nodded to accept she might partake a little. 'What do we do if no wine each night?' The dessert arrived, a walnut and pear flan that shouted for it to be wolfed down.

'We read, "Paradise Lost", everyone who is everyone is reading it. A fad, championed by the BBC and a response to the storm.'

'"говно", I am going to live in a church.' She glugged more of the Sauvignon Blanc.

'It's a good story. All about the fall of Man, Adam and Eve, Satan and the Garden of Eden.'

Natalia bumbled away, '"да", like my garden! I am Eve and Bert is Adam.'

'Probably not, neither of you are pure enough! But Satan was supposedly the most beautiful of the angels before he was cast out. "Better to reign in hell than serve in heaven," was what he said. Maybe that's what Bert sees in going into the Deeps.'

'Depending which way you interpret! No, my Bert is not Satan, he is my God and always will be.'

The ladies lunched in paradise, whilst chatting about the competing factions in Somalia and the Central African Republic who lynched. They talked about how the intensified political rivalries in parliaments across the EU. Briony asserted her left wing credentials and stood up to Natalia's capitalist right wing ethos. They did agree that the storm was an excuse for some governments to tell their poor and illiterate populations that their opposition was failing the people and should be eliminated. Natalia told her friend that she could see how law and order had ascended in civilised countries but descended in the fourth world. She said she had found her social conscience on the road to Convergence and was sorry for the down and outs caught up and dumped in the battle to survive.

★ ★ ★

Later that evening, Sam and his daughter were sitting alone in their lounge. They were watching a soap opera on TV. Liam was playing on his PS5 in his bedroom and Briony was working in the study. Sam sat with his arm around Hannah. It was comforting for them both. She received a text from Allie. 'Four days more and then we can wreak havoc from the same house!'

Hannah texted back immediately. 'Different rules here. Prepare yourself for poverty and deprivation.'

'Who was that?' She looked coyly at him. 'I am your dad, I always have to ask my dearest daughter.'

'Just Allie.'

'Daughters always reply vaguely, don't they.' He waited a few seconds. 'And remember Dads don't give up.'

'And she can't wait to come and watch a soap opera like "Corrie" with us.' She was smiling as she said it to his face.

'Umm, and I know she will never do that.' He resigned himself to his daughter taking control, it made him feel warm inside. Hannah walked across to the TV and turned it off. She perched on a chair facing him. He asked her directly before she could broach her subject. 'Are you and Liam OK about them staying here?'

'Course. They're our friends, period.'

Sam was happy with her answer. 'It may only be for a short time anyway.'

She was a clever girl. 'I've inadvertently listened to you and mum chatting, sometimes, kind of…'

'That is so bad, young lady!'

'C'mon, dad, tell me some truths about what other countries are doing?'

'You know I can't give away any secrets.'

'Just an example or two, so I know what my superhero dad is doing.'

Sam thought about a politically correct example. 'Well, Russia is sitting out on a limb. They don't want anything to do with Europe and the USA since the big fall out over the invasion of Estonia last year.' She nodded for him to tell her more. 'They hope to find a different solution to The Envelope, an electronic shield made from an injection of charged particles, high up in the space above us. It's termed "geoengineering".'

'That sounds impossible to achieve in a few months.'

'You're right love, and I can't possibly comment. Except, in the end it makes me angry and frustrated because it is a sop to the Russian people.'

'By default they will die.'

'No comment.'

'What's happening in the fourth world?'

Sam stretched his arms to the ceiling and yawned to cover his embarrassment. 'The fourth world?'

'Oh Dad, you know I love reading lots about politics and sociology. The fourth world is the third world countries who have unstable governments.'

'Yeah, of course, umm…where the governments are strong, they are following the CCOW advice. But where they're weak the opposition is fighting to take control of the country. Saying they could do a better job.'

'Well, that is stupid as it takes time away from the preparations for Convergence.'

'True, and how is the cooperation in the Leinster household?'

'Allie is angry with her dad about nothing.' Hannah preened herself as she spoke in a higher pitch. '"Daddy, I can't even buy my favourite face cream as they are making medicines instead."'

He giggled. 'Well, maybe she is taking her anger out on small things when really she wants to be safe with a loving family.'

'I think she's blaming him for any tiny thing because he is so nasty to her mum. Like, Uncle Bert has gone a bit mad. She told me that he's even talking to flowers!'

They laughed until their tummies hurt. Sam gasped, 'Maybe he will start texting them soon!'

'Or WhatsApping, with flower emojis!'

Sam wiped his eyes. 'But being serious, we need to help Allie cope through all this.'

'How do I do that?'

'Darling, there are TV newsflashes showing stockpiling of food in bunkers and she is truly worried about face cream?'

'She seriously is.'

'Well, encourage her to face up to reality by sitting and watching the news with you. Like we did tonight. As in the book of Job. Sit in the dust with her.'

Hannah questioned, 'On the news there seems to be rioting all over the world?'

'People are angry with governments and us scientists. They need someone to blame. But relatively, a few thousand people in the odd capital is nothing, yeah.'

She thought about it. Her head held lower than normal. 'I know more than I let on.'

'I know you do, Hannah. Are you scared, love?'

She walked across to the sofa and gently climbed onto his lap as if she was seven years old again. He patted her back as she curled tighter to keep the bad thoughts away. 'Mum says we are going to stay in Bex, in the salt mines.'

'Well, we enjoyed our visit there.'

'But dad, it's damp and dark.'

'They will have made it lovely by the time we arrive and remember, it may only be for a week or two.'

'Dad, you think too much and want to save us. But you can be open with me, I'm nearly an adult.'

'No, you are not. You are my little daughter who needs a dad to look after her.' He kissed her forehead as they sat in silence. Briony walked into the room with Liam. Without a word she joined in the cuddle on the sofa and after a few seconds even the teenage boy could see it made sense and joined the family huddle.

★ ★ ★

Bert was in the garden when he first noticed the absence of bees. He knew that no bees meant no pollination, no fertilisation and no food, no fruits, no medicines and numerous other products . It was in an instant of a day, an overnight atrocity. They always came to the lavender that bordered the ancient roses in front of the chalet. The swarms arrived at the start of the day, as soon as the bees considered it warm enough to fly. The honey bees came from the brightly coloured hives sat in the pine woods above the house. A garden alive with buzzing, the noise that had crescendoed in May, died on a single day, August 26th. The legions were lost from Bert's garden but also lost from most of the world. An instantaneous global event. Bert confirmed it the day after. It was early evening as he pinched out the 57 deadheads in his shorts. He normally avoided edging his bare legs into the stalks of lilac and grey. He edged forward and around the tall roman pots and kept going without a care. It was only later as he closed his eyes to sleep that a buzz echoed in his mind to prompt him of their demise. Quickly he ran into Natalia's bedroom. He lay down beside her and whispered. 'It's started.'

'"Het", Lyubov, I was asleep.' She squirmed close to him, warm and soft.

'The bees have gone.'

'They will be back, come here.'

'No, they are gone forever, I know it.' He pulled away and swung his legs off the bed.

'Do not worry, CCOW have pollen.' She yawned, 'Go to sleep.' She turned on her side and stretched her legs before tugging the sheet over her ears.

Bert left immediately; he wouldn't compromise her emotions anymore. He knew there would be an instant assumption that technology would ride to the pollinators rescue. No one would credit mass manual pollination by people clinging to ladders and dabbing stamen to stamen with delicate paint brushes. The naturalists would investigate why the bees died. They would be too busy analysing flesh and organs for macro changes on a cancer level to learn the truth. But the death of the bees was more subtle, only he understood and he wasn't saying anything to anyone anymore. It was of course down to the HBs, there could be no doubting of that. A few a day were colliding with the smallest particles of a body, human or insect and creating a disturbance. An odd quark here, three electrons there and many other particles of the flesh that CERN had no time to discover. It was a particle change, not an elemental change like cancer.

Much later, Bert woke with a start. He was lying on his side cradling his beloved wife. As his brain woke fully, he hugged her tighter to show his undying love and then he felt the empty space beside him. 0.1% of all that is matter, the real her, had gone. Her matter was in the spare room on the third floor and would soon be in Blonay.

★ ★ ★

In the neighbouring valley it was midnight, the time for dark thoughts. Neither Sam nor Briony could sleep. Sam lay still on his back in the dark. His back was drenched from fear and not the heat of the night. Briony turned towards him and gently rubbed her fingers across his moist forehead. Her words jerked the shadows: 'I'm worried about the bunkers. Well, I am happy to go below but, the conditions will be rank, won't they?'

He replied evenly enough, confident enough, 'Once we are in the bunkers, we will keep on digging. From bare necessities, we can improve things each day for us all.' His breathing was shallower, his heart pumped harder.

She was brighter. 'Of course we will, darling. We will learn new ways of coping and doing. And that will make people better in every way.'

Sam turned on his side and put an arm around her. 'I may be a pain at times but I am right and now is the time for the world to get serious.'

'It has always been serious, Sam.'

'So I am a pain?'

'Course not, that is…apart from buying inappropriate Christmas presents.'

'You're funny Mrs Murray. That is why I love you.' He pecked her cheek. 'It was just that I was lying here thinking the world hasn't taken the storm seriously enough.

'I don't see it.'

'It's not like a serious war, you know, so there is less emotional change. Thousands killed in some unholy way. Really, I don't understand it. It's too…I don't know, lighthearted.'

'Darling, life isn't as black as in say a World War. We don't focus on one thing because we can electronically cover the world. It's a lighter place, dare I say dumber even.'

'Umm…maybe'

'Are you seeing in your role that countries aren't serious, are you saying that?'

'Yeah, it's a game for some, the worse aspect is the way some populations or classes within them got angry because the game mattered. But now they have forgotten about it and will keep forgetting, until the moment they have to go below.'

'That can't be all true, Sam. Anger is part of their grief and within that people are capable of the greatest good as well as the worst evil.'

'What do you mean? You have never said anything like that.'

'I believe there is a catalyst for seriousness, when good challenges evil, if you like. That would explain your view that there has not been an emotional change. It's not like a war.'

He kissed her lightly and ran his hand through her hair. 'God versus the Devil then?'

'Hmm, maybe, but that is such a basic concept it is easily understood. A complicated concept is something humans don't understand. There has to be an emotional trigger to completely understand it and accept it.'

Sam was quiet for a few minutes. 'I guess the HB storm is a trigger but it's not the catalyst for seriousness. There must be a missing ingredient, so we can call it x. And x is not apparent yet.'

Sam reached two arms for her and she snuggled in.

'X as in any three letter word you know?' He rolled on top of her, with her hands running down his back and pulling him tighter.

★ ★ ★

It was three o'cock in the morning and Sam had tiptoed down to the lounge. He opened his emails and started to wade through them. He had created four folders. Donally personal, protection, CCOW and one dubiously entitled forget too late. His inbox contained the new day's CCOW briefing, which he moved into junk. He then opened one from the deputy head of CERN protection about the current supply status of The Envelope. It was depressing, barely 30% of target had been met despite China being paid double the price versus the previous month. He threw his keyboard to one side and reached into his left hand drawer to find the tranquillisers. He tossed two back and held them on his tongue as he walked to the half empty Merlot left over from supper. Swigging a large gulp, the pills still stuck on their way down his gullet and so he swigged more and then again and again. He stabbed the bottle back onto the table and stumbled back to the glare from his PC. It was guilt that made him click open the CCOW briefing and move it into the correct folder.

CCOW – Central Control Of the World

Briefing

Countries not joining in the world accord and our consolidated actions will be pushed to one side. CCOW backed by the military might of the USA and Europe will contain any contagion. Countries will be placed in isolation.

Recent riots in most countries have now subsided. The latest sociological research has identified the cause of the unrest. It mostly occurred in democracies. In each case, there was a perceived transgression by either the country's scientists or the government. This perception grew and spread without the facts across many large cities but with the focus on the capital of the country, usually the seat of its parliament. In all cases, the national governments have confronted the psychology of the spontaneous crowds. Arrests have led to the first firing squad executions. All governments were lenient in many respects and only chose to capture and execute the ring leaders.

He slapped the desk, fucking lies, so fucking untrue when they've executed more than three million people worldwide.

News has reached us that Kenya is conducting airstrikes on its neighbours, Somalia, Burundi, and Ethiopia. In addition to this and making the African scenario much worse, we have learned that Rwanda, Nigeria and The Cameroons are also conducting ground and helicopter attacks to subdue the jealous natives of their neighbours in CAR, Benin and Chad. All the African aggressors say their objective is to protect their people and their rights to the limited numbers of Enveloped bunkers. There are no dangers to the developed world because of these actions in poor parts of Africa. We will be monitoring the situation closely. Any dangers would be minimised by joint actions of the CCOW forces. Please view this news calmly.

No danger? When there are hundreds of thousands of migrants in rubber boats heading north to the EU. Fucking liars.

Rumours of a decline in the bee population and the loss of pollen for food production are untrue. Our scientists say that the prolonged summer rains in the northern hemisphere were unusual and caused by a radical change of the jet stream above Europe. This is expected to return to normal in late September. They say the extraordinary cold and wet weather has reduced the number of bees by 65% but this is a fact of nature and has been experienced many times before. You may not notice the bees return as the winter is approaching if you live in the northern hemisphere. All this has impacted very slightly on the southern hemisphere and will be explained after the naturalists have completed their studies in November.

And my best mate says we have no pollination anymore which means no fruit or crops and no food. So if we have less food for storage we should kill off the old gits now. He wondered what age they would decide on as it was logically the only way. After a momentary panic, he decided he was way too young and swept on with his reading.

A minor inconvenience. Green light
Troops that were deployed on the streets of most major cities will be withdrawn as soon as peace reigns again. Calm is returning now.

A moderate inconvenience. Amber light
We recognise that closing down areas surrounding major government buildings may cause you inconvenience but peace and quiet is essential for the teams of people working on your behalf to prepare the Deeps.

A major inconvenience. Red light
We are listening to you!

Recognising that most riots are down to ignorance, CCOW have increased their information bulletins. Each one is now being broadcast on national TV on the hour, every hour.

Please telephone the new free helplines to ask your questions or come online and chat with an expert psychologist to understand your worries.

No, we are fucking not listening, fuck you all as we are making ourselves safe and secure and most of you will die you fucking proletarians. Sam slumped onto his forearms and wedged the keyboard onto endless input. When he would awake in the morning, the CCOW briefing would have been accidentally edited with the addition of thousands of Zs.

HB Predictor today
CERN have confirmed there has been a negligible change to level 57.

> *"A riot is the language of the unheard."*
> *Martin Luther King.*

"Passion is the mob of the man, that commits a riot upon his reason."

William Penn.

★ ★ ★

It was their last day in the chalet. The children had gone to the beach in the late afternoon to meet Hannah and Liam, leaving Natalia and Bert alone. The children had said goodbye to Bert as normal, in expectation of seeing him soon. The adults sat face to face above the pool house. He hoped she would listen before she left. His right hand clenched his left fist as he expounded his views. 'Imagine yourself one hundred and fifty years ago, when this house was built. Imagine looking at the wash basin and dribbling toothpaste from your mouth to drop into the water at the bottom. You are using an electric toothbrush and total protection toothpaste. Nowadays, we have batteries, we can explain the chemistry of the toothpaste, the physics of the dribble and the meniscus and wave theory of the collecting waters. But when the house was built, the Victorians couldn't have explained any of the science. All they had were the basics of cleaning teeth with a bristle brush and salt paste. They still dribbled into the basin, so nothing changes except for the level of explanation. That's where we are now, we can't explain what is happening and by the time we can, we will all be dead. So nothing changes, right?'

Her arms were crossed. 'Only us, Bert.'

'We have not really changed. We still cling to the basics, don't we? And neither will our love for each other change or die.' Her jaw felt numb so she couldn't reply. He continued on: 'Did you know they are putting brominated vegetable oil in the water supplies now? A fizzy pop chemical to reduce everyone's sexual urges induced by an artificial hormone.'

She spat her words at him. 'Billions do not know. Less urges, less violence, more happy drug. I say perfect, keep everyone happy and under control to survive.'

'Natalia, don't be angry, be realistic. When you look someone in the eye, can you tell whether they are your friend or foe? Even your best friends… Don't you think that they will soon revert to their basal core identities?' She resembled the statues in the garden. He tried again, 'Will they stay or will they run? If they stay, they will fight and you have to ask yourself, can you win that fight?' She didn't respond to his lecture. He smacked his palms on the armrests. 'I can always tell the world, can't I? The Envelope won't work and it's too late for us all.' She remained silent. 'How shall I do it? Via Facebook and Twitter? Or shall I call my own media conference?'

She turned to face him and smacked him on the shoulder. 'It would not work "да". No one will believe you, because you are a has been.' It was brutal and the truth hurt him.

He responded bitterly, 'And you have your God to protect you, I suppose? Have Briony and Sam rejuvenated your beliefs that subsisted for the last forty years?'

'Damn you, you shit. Why bring them into us. Us, Bert, us!'

'God, God, God. That's all you sodding think about.'

'I am and always have been a Russian Orthodox. It was God who created man. Not you, you shit.'

He sprang at her and shook her shoulders. 'No, God is what you see now as there is nothing else for you.'

She pushed him away, 'That is unfeeling, Bert. You say you know nothing about your particles, your universe. And all you search for is the truth about matter and antimatter. Maybe you search for the wrong thing. Maybe what matters is the emotional and subjective, after all.'

'A fine speech from the ignorant. Do you think I know nothing about religion, about God, woman?' He crossed his arms, a mirror image.

'I believe in God, but you do not, Bert. I believe in "The God of this world" as in Corinthians. I believe in Lucifer, the opposite of my God.'

Bert put his fingers to both temples and squinted. 'The Book of Job describes when God created the earth and God asked Job, "Where were you when I laid the foundations of the earth? When the morning stars sang together, and all the sons of God shouted for joy?" The stars of course were the angels or sons of God.'

She copied his oft used phrase: 'And your point is?'

'It says all of them shouted and sang together. There were no demons at the time of creation.'

'That is like saying there was no antimatter...'

She had beaten him. He retaliated in the worse way. 'Bollocks, bollocks, bollocks. Big Bang made matter, say material; you call it God. As for the Devil, well maybe he was immaterial.'

She stood and laughed in his face. He slumped deeper into his chair and wondered if Lily was listening. It took him a few moments to recover. But he spoke with less venom now: 'The application of physics cannot in my mind be related to subjective idiosyncrasies, applied by humans in the last three thousand five hundred years to something they don't understand, so they make it up.'

Natalia was triumphant. 'The mystery schools of the Greeks always looked at mind before matter. Then we, so called clever people, changed it. Now we look at matter before mind, science before feeling.'

'That's me, wife, a frigging sceptic talking to a plant and predicting the end of the world. Joy of frigging joys.'

'You talk nonsense, man. Your life is one…what you say…undecipherable set of equations. You are married to a whiteboard, huh, and to prove what? Most people see it as… shit, you need to get a real life, Bert.'

Bert whispered, 'Do you still love me?' Natalia didn't answer at first.

She was standing, quivering with rage. She placed her hands on her rounded sides. 'Do you truly want us to leave?'

He didn't respond but stood to grasp her. He tried to pull her close but she resisted. 'It's for the best, Natalia. You must leave.'

'What is it, Bert? Sex, love, going into the Deeps? Or has normal living got in the way of our marriage?' She stared at her husband. But there was only one life; they both knew it wasn't a rehearsal.

'Much more than our living, so much more, that you can never understand. Just know, I will always love you.' Bert had too much on his mind to think properly. As he turned and walked away, he whispered, 'Be a believer, stay faithful.' He thought it was Oscar Wilde who had said "Scepticism is the beginning of Faith", but he knew he had lost her. It was a question of choices now and not circumstances. He spoke to himself, a poor comfort. 'And I will always love you, even when you are wrong.' Most thoughts don't build bridges, and the only listener was Lily and Lily stayed quiet.

★ ★ ★

Sam called in at the chalet the next morning and saw his friend slumped on a deckchair near the pool. Bert told him about Lily and how Natalia didn't believe him. His best friend dismissed the notion out of hand. 'Flowers can't talk, Bert. You have lost the plot, mate.'

'I have not lost the fucking plot.' He drew breath before shouting. 'The world has lost the fucking plot.'

Bert's response made Sam shiver, in his mind there was a single and correct reality; the journey to the Deeps. Bert stood to grasp Sam's lapels and spat the words into his face, 'Higgs Boson didn't exist until 2012, it was only in our minds. Who knows how Lily is communicating? You of all people must understand that humankind truly knows nothing. I hear Her and that is factual. Not your fact, not scientific fact but it is a fact.'

Sam stayed in factual mode as he gently pushed Bert away, 'Your wife is OK, if you care to know, so are the kids, Bert. All settled in.'

'She has gone forever.'

'No, mate, nothing is forever. You can always come with us into the bunker.'

'I forget. Which one?'

'Bex salt mines.'

Bert rolled his eyes. 'What a pit.'

'Are you OK?'

'Fine. All Natalia wanted to talk about last night was God.' He was going to add and that's your fault.

Sam was bouncing with positive energy. 'Faith helps at a time like this. In fact I have just been up to the church at Caux to pray for us all.' Sam turned to his left and pointed heavenwards to the church across the valley. 'I didn't realise that you can see the tower from here.'

'Why?' His flat tone matched his slumped shoulders.

'Why? Because I wanted to pray of course.'

'No, why Caux stupid?'

'Oh yeah, umm...I guess because it's solitary and beautiful. It has a special feel and you can sit there without being disturbed.' Sam held his old prayer book in his hand. A battered black leather book that was the size of a wallet. He glanced down at it and flipped through the pages, seeking a passage to give solace to his friend.

Bert was non-committal. 'I can understand you saying prayers for all of this to end nicely. But I hope you haven't been bargaining your life for that of your family and friends.'

'Of course I have. I'm weak and you are strong. We've always been opposites.'

Bert complained bitterly: 'Next you will be quoting me something religious. "In the beginning was the Word, and the Word was with God, and the Word was God. He was in the beginning with God. All things were made through him, and without him was not any thing made that was made. In him was life, and the life was the light of men. The light shines in the darkness, and the darkness has not overcome it."'

Sam stared hard at Bert. 'I'm impressed. How do you know that, Mr. Clever?'

'Manchester Grammar School, an elementary thesis to teach us about Good versus Evil.'

Sam sat in silence for five or ten minutes. He stretched his legs out and closed his eyes, 'Bert, if I quote anything from the Bible it is this.' He opened his prayer book. '"James 2: 14-26. What good is it, my brothers, if someone says he has faith but does not have works? Can that faith save him? If a brother or sister is poorly clothed and lacking in daily food, and one of you says to them, "Go in peace, be warmed and filled," without giving them the things needed for the body, what good is that? So also faith by itself, if it does not have works, is dead. But someone will say, "You have faith and I have works." Show me your faith apart from your works, and I will show you my faith by my works."' He paused for a minute. 'And that is what we are doing. Working together to save humankind and not talking to flowers and pondering why the frigging HB storm started.' Sam leaned across and touched his friend's arm. 'Bert?' It was a last plea for normality.

Bert looked away. 'God is delusional, any God. Yours, Allah, Krishna. It is all a load of cock.' It touched a nerve.

Sam raved at Bert. 'We have The Envelope. We have a plan and we have our faith. Why can't you get in line and look after your family?' He stormed off the decking, throwing his prayer book into a corner by the wall. 'There you go. A present for you when you need to believe.'

Bert was stunned by the ferocity of Sam's words. Each of the three points hurt him, but the last comment hurt him the most of all. He sulked his way into the basement to find his special tool for collecting myrtle berries. It was nearly dark outside but he could discern enough of the blue berries with their matt waxy sheen.

'Bert. Don't be angry. Listen to your friend.'

'I am not angry with my friend.'

'He shouted at you. Your best friend thinks you are a fool.'

'You see humans on a superficial level.' He started to comb the branches with the small wooden box until it was filled.

'No, I see their emotions. The vibrations of their souls.'

'Next you will be telling me we vibrate at a certain frequency and are cosmic beings linked to a divine source.'

'*You stupid man. Only humans would think such inane rubbish.*'

'Yeah, they do and they would probably put it in a blog and share their visions immediately after dancing naked around a fire at midnight.' He tipped the fruits into his bucket and started on the next branch.

'*The last refuge of modest and chaste-souled people when the privacy of their soul is coarsely and intrusively invaded.*'

'Fyodor Dostoevsky, writing about sarcasm.'

'*You are clever, Bert. He was an orthodox christian who lost his way like your wife. You are surrounded by God worshippers.*'

'Not now.' He continued to comb the small tree. Why should he bother to argue with a lily, when the world was tumbling into the depths of despair? The berries sacred to Aphrodite, the Greek Goddess of love, beauty, pleasure, and procreation, were sweet and full. They would be the last he would eat.

[6]

Lonely Reflection

SEPTEMBER 2018, THE EOTW autumn, was in sharp contrast to an apposite autumn. For Bert it was a question of containment. Containing the memories undisclosed, holding the thoughts of another day in another time. But he was mired in 2014, the cool and wet summer had been the worst in eighty five years but had given way to a glorious autumn. The pretty village above Chalet Suvarov had been the wettest place in Switzerland. It clarified the historic reason why the city of Lausanne sourced its water supply from the permanently damp valley of the Chauderon. One spring alone disgorged twenty eight thousand litres of water in a minute. That is nature, naturally unforgiving and unpredictable.

Therefore the hot and sunny days, had been a blessing for all the locals who lived a café culture, with long lunches and a siesta. That year the Leinster family enjoyed fun and laughter enclosed by the beauty of the Lavaux. The ancient vineyards, once tended by Benedictine and Cistercian monks, were astonishing enough to be a Unesco Heritage site. A glory of terraces following the curve of the lake, with steep rushing torrents punctuating the straight lines of vines. The family had joined in the Route Gourmand starting nearby, a traditional fiesta to celebrate the end of the grape harvest. They had meandered for many kilometres between feeding stations, drinking as much local wine as they wanted and tasting the local food. They had met a dozen friends from CERN and Nestlé. They had laughed, chatted and danced to the jazz that serenaded their passage. The exertions necessitated an enjoyable siesta on a dry grassy bank. Natalia and Bert had walked and talked, kissed and had fun. They had admired the remaining heavy bunches of grapes, which hung temptingly but were sour to the taste. Four years before the HB storm, the start of autumn had been perfect, but paradise was now truly lost.

September 2018 was damp and overcast, the weather engaged Bert and won. The atmosphere had absorbed the lake and had steadily rung itself dry on the humans. Not every day was bad, but it was a depressing and dark series of wet days that matched the mood of the Swiss people. Bert had enjoyed listening to the radio; now on many occasions he switched it off to avoid the new emotional terms bandied about in the media. Pre HB, living with HB, and a positive, if optimistic statement, of post HB. The Route Gourmand had been cancelled and the well kept vines were dishevelled. Most of the grapes rotted on their bushes, there had been no good reason to spray them with fungicide, Botrytis cinerea was rife, a grey mould erupting from the bunches of grapes. A quick look and one's animal instinct would arrest the urge to eat. And there was little laughter in the small vigneron communes. Oh so quiet, with few visitors strolling across the grand terraces. At Chalet Suvarov there was no laughter, no family or visitors and no perpetual movement of people. Bert remained encased in the dark interior and brooded with the Victorian ghosts.

He stared blankly at the leaves on the trees, puzzled as they were starting to change colour but it was ridiculously early. Dendrologists from the University of Fribourg attributed the change to abnormally low chlorophyll levels due to a decrease in magnesium. Everyone, even the cleverest people, denied the HB storm was responsible. The leaves were already falling, a full month in advance of a normal year. The norm was based on previous human experiences over mere centuries but this was a blink of an eye in comparison to the age of the universe. The aster flowers of intense purple and Caribbean blue had appeared at the normal time in the garden and the marguerites continued to thrive. But for Bert the norm was changing. He was awake early each morning and late into the night and he alone noticed subtle mutations in nature. The roe deer that frequented his roses to snack on the dewy buds, exhibited no breeding frenzy as they grazed at the foot of his woody knoll. He saw that the stag's antlers were late in growing and still covered in velvet, untouched by territorial fights. Caught in his torchlight, he saw the deer were still red coated instead of the darkening brown of a normal year. And underfoot, Bert's boots squashed few ants, as if they had assumed a winter dormancy a month or two early.

The humans were also mutating but refused to acknowledge the differences. A slight memory loss was considered normal, and put down to worry. The fatigue after jogging or swimming was eliminated by a person trying harder. Bert didn't feel ill, but equally he knew he wasn't feeling "right"; he knew the difference. His personal stress and anxiety was reduced as he spent the minimal time at

CERN and the maximum time at home. He contemplated the HB storm and its cause and nature helped him search for his answers. In the morning, he would stand for an hour in the shower. Cupping his hands under the silver flow, he watched hydrogen and oxygen bubble up and over his fingers, enlightened by the sun slanting through the bathroom window. At night he would sit in bed and stare at the mirror on the wall opposite. A phantom of Bert Leinster was visible in the dim light of his bedside lamp. Twisting his head from left to right, he used both hands to rub away the pain in his temples. After an eternity, a time lost to him, he would change the movement to up and then down, nodding in affirmation of his selfish but lonely plight.

There seemed little to live for and so he experimented with life itself. Sat in an armchair on the veranda, he stared at the sun. The brightness caused him to close his eyes and hold onto a blind hallucination of red. He took a deep breath and held it, determined it would be his last, determined to die. Reaching thirty seconds was easy; at a minute his heart was pounding. Some time later, when he had stopped counting the seconds, the hypoxia made him lightheaded. He looked down at himself from above. He tried to move and failed but he held on, he was determined not to breathe. His fingers started to tingle and his head to ache. He watched the three roe deer somersaulting across the lawn with a water lily chomped between their jaws. The small fawn managed a triple loop, then he jerked awake. He couldn't remember his first breaths, the elixir of life. But the terror of dying had been experienced and he vowed he would never commit suicide. He had to face the true end for humankind, he knew that his presence was somehow important.

The only excitement at the chalet was a day of frenetic activity, when the army installed a huge electricity generator designed to power the whole house. A secondary oil tank of twenty thousand litres doubled up the existing capacity. They also installed a petrol tank inside one of his garages so he could always travel to CERN as the last bastion of Man on earth. The media had dubbed him "the predictor keeper" and had photoshopped his publicity pictures with a superman's outfit. The following day, a bunch of technicians arrived to set up a direct satellite link to the HB experiment. When the predictor level reached 10, everyone would start to go below. It was a new CCOW directive, a way of introducing a safety margin before level zero and Convergence day. It was arbitrary, as no scientist or doctor had a clue as to what would happen to the human body at this point or even before. And Lily? Lily watched; she heard and saw every movement. The host watched for her, and nature reported back on humankind's backward progress as they raced towards their short future.

★ ★ ★

The four children were sat with Sam, Briony and Natalia eating Rösti, baked grated potato coated with Gruyère cheese and small pieces of bacon. The TV droned in the background as they chatted. The tribe stopped eating and turned as one to watch the BBC news. The familiar fanfare preceded the announcer declaring in a loud serious tone, CCOW – Central Control Of the World briefing:

Important news, take action now! The World Council asks you to go to where your family intend congregating in the next four weeks. Don't wait! Go and register in the town where you want to be for entry into the Deeps. Go as soon as possible, as the pressure is increasing on all our transport systems the closer we are to Convergence day. Transport resources are already stretched to breaking point to enable workers to complete the bunkers. We know we can cope over the next four weeks but after this period we may have to introduce emergency measures limiting personal travel.

Be with the ones you love now. This will help the local authorities to monitor numbers of clients for different bunkers and keep all families together.

The children pushed their food around the plate with their heads down. The adults looked at each other but kept quiet.

Multi-faith services will be held next weekend to celebrate our wonderful lives. We are delighted to report that every faith and every single place of worship have committed to this global event. Find your nearest service and join in the joy of life celebrations. Spread the word.#EOTWmultifaith. There are more details on our website under the banner advertisement.

Briony latched onto the good news. 'Won't that be lovely guys, I expect the Anglicans will use the same location as last Easter. Do you remember, we went a few years back, down by the lake at dawn.'

Sam joined in with a cheery, 'Gosh yes darling, how delightful, I can't wait.' The children said nothing and ate nothing.

A minor inconvenience. Green light

The shortage of petrol is because oil refining has been geared towards creating more derv and heating oil. We must put as much as possible into storage for generating electricity and powering our boilers. Most countries have already hit the three hundred days reserve set by The World Council. New pipelines have been installed between storage facilities and the bunkers.

The motto is: use public transport wherever possible.

A moderate inconvenience. Amber light

There has been a shortage of paste to secure The Envelope to the walls of the bunkers. However, a mighty effort in most countries will ensure full and adequate supplies again from next week. This will not delay completion of The Envelope in our bunkers. Its attachment to walls is non-skilled work, and we have a surplus of help.

A major inconvenience. Red light

Please discuss with your employer the Convergence payments to supplement your income during the period between leaving work and going below. This is a generous payment equal to 80% of your salary. It allows you to leave work now and be in the home location that you desire.

Also remember to log your CV online to help us utilise your skills in your new area. Report to the local council immediately upon arrival in a new town. We have so much for you to do! If you are under 35 years old, we would like you to populate the bunkers early as we need your enthusiasm and energy. Hard work awaits you but it will be incredibly rewarding.

Sam already knew the answer, 'Can you leave work soon darling? I don't know how generous Néstle will be, do you?'

'Well, the good news is we discussed the draft proposals in our team meeting last week and I think I'll be able to sit in splendid retirement next month.'

'Oh gosh,' Sam clapped his hands together, 'What wonderful news children, don't you think?' There were four low grunts around the table from the top of four heads with Natalia remaining coy.

HB Predictor today
CERN has announced the level is 30. This is not a shock. We all expected it could happen.

Remember the level could also increase, as we experienced last week.

But take time for quiet reflection. Do not be alone. Search out your neighbours and talk about our future, our new world.

"Life is full of misery, loneliness, and suffering – and it's all over much too soon."

Woody Allen

"If there is a look of human eyes that tells of perpetual loneliness, so there is also the familiar look that is the sign of perpetual crowds."

Alice Meynell

End of broadcast.

Allie broke the silence first. 'Who's Alice Meynell?'

'She was an English writer and suffragist but mostly she is remembered for her poetry.' They all stared in astonishment at Natalia. 'I am not stupid, you just never talk about the arts in this house. Only science!'

Sam was visibly upset by the quotations. 'I can't believe they have tried to inject humour into the situation by using Woody Allen. That stinks.'

Allie urged him to relax by passing him the hot dish of Rösti for second helpings. 'Uncle Sam, most of us have never even heard of Woody Allen. Anyway, I think it's quite a funny line.'

Josh interrupted her before she could assuage Sam further. He was using his iPhone to surf the web. A favourite site had come up and he told everyone the news. 'Wow, Bet365/24/7 has just changed the odds on The End of the World to November.'

Liam was leaning over his shoulder to look. 'Bring it on mate, it's five to one now.'

Sam looked askance at the them: 'I hope you two haven't been betting.'

They were unapologetic. Liam answered for them both: 'Sorry, dad, but we thought we had excellent inside knowledge through you and Uncle Bert and could make some good money.'

Briony wagged a finger at them. 'Very enterprising of you both, but so wrong. By the way, whose bank account did you use?' The boys deliberately ignored her query. 'OK, in which case, what are the odds on me getting my money back?'

Liam replied with a smile. 'I reckon we could split the bet three ways, mum.'

'And I reckon not, young man. By the way, what are the odds on the return to the surface before June 2019?'

Liam continued quickly as cover, 'I'm glad we live here in Switzerland. The Swiss are really good at creating bunkers. We have some left over from World War Two and of course there also the old nuclear ones.'

Allie helped Liam out, 'I heard that some shopping malls in Zurich and Geneva are going to be amazingly beautiful bunkers and they say that there will be food and water to last three years.' The children were seemingly desperate to go below now. Lessons at school were ground out each day but the teachers had no motivation without an examination certificate for their pupils to obtain. All types of educational award had been suspended. Teenagers especially ignored any potential damage to their bodies from the HBs, it was out of sight and therefore out of mind. They wanted to accelerate the transfer into the Deeps in order to move closer to The Return; it was a youth strategy. Psychologists working for CCOW had anticipated this fresh wave of enthusiasm. They had determined the method of deceiving humankind using the briefings, subliminal adverts and hidden drugs in food and water, it was a successful regime for all those marching happily to Convergence.

Josh always argued with his sister. 'C'mon sis…it's not going to be a hotel, not even a budget one at that. No family room with a kettle and ensuite toilet and shower.'

'I know, doik! Girls will cope better than any boys as we can multi-task, OK ya. Whatever we need to do to survive, we can do. So long a there is a hairdryer, of course.'

'And some nice Chardonnay,' added Briony.

Sam cheerily concurred, 'Don't forget the beer, ladies.'

The happier group carried on discussing the bunker facilities, the pleasure of meeting new people and the bonhomie when helping each other create extra space and new facilities such as a gym and perhaps a swimming pool. They were confident the time below wouldn't extend longer than a few weeks, three months at most.

The mums were smiling, proud of their sensible and brave children. It was only Sam who kept his thoughts private. There is survival and there is life. Is it better to live a shorter life than survive a longer period? Is Bert right? The concept constantly gnawed away at his insides.

★ ★ ★

Bert's month was monotonous. A fast drive to CERN twice a week, breaking every speed limit on every road. The notices from the police piled high in his letter box with the penalty fines, house bills and council advices. The good news in the crisis was the free newsletters and flyers had dried up. He dozed during much of the day and any lunch was always taken with a bottle of red wine, which then necessitated a long siesta. He bought food at will from the local Denner express. Bread, cheese and ham became his staple diet. Breakfasts occurred any time between 5am and 5pm and were a selection of whichever cereal he had purchased on impulse. This was driven by the packaging that mattered to him. He selected the ones with children's toys, games and offers, usually with comic strip characters emblazoned in multi-colours. And always full cream milk; cholesterol held no fears for him. Most nights he walked. Starting at sunset he headed into the Prealps behind the chalet. There were dozens of walks, all marked with yellow signs "Tourisme pédestre", or yellow diamonds painted on tree trunks and rocks. When there was no moonlight to guide his way, he took an LED head torch with him. He walked himself into exhaustion. At the start of the month he could barely manage an hour of the steep gradients but by the end of it, five hours of punishing walking was easy for him. It gave him extra thinking time in the midst of the nature he loved. He watched the deer, foxes and stone martens. He leaned against the limestone cliffs gracing the Gorge de Chauderon and looked upwards to watch the bats flirt with his torch beam. And as he became fitter, he would end his walk at a panoramic view to enjoy the beauty of the washed yellow sunrise. The rays heating up his body that had gone cold after the sweat of his exertions.

Briony now acted as intermediary between Bert, Sam and Natalia. That morning, her husband and friend had been in the kitchen at Blonay as she cooked a cottage pie. By the time she started to coat the mincemeat with mashed potato, Sam had asked a second time for her to invite Bert to stay with them. As the cheese was grated on top of the potato, Natalia reiterated that the family wanted Bert to go into the Deeps with them. A lot of love went into that particular dish.

Briony performed her duty later that morning. Arriving at the chalet, she found Bert asleep. He was slumped across a sofa in the salon and snoring heavily. She nudged him awake with the peace offering and wafted it under his nose before taking it into the kitchen and putting it in the fridge. Returning to the salon, she found he was now semi-revived.

She sat, crossed her legs and looked down her nose, 'You know why I'm here, don't you?'

She barely caught his languid reply: 'Natalia wants to come home?' He gave a dishonest answer with an underhanded question.

'No, Natalia wants you to be with us, of course. In fact, Sam and I and all the kids want you to come and live with us for the last few weeks before Deeps Day.'

He sat up and stretched his arms above his head. 'I'm not lonely on my own, you know. I can talk to flowers all day and even in the night.'

'Very droll, Bert,' Briony continued. 'Eat the pie tonight and think of us, at least please come and stay. You don't have to commit to the Deeps because I think I understand your need to be the last person above ground.'

'I'm not sure you do, Briony.'

'Well, some of it is your ego. Some of it is because you cannot fail in your own mind, which seems quite autistic to me.'

'But that's not all.' He stood up. 'Let's walk up to Caux. I need some air.'

They set out towards the ridge east of the chalet. There were no passing humans and no conversation between the two of them. After half an hour they had strolled past the gigantic Grand Hotel that was now a hotel school. It had been the centre for moral rearmament after the Second World War. Also, a haven for nearly two thousand Hungarian Jews, bought off Adolf Eichmann and transferred to Switzerland on the Kastner train to avoid Auschwitz. Bert and Briony stopped near the old coaching houses to collect walnuts. They took the five metre long stick that leaned against the lava-like bark and knocked some fresh nuts off the lower branches.

'You'll...hmm... lose Natalia if you don't make an effort.' Briony swished the stick into the leaves and three nuts fell nearby. 'Can't you give in and be with her?'

Bert took the stick from her and hit the tree much harder. A dozen or more green roundels fell off. 'I can't, otherwise I would.' He stooped to gather the nuts and left the pole leaning where they had found it. 'I only do what I believe in and none of you can change my mad beliefs, can you.' He remembered asking his wife if she still loved him and obtaining no response.

They walked further up the steep and winding road towards Sam's favourite church. Briony touched his arm. 'So you actually welcome separation then?'

'Exactly, and from the kids.' Bert slowed to look at her for the first time during the walk. 'It has to be like this. I know it has to happen as it's a test in time. It's not real, Briony.' He smiled at her, a warm, generous smile. 'Whether we die together and simultaneously as a family, or die separately and a month apart. Someone who matters cares. But I think I care the most and I can die the last.'

'Of course someone cares and we all matter.' He didn't answer her. 'Look, here we are at the top of a mountain and you have a prime example of human emotions.' They had stopped by the grand entrance to the Lectorium Rosicrucianum, the headquarters for gnostic spiritualism. 'This whole village has been devoted to peace for decades and all we want is peace for our two families. Why not give in?'

'Because, Briony, I am bonkers and talk to a lily. I guess Sam has told you.'

'Yes, of course he has, and yes you are mad, Bert. It would be like me talking to a yoghurt.'

'Very fucking funny, and I think dying in a darkened hole is a waste of what little life remains. That is why the world laughs at me – because I'm different.'

She stamped away from him. After a minute she halted next to the Rosicrucians' noticeboard and paraphrased it to Bert, whilst he stood gormless, examining the rhododendrons above. 'Listen here, monsieur, the gnostic teaching is based on an understanding of man as a multi-dimensional entity with an immortal spirit-spark, the germ of a new microcosm.' She looked around and saw him motionless. She carried on regardless but spoke more loudly. 'The destiny of man is the path of return to the original, overcoming the limitations of his present consciousness that is limited by space and time.'

He spoke briefly without looking at her: 'That is very apt. Very apt indeed.'

She had forgotten his gift to think on many levels at once. So she continued. It seemed right for them both to heed the teachings. 'Man gains self-awareness of the original creative force.'

Bert turned to her and replied, 'Man's immortal spirit-spark. How often do religions talk about it but in a slightly different way?' He came behind her and looked at the noticeboard. He read aloud: '"The Light is the teacher and master. The direct knowledge resulting from the Light is called Gnosis – knowledge of God."' He strode away down the hill and left her to catch up. He called over his shoulder, 'Anyone could make that up and anyone has always done so…word confusion equals enlightenment blah!' The host in Caux heard the comments and interpreted his emotions. The village had been chosen by Man but it was nature which had called them to the place.

★ ★ ★

'I saw you when you stopped breathing, Bert. Your soul hovered nearby and yet you couldn't depart this earth.'

'Go away, Lily, you are unwelcome in my bedroom.' He turned onto his left side and looked at the alarm clock on the table. Three in the morning; he put a pillow over his head.

'But you were a coward and breathed. Why don't you try some of the rat poison in your garage mixed with a bottle of cognac?

Drink a bottle of neat cognac first and then a second laced with the poison. After a few seconds, with no pain, you can find the oblivion you crave.'

'Just fuck off, Lily.'

'Or go for a swim in the lake on a dark night, swallow a packet of your wife's Zopiclone tablets. It will be easy. Drink a couple of bottles of red wine and swim until you feel no pain. You can let go now as we are nearing the end.'

'I may be depressed and dull-headed and I have nothing to live for apart from my thoughts. But thoughts are life.' He turned on his back and stared at the ceiling. A patch of yellow moonlight crept between the curtains and splayed across the white emulsion. A ghostly phantom that diluted his solitude.

'You could be brave and jump head first off the Pont de Pierre. A five metre drop is enough to cave your skull into your brains and the stream will wash your thoughts down the gorge to Lac Léman. A clean ending.'

'My brain is being shredded by HBs, so I don't want to pollute the pristine lake with them.' He was wide awake now and listened intently.

'No, you won't do that? Too scared? So go to your doctor and make an appointment with death. Millions of people around the globe are taking the quiet and dignified way out.'

Bert probed her motives. 'Brian Greene, one of our foremost physics and mathematics professors said something like: "When you die, I believe you die. The interval of time in which you are alive are moments that exist and persist. But outside of that, before you are born or after you die, you don't exist."'

'And your point is?'

'You are very astute, aren't you? Using my phrase to rile me. To deflect me.' After a short pause he continued, 'Greene based his answer about death on a belief. A faith that life, and consciousness is the result of particles being in specific, highly specialised arrangements. When particles cease to be in those arrangements, life and consciousness cease to exist.'

'So you don't believe in God then, Bert. You only believe in science?'

There was a vacuum created in the bedroom by Her statement. He spoke so softly a cat wouldn't hear. 'I believe that we as humans barely touch the reality of life. So there may be God or there may be the Devil. I don't know. Maybe plants can talk to us, maybe they can't. I really don't know.'

'You are a fallen angel, Bert. That is the first time you have ever said, "I don't know". All the power and the glory you held and have now lost: If you worshipped me, all the world could be yours. Is that why you want to be the last human alive?'

'My imagination gives me my power. But I am a humble man when I don't know the answer. I cannot imagine my children and wife entombed in the Deeps. Young kids running riot, bad medical care, basic sanitation and of course not everyone can fit into the bunkers. So what must happen to the remainder? That is my weakness but also my strength. My imagination.'

'You came from the soil and you will return to the soil. You are us and we are you.'

Bert closed Her out of his mind and drifted off to sleep. He pondered Her questions and suggestions. Did his ephemeral Lily want him dead? An early death, leaving a humble Lily to thrive in the chaos that must ensue post HB. The last thought before sleep was an old conversation with Her. He murmured it to himself and slept deeply for the first time that month. '"I love all my host. The legions love me. We are one".'

★ ★ ★

The best outcome of the walk in Caux came twenty four hours later. Peace had reigned when Briony and Bert had arrived back at the chalet and Bert agreed to meet his children on the following day. The two teenagers stood adjacent to the Freddie Mercury statue in central Montreux, and were looking at the lake. It was still and so were they. Calm and content. Freddie was solid in his bronze effigy, leaving only Bert as the nervous one. He walked down the steps from the Eiffel-designed market and quietly came up behind them.

'I swear you have both grown taller in the last few weeks!' Both children turned upon hearing his voice and stepping forwards they hugged together as a tight group. Bert felt the aura of love around them. A passer-by paused and then completely stopped for a double-take and realised it was the famous predictor-keeper dwarfed by Freddie. The man immediately took a photo with his smartphone and uploaded it to Twitter with the ironic words, a song title by Queen. "#Who wants to live forever". It went viral across the globe within an hour of being posted. Bert saw it after his kids made him aware of the retweets #goingtodiesoplaymoremusic.

The children and their father strolled slowly by the side of the lake. The depleted flowerbeds were bare dry soil with a smattering of cigarette butts. Only the rare specimens of tree and perennial plants enlivened the promenade now. Far fewer humans stretched along the three kilometres that usually bounced with life. Normally, the threesome would be competing with families sporting pushchairs, cyclists, children on scooters, dogs unbridled by their extendable leashes, but today was inordinately quiet. It made it easier to chat.

They discussed school, the food and sleeping arrangements at Sam and Briony's home. Everything mundane and nothing about the bunker at Bex or the HB storm. They joined what Natalia had once described as "the proletarians" in a short queue for a Mövenpick ice cream. There were only three choices now, compared to 30 before HB. Crème brûlée, cappuccino, and banana. Bert let his children talk. They didn't ask him what he was doing, they only reassured him that they were OK. As teenagers they had assumed their adult responsibilities. They walked further and constantly talked at him. Distracted, he looked at the passing tourists and an odd local. He considered how they might blend together when they knew the truth about their incarceration. It would be an impossibility created by humankind's many varieties. A fairy tale that everyone assumed was true. Possible was the love and emotion of a father and his two children strolling along the promenade by a beautiful lake. He was sad, infinitely sad.

★ ★ ★

The blackness clung to Bert on the small hillock at the edge of his garden as he watched the red fairy lights slowly spinning on the big wheel in Montreux. The fair was part of the annual Federal Fast arranged by the government since 1619. The government had chosen "Unity" as the fasting focus for all of its citizens in 2018. It was in response to the odd riot and general angst felt by the population during the weeks before. Unity in finishing the bunkers as soon as possible. Unity in going below. Unity in the belief that there would be a future. Bert could touch the nadir of his depression. He could feel his health ebbing away in his aching bones. Every waking moment was a struggle, a test of his strength of will, but enough was enough. It was time to move forward towards his version of Convergence. The big wheel moved a touch, he'd seen it that afternoon but it had been closed. He had wanted to be suspended with his children, eating waffles dripping with chocolate and chantilly cream. He could feel the waves of emotions billow upwards from a thousand families having fun. He collapsed to his knees and bowed to the ground. His form dulled but his mind burned brighter than ever before.

As the churches' bells in Montreux tolled tenfold, the sky splintered horizontally with the first flashes of the fireworks. He squinted through the rainbow colours that cascaded from the star bursts hanging high above the lake. Behind the man-made pyrotechnics hung a crescent moon, a small mouth laughing at the humans fun, enjoyed despite their plight. He started to weep, his body shaking in its crouch, his hands digging into the soil around him. He saw and heard nothing now, only the quiet blackness of the lake until more spurts soared skywards around the French resorts opposing the promontories of Montreux. A picture of paradise entangled in the stars and mirrored in the lake.

'Dying is easy, isn't it?'

'You are too harsh, Bert.' He thought it was Lily, but it was a resonance of his own mind. 'But it is only a question of oxygen. Heart, stroke whatever the illness, you gasp for a couple of minutes and lose consciousness and bingo, it's all over. Completed, shoved off.' But he had already suffered a slow death during September so he knew the mental pain associated with death. The realisation that dying is about memories and the loss of subjectives like love and happiness.

He wobbled unsteadily to his feet and wandered back to the house at a slow tramp. In his study he picked up the book he had been reading in every spare moment. He started to thrash himself across the top of his head with the hardback. Slowly at first, as he clapped the book, "Hard-boiled Wonderland and the End of The World" by Haruki Murakami, onto his receding forehead. Then faster and harder until it hurt. But the literary bombardment didn't dull his pain. He gave up, his smarting head ringing violently, and staggered into the kitchen.

Through bouncing eyes he saw a dozen electrical devices spread around the worktops. He gravitated to each one, starting with the Sonos wifi radio receiver. He grabbed it using both hands and raised his arms above his head. Then he dropped it onto the travertine floor to shatter every component. He continued around the room and did the same to his iPad, a laptop and finally the two TV sets. Trembling, he booted the smashed bits, they screeched before lodging against a cupboard. After five minutes he collapsed against a worktop, his breath condensing alongside the sweaty palm marks. There were no factual answers to why there was a HB storm, only emotional and subjective suggestions. His tears started again. He wanted his family with him at their home. He wanted them to stay above ground. He wanted to die with them. He slapped his hands across the marble; he shouted to the ceiling that he had failed. Until that smell, Natalia's fresh baked bread, a culinary figment of his imagination. How he longed for the genuine smell and taste of her food, of her person. It was over, he knew his anger at their desertion was dulled, the smashed technologies merely symbolic and he desired the stability and reality of CERN to understand his current deliberations. He went to shower and then he would drive to Geneva.

★ ★ ★

Sam banged hard on the door of the chalet but there was no answer. As he walked past the Merc garage he saw the gaping door. He sighed heavily. They were running out of time together and he had questions that needed asking. Sam was surprised about Bert's absence, he thought he had given up. He tried his mobile but the ring bleeped then faded and so he set off to the experiment, hoping his friend had gone to CERN. The offices in the LHC were disembodied, eerie with echoes of a chair scraped, a light drumming of the air conditioning. There was a faint electrical hum from isolated servers, separated from their researchers who were now bound to the CERN campus. The experiment to find life had adopted the silence of the dead. Sam wanted to verify he had made the right decision to go below. He wanted to ward off his assumed responsibilities. He had forgiven his friend and wanted peace. He breathed deeply as he approached the shed door and flung it open. Bert sat calmly drinking a machine coffee, the plastic taste that had become a drug over many years. A shared dislike since their first days together at Manchester University. Sam nodded his head and wiggled his hand at his mate. Bert put his thumb up for another.

They sat head to head and talked quietly. Sam was telling Bert about the final work undertaken by their team. He was surprised but pleased that Bert truly wanted to know. 'Before everything closed down last Friday, we let some post graduates perform an experiment on a new type of Cherenkov.' Bert listened silently. 'They found sodding HBs. They had generated HBs when colliding electrons in part of the collider that has never been part of the HB experiments. Bert, can you frigging believe that?' Bert remained silent but waved a hand to indicate Sam should proceed. 'I asked them to repeat their experiments and to crosscheck the result. It was correct but without years of work, I assume they had discovered a new particle, something akin to HBs and it also gave other particles mass.'

Bert yawned. 'But an ad hoc experiment like that is outside of any protocol and therefore the results are very likely to be erroneous.'

Sam was insistent: 'Mate, I thought you should know. It might help you work it all out later.'

'There is no later, only now, and now is coming to an end.'

Sam ignored him and pursued his thoughts. 'We also saw the new particle can decay down five different channels and then some and then and then... It was infinite, so if particle physics is infinite then the multiverse is infinite and you know the theories that say that can't be true.'

Bert smiled gravely. 'It took fifty years from predicting the Higgs Boson to finding it. I repeat, we have no time left.'

Sam's voice was shaky. 'We used the LHC to find out the truth concerning matter and antimatter. Maybe we did find the ultimate truth in our universe.'

Bert was adamant: 'No, not that old argument again. We did not create quantum black holes. Besides, none of our detectors were compromised by them. So we have not seen them to prove your fear. Get real and forget it, pal.'

Sam was searching for answers and he had always asked Bert. His best friend always had the answers. 'The Higgs Boson gives mass to everything, so apart from the onslaught of radiation, what are the other physical effects? What interactions are we missing?'

Bert cut him short: 'The answers don't matter. As Ralph said. You die if you worry, you die if you don't, so don't worry.'

'But I do worry. I want to tell people the truth.'

Bert was sharper than normal with his friend: 'You can't, Sam. No one can accept the truth, everyone must believe in the lie. That is, until we spin off this planet into nothingness.' He paused. 'By the way, where is Ralph nowadays?'

Sam tossed is plastic cup into the bin. 'Gone, retired. He up and left with his family and headed for Provence.' Bert nodded his approval as Sam headed back to theory land. 'String theory predicts extra dimensions, so have the HBs come from another universe?'

'Sam,' Bert was emphatic, 'we cannot search for the cause in one of the infinite other universes of our multiverse model. Yes, we predicted them using string theory but finding the cause in our universe or any other solves nothing. So listen to me, keep treating the symptoms and take your solace from the great work you have done for humankind.'

Sam gave it one last attempt. 'We discovered four statistically unlikely circular patterns in the cosmic microwave background. The researchers think that these marks could be "bruises" that our universe has incurred from being bumped four times by other universes. Bert, might we assume a bump led to the HB storm?'

'Sam, my dear Sam, I know you want closure but…we won't be around to verify it. So go and do your work, go and look after our families and stop worrying about nothing. Worry about everything real and immediate and leave the unreal and future to me.'

★ ★ ★

But Sam always worried and he needed Bert like they were toast and butter. He visited Chalet Suvarov after finishing work on the same night. They sat on the veranda drinking bottles of beer. After the fourth one each, they talked seriously again.

Sam spoke in a monotone: 'It's the utter depression of it all. The magnitude of losing a lifestyle, which feels more like a life.'

'Yep, every day is a grey day, wet, foggy and cold. A horrible day, everyday. And it's all in our minds.' They drank deeply. He looked across at Sam, 'How is my family?'

'They're umm…calm. Enough said. But you never care to ask about the rest of the world or even Switzerland anymore?'

'I don't care about anyone other than my family and you guys, the rest is work.'

Sam grunted as he stared skyward. 'I need an explanation, mate. ALMA, Hubble, they've clocked nothing. We see our past for millions of years but can't predict our future for the next month. That's it, tick.'

Bert made a whimsical, throwaway comment; 'There is an explanation, hard to find, difficult to accept but definitely not philosophical.'

'It is an act of God, Bert.'

'Absolute bollocks.' Bert threw his empty bottle onto the lawn. 'Look, God doesn't exist, it – him, is a figment of human imagination, a crutch to lean on when times are hard.' He pointed a finger at Sam's temple. 'I thought you were a scientist before a friend?'

Sam shrugged. 'God exists as an antithesis of science, no different to the Higgs Boson as the glue of our universe.' He was confident in his view. 'I don't need to see you again, Bert, not for me, nor for your family. You are alone at last, do you really crave that?'

Bert answered slowly, 'I don't need to see you ever again. Forget me, as I will forget you.' Tears welled up in Sam's eyes. He couldn't look at Bert. 'It is alright, I have a new determination now that I am alone and fit. Now I can concentrate on the enemy. Maybe we should all accept death and go to your fictitious heaven? We transform particles into pure energy to make things that don't exist, so by default, the things that don't exist can do the same to us.'

His best friend was talking rubbish; he was best left alone but he had given him a gift, the confidence to accept Convergence. Sam stood to leave. He reached out his hand. Bert took it and held it tight. Sam looked into his friend's eyes. 'It feels like a final goodbye.' Bert's mouth was taut and grimaced as if he had sucked a lemon. A tear ran down his right cheek.

★ ★ ★

The two girls crouched with their arms grasping their knees on the sofa in the lounge. There was no TV to distract them, all they could hear was Briony in the kitchen as she banged the pans for dinner and the rush of water in the pipes as Natalia showered. The echoes filled the space of the glass walled house. The hard ceramic floor enhanced the reverberations and the lack of furniture provided no absorption.

Allie was speaking quietly so that Briony wouldn't hear. 'The most depressing part of the crisis is the way that old people like mummy keep talking about the good old days.'

Hannah rolled here eyes. 'I agree, but you know, I also keep thinking about things from my childhood.'

'Like what?'

'Like when I was five years old and I got my first bike and a huge doll's house. We lived in a big house near Manchester

University. It was lovely there, my dad used to take me cycling in the park.'

Allie murmured in her friend's ear, 'I keep thinking about my daddy being lonely. On his own in that spooky house.'

Hannah gently touched an elbow into her side. 'Dad says he has crucial work to do, benefitting all humankind. That makes your daddy very special, Allie.'

Allie started weeping. 'But without The Envelope and the Deeps, he's going to die and I don't want my daddy to...'

Hannah grasped her and held on. 'You don't know that. Your dad is the cleverest man on earth when it comes to the Higgs Boson. I think he is thinking stuff that we haven't got a clue about. Trust him yeah.'

She dried her eyes. 'I do trust him and also my mummy. But it's hard when we are all apart and mum is so depressed.'

'You must have something, though.'

'There's nothing to look forward to, nothing that I love like my skiing.'

Hannah pulled her to her feet using both hands. 'Hold on there. Let's go and plague the boys.' They went up the open circular stairs and found their brothers silently playing against each other on Liam's PS5. Interactive Call of Duty 8 was usually accompanied by wild shouts. Hannah walked across to the TV and turned it off. They were so astonished, they stared at her without a comment. 'I know, I really do know, but Allie needs all of our support at the moment.'

'Why?' asked Josh. He wasn't too bothered about helping his sister.

Hannah answered, 'Because she misses your dad and because we are all in this crisis together.' She looked at both boys in turn. 'Are you OK with that?'

Josh demurred. 'OK, I guess. I have read on a psychology website that it's important to reflect on stuff as it's part of the grieving process.'

Allie wanted to know what for. 'You mean grieving for the loss of dad?'

Josh answered, 'C'mon sis…not for dad. He's OK. I think we are grieving for our old lives. It's normal, apparently.' The others looked for his help. 'It said if we reflect on it, then it puts things into their true perspective.' He shrugged his shoulders and threw his headphones to one side.

Liam pulled a face. 'I'm not bothered about the past. My only wish is I could do my school exams and go to University like mum and dad.'

Josh replied, 'So you're grieving for not doing your exams! Do you get it now?'

'I do but I have never grieved for anything in my life before and I really don't want to. Sometimes you are just too clever, mate.'

'I agree and sometimes my cleverness depresses me and I guess that's how dad feels.'

'Josh, we are all grieving, don't forget that,' Allie placed a hand on his shoulder, 'day to day things come to mind. Strangely, not going to school has left an empty space inside of me.'

Hannah snapped them out of it. 'Don't let's be morbid, we aren't dead yet and I for one believe we have every chance of surviving all this crap.'

Josh told them what he had seen on Swiss TV the night before. 'They had a debate on assisted dying at the Dignitas place in Zurich. It was pretty chilling and filmed on this featureless commercial estate. They were saying that even though France and Spain legalised suicide last year, the numbers had barely increased.'

Hannah stood up with her hands on her waist: 'It gives terminally ill, mentally competent people the option. Which is right, I think, but my beliefs wouldn't let me do it.'

Josh was hard on the group. 'People don't want to die, that's a fact. They hold on just in case. The ultimate vanity is to remain living.' No one commented and so he carried on. 'In a state of unreality, people can only submerse themselves in reality. And each and every one of our realities is completely unreal to each other person.' The girls eyes looked away from him but Liam remained interested.

He spoke: 'That is so like your dad, so overly responsible, like you are 40 or something. I overheard him say that combining knowledge and action on food, shelter, energy and medicine won't stop the unstoppable.'

Allie clenched her fists: 'So what do you suggest we do then? Give up because no one can find an answer. My dad is the know it all who finally failed. Is that what you want? To give up?'

Liam retaliated: 'No, of course not, I truly don't think that any of us will give up, including your dad. We are all together on this, aren't we?' He waited for a response.

Allie heaved a huge sigh, 'I'm so sorry everyone. Dad is the greatest but it's just stuff, you know.' She collapsed onto a bean bag in a heap.

Hannah gently sat next to her and spoke to the boys. 'Personally, I am shit scared. Everyone is taking this new emotional drug. A survival medicine, with only two ingredients. Life or death.'

'Sounds like a cue for Call of Duty, sis.' Liam rebooted the PS5 and the boys donned their headphones and carried on killing.

★ ★ ★

The Swiss Riviera was in the grip of an explosion of crane flies. The gangly onslaught was due to the combination of a hot summer, then heavy rain showers and a warm September. Their numbers always peaked at this time of year. The larvae, known as leatherjackets, feed through the autumn, winter and spring on decaying plant material below the soil. This year's cloud of wobbling flyers would not survive to turn to pupae. It was a pointless purpose to mate and to die over the next few days. They don't eat during their short lives as they can survive on reserves stored in their bodies. A parody of human life to come.

By the end of September, the leaves on the aged beeches in the Suvarov garden were constantly ruffled by the autumnal breezes that whipped down the valleys leading to the lake. The tree was yellow at the summit, tending to green at the foot with layers of hesitant leaves between. Across all the trees of the Chauderon, the yellows and browns were startling in their early ferocity. A single leaf dropped and floated first to the left and then to the right on a dizzy descent. Bert watched the nervous drop, a first move towards composting beneath the end of November snows. It felt like the last leaf he would ever see. Earlier in the month, he had walked into a snowstorm of betula leaves, whipped off the trees and flirting like a thousand butterflies across the forest path. It was the Monday de Jeûne, a day of fasting, of thanksgiving, of repentance and a prayer for families. But Bert had no family now and no friends and he certainly didn't repent. He remembered he was only supposed to eat plum tart all day according to tradition but he had no tart and in fact he had no food in the house at all. His problem was there were no shops open as it was a bank holiday. So shots of espresso coffee would have to suffice. He pondered his internal physical changes, his lack of hunger. He felt slower, different to lethargic, heavy and ponderous without any body weight, so food didn't seem essential anymore.

The air was musty in the chalet and there had been a fall of soot into the fireplace of the grand salon which added an acrid taint. He walked out to the veranda and stretched his arms skywards. The sun was still hiding behind the Rochers de Naye but it would be a beautiful autumnal day once it rose above the peaks. There was little noise from the autoroute far below him. Occasionally a lorry thundered by to fill a bunker with the essentials for living and the necessities for dying. His immediate thought was to take a walk, one like he used to take with Natalia. As a couple like Heidi and Peter but with cows rather than goats. It would be an escape away from his prison, away from his mind circling like a buzzard above his trouble and strife.

He walked down the hill towards the gorge moving so quietly the herd of deer nibbling the long wet grass remained feeding. They looked up before stepping languidly out of the steaming sunny field and into the shade of the pines. He felt slowness in his own pace across the rough tarmac, pausing to examine a squashed yellow salamander. Its short yellow and brown stripes were concertina'd into a lump of death. At least the choice of life and death had not been its own responsibility. He wondered if lizards were responsible or did they live a carefree and irresponsible life? As he approached the Pont de Pierre, he felt the random drumming of the tumbling waters as they cascaded beneath it. Water, the source of life, a spiritual cleansing of the earth from a baptism of rain until its clouded rise back to the heavens. On the trees there were a few transparent green leaves edged with brown, clinging desperately to bare branches. A slanting sunbeam penetrated the depths of the forest, spotlighting the reliant nature beneath the canopy.

There were no cars on these fenceless lanes. No one could really afford petrol now, plus of course there was the rationing. It was also a fete day, a stay local day, a family day. He walked past a huge stone landslide awash with last night's rain. It had collapsed willingly into the bank of the over full stream to create a collusion of brown and clear froth. The amplified churn of airy silvered water sped past, smoothed by the flow and hiss of escaping air mauled on the polished limestone. Pine cones lined the edges of the road, kicked into position by the passing traffic. They looked like armadillo plated excrement. He swung his right foot and kicked a pile over the edge of the precipice to his left.

Occasional birdsong caught him unawares; it denounced the birds' retreat. He wasn't sure whether the population of birds had plummeted like the bees or they had consciously decided to fall silent. He would have liked to ask them. A clanking train passed above him on the funicular rail up to Rochers de Naye. It was carrying The Envelope to the workforce who were creating the last bunker required on the Riviera. He could see dozens of rolls of the immortal plastic, see-through, a film of nothing to stop a nothing particle. He looked again and judged it to be empty of all hope. At the highest point on the road before turning homewards, he noticed the first snow of the year on The Dent de Midi. The mountains nestled in fluffy white clouds that allowed their white peaks to poke through and reach for the blue sky. By the end of the afternoon he was back home, exhausted but happy to be alive. His plans were coming together, unseen and unheard and that was the way he wanted. He went to water his flower pots and picked 30 dead heads off the celestial sphere of the marguerites. He carried on along the path to the etang and stood to listen. There was no conversation today. He thought about his counting of the flower heads, the sampling undertaken since the start of September. Everything seemed to be dying now. Dead flower heads as dead as his marriage.

★ ★ ★

That night he thought She would come to him. He lay in the dark in anticipation of Her. He pondered her instant access without preamble, the reasons why She accessed him alone.

'People will go below, Bert. It will be easier; no responsibilities, no daily challenge of living. The fetching, carrying, struggling and existing will be easier than normal day to day life above ground. So people will take the easy option. They always did.'

He replied quietly, happy with the tired calm surrounding him, 'But they won't be living, will they? These new moles. They will be existing with nothing except hope for a new life above and that is truly a dream. They think they will return to the same house and car, the same TV, the same job but they haven't thought it through, have they? They will plummet from living to existing and ever downward until just breathing'

'Correct. There will be no trees, or seeds, grass and animals. The essence of life will have disappeared. So they have no future, it is irreversible and the past will be irretrievable.' She paused. *'You do know that, Bert, don't you? So will you admit it?'*

'I admit it, I have known that for a long time.' Is she gloating at us?

'*Surely the truth is more important. To die in truth is honourable for your God, Bert. Don't you want the ones you love to know the truth?*'

'Avoid the truth and you invite evil into our world, the Devil that Sam believes in. The Devil would enter this world. My path is sure and true, don't make me question it now.'

Bert was weaker than he imagined, he started crying but she didn't read his thoughts and he didn't want her to relish his weakness. The words of Sam returned to him: Save the world if you can, Bert, be yourself, be brilliant and tell us how we can exist. Bert looked into the shadows to search for his friend. He spoke to his phantom in the corner. 'I don't think we can exist here, nor now. I think we will exist in a future that we proved, Sam. You and I together. A mathematical conundrum that no one believes in, a fifth world. As unbelievable as a Nobel Laureate talking to a lily.' He turned onto his side and slept, death's twin brother, plunged into the night for a full twelve hours.

[7]

The Upward Turn

B RIONY STOOD WITH Jack, her senior lab technician. Despite the temperatures dropping they breathed the natural air inhaled through an opened window, its stile catching the October breeze. Half her team had already given up working and she was due to follow shortly. She listened to Jack and felt more depressed by the minute. He was frowning as he pointed out the trees fronting the lake which had no leaves for the first time in his 30 years in the laboratory. She knew the rustic shades of autumn had lasted a bare three weeks. In the southern hemisphere, spring had arrived but, in pure symmetry, the trees were also bare and lifeless. The Xylem and Phloem saps, the two vascular arteries of the ecosystem, appeared to have called a worldwide strike according to the botanists. Across the globe they issued conflicting arguments for the failure of the tree saps to translocate. A tiny minority suggested the pressure flow hypothesis had been interrupted. The informational signals sent via the sap were not being accepted by the plant. The plant signalling systems had been short circuited by something, as if all the plants and trees were acting in unison, coordinated by their union leader.

On her way into work that morning the train had trundled past the allotments to the west of Montreux. Many were fields of orange mush, they were crammed with rotting pumpkins, disappointing the local children who anticipated hollowing them out for Halloween. The fibrous pulp oozed out of cracks in the hard orange skins. When the shells were split in half, the normally cream coloured seeds had turned black. On the borders of the allotments were apple trees hung heavy with red Florina and Idared fruit. But the leafless trees supported sour and inedible baubles that dropped and bounced onto the ground in the slightest zephyr of wind. Now the same breeze touched her face and she felt sad and alone amidst her remaining work friends. Jack left her to return to his PC; it was time for the CCOW briefing. A religious fix for all her staff that she deigned to enjoy in an act of rebellion. She avoided Bert's Lowest Common Denominator, it felt wrong, the CCOW preaching, the scientist in her wasn't sure it rang true anymore but she had faith in her husband.

CCOW – Central Control Of the World

Briefing

The time for humankind to take a short holiday beneath our green, pleasant but dangerous surface has now arrived!

This is an emotional day, an uplifting day.

You have achieved the impossible dream and created bunkers to house all the human beings across the whole of the world. You have been amazing. Congratulate yourselves.

Your strength and commitment has been matched by man's ingenuity.

Follow the Convergence plan for your zone. Everyone will be safely and securely housed in the Deeps within the next three weeks.

Jack shouted at her white coated back, 'Briony, you need to see this.' She walked across to him and started to read from the top, her depression dipped into a darkening afternoon.

A minor inconvenience. Green light

The supply of tinned tuna exceeded all expectations. But many batches tested in our laboratories appear to have abnormally high levels of mercury. This is dangerous for your brain. There will inevitably be a shortage of tinned tuna in the Deeps.

A moderate inconvenience. Amber light

We cannot guarantee 5G communications in all the spaces of your bunker. Facetious usage of the signal will be restricted to ensure basic communications are guaranteed.

A major inconvenience. Red light

Please help us to help you. All older persons should undertake the free and comprehensive medical examination before entry into your bunker. This means that any health issues can be resolved before entry. It also means you will then receive specialist medical care during your time below.

HB Predictor today

Level 10, time for Convergence.

Our scientists do not anticipate an increase back to previous, higher levels. Therefore, we must play safe.

The last man on earth, Professor Bert Leinster, will continue to monitor the predictor levels and report to CCOW. We wish Professor Leinster good health and thank him for volunteering to be the predictor-keeper.

"There is only one thing that makes a dream impossible to achieve: the fear of failure."

Paulo Coelho

"It doesn't matter how slow you go, as long as you don't stop."

Confucius

★ ★ ★

Briony telephoned Hannah who was shopping in Vevey with Allie, it was a moment after they had read the briefing on their mobiles. 'Hannah, have you seen the CCOW briefing yet?'

'Oh mum, what a mess here. There are hundreds of people stopped all around us, it's like they disbelieved everything over the last five months and have now cracked. There are people screaming everywhere.'

'Hannah, you're breaking up, are you OK?'

'Mum, mum…can you hear me? With Allie, got it?'

'Got you, got you. Oh my love, are you OK?'

'We are both fine but loads of people have collapsed on the street, others are leaning on their friends, kinda spaced-out.'

'Stay calm, love and I'll meet you at home as soon as possible.'

'Yep.'

'Where's Natalia?'

'We left her in a coffee shop by the market, so we'll be with her in a couple of minutes.'

Briony sighed heavily, her chest hurt, 'OK…hmm…right, it's OK, well take Allie with you and go and find Auntie Natalia and bring her home. Yes? Bring her home as soon as possible and wait for me there. OK?'

'Yes mum, don't panic so. Bye.'

Briony immediately telephoned Sam on his mobile at home, 'Just a quick call, love, I am so sorry to interrupt you, darling, you must be so busy today. Have we got our date to enter the Bex bunker yet?'

He sounded sleepy as he answered, but it was a drug induced lethargy: 'Why?'

'Because, as if you didn't know, CCOW have just announced Convergence over the next three weeks.'

'Umm…of course, sorry, couldn't tell you and all that.' There was a long pause, she heard him shuffling about. She thought she heard him muttering something like fucking bastards in between the scrapes and bangs, she wondered if he had been in bed.

'You sound unsure about it.'

'No, of course not. I've been trying to confirm our date for the last few days, so I will double check and ring you later on. OK?'

'Great, thanks, my darling. You did know about this, didn't you? You sound so hmm…off.'

She noted the slight hesitation again. 'Sure, leave it with me. I will confirm the day to everyone by email and text. Then we can all be positive about our escape.'

'No Sam, not like that. Tell us all face to face this evening. OK?'

'Yeah, sorry that was a bit thoughtless of me, but you know, lots on and all that.'

She blew a kiss down the receiver. 'Love you.' But there was no reply as per normal, Sam had cut her off. Strangely, the call to Convergence had lifted her spirits and she started to make a list of extra supplies she would buy, deodorant, face cream; now she could feel organised.

★ ★ ★

Bert was kneeling in his study at the chalet, shuffling papers across the parquet. Pinned to the walls were hundreds of excerpts from old scientific journals, many butchered from the years of stock on his library shelves. Others had been copied, pasted and printed directly off the internet. His mind whirled as he read, he printed and pinned in a mad frenzy. His core focus for the last three days had been the true meaning of time. He scanned the reports on the wall. He had highlighted interesting phrases with a green marker pen.

Nature Physics Journal

The team trapped 38 anti-atoms for just 172 milliseconds. "The question is really very simple," according to the lead author of the report Professor Jeffrey Hangst from Aarhus University. "Do matter and antimatter obey the same laws of physics? Eventually, we will use this technique to compare the structure of anti-hydrogen and hydrogen atoms, to search for differences between matter and antimatter. We do not yet have enough precision to test these fundamental symmetries."

"The Universe has shown a preference for matter over antimatter as it has evolved, but so far, no measurements can explain why this came about."

Bert tapped the article twice in quick succession with his forefinger. 'What if matter was a creation of a God?'

The article continued: "If matter and antimatter were truly identical, the Universe as we know it could not have come about." He moved quickly to his left and looked at a different note.

"Chaotic inflation, in which inflation events start here and there in a random quantum-gravity foam, each leading to a bubble universe expanding from its own Big Bang. Proposers see the Big Bang as an event in a much larger and older universe, or multiverse, and not the literal beginning."

He went back to the laptop on the desk and jabbed at the keys. It was all making sense now. He had no thoughts for his family, only the cause of the HB storm mattered. He wanted an answer for humankind, a justification of his conceit. The CCOW briefing pinged onto his screen at the same moment that his daughter was reading it in Vevey. He immediately checked the predictor level on the HB ancillary device in the corner of his study. The result was confusing. He glanced at his watch, he didn't want to go, but a trip to CERN was required. It was only two in the afternoon. Just time for lunch and then a quick trip into Montreux for a haircut. His hair was down to his shoulders. He walked out to where his marguerites still flourished and picked off the dead heads. There were far less than normal. Only twenty and now with very few new flower buds to replace them. Sadly, their season was ending and the first hard frost would instantly wither them. He leaned forward to check underneath the rear of one of the plants and picked two snails from the frail leaves. As he returned to an upright position, his forehead scratched against the climbing rose that clung to a trellis. Rose thorns had caught his head and deeply punctured his skin in a few places. Annoyed with his recent instability, he quickly went inside to clean up the wound.

Entering the downstairs WC he looked at his forehead in the mirror. It hurt more than it should and instead of a trickle of blood, there were several large globules of it hanging from the punctures in the skin. These pushed through the epidermis and were encased by the usually hidden dermis. He put on a light and stared at the wounds for a few more moments before wiping the traces of thorns away with a damp towel. He chuckled to himself as he thought his reflection resembled that of Christ's depiction on the cross.

★ ★ ★

In the old town of Montreux there were plenty of parking spaces near his hairdressers. He pulled in and walked. As he passed the junior school he could see the children playing outside. Another week and it would be closed like the senior schools. There was a cacophony of noise. Boys shouted and girls shrieked as they chased each other around the playground in a world that he would never understand. But he heard the laughter and remembered Allie and Josh when they didn't have a care in the world, avoiding the hopscotch of adulthood. He was smiling as he sat in the hairdresser's chair.

She started his cut. 'I don't need to ask you what you've been up to in the months since your last visit. All those predictors and tunnel collider things.'

He just smiled at her and flicked the locks of his shoulders. 'Big trim on the sides, yeah.'

'Well, there's nothing much left on the top, is there.' She laughed as she gently placed a pale blue cape around his shoulders.

'No worries, hey.'

'Everything is slowing down now and from Monday people will start to disappear and leave for the Deeps. How incredible is that? Me, you ask? I have to keep working to the bitter end. I wouldn't let my clients down.' She snipped to length first. A layered cut of 15 to 20 centimetres. She was excited he was there. 'I am so glad it was you who made the decision to go below. It just makes me happy to go. Knowing it's safe to move in, move your head dear, and move on past this crisis to a new paradise.'

He murmured, 'KK.'

'That's a nasty wound, how did you do that?'

'I wore a crown of thorns all day, given as a symbol of ridicule by the people who mocked me.'

He knew she wasn't smart enough to understand the allegory and waited patiently. She changed to what she knew about her illustrious client. 'I suppose you will be going below at CCOW, won't you?' He didn't answer; she hadn't bothered to read the briefings properly. 'I bet it's like a luxury palace.' She rumbled on, unstoppable in her mundane world. 'And me, well, the kids and I are going into the Hongrin tunnel, where the hydro-electricity comes from. As for the ex-husband, I hope he rots in hell on the surface.' She brayed loudly, her persistent happiness was upsetting him deeply.

Bert brought her attention back to her work. 'I'm really sorry, but I have an important meeting in CERN. Can you tidy it up now so I can leave, please?'

'Sure,' she replied, 'anything for a Nobel Laureate.' When he left the salon, she hugged him and gave him three large kisses on his cheeks. 'Thank you for all you've done, Professor, we all appreciate it.'

His sarcasm was lost on her, 'No, I mean really, don't waste your breath on me, as you'll need it in the dungeons. Thank

Professor Murray. He discovered the HB storm and he has driven you all below.'

There was little traffic on the autoroute as he headed along the north shore of Lac Léman. The CCOW announcement had stunned the country and people had stopped travelling to sit at home with friends and family. The services were also crammed with stationery cars. He noticed the latest graffiti on the concrete bridges as he sped past. "Man conquers with technology." Then came a Banksy quote. "Follow your dreams," with "cancelled" sprayed across it in red. At the next bridge, there was a giant panda with a cross driven through its heart like a dagger. The caption read "well at least we tried." Bert swerved into the experiment carpark past a lone bewildered guard. The CERN outpost was a ghost town, bereft of the thinkers who were now pre-occupied with their families and safety. He was recognised immediately and allowed to proceed to the building entrance without any security checks. Pressing his eye to the retinal scanner he gained access and walked down to the control room. Bert sat in front of the predictor computer that was directly linked to the detector one hundred metres below him. Tapping a few keys, he searched through all the key components to verify there were no malfunctions. The answer was the same as on the ancillary predictor at home. Level 20. He didn't really need any more confirmation that CCOW had lied and manipulated the population. That had already been confirmed many times. But putting his name to a global deception meant his work was dispensable. He left the predictor running for his own benefit but decided it was a waste of effort sending any more predictor reports to CCOW. The scientific insulation between fact and fiction had now burnt out.

★ ★ ★

Convergence day was set as October 7th for families Leinster and Murray. They were told to assemble at the market place in Montreux. Four children, three adults under 46 years old, one adult over 46 years old. The age separation on the e-tickets was noted by Sam; he had seen and deleted an email at work which alluded to the need for a few health checks. The destination shown was Bex salt mines, a few kilometres to the south. He had resisted the temptation for months but had finally manipulated the reservations to ensure his extended family went to the best bunker in the canton. The airline-style boarding passes were only downloadable twenty four hours in advance. Whilst downloading, it had dawned on Sam that they all used iPhones and was heartened that they would be able to FaceTime each other in the Deeps and even contact Bert. He had also set up family sharing on iCloud, with him as the organiser. Whatever happened over the next few months he reasoned that at least they could stay all in touch.

He knew that any persons without e-boarding passes had to arrive for embarkation two hours before their allotted time and with one, was just half an hour. So he had ordered two taxis for a quarter of an hour before their slot. When they arrived, the taxi drivers helped them to unload in the pedestrianised zone leading down to the Freddie statue. Above them swayed wires restraining a thousand coloured light bulbs from the whistling wind. The spots of colour danced in time with the jazz band playing beneath them. Twenty musicians were knocking out Glenn Miller tunes that faded to nothing as the notes clung to the gusts. Sam made everyone double check they each had their one allowable piece of luggage, the same size as carry-on airline bags. Each person had also been advised by CCOW to don a second layer of coats and to wear a warm hat. He knew that storage space in the bunker would be at a premium and regretted not finding the time to make a pre-visit. Sam ushered the families towards the large green covered market, he was tetchy with them all because they were so carefree. 'Keep moving you lot,' they paused to admire the white-capped waves on the lake. He was walking on hot coals, 'No time to waste, turn that music off boys.' They entered and joined a short queue of fellow travellers who were happily chatting away. They were wishing strangers well and anticipating what would be served for lunch once they arrived in Bex.

It took no more than ten minutes to pass through security. Most people knew the procedure as it used exactly the same rules as applied at airports. Natalia's face creams were over the 100 ml limit and had to be binned. Briony's corkscrew was deemed a dangerous weapon and joined the sharps discard pile. Her bottle of wine was more carefully placed to one side for recycling. But Sam breathed easier as the efficiency was very Swiss and filling the thirty waiting coaches was fast and untroubled. The boys sat together, the girls and mums too, leaving him to sit alone and stare out of the window at the cafés and shops of the town centre as they left. He slumped with his forehead against the window and thought of Bert. Bert's freedom to wander the empty streets and to window shop the retailer's detritus. To sit on a bench by the lake and watch the sunset. As the women revisited whether they had packed the right clothes for the heat or for the cold, he sat without speaking, without thinking and now devoid of emotion. It was all over.

★ ★ ★

Natalia crossed and uncrossed her arms, wriggled in her seat and every few minutes she leaned sideways to gaze down the aisle of the old coach. There was a little talking as the passengers engaged with the slammed gear changes. The driver demanded that all the teenagers turn off their mobiles in respect of the moment. It was sombre and quiet as she watched the children sat deeper in thought than any other time of their young lives. She listened quietly as Liam and Hannah shared a fear with their mum about the numbers of coaches, the gaggle of new acquaintances. Natalia realised the close proximity of others had never impinged upon their middle class lives. Whereas Allie and Josh were used to living en masse in their private boarding school. She sighed deeper than the bottom of the ruffled lake as they left it behind. Whilst sat in the taxi Allie had asked her if their daddy had changed his mind. She had gripped her shoulders and reassured her their dad was staying above ground to fulfil a vital role as the predictor-keeper.

The ascent from the alluvial plain of the river Rhone was punctuated with hard domes of igneous rock that the alpine glaciers had failed to erode. Natalia looked out of the coach window to her left. There was a pretty stream, a set of Victorian weirs and a short cascade that tumbled over a series of arches forming an ancient bridge. She dwelled on Bert and then with a new found strength she managed to dismiss him from her mind. Bert was OK, Bert is always OK, concentrate on the children. The coach was held at a red traffic light for ages. She stared at it, she couldn't take her eyes off the dragon's eye; it represented the stop and go of life. She tried to predict the moment it would turn to green by counting down from ten, but failed the four times that she tried. Eventually, the delay became obvious. Because they were ascending a single track road they had to wait for earlier coaches which were now descending. The vehicles had to make it back to Montreux for the afternoon embarkations. Natalia put her handkerchief to her nose after spraying it with Lalique. The coach stank of B. O. and pulsed with the tinny sounds of the travellers chatting impatiently about the bunker ahead. She herself remained quiet, withdrawn into her seat. She eavesdropped on the cranky old couple sat in front of her, berating the predictor level and deciding they must all be affected, they must all be dying. They negatively concluded it was time to go below but they probably already had terminal cancer. Natalia had seen the horror stories showing putrid tuna, apples and pumpkins and also wondered what was changing inside her body cells. The passengers gasped as the coach crawled forward twenty metres but the light returned to red. Natalia now sat opposite a dull yellow auberge on her right. It was heaving with personnel from the local commune who wore safety vests, like greenfly crawling across a yellow flower. These controllers strode purposefully in and out and were clearly in charge. It was obviously a place of instruction, a place to eat and change their clothes between shifts. At last the coach moved again and after a few minutes it had reached the turning point at the entrance to the salt mine. As the engine died, they could her the tumbling stream mingled with the barked orders of the controllers. Everyone peered out of the windows at their surroundings, faces pressed on glass, shoulders leant on. There was a towering limestone cliff with its hanging shrubberies engulfing the reception office. This consisted of the old shop and café as used by the tourists pre the HB storm.

As they disembarked with their single bag, it was Natalia who tried to make light of it all: 'There is no going back now, only forwards "да". I am very happy,' Allie asked why, 'at least we have plenty of salt to sprinkle on our chips.' They all laughed except for Sam, who dropped back as they walked towards the check-in area.

He made a comment to the clouds that they didn't catch. 'Nothing is predictable, or is it? At the risk of walking to our deaths.'

Allie turned to her mum as they waited for a few moments in the arrivals queue. 'Is there absolutely no chance of daddy joining us?'

Natalia looked into Allie's eyes. 'No sorry, daddy is helping to save the world. Keep that in your mind, my beautiful daughter.' They were the right words. Allie pushed her arm through her mum's and leaned her head against her shoulder.

Natalia turned to Briony, her friend looked at her but said nothing. The two boys were also quiet. She then turned to see if Sam was alright and caught his eye. For the first time, she noticed his despair and it made her choke. She swallowed a few times, after a few moments she spoke to him in a fearless tone: 'Come on, Sam, we can only try. We always knew trying is better than dying.'

He smiled at her before turning to his wife and put on a brave face to match Natalia's voice. Pulling Briony close, he kissed her hard. 'I love you so much, you will never know.'

'I do know, darling. Because I love you even more.'

Natalia turned away from the couple and stifled a sob.

★ ★ ★

"WELCOME TO BEX – YOUR PLACE OF SAFETY"

Sam took a few deep breaths as he stared down at the blue and white sign sitting on the young receptionist's desk. They were now inside the old museum shop and starting to sweat out of the biting wind. The lights were dimmed but still intensified the burnt orange of the interior emulsion, making it warm and welcoming. It was comforting, so he relaxed as they were now safe, his job done. Rebecca, her name badge said, shook all of their hands. Her navy starched uniform added to the air of efficiency. 'It is such a pleasure to meet you, Professor Murray. You look much younger than on the television!' They all laughed as he went bright red and shuffled his feet.

Briony commented. 'That's why I married my Sam. He has found the secret of eternal youth!'

Rebecca answered brightly, 'If only we all had some of that, what an invention that would be.' She continued, her eyes flirted with Sam. 'So Professor, as you are over 46 years old, even saviours of humankind are entitled to a free medical check. You will appreciate how we can then keep an eye on the statistically less healthy in the bunker, although you really do look great.' She smiled and giggled; Sam watched his son poke two fingers in and out of his open mouth.

Sam gushed, 'You're very kind, umm…Rebecca. If all the staff are like you, our short stay will be better than a five star hotel.'

'It is our pleasure, sir. Now then, if you go over there to the cubicles, we will get the family safely underground and ready for lunch, then you can follow along later.' The families glanced at the series of ten cubicles formed using blue hospital curtains. Five sets of curtains were open and they could see a nurse in each, sat at a desk with a series of instruments. Blood pressure monitor, cardiogram machine, stethoscope, it all looked very professional.

'What happens if they find anything wrong with me?' Sam enquired as he walked a metre then stopped.

'Well, Professor, it has happened in maybe…I guess 5% of check ups. Depending on the diagnosis, we have kept people here and prescribed drugs, or they have been taxied into the hospital at Montreux for treatment before coming straight back. We really do take care of everyone to the best of our abilities.' Sam said a brief goodbye to the others and promised to meet them later. They left him with soft words of reassurance and proceeded into the hustle and bustle outside.

★ ★ ★

Briony started as the three high pitched peeps sounded from the train's whistle as it crossed the points after leaving the tunnel. Above the opening there was a name and date carved into the rock. "Galerie de Bouillet 1726". The train driver sounded the whistle again to keep people at a safe distance from the carriages as it screeched to a halt. The whistle was a freedom of noise escaping to the atmosphere, an act of rebellion against the Deeps. The upended parabola shape of the mine train was no more than 1.5 metres tall. It seemed too cramped for the latest batch of newcomers to journey inside. Briony saw the roof was rusty, but as she closed on the train, she realised it was dust from the workings that lay on the stainless steel cover. The seven coach train had pulled to a halt under the raw cedar boards of a new lean-to and was now ready for the newcomers to embark. The bright white headlight on the tiny locomotive shone star-like in the gloom of the shed. Briony looked around, everywhere was also infiltrated with dust. The external walls of the reception, the train's dusted wheels on dusted rails and the floor around was permanently stained. She realised it was anhydrite, otherwise known as dehydrated gypsum.

She dragged her son and daughter close as they forced their way into the parabolic coaches. It was too small for comfort. Natalia grabbed Allie and Josh and went for the second coach. After a few minutes, the controller walked the length of the train and locked all the doors. The external bolt grated into the eyelet. She heard a few passengers question this but the controller appeared perfectly calm, saying it was for their safety. He also instructed them to keep their hands inside the coach at all times. 'Twenty minutes maximum to reception "two", enjoy the ride, guys. Tourists used to pay good money for this trip!' And then they set off. The drawn out squeal of the wheels on curved rails grated on their teeth and then with a whoosh the infernal machine sank into the Galerie at high speed. Once inside the tunnel, the dull repetitive clank of the wheels echoed in a steady roar. Everyone remained quiet, Briony and Hannah were clutching each other's arms. They could see shadows leaping by as they passed an occasional low wattage light but everything was hazy through the scratched plastic window. Briony found her knees were stuck hard against the cold door. She could smell the ancient rusting chassis through the charged atmosphere. Closing her eyes tightly, she grasped her daughter's hands; they were somewhere to her right. As they went faster and deeper, she tightened her grip and closed her eyes. Flashes of light touched the inside of her lids every ten seconds and her ears popped with the pressure change.

The knees of an unknown man on her left touched against her. He pushed against her with his knee a second time, making it an obvious approach. He leaned close to make himself heard. 'Don't worry, love, we can all look after each other now.' He squeezed her left leg at the top of her thigh, a finger lingered on the inside of it, hidden by the dark. Briony shuddered. She didn't complain because she might scare the children. He spoke again. 'I hope to meet you later and give you some morale support, love!' She could smell his stale garlic breath fogging the journey which seemed to take hours.

Then there was a relieving flood of steady bright light. They had nearly arrived at reception "two". Briony quoted Genesis under her breath, the words rattled out of her chest. 'Then God said, Let there be light...shit. He saw the light, and he knew that it was good. Oh my God, my God, keep us safe God.' As they clambered out of the tiny train, they were all shaking with fear. Their tourist visit hadn't felt like a dive towards the devil. But now she understood that day and night had merged. She had hoped to be in heaven but had already seen it might be hell. Slowly, the large group of prisoners in front of her walked along a small tunnel towards the yellow light that was framing an opening about two hundred metres ahead. The wall of the tunnel was grey and rust coloured. It still showed the hammer and chisel marks of its creators.

A burst of chatter bounced around the large reception area. It was the place where tour groups used to receive a safety briefing and where the Murrays had watched a short film showing the history of the mine. Hannah and Liam told their mum that they only vaguely remembered it. The six of them sat in a semi-circle on hard wooden benches set close to the outer wall. The light was a sodium yellow but gloomy as it reflected off dull walls and low ceilings. Behind her she could see the glistening Envelope, their saviour. It resembled clingfilm with dabs of glue holding it to the wet walls. Some of the dabs had come loose and the plastic hung in heavy folds, threatening to tear its integrity. Patches of condensation formed small droplets where The Envelope touched the wall. This glorified the many colours of the rock but also caused more condensation, in a vicious circle of magnificence. The drops of water ran like tears behind the fragile sheath. Looking around her, she could see that the cavern was fifty metres in diameter and about three metres high. In odd places she noticed and worried that the magical Envelope had a tear and had been patched up unevenly and probably in haste. Around the outer wall was a line of beaded yellow eyes. Stood between each spot of jaundiced light was a soldier armed with an assault rifle. Soldiers also stood at each of the three exits, where there were three sealed glass doors controlled using card access systems. There was a tunnel to their right with a new sign at the entrance announcing access to the WC, mess and rest galleries. The circle of lights contained but missed the central area, where the old cinema screen remained dark and fixed for future tourists. All of them had cold feet and jiggled them nervously. Briony suggested they added a layer of clothing and so whilst they waited, they rummaged for an item in their luggage. She decided on a warm fleece. Pulling it over her head she smelt a waft of lemon fabric conditioner which purified the clinging damp of the chamber. She remarked to the rest that it had been wise idea to bring along GoreTex clothing. The rust smell was also stronger now she was stationary, with an occasional waft of sewage. There was no talking. She looked around and hoped that this was nothing like the billet. It was contrary to everything she had imagined.

★ ★ ★

Sam had turned to watch the others leave and as soon as he lost sight of them, he marched positively into the first cubicle available. The nurse smiled and fawned over the famous Professor as she asked him to strip to his underpants. He then lay down on a cream coloured metal bed and allowed her to attach electrodes in nine different places. Once he was attached to the heart monitor, she pressed a red button on the front of the machine and within two minutes she had a read-out of his cardiac statistics. They were all fine. She used a stethoscope to listen to his lungs via his chest and then his back, tested his reflexes and completed a questionnaire about his family medical history. The second to last test was the one he always hated. It was so long since he had had a blood test, that he didn't realise that once a needle was inserted in the vein on the inside elbow, it was simple. Fast vacuum extraction and no long winded wavering of needles. He looked away as most people do.

'It will be all over in a minute, close your eyes and count to sixty.' She placed the first vacutainer onto the needle then set aside the full phial. His eyes remained scrunched up as she attached the second vacutainer. As the blood slowly and abnormally eased out of Sam, a clear fluid went into him.

He chatted, 'Are the wages any good in this job?'

'Of course, Professor, they are paying me double what I earned in the doctor's surgery.'

'Gosh, that's excellent, isn't it.'

'And as an added bonus, after another week of intake duties, I'll be allowed underground early.' She wiped the injection hole with an antiseptic pad. 'Open those eyes, Professor, we are all done here.' He had only counted to 15. She didn't say the painless barbiturate would take effect after ten minutes and after 20 he would be dead. She said, 'Please dress and then exit through the rear of this cubicle to my colleagues. There you can use the toilet for a urine sample and afterwards you can sit and relax with a tea or coffee. And so far, the test results are just fine.' She reassured a smiling and relieved Sam, with a cheery, 'Have a nice day, won't you?' Then she sat and calmly waited for the next over 46 years old person to arrive for their health check.

Sam walked into the second area thirty metres beyond the blue curtains. It was isolated from the rough and tumble of arrivals and much more private and quiet. He felt extraordinarily happy to be going below at last. What a frigging relief, it was much easier than he had thought. Having given his urine sample, he went into a cubicle and sat in the armchair to wait for his tea. He thought he should text Briony but it seemed a bit pointless as he would soon be reunited with her and his children. He left his mobile turned off in his pocket; in every way it was a relief knowing the constant CCOW emails were coming to an end, the constant telephone calls and meetings. He was far happier than in the previous five months, the stress of the HB discovery was over. After a few minutes he had nodded off, relaxed forevermore. He was searched and then like a sack of potatoes the two controllers grabbed him under his armpits and dragged him through the rear curtain. With a sharp heave they dumped his body with a dull thump into the back of a waiting army truck.

★ ★ ★

Natalia blinked and then squinted her eyes to scan the crowd enclosed deep inside the mountain. She thought there was close on two hundred, all with something to say about their new surroundings. The level of noise had risen as they competed to be heard. They were human beings after all and not cattle to be herded into stables for the harsh winter.

A short dumpy man in an immaculate army uniform marched with an escort of four soldiers to the central dais. He tapped the microphone to gain their attention. 'Good afternoon, ladies, gentlemen and children. My name is Major Raphael Cachin and I am the commanding officer of this safe centre at Bex, one of two hundred safe centres that are dotted around Switzerland. First impressions may not impress you, but remember this; it is safe! We all know that this place is a brief stop before we begin a new and better life back on the surface.' He paused and watched for any hostility before continuing. 'This is our safe place-' he emphasised our, '-and we can make it work better than any other in our wonderful country. Consider this, none of us are gainers or losers on the surface. Nothing will have changed when we return except…' He drew himself up to his full height, his chest expanded with pride. 'Except we will have worked together for the sake of humankind and achieved the impossible dream.' There was some light applause. 'My adjutant, Lieutenant Clement, will explain some of the basic regulations that will keep us all in happy harmony.' Major Cachin stepped off the podium to allow the Lieutenant to speak in a clipped voice. A neat thin man to match his tone.

'Exercise consists of compulsory walks and will be held at 10am and then a second session at 4pm. This is for your sector alone. Remember, your sector is nominated as sector C. We have sectors A to Z spread across twenty four tunnels and caves. So please remain in your sector as it is easy to get lost in the 100's of kilometres of old workings and they are very dangerous indeed. By the end of next week we will be full. That means we will have approximately twelve thousand people in our safe haven.' Natalia thought the Lieutenant was pompous and then aggravating as he spouted on. 'Be assured it is absolutely safe. You are four hundred and fifty metres below the top of the mountain and 1.2 kilometres inside of it.' She heard many gasps and quick asides between families; they were safe at last. What a relief. He clapped his hands for quiet. 'Do not worry about the temperature. It stays fairly stable at seventeen degrees centigrade. But please keep warm as previously instructed.' He checked his list of points on a clipboard in front of him. 'As you would expect, no smoking is allowed. And one last thing, and I understand that some of you might find this disappointing, we are going to take all of your mobiles, iPads and laptops from you and keep them in safe storage until The Return.'

There was a roar of disapproval from the crowd that bounced around the cavern time after time. Natalia was the first to react in her group. She reached into her carry-on and pulled out a small clear plastic bag, which she quickly hid under her coat. Taking her iPhone from her pocket she tipped out her eye cream from the bag and turned the mobile completely off before slipping it inside. She looked around, no one had seen her, so she pressed out the remaining air, then she knotted the neck of the bag to make it watertight.

Briony was sitting next to her. She had frantically removed her mobile from her handbag and was listening intently to its ring as she urgently called Sam. She was shaking as she yelled at Natalia. 'I can't raise him, girl. What bastards, deceiving us all about the use of our mobiles. Fucking bastards.'

As the officer shouted for order, Natalia took advantage of the commotion to gently drop her package into the salt water pool immediately behind her. It steadily sank 60 centimetres to the bottom and settled into the orange deposits. She hoped to God that the bag would remain watertight until she might be able to recover it. Looking straight ahead, she thought the guards would be bound to take chargers off the inmates as they confiscated their equipment and heaved a sigh of relief that she had turned it off.

Natalia turned and closed her arms around her friend. She sniffed the Chanel between words. 'Do not worry,' she inhaled, 'he is just having a few tests "да" and will be with us soon.' Natalia was disappointed at the announcement but kept her thoughts to herself as she memorised their seating location. 'Briony, it is another lie, giving no chance to tell those outside.' She leaned across and noted that her friend had four bars of signal on the mobile's screen.

The officer shouted above the noise: 'Despite heroic efforts by our technicians, there is no decent 5G signal achievable at this depth and wifi is impossible as we are living in long tunnels. Nor do we have sufficient electricity to keep the appliances charged. We understand it is all a bit basic, and a bit of a shock. Please cooperate with your controllers immediately and without question.' A group of twenty controllers started to walk around the seated group to collect the devices. 'At any time please do ask the controllers for any help. We will broadcast an update on the situation above ground and also any news about circumstances here below ground. There are speakers set in each gallery. Listen out for the klaxon asking you to remain silent for the briefing. This broadcast will usually take place each evening at 6pm sharp.' He stepped down from the rostrum and walked towards his commanding officer. Together they watched the angry exchanges, pushes and pumped fists generated by giving up the most prized possessions. After ten minutes, the controllers had assembled all the instruments in plastic tote boxes that were stacked on a small golf buggy. The buggy drove out of the room with every person watching it leave.

The controllers moved between the newcomers and ushered them towards the tunnel signposted "rest galleries". The exit had an airport style metal detector, through which everyone was forced to pass. The second person to be caught with his phone hidden inside his boot was arguing loudly about the injustice of it all and the lies they had been told. A small group of men joined in the row and it quickly overheated. Punches were thrown between the controllers and the newcomers and then the controllers started whacking people with their coshes. Natalia sat hunched over as if she had stomach cramps. She turned away from her friend Briony and the four children, so that she could cry in private.

★ ★ ★

Bert was in the master bathroom in Chalet Suvarov. He was luxuriating in a hot foam bath, illuminated by a single lavender candle that he had found in one of Natalia's drawers. The cosseting heat was the only solution now to his aching joints. The pains were worsening and had to be due to the HBs but the cause and final result were unpredictable. The bathroom shone in all of its original opulence. He lay in a giant Victoria and Albert freestanding bath, splendid in white and stood on magnificent bronze feet. These perched beautifully on the dark green Udaipur marble floor. The double sink to his left longed for a human companion but behind it sat the remaining pots of Natalia's beauty products. The metal lids flickered in the solitary candle light, an epitaph to beauty no longer relevant in the darkest shadows of the earth. Bert stared at the dozens of defined shapes, immortalised as silvered and golden reflections, half full precious glass that contained nothing important. And nothing was now required by his lady, away from any sunlight, unadorned and pasty-faced with those who shared Bex. He groaned out of the bath and wound a white towelling dressing gown around himself.

The cold wind had dropped, the noise had abated. So he grabbed a blanket from the linen cupboard and walked outside onto the first floor balcony. He pulled the blanket closer to his warm body to maintain the relaxing after effect of the soak and stared at the view. The sunset was unspectacular, the lake free and unpolluted by any glimmer of red. There was no noise, nothing from the autoroute, no cow bells anymore as they had been removed from the freed beast's necks. Some church bells tolled in the distance; he thought the mechanism must be electrically driven. Across the lake on the French shore he saw no headlamps, no scurrying of cars along the lake road on the way home to food, family and love. There was a low whirring sound in the distance near Glion. After a few moments he could make out the four coaches of the funicular train heading up to Rochers de Naye. He imagined it might be the one of the last runs to the bunker at the top of the mountain.

★ ★ ★

'The end has come, Bert. The weakness of the human race has prevailed. That ability to compromise when disagreement and disharmony would have made the strongest stronger and built a new generation. It is pathetic. Nature would never have compromised, only the strong stay alive in my world.'

'What do you call a strong human being? What are the examples that you would have chosen to survive?'

'Some of you humans have been strong.'

'I said give me examples.'

'Hitler and Stalin in the previous century are the names you would know.'

'They were all evil men, not strong.'

'They were strong, they had a vision and they lived every moment to achieve their aims.'

'Who else in history caught your eye?'

'Atilla the Hun and Kubla Khan listened. Maximilien Robespierre, Pol Pot...'

He interrupted Her. 'But there are no women?'

'There were strong women. Ilse Koch was particularly bad; I watched as she collected the tattoos from the murdered inmates of a Nazi concentration camp. However, your Godly court never judged her correctly, did they; they were too scared to admit to her barbarity, the reality of her beautiful lampshades made from human skin. Irma Grese also excelled in torture in those camps and of course Myra Hindley was a devil with children.'

Bert dug his nails into the railing, he felt physically sick. Nauseated by the venom in Her voice. 'That is a terrible list. For each evil person there are far more good ones, Christian saints for example.'

'You are thinking of religion, rights and wrongs? You heretic, *you have no God. Your Christianity was a whim of a Roman Emperor, a development from a small tribe of Jews. You have played with the days to make Sunday important when it never was. And now you have shunned it. Christianity could have been Mithraism or Manichaenism. You choose, Bert.'*

'No, you tell me for once. I choose nothing and no one. My quest is the logic of truth. The meaning of time since the Big Bang.'

'I tell you I was there with the host. We have had to listen to humankind's tormented souls over the last four thousand years, when before...'

Bert listened, she ranted on, drunk with euphoria now that most of humankind had gone below.

'Before, for nearly the whole of time now and also, Nobel Laureate, time that you do not know; the time before. We always listened. We heard each other and now we hear you, as you hurt and kill, kiss and love. But no more, you will all be gone very soon.'

Bert was learning more than he had expected. 'So, Higgs Boson, the particle that gives mass to everything. You must have a view on when it appeared in time. You must have that knowledge, because you say you have been alive forever.'

'You fool, you have answered all the relevant questions since you found the Higgs Boson in 2012. You, only you, could have found it. Only you could have pursued the collision of matter and antimatter. You are the one and now you are going to die.'

'I have answered nothing, Lily, but I will. The time will come and I will be ready.'

Bert had gone cold. He walked back into the bedroom ready for his warm comfortable bed and a long refreshing sleep. He lay in the dark and thought. The last article he had pinned on his study wall was about quantum entanglement. Where particles were separated by any distance but their states are linked. It said it is impossible to predict the state, but pairs of particles reference each other, they mirror each other's changes despite any distance between them. He wondered if his wife was sleeping before he introduced time into his matrix and thought back to before the Big Bang. Before any concept of universe there must have been two particles that existed and that referenced each other. Was it matter and antimatter and what did they represent? Where had they come from? Two particles, two entities that were inevitably linked to the start and ultimately the end of time.

Lily couldn't read his mind and he would never tell her his true thoughts. But whatever happened, he was determined to live longer than Lily. His will would see him through. He understood Her now and that only his soul could battle with Her. There could never be a physical contest on this earth, in this universe.

★ ★ ★

The women and children were separated from the men after they left reception "two". It prompted Hannah to search the faces of the departing group in case her father had belatedly arrived, but there was no sign of him. Her mum reassured her. 'Maybe he has been sent to the hospital in Montreux for more tests or something?'

Hannah was close to tears. 'But what could be wrong with my dad?

Briony gave her a quick hug as they padded along the worn rock floor. A dark line of bodies marched in front of them and disappeared into the gloom. 'I'm sure they will let us know.

Anything could have happened. An ear infection, low sugars on the blood test. We just need to be patient as we saw he went into professional hands.'

Liam was listening. 'Without dad, we have no iCloud service, him being the fucking "sharing organiser". But it's pointless anyhow, giving up my phone and iPad has really pissed me off.'

Briony grabbed his arm and shook him. She pulled him face to face: 'Liam, just because we are all a bit touchy, it doesn't give you the right to swear.'

'But it's fucking wrong, mum, and this place is just a foul hole.' Briony couldn't argue with him. She could see they were all disappointed, their shoulders sagged, their spirits gone like she had never seen before. It made her sad but she was determined not to show any weakness.

'Come on you lot! Pull yourselves together; we have barely been here an hour and you have written-off our temporary holiday without giving it a chance. It is just a fucking mobile!' They laughed at her, Briony never swore. She glanced over her shoulder and could see people moving into the gloom. 'Right we're off. Keep alert and stay close to me so that we can meet any contingency, as one positive, happy family.'

They came to the sleeping quarters, gallery sector C. The controllers lost control again as the women pushed forward to grab the best perceived beds. The one nearest to a light. The one furthest from a wet wall. They pushed and shoved each other and fought for their children as they crammed into the wooden walkways that were set in four tiers of gloom. Layers of wooden bunk beds formed laths and rafters as if supporting the low roof, which itself was an ugly honeycomb of rock made from flooding the galleries to leach out the salt. There were kilometres of dark nothing that disappeared into nothingness. Some of the bunks had brand new mattresses, but most had mattresses that had come from the empty hotels of Montreux. The majority were old, soft and worn out by humanity with the occasional inhumane bed bug. It took an hour of arguments and placing and throwing luggage off beds before the gallery was peaceful. The newcomers called the controllers the "inappropriates" for the rest of their time below. As the people hurled abuse at the controllers, they had been trained to civilly reply, 'That is inappropriate, madam.' Briony tried with them. She asked for clarification about her husband but all she got back was a polite, please wait patiently madam.

The Leinster and Murray families had remained aloof from the human turmoil. They had carried on walking to the very end of the sleeping quarters instead of stopping to argue at the start of them. Briony was in the lead, she barged her way through the logjam, digging her elbows into the squabbling mass and encouraging her little ducklings to follow her into the gloom. She kept turning back to make sure none were lost and could see Natalia frantically waving to encourage her onwards. In Briony's mind, the most important bunks were those closest to any fresh air; she searched left and right, hurrying forward, tripping on the uneven floor. After a short period of chaos she found seven bunks lying together near a vertical shaft. She sniffed the pure air and gestured for her family to immediately grab a bunk. All of them dumped themselves and their bags onto the bunks to claim possession, waiting patiently until the mayhem had dispersed into the gloom. She breathed hard, Liam lay across the very narrow aisle between the bunks with his head on his and his feet on his dad's. Her breathlessness was compounded by her loss, where was he? She needed her sun sharer now.

Reverberations of anger splashed on the litmus of salty rock and was soon sucked into the damp walls.

★ ★ ★

An hour later and an uneasy peace had settled on the gallery. Low conversations were inaudible as the new occupants adjusted their volume to match the lack of privacy. Natalia whispered to Briony, careful the children didn't hear, 'I kept my mobile.'

'Wow, girl, where is it?'

'In reception "two", in a plastic bag at the bottom of the pond where we were sat.'

Briony reached across and held her hand. 'Brilliant, well done. We can try Sam later if we can recover it. But I think the security is pretty tight.'

Natalia squeezed Briony's hand. 'Or we could telephone Bert.' They both fell quiet, the enormity of the change overcame them. She continued quietly, 'I am going to see what the toilets are like. Always leave one of us here, near the children.' She twisted off the bed and stood up. 'I think that's the safest plan. As moya lyubov used to say, we have to allow for the Lowest Common Denominator.' She stared into the gloom. 'I never thought people were such animals. Never, in my whole life.' She shook her head in wonderment. 'And it will only get worse. Give me half an hour to get there and back. If I am not back, come and find me "да". Remember, I am going direct to the WC.' She received Briony's assent and slowly made her way through the lines of bunks.

The hole stank already. A mixture of body odour, perfume and farts. People stared. Hunted looks like animals parading around an amphitheatre, ready to fight the gladiator in their midst. It was a disturbing sensation, the look, the weighing up, the protective scowl, welcoming smile or defeatist turn of the body. It was the first time that Natalia had appreciated that people, humans, were mere animals in every physical sense.

After five minutes she crossed a shallow reservoir of salty water via a suspended walkway. The new boards were placed on those laid a century before. Her path meandered between hewn columns that looked in danger of collapse beneath the weight of the roof. Spikes of dirty brown salt crystals adorned each column to a height of one metre. The salt stalagmites amazed her. It took another five minutes before she arrived at the puits, the old wells. She leaned over a wooden balustrade and looked into the circular hole and down a one hundred metre drop to the stream running below. Fresh water to wash away the detritus of human excrement whenever people used the communal toilet.

A male controller blocked her path. He spoke severely. 'Madam, you are only allowed in this area at set times. Please return to your sector.'

Natalia took affront. 'What, I cannot use the toilet?'

'Because from now and for the next hour it is a male toilet. We have to maintain decency.'

'So why has no person told us "да"? It is a basic right man.' She was indignantly loud and the rebellious tones bounced across the low ceilings and back to haunt him.

'Madam, just go back to your sector and use the bucket beneath your bunk.'

'"Нет", You are joking aren't you? What "говно."'

'Please madam, whatever you are saying, it must have been a trying day for you, the shock you know. We can't tell you everything instantly, we are only human.'

She thought not, but she did as ordered and walked away from him, following the dim passage and barely visible signs to gallery C. The communal toilets had finally stripped her humanity bare but she resolved to stay positive and strong for the children. As she re-passed the balustrade she looked into the puits again. After the first three metres she could see old metal handles partially hidden by the darkness and the merging of the rust with the anhydrite. She hurried back to her family. On her return journey, she noticed the black conduits of varying sizes hastily looped along the walls like loose entrails. Inside she thought must be electricity cables. Further along there was a methane detector. It looked like something from the 1970s. A short broken pipe protruded from the top of the black box and its coloured dial announced red for danger. It was totally inadequate and probably not working, but it reminded her that humans and their technology changed as quickly as nature. Only now mattered, she could see that, but it came as a shock. As she turned into the small cavern that would be home, she saw the glow of a candle on her right. A controller must have lit it and placed it on a ledge by a beautiful natural picture made from an accidental mixture of rocks. The wavering illumination enhanced its astonishing beauty. She read the tourist signage below it. "The Window of Hope". It resembled a snail shell of rocky striations in red grey and yellow. The sign below it also told her it was a mix of halite, gypsum, pyrite and rock salt. A melange that must have been created pre-humankind.

She felt sad that they were in a place where visitors used to gaze and relish the beauty of the salt mines. She imagined how they had marvelled at the bravery and ingenuity of the miners and had chatted happily with their guides. Oppressiveness can't have been a consideration during a two hour tourist visit. Now she passed new inhabitants, a pale face at every step that gazed at her before fading into the blankness. She heard as some swore at the patrolling "inappropriates", safe from identification in the darkness and she wondered if this was the biblical hell on earth.

★ ★ ★

Bert woke refreshed the next morning. He walked out onto the grass in front of the house and stretched his arms wide to welcome the day. To his right he could see the Jura mountains looming over Geneva; they shone with the first thin capping of winter's pure white snow. To his left ran the verdant Rhone valley, with a cloudy blue outfall at the mouth of the river. It was beautiful, astonishing and made his soul soar to the heavens.

'It is all your fault, of course. You should go and join your family; it is a penitence to die together.'

'My fault? A cosmic explosion?' He acted deliberately ignorant.

'Tush, a man of your intelligence. Acting like God without understanding the implications.'

'Do you mean the last experiment?'

'Of course, you fool. Colliding antimatter with matter. You didn't calculate the maths, did you, Bert?'

He was honest with his reply. 'I thought we would discover the meaning of life.' He felt the full force of her rant as if a hail storm was streaming into his face.

'You did, didn't you, Bert, or shall I call you God? You are responsible for killing all the insects alive on earth. That is ten quintillion lives. Then you must add eight billion humans.' He couldn't reply, the wind was knocked out of him and had bent him double. 'Do you realise that in 70,000 BC there were fewer than twenty thousand Homo Sapiens on this earth, do you? But we were a million species, and nearly half of us were plants. Look at you! You have spread like a virus. And now you are the *biggest mass murderer of all time. You! A single human being has undertaken a divine action to put an end to this miserable human world.'*

Bert staggered to the pool house nearby. He went to sit down but noticed the prayer book thrown into the corner by Sam. She watched him pause, tempted to pick it up.

'Why bother with religion and God now? The damage is done.'

He walked deliberately across the grey marble and bent to pick it up. Clutching it to his chest, he eased his way into a low seat, grunting in pain. Then he laughed, a maniac laughing at himself talking to Her, a lily. He thought to himself, so she believes God and religion may have helped before? And then he spoke to the sun; his eyes were closed to help him listen, a red mist clouded his sight. Because maybe I have missed a heavenly ingredient? He laughed again, it was a good thought, a crazy thought. He started to cough and couldn't stop. His guts retched in spasm as he spat blood from his mouth and it sat as globules spewed across the grey tiles.

'Go below, don't be alone, Bert. Be with your family and see a doctor; you need medicine and all will be well.'

He knew that medicine couldn't save anyone. He opened the book at random. It was the first time he had done so since he was a young boy, before he started to worship science. He read the words to himself.

Matthew:10:28

"And fear not them which kill the body, but are not able to kill the soul: but rather fear him which is able to destroy both soul and body in hell."

Underneath the excerpt was Sam's writing. The word "soul" equals the capacity to live. We may be killed, but we still have the capacity to live again, through resurrection, a gift of God. 'Do not fear physical death. Jesus said, We should not fear man, but God. But the fearful, and unbelieving, and the abominable, and murderers, and whoremongers, and sorcerers, and idolaters, and all liars, shall have their part in the lake which burneth with fire and brimstone: which is the second death.'

Bert spoke to Lily: 'So what are you going to do when we are finished?' She didn't answer. In the corner of the room he could see Sam again. The phantom of Sam but this time his friend was white, bright and truly there. He wasn't moving or speaking but carefully watched his best friend. 'Look, pal, don't you think your God is sat there on high looking down at the miserable human race and thinking what the hell did I create?' The phantom wavered slightly. 'And God spake – Why did I do such a bad job?' But Bert knew the answers. He walked out of the pool house, afraid to face his ghostly friend.

★ ★ ★

Most of the cows had been taken off the mountain pastures as usual in early October, before the frosts iced up their water supplies. They needed about sixty litres a day to survive and so the farmers had made sure that they had freedom of access to many square kilometres of unfettered fields by low level rivers and lakes. The cows looked lost, they had no farmer to manoeuvre them through their day. CCOW had decided that 20% of all stock animals should be left to roam free but the remaining 80% would be slaughtered and frozen for the Deeps. No one could predict what would happen to the roaming cattle.

Most people thought the goats and sheep stood a better chance of survival than the cows, but the reality was they all started to die at about the same time. Only the birds seemed as happy as normal in the HB storm. The whistling noise of the flocks of starlings heading between Holland and Spain continued. There were fewer flocks but still enough to cause a show. Black clouds of birds swooped across the valley of the Chauderon until alighting as one in a field or a tree. Like scared shoals of fish he had seen when scuba diving, zigzagging across the liquid sky, they made shadows on the prairie below them. And then they whistled off again on a pre-planned track to the winter sun. Migratory perigrinations that had taken place for millennia before man had settled the valleys above Montreux.

Bert stepped around his flower beds examining the damage. He supposed all gardens were now the saddest memorial to humankind. He thought it was a shame because humans used to make time to stand and gaze at flowers in times of crisis. At funerals and weddings. He knew that for many centuries flowers had played a significant role in human life. They made Man happy and cheerful or were used to express Man's emotions and feelings. The presence of bright multi-coloured flowers intensified feelings of contentment. Often beautiful flower arrangements were kept in hospitals, so as to reduce the stress and pain felt by patients or some species had even been made into drugs that would cure them.

He touched a red carnation and it crumbled in his hand, the vibrant symbol of change fell to dust and was swallowed by the earth. It was a get-well-soon flower, or for telling a friend that you feel for their loss. But the carnations were all compost. And he knew there were no flowers in the bunkers. There was no natural light to nurture them. There were no birds to sing and swoop in the enclosed air. There were no animals apart from the human beings. All the subjective and emotional aspects of an open nature had been subdued into the bitter ignorance of humankind, in the closed creations called the Deeps. He wondered what they were doing in their nothingness.

★ ★ ★

Bert had taken to walking again. He wanted to maintain his fitness as long as possible. Each day, he headed upwards, drawn to the Dent de Jaman. A pinnacle of hardened limestone, nineteen hundred metres high with an old wooden cross perched on the tiny summit. He talked to the animals wandering in his path and sometimes they would follow him in small groups, two by two, glad to be in the presence of a human owner. He talked to them because there were no other living persons who remained above ground. He was never bored with his last days and nights. He used the time to think. There were no more research papers to be had, since all surfing had been stopped on the internet. The great worldwide brain was in the latter stages of dementia. Bizarrely, he still received emails from CCOW demanding the predictor level but he ignored them. CCOW was dead to him but he let his family and friends into his thoughts in a controlled way. For the last few months he had presumed they were going to their deaths and had grieved for them before they left. Now he concentrated on his health and realistic solutions to the day's new problems, because there might not be a tomorrow. The generator needed repair. There was a blockage in the fuel pipe. Fix it if you want electricity – simple. But when he thought of his family, it was invariably Natalia who held his attention. He remembered her making Vin Cuit, a delicious tart she served with vanilla ice-cream. He could still taste it. But of all the flavours in her autumn kitchen, the best in every October past had always been the apple pie served with hot custard. October had been a gastronomic delight, the last days of summer merging with autumn and a plethora of yellows and browns, with a smell of must, as the vineyards had been stripped of their grapes and the pressings returned to feed the soil.

But Bert was bored. He thought he was the last person on the earth's surface and still in reasonable health. He had a car, food, electricity and all the space in the world. So he chose to explore it. He had accompanied Natalia in the spring time to The Fondation Giannada near Martigny. Her father had loaned the art museum some of his famous works. There were Monets and Cezannes and the exhibition was now frozen in time, awaiting The Return. He wanted to see the Cezanne paintings depicting nature for a last time. A last check on his reality, and he knew "The Small Forest" and the "Forest," were on display for no one to see anymore. He decided he would steal one, maybe more and keep them at home to remind him of man's greatest talents, the ability to create beauty by copying nature. When they had toured the exhibition as a couple, he had paid little attention to the endless display of water lily paintings. Monet had painted two hundred and fifty canvasses of lilies and thirty had been sat in the Fondation. Now he wanted a few in his house. He had read that the elderly Monet had started his water lily series after planting hundreds in his garden at Giverny. Monet had declared, "One instant, one aspect of nature contains it all." He had painted the opposite effects of light versus dark as they fought each other across the water of his giant pond. They were painted at the end of his career, at a time when his sight was failing due to cataracts. If he was angry he destroyed his works. As a perfectionist, he would ruin many paintings rather than exhibit them.

When Bert and Natalia had visited the Fondation, he had been impressed by the Chinese Empress Tree. It was adjacent to the pond with the horizontal fountain that reflected the reflections. The beautiful lilac and orchid-like flowers and the large heart shaped leaves had entranced him. But he couldn't understand the lack of security at the time as its location gave easy access to the roof. Bert's final HB theory was corrupted in his usually clear mind and a visit to the lilies would help return some clarity. He set off in the Merc and drove to the autoroute as if the tiny country roads were the race track at Le Mans. The joy of speed was a relief from science as he let his emotional self rule his subjective and over logical psyche.

Halfway to Martigny, it started to pour down but he maintained a crazy but constant speed of 300 kph. For the first time in his life there was no dangerous spray on the autoroute and he could keep his foot hard on the accelerator. He slowed to the speed limit through the centre of the town itself but only because he was searching for any fellow human beings. It was completely dead; everyone had gone below. Thousands had left their dull concrete blocks and no one had rebelled. The only occupants of the town centre were five sheep and two cows that were forlornly searching for fresh foliage. At The Fondation, he dumped the car outside of the front entrance and climbed over the fence to his left. The beige block of the windowless building resembled an alien spaceship. Bronze heavy doors were firmly shut but he rightly judged that if there was an intruder alarm, nobody would appear to challenge his entrance. At his favourite tree he started the two minute climb to reach the roof. He laboured upwards for half an hour bent double under the weight of the ropes, belays and the cordless angle grinder he had brought with him. The tree had no leaves but held onto its brown seed pods and bunches of light brown fruits. These crackled under his feet as he clambered up the branches. At the peak of the spaceship was a huge skylight that gave natural illumination to the centre of the building. Quickly, he cut the plastic glass with the grinder and dropped the rope to the floor twenty metres below. After tying it to the ventilation duct just beneath him, he dropped down using a belay device. There were no lights on and no alarm either. They weren't expecting burglars and if anyone was still above ground they would be dead.

Halfway to the floor he glanced around at the glass cases of Roman remains that stood against the dirty brown walls of the balcony. He wondered if another species would take the remains of his modern world and create a similar museum. That made him laugh crazily, the bark reverberating around the exhibition hall. The acoustic design made bad laughs better and crazy laughs crazier. He dropped onto one of the black chairs in the centre of the hall which was an ancient temple. Knocking several over, he landed heavily on his back and struggled to regain his feet. Slowly, he stepped over the low walls of the temple, onto the coir carpet and gained the travertine walkway. There was a light switch on the wall by the bookshop, which he flipped down. Light poured onto the paintings around him. It made him gasp with delight as he felt privileged to be alone in such beauty. It took him two hours to walk around all the Monets and Cezannes and then he chose his favourite pictures and took them out of the front doors to gently place in his car.

His last act of rebellion was to shout at the top of his voice, 'Natalia, Allie, Josh.' The loved ones' names bounced and collided around the room. He repeated the shouts again and again until his voice was hoarse. Pulling armfuls of books from the bookshop into a pile, he took out his lighter and torched the pages of a guide to Roman Martigny. It set fire easily; caught and spread, engulfing the metre high pyre which grew as he threw more books on top of it. And when he was happy that the building must inevitably burn down, he turned and walked away. Art and beauty died in the heat of the flames and now it was time for science.

★ ★ ★

That night at home, he noticed the gleaming eyes of Glion and Montreux had darkened, the electricity particles vibrated no more. Lights were the first particles on earth's surface to extinguish forever. Only natural light would suffice for the rest of the life of this universe. And there was no one. No noise, no sharing of life with hate and murder, love and birth. It was easier for Bert the loner, than anyone could have imagined. No TV coverage of the Moslem Caliphate in Syria and Iraq. No arguments over the rights and wrongs of endless terrorist war. No comments driven by power, money and sex in a modern media-driven and lying fake life. Only the stars staring up from the lake and a solitary bulb shining in a French village called Novel. There was another loner on the mountains opposite Bert's house. Someone with a generator in a refuge for the sane or maybe insane. Someone who shared paradise.

[8]

Working Through

R ETRIEVING NATALIA'S HIDDEN mobile proved to be very easy, it was their talisman for contacting the two husbands. A few days after their arrival, Bex salt mines had completed the intake of their esteemed clients. The day after the last group had been sorted through reception the compulsory walks at 10am and 4pm had commenced. The reception area was an obvious choice; it was circular, it was big and it was "safe". The truth was that no one could escape, everyone was easily monitored as they transferred between the galleries and the exercise area. The tunnels allowed the humans to be channelled through security as on intake, but now there was no need for the airport style metal detectors as the mines were in "lock-down".

The first exercise period was a relief to everyone involved. It took some stress off the controllers but much more off the inmates. 100 women and children circled the reception in a lethargic stroll. They wanted to walk faster but the gloomy crush punctuated by the baleful yellow lights enticed many to be lazy and sit it out on the benches adjacent to the outer pool. From this periphery vantage point, they watched their more enthusiastic family members swinging by. The swirl of humans ebbed and flowed from two to seven abreast, a whirlpool of beings with an occasional escaping drop that splashed onto the surrounds. The still water of the outer pool beckoned for a hand to stir the calm surface and make patterns to entertain depressed minds. The liquid soothed the angst and extinguished the thoughts of home. Retrieval of the mobile was thus a natural action. It simply required a concerted family huddle to hide Natalia as she plucked it from the pool and hid it in her pocket.

She was now lying on her bed in the gallery of sector C. The mobile was still dry and functioning. She whispered to Briony. 'I've got a 5G signal!'

Briony came to lie on Natalia's bed. She huddled close to keep their secret. 'That's amazing but why don't you save your battery life by just using it for texts?'

'About what?' For the first time in her life, Natalia was at a loss as to who she might text.

'Well, you can text Bert to see if he's OK?'

However, Natalia decided on the first priority. 'Here, take it and text Sam. The living come first.'

'I'm sure Bert is still alive. So no, I'm sorry Natalia. I can't take away your privilege to go first.'

'Nonsense, Sam wants to be with us and Bert may be dead.' It was a harsh reality but it encouraged Briony to accept the mobile from Natalia and input a text.

'We are worried about you, it's me! Love Briony. Natalia kept this mobile but they are generally banned here. Beware when you arrive! Let us know you are safe and well. Tell us when you might join us. x' She handed the iPhone back to

Natalia. 'Go on. Text him.' Briony could see the wet glint in her friend's eyes. 'You want to. So just do it. Tell him how you feel.'

Natalia considered her words carefully. After five minutes' thought she sent her secret text. 'You were right, Bert, it is awful in the Deeps. I would even say inhuman. We are all growing weaker by the day now. No other symptoms; we are invisibly dying. I sense you are still alive and I just want to tell you that I love you. No matter what, I will always love you x.'

Briony leaned across. 'Did both texts go?'

Natalia looked at the sent folder. 'Yes, it says they did. But I can't believe CCOW lied to us about so much.' Briony said nothing. She hugged her friend tightly and stayed next to her as they both pondered their predicament.

She was still lying prone when Natalia saw the controller and accompanying soldier walking along the gallery. The controller held a small antenna attached to a black box which had a meter on the top and was used to detect 5G signals. The two men stopped next to her bunk and the controller brought the detector close to Natalia's pocket. She jumped as she caught the movement out of the corner of her eye. It was hard to catch her breath as she twisted to confront the men. She watched as Briony rolled out of the bunk on the opposite side and also stood, fists clenched and arms straight down.

The controller's voice was rough: 'Hand the mobile over immediately.' Natalia meekly gave him the iPhone and mentally kicked herself for leaving it switched on after texting. The controller waved the mobile like a magic wand in front of both Natalia and Briony. The four children protectively gathered around their mums, worried about a punishment. He had a low and menacing voice. 'You were told the rules and we expect you to live by them.'

Natalia replied for them all: 'We were never told that there would be rules and now you expect us to die by them.'

Without any argument the controller and his bodyguard turned on their heels and walked away into the gloom of the gallery. There was a stunned silence from the families.

Allie broke it first: 'Did you telephone dad or Uncle Sam?' Her mum was shaking uncontrollably and as she tried to reply she convulsed into huge sobs. Allie and Josh sat and enveloped her with their arms. Allie looked up at Briony who still stood by the bunk.

Briony shook her head. 'No, we tried a text to both dads. The texts went. At least we think they went but I guess the controllers intercepted them, hence they knew we had been on the network.'

Josh said what they were all thinking: 'If a text can't leave here, I doubt if anything will ever leave here.'

Natalia clutched at Briony's arm and pulled her close. 'Don't think of Sam now. Think of your past life with him, your loving husband and their fine father.' Briony jerked under Natalia's clamped hands.

After a few minutes she whispered, a wet face close to Natalia's ear, 'I know I will never see him again. I love him so much and I,' but she couldn't complete her sentence.

'Just love him and be strong Briony. Be with us, for us and now.'

★ ★ ★

Bert never cared for classical music. He would reluctantly listen to a sample on the occasional winter's evening, always sat by his wife and inevitably facing a glowing log fire. But his attendance was only upon request and when enticed by a smile, a cognac and something more, a little foreplay. He was still drinking the cognac and the fire still crackled beneath the slate mantelpiece as he admired his stolen paintings by Monet. He was playing Natalia's favourite song on the CD, "Una furtiva lagrima", sung by Pavarotti. It was the only song she ever played from the Italian opera by Donizetti. Natalia had always whispered her love into his ear as she had listened to it, claiming to have been drugged by Bert's love potion, secretly administered in Stockholm twenty years before.

His body was too broken to cry. All his strength and emotions fought to glue his cells together to combat the fraying by the HBs. He looked up at the three new paintings in the salon. They had been hung from long nails that he had haphazardly hammered into the yellow stucco walls. Near the door to the veranda was "The bridge". Two white bars arched across the water supported by an inadequate number of uprights. The bridge broke the uniformity of green with a patch of purple shade to the right. Bert counted the number of white lilies spreading into the distance of the pond and reached an unconvincing 54. He repeated the process again and again. Each time the number changed as if the lilies were playing a game of hide and seek with him.

Near the stopped Louis XVI clock was the second stolen piece, "Water lilies and agapanthus". The number of lilies was easy to count this time. The four purple heads of the agapanthus nodded in obeisance to the couple of nymphaea. The painting exuded purple, it reminded him of his university days and his penchant for the "Purple Rain" and "Purple Haze" songs. An odd cacophony of guitars to add strident memories to the soft classic voice of Pavarotti. But his favourite Monet painting was the third, "The clouds". It was atmospheric, oozing humidity from the oils, a start and end from within deep shadow. The best part of this Monet was the absence of lilies. He was thinking about Her and creation. The equality of light and darkness created by God. "God said" was the phrase, and He commanded the division of the waters to create land for plants to germinate. And the creation of stars, the universe, and above and beyond. Like God, Bert had decided to take the seventh day of creation and take a rest as his work was done. The Higgs Boson detector was still working and showed a level of ten. He turned the volume of the music up. Level ten, in Genesis the phrase "God said" repeated exactly ten times. God gave the ten Commandments to man. The tenth day of the seventh month is the Holy Day, the Day of Atonement, where man undertakes a spiritual spring clean. A day of fasting that encapsulates the removal of Satan, the creator of sin, before the reign of Jesus started. The final rules of the kingdom of man under Satan was symbolised in many ways by the number ten. Ten days knowing his family were incarcerated under the salty crust of Bex. Ten glasses of cognac distorted Bert's thinking until oblivion.

He remembered. Allie and Josh were holding his hands. He looked down at their innocent young faces, bright with excitement. The paddle steamer sounded its steam horn, a hot exclamation mark that reverberated around the valley above Montreux. Much to Natalia's distaste, they had taken the electric tram to the Château de Chillon. An exciting journey for the seven year olds followed by the dread of the dungeons where the lake waters lapped close to the barred windows. But the boat was the most exciting part of their family trip. The steam paddles whirled and churned the water to froth behind its protective glass. And now they were excitedly pointing at their house set high on the hill above the town. The toot of the whistle was sharp in Bert's ear. He looked towards the steamer's funnel to see if it had moved closer to him. But all he saw was the golden eagle on the top of the clock as it chimed midnight. It slammed him straight back into the truth of despair and so he eased his carcass off the settee and staggered out of the salon door and onto the veranda.

Orion's belt stood upright in the sky above Rochers de Naye. He looked to the lake and saw three dim white lights of fishing boats making a reflection of the celestial beauty. He stared again, puzzled and realised they were reflections of the past, stars beaming in from outer space, an unreality floating on an abandoned lake. The invincibility of nature calmed him sufficiently. A satellite, direct and purposeful and seemingly in a straight line, crossed his view with astonishing speed. He thought it was going to collide with a star. Not that it mattered anymore.

He took a few deep breaths, filling his lungs to bursting point each time to clarify his will to live. Still alive, and wanting to live, he walked back inside his home. Bert changed the CD on the Hi Fi to Chris Rea. "Tell me there's a heaven". The song mourned its way across the salon as he sat. He remembered the comfort brought to him by his laptop. The feeling of being in touch with the world as breaking news flashed across his screen. A month before and he had randomly keyed the word "heaven" into his search engine. "I'm feeling lucky", said the caption. Between the adverts for gay bars and music clubs sat the truth. The truth or man's perceived truth made unreal by an analyst in Wikipedia, because what was Googled had now become fact. Man would not search further anymore, it was too difficult, too time consuming. "Heaven, in many religions, is the holiest place where God lives, a Paradise to ascend to upon death. The opposite is Hell, a place to avoid because the Devil resides there. Human beings can go to Heaven if they have the right based upon what they have achieved in life. Being good or pious. Being right and having faith in God. Many believe that Heaven will be found on Earth in a different time."

'But no one gives a shit, do they, Bert?'

Lily had been absent from his psyche for a long time, blocked by his consciousness. 'I think they do now, Lily.'

'When you are going to die, well, then you give a shit. Is that the sentiment for your people?'

'My people?' He thought about the term and then ignored it. 'I'm too old to worry about dying, let death find me if it wants.'

'You are right, Bert. Let death come now. Die whilst you can think, can understand your ending.'

He asserted himself: 'I do understand my ending and also my beginning.'

'You are so young, Bert. Go to Bex, there are no solutions here. Go to your loved ones.'

'My loved ones are the people of this planet. I have always strived to give them the truth.'

'Be selfish, you are ill but your family love you and will care for you until your death.'

'Life is a meaningless swim around nothingness for most. But not me, I understand much more than most.' He walked into his study and picked up the same book he had hit his head with a few weeks before. He opened up a well-thumbed page. "The gatekeeper said to the hero, 'If you endure, everything will be fine. No worry, no suffering. It all disappears.'

It was a walled town, a place for a dream reader and Unicorns. The gatekeeper said, 'this is where the world ends. Nowhere further to go.'"

Bert addressed Lily: 'Aren't we in that same world? A meaningless wandering around nothingness?'

'Bert, you need to get a grip. You are the ultimate logical man and now spouting Marukami Kafkaesque type drivel.'

'One man to save the world. So logically, I am the new Jesus?'

'Either that or you are completely bonkers.'

'Well, maybe I am bonkers and you don't exist, maybe I am a true existentialist.'

'But I do exist, I am here, you can touch me, smell me and kill me. It's your choice; believe and be long dead.'

★ ★ ★

Briony marched with purpose. The tortured reality of a subterranean Bex village bore no resemblance to the real article above them. Below, there was an over-density of living, a darkness without horizon. Above, there was space and light to the extremes of the universe. She and the rest of the Leinsters and Murrays were walking in reception "two". They had been going for 15 minutes and knew that they would be consigned back to the gallery in another five. It had been Briony's idea to walk as fast as possible and try to get out of breath. They had started arm in arm, a six fold barrier, an antiseptic to the drudgery of walking in partial light. After a couple of circuits they gave up their mutual support and stayed independent, which allowed them to speed up and overtake the dawdlers. It helped because they were now puffing and panting as they made a game of keeping up with each other.

Allie put on a spurt and surged past Hannah. 'Just like the Roadrunner, catch me if you can, coyote!' She had pulled two metres ahead before Hannah could respond.

Natalia gasped as she walked. 'Never mind an overfed bird, I feel like a fucking bat.'

Josh remonstrated, 'Mum, humans don't possess echolocation. And dad wouldn't like you swearing, would he?' He skipped ahead of her after a quick shove, shoulder to shoulder.

She laughed at her boy. '"Het", he would not, but I do think he would swear in here.'

Allie dropped back to her mum; she had given up trying to beat Hannah. 'Too fucking true!'

They all laughed. There was no point in crying anymore. Nor complaining. The damp air made the women's hair curly and there were no heated tongs to smooth out the ringlets. In fact there were only six electrical sockets to power hair dryers or tongs, for the 100 people in their gallery but no one had been permitted to bring them underground. They were a safety hazard. The females ate at the same time and were always kept separate from their husbands, partners and dads by their five controllers. It was rumoured that the men's areas had twice the number of controllers per head. Three meals a day were served in the Salle des Cristaux, a wide but low area with giant columns of rock holding up the roof. At one end were the kitchens, a series of ovens, hobs and microwaves set in stainless steel cabinets and worktops. Adjacent to these was a stainless buffet bar with bright overhead lights and then there were a set of wooden trestle tables. The food resembled sludge. Green frozen spinach sludge. Brown mincemeat sludge, a sludge of mashed potatoes but never any dessert sludge. Water was the only drink apart from tea and coffee, which was only ever served at breakfast time.

It was a rumour, there were always rumours. A controller had told someone in sector G that nitrogen gas had been pumped into many of the bunkers in France. The someone had passed it on and finally it came to Briony in hushed tones via the lady next door to her bunk. A scientific fact or a rumour, she thought? It was certainly more humane than cyanide gas, less painful. And did the controllers know it was true because the border was only twenty kilometres away? She thought about the implications for a day before asking her neighbour for more details.

The neighbour helped her think it through to the dread reality. She whispered: 'A few stragglers who had refused to go below in France, in Evian to be exact, had crossed into Switzerland and sought help. One, a man, ended up here at the bunker and pretended to have family from Vevey.'

'Did they let him in?'

'Yes but after a day he disappeared.'

Sam flipped across her mind, she missed him. 'And your point is?'

'A young controller reputedly told him it was not a CCOW or World Council decision. Each government recognised the realities of the low food stocks and each government made the decision to kill humanely. This would leave some chance for the remaining population and of course 100% certainty for their administrators survival.'

'For the love of Jesus.'

'Yes, my dear, and then the man disappeared an hour after that conversation. But no one has seen the controller either.'

Briony kept quiet. She could only think that there must be so little food there could only be a few more weeks to live.

It wasn't something to share with her extended family, only Natalia. She had her worst nightmares that night because the logical truth swept through her dreams. The world's governments, the powerful and rich would have conspired to keep the Return as clean and tidy as possible. When she woke, the stench of her own sweat appalled her. It was a simple equation, maximising the survival rate of the few.

[9]

Acceptance and Hope

L ATE OCTOBER 2018, and home is where the heart
is. The first use of the sentiment was attributed to Pliny
the Elder in Greece, sometime before 79 AD. One's own home
is preferable to all others, but some homes like the chalet are
special because of the view. Bert sat on the steps facing the
lake with a handful of gravel gathered off the path under his
feet. He threw a stone at a lighting bollard twenty metres
away and missed. His home had become extremely ordinary
without his family, because the heart had left. He looked to his
left at Glion. Panes of glass glowed red-gold, the whole was
brought into perfect perspective. Soon to be a last sun going
down on humankind, the end of light and the beginning of
darkness. In front of him, the meadow saffron was sad, the
lavender flowers drooped across the dry earth. Beyond this
dropsy, vines marched as yellow soldiers, their serried ranks
ran towards the lake as line abreast or astern, disciplined in
two directions alone. He thought it was a shame the grapes
had been left to rot, a victim of an invisible war. He threw

another stone and missed; sod the vines, I never liked Chasselas anyway.

This October had been an Indian summer with the odd cold day, but no one promenaded by the lake. No fashion conscious crowds licked the ice-cream or lounged with a happy aperitif. But there was an airshow for the missing to watch with the solitary Bert. A biplane appeared from behind the sharp cliff of Rochers de Naye and headed towards the lake. Halfway across the water, he thought it commenced a carefree and cavorting loop the loop. Turning back towards Montreux it barrel-rolled and then snaked left and right as it re-crossed above the small villages of Caux and Glion. The finale was unexpected. Once more it headed out towards the centre of the lake but above the Château de Chillon, it climbed forever. The engine thumping and straining for air before performing a final silent loop. Up and over in a graceful arch without end, but excluding the recovery phase. Straight down it plunged, down and down until it broke the meniscus of a perfectly calm lake.

The next day, he was outdoors again, drawn by nature, searching for the horizon. He was looking at the ground a step in front so he missed the cloud momentarily drifting across the sun and eclipsing the glint of the lake below him. After a few seconds it was dragged beneath the still waters as a black hole swallowing matter. Bert had been collecting mushrooms for his breakfast since early morning. It was a change from the dried and tinned food that CERN had put in his larder. He had carefully cut the stipe and gently laid the mushrooms in his wicker basket. The wicker allowed the spores to fall through the holes and ensured re-propagation. He hadn't been careful about which varieties he had picked and many, he knew, might be poisonous. But there was no free telephone advice anymore, to verify which were safe. He left the basket in the prairie, a decision finally made, accidental death by fungus toxin was stupid.

His wandering snaked downhill and eventually he sat in the Montreux cemetery by the family burial plot. Dwarfing him was a large red granite headstone, two metres tall and two metres wide. Behind this stood a giant sequoia tree, planted 150 years before when the resort town had become popular with the Victorian English. The highest entry on the gravestone read: "Natalia Suvarov Leinster". His name was carved below and the children last of all. All their dates of birth were shown and a space left for the date they died. The dedication at the bottom had been Bert's idea when they had reserved the plot from the local commune. "Together through space and time". He hoped so, sincerely he hoped he was right. But the engraving would never be completed and the true dates would be left untold.

As he walked around the cemetery, he mourned the absence of flowers and candles. Every year on November 1st, Christians in Switzerland honoured all their saints, and the cemetery would be alive with visitors chatting, drinking wine and breaking bread to eat with cheese and ham. But not this year. The tradition of All Saints' Day, celebrated since the fourth century, was now lost. There were no symbols displayed, nothing at all. He saw no sheafs of wheat, hands of God, or crowns. The only symbol was Bert himself, who had remembered to wear bright white clothes in honour of every saint and martyr in human history.

★ ★ ★

He meandered towards the centre of Montreux, stopping on occasion to look and listen. But the place was as dead as the cemetery. Flowers had turned to mouldy dust. The dead heads collapsed as he passed them, disturbed by the slightest breeze. At the wooden deck adjacent to the Freddie Mercury statue he decided to swim. Stripping naked, he stood and saluted the sky then looked into the blackness of the water as he contemplated death. With a small jump he arched towards the water and pared his way beneath the surface. The cold clenched at his heart, an icy grip trying to stop the pump of its beat as he plunged downwards; opening his eyes he couldn't see anything in the depths. Desperate for breath he kicked upward but saw nothing. He weakly kicked again, three then four times until the light beckoned him to the surface. He gasped as he floated on his back, fighting to take in enough oxygen to survive. In the distance he saw the snowy peaks. They called to him, to leave the waters where man had been created and to rise to the heavens. He swam frog-like making barely a ripple with his hands as they cupped then pushed the water into his sides. It was far colder than he had anticipated and his breathing was shallow.

He heard Lily speaking. *'Not long now. Go if you want, why wait?'*

He flopped over to his front and with a weak crawl he covered the thirty metres to the lakeside. He dragged himself out of the water and lay shuddering with cold.

'Lily?'

'As long as there is life, there is hope. As long as there is hope, there is life. Is that correct, human?'

Bert snorted with anger as he walked back to his clothes. He posed Her a question: 'The life of what not whom?' He tried again: 'The hope of the what, not of the whom?'

She despised him. The venom oozed between the words that she spat out. *'Firstly, define life, Bert. Are you God, can you take on that responsibility, human?'*

He answered slowly, without anger now, 'Man has co-existed with each other and with the eukaryotes. Man has not lived together, instead we have fought, improved and forgotten together. This was not life. Living is understanding our existence, our time and our space. Understanding our minuscule point in infinite time and realising that we are nothing within something.'

She laughed at him. The long drawn out laugh of a lunatic.

It took him four tedious hours to reach home; a journey that would normally take 45 minutes. Each step was torture. But he wanted to be wet and cold again. He waded into the etang with his mushroom knife and cut the heart out of Lily to take into the house to cook and then eat Her.

★ ★ ★

Home is where the heart is, but Natalia's heart was not in the Deeps at Bex. She lay on her back in the bunk next to Briony. The children had made friends and created a hopscotch court. They were playing with them at the end of the gallery where the light was slightly better. Briony started in her doze and gasped.

'I can't stand any more.'

Briony slowly turned on her side to look at her friend. She wasn't going to argue. She recognised the fatigue in their bodies was growing exponentially. The children were always tired, she presumed they were being attacked faster than the adults. She presumed the Envelope wasn't working to expectations. There were so many episodes of sickness and diarrhoea across the spectrum of ages but more and more children were taking to their bunks, motionless even without a mobile to gawk at. The controllers didn't help. There were insufficient doctors and they were confused which medicines might alleviate their inmate's conditions; deep down Briony knew there was nothing they could do that would truly help. Briony whispered. 'I don't think you can escape, if that is what you want.'

'I think I can and I think no one will try to chase after me.'

Briony pondered for a moment. 'You know I would look after the children for you.'

'I know that and I also know I could not return. So it is final if I go.'

'Return you say, who would want to return?'

'No one.'

Briony slipped across the darkness and huddled close to her friend. 'You have been the best friend that has made my life complete.' Both women cried silently; they stroked each others hair and gently kissed cheek to cheek. 'Natalia, my love, we all know the end is soon. Just go if you want.'

'So I will speak with Josh and Allie after dinner and go in the middle of the night.'

Briony asked her a last question. 'I don't want to know how you will escape. Then I can't be interrogated and give your secret away. But tell me why. Why must you go?'

Natalia drew every word from deep inside her subconscious. 'It feels as if I have been living a dream since the announcement of the HB storm. I have always believed in Bert but I did not accept his idea.'

'But we all do now, right?'

'We all know the truth, but still no one will accept it. So I want to die in the midst of truth and not deception.'

Natalia spoke gently with the children that evening. She didn't try and justify her escape attempt or amplify they had all been deceived because they knew. She told them she loved them and Briony would look after them. She added nothing extra to their lives in the Deeps, except love, and they knew they would have that until the bitter end. They made a single, joint request. 'Tell dad that we love him forever.'

★ ★ ★

'You'll make it, girl, be strong as we are all growing so weak, so fast.'

Natalia kissed Briony's forehead. 'The ending cannot be good. Believe in God and an afterlife of joy and happiness. Death is not an end but a beginning.'

Briony whispered, 'Sam was definitely left above, wasn't he?' She stumbled through her request. 'If you see him,' she sighed deeply, 'If there is any chance of saying goodbye to him, tell him I love him forever.'

Natalia's last words trembled. 'Of course but I fear that all we believed in is untrue and all that we left has all but gone.'

Briony gave her a last hug before pushing her away into the gloom. It was 3am, and everyone was sleeping. The walk to the puits was innocent but purposeful, a quick trip to the toilet if she were caught. Lowering herself between the wooden barrier surrounding the old shaft, Natalia searched for the first metal rung with her left foot. When she found it she took a deep breath and slowly descended.

At 5am Briony heard the sound of drills from behind the wooden doors leading to sector C. She was puzzled, the banging and drilling noises increased and came at her from many directions, echoing off the rock walls, waking a few others. She knew if the controllers were busy they might not detect Natalia's absence which made her happy. After half an hour there was silence. Those awake lay or sat on their bunks and waited for an instruction through the tannoy. She sat and watched the children sleeping peacefully, the flickering candle light dulled to an orange colour and she curled onto her side and drew her legs into a foetus position. Natalia had escaped, they would all be alright without her. Her last thought was of her school and orange flames, she was in the lab experimenting on the effects of carbon monoxide.

★ ★ ★

Natalia escaped into November at the foot of a cliff in Bex, she gasped for air as she lay on her side at the end of the puit. Her shivering was from the fear of being lost, of the dark and the choice she had made. Barely lit by a rising sun she thought of those below. How human beings were learning a new type of existence. She looked towards France in the distance, no one could appreciate the sprinkling of snow on the Prealps anymore. The first ski trip of the season was close but now so far for them all. Shades of grey coloured clouds hung across the mountains at different levels, a sandwiching of temperature and humidity not dissimilar to the galleries of the salt mines. Plain stratus slit across the cold slopes, cumulonimbus frayed above them as sheared wool hugging the peaks. She was alone and in pain as she struggled to her feet. Pushing one foot in front of the other she dragged herself back into the real world and walked unsteadily towards the village in search of a way to get home.

[1 0]

Now the Earth was Formless and Empty

A COMPLETE DARKNESS SURROUNDED Bert as he sat on the veranda. There was no artificial illumination and a dearth of the noise that once dominated his environment. Only a fragile finger of moonlight swept across the lake from an orange segment of the moon that hung above Evian. Genesis 1: "Now the earth was formless and empty, darkness was over the surface of the deep, and the Spirit of God was hovering over the waters." Bert mouthed the words he had learned at school as an innocent nine year old. "In the beginning God created the heavens and the earth." The words felt like they were for The Beginning not The Ending and that puzzled him. Bert felt his loneliness. There were no emails, no texts, no telephone calls. A life empty of communication. That must have been the same at the origin of Man; communication could only have been made on the particle level. He existed completely in his self, but he shared no life because life was about sharing. Occupying space and time with another particle being. He only talked to plants and their particles were different to humans.

★ ★ ★

Dawn broke and a grey light touched the trees. They reached for the skies with their bare and lifeless branches. A supplication to the fog upwelling into the Chauderon valley, hugging the warmer roads. There were no snow poles alongside them this year. No bare and lifeless branches glorying in a new life, painted orange and planted by Man.

Bert's mobile phone rang out, an impossible call. He had turned it back on the day before, in hope and desperation. He wondered if it was Natalia, the only reason was to hear her voice again. So he could say he was sorry, sorry for everything. The tune was Biffy Clyro's song, "Machines". "I would dig a 1000 holes to lay next to you..." He let it ring, he was afraid to look at the number, the song rang hollow at the end of the ringtone. "I've forgotten how good it could be to feel alive". He snatched at it as if it was hot and answered abruptly, 'This is an impossible conversation.'

'Why?' It was a young female voice.

'Because most of us must be dead.'

'But we are all nearly alive too, Bert.'

He thought about the contradiction for a minute, whilst she breathed gently down the line. He heaved a sigh of relief and controlled his emotions as he asked. 'What's your name?'

'I am Eve.'

'No, your real name before you went mad.'

'Lily.'

She couldn't have known. This wasn't in his imagination. 'And where are you, Lily?'

'CCOW.'

'Is there anyone left?'

'Not here in the control centre, the final few went further below, to the ultimate depths, a week ago but because I had been the one monitoring your reports.' She paused for a full minute. Bert let her think. 'Well, I have something to tell you.'

The human Lily buried in a distant USA couldn't have known the phrase Sam had said on the very first HB night. Bert swallowed a sob. 'What can you tell me, now I know everything?'

'You were right.' The line went abruptly dead.

★ ★ ★

November always encompassed the first large falls of snow. A pure coating on each tree branch, caps for the mountains above the chalet. It deadened sound that existed no more and melted as quickly as it came. A presumptive start to a winter that no one would see in its cold isolation. Bert constantly sat on the veranda; he watched the sky change and the symmetrical equivalent in the lake. The cane settee allowed him to stretch out beneath his blankets as he watched nature die in parallel to himself. He jerked up and looked down his lane. There was an unnatural whirring sound approaching. An interruption of nature by a manmade machine. He stood slowly and let the blanket fall to the mosaic floor. He walked to the edge of the veranda and looked more closely to see what this noise was as it wound its way towards him. A slow moving spot appeared and gradually came into focus. There was a lone figure astride a moped that struggled manfully up the steep incline. At 10 kph it was easy to see the long platinum blonde tresses that barely moved in the slight headwind. The machine stuttered to a halt beneath the Tilleul tree on their roundabout and Natalia let it fall to the floor. Her movements were slow and deliberate, each slight inflection hurt her. Bert waved once to show where he was and she altered her course. It took a while for her to arrive; her steps were deliberate but unbalanced. Her long navy Barbour jacket covered a walking skeleton. Bert hugged her tightly at the bottom of the steps. He helped her upwards and let her collapse on his settee. She was completely spent. Her face was hollow and her eyes haunted. She blinked slowly whilst searching his face. All he could see was the love they had lost. He asked her gently, 'I never thought,' he changed his mind and asked a different question, 'Was it bad?'

'Worse than you predicted, moya Lyubov.' She slumped backward but remained grasping his hand.

Bert struggled to say anything sensible. 'Why did you return?'

He leaned forward to listen, her voice came in rasps: 'I would rather die naturally with you, my husband. To have and to hold, in sickness and in health.'

Bert sobbed gently; it took him a minute to compose himself again. 'And the children?'

'They were sad. Shadows within shadows.' She fondled his left cheek with her fingertips. 'But they want you to know that they love you.'

She had come home but there was no escape from prison, no escape for their imaginations in this infernal hell they were still alive to witness. 'And my Sam?'

'He went for a health check for the over 46 year olds and never came back. So he didn't suffer in our hell.'

Bert couldn't breathe properly. 'So they were full, then?' He knew the answer.

She didn't answer him. Her spirit was fading and her body already wasted beyond what it could stand. She choked as she spoke, 'I wanted to be here with you, in the comfort of our home, that's all I needed, and now I am satisfied.'

He spoke again: 'Not hell, Natalia, but heaven.' He spread his arms out to the view but she only watched him without reply. 'This is heaven and we will see the end of it.'

She smiled. 'So you believe in God now, my husband?'

Bert nodded. 'I think I always did. I just didn't want to agree with Sam, my constant opposite. But I always believed in nature, the universes…'

'And Lily? Do you believe you were talking to her, as a girl can become jealous?'

Bert was serious. 'Yes, of course. I am the most rational man on earth and I believe I was.' He squeezed her hand. 'She hasn't gone yet, she is hanging onto humankind's demise and waiting for us to fail.'

'Fail?'

'To lose all of our goodness, to become animals and at that level she will win.'

'Who is Lily?'

'I said I believe in God, yes?' He felt her going, there was little time left, he saw she had no energy to answer him. 'So therefore every positive particle must have a negative one according to the simple laws of particle physics. Any plus has a minus.'

She inhaled deeply and pulled him tight to her breast so that he could hear her. 'So humankind is being judged?'

'Judged until final extinction in the now and judged when

we reappear in the future, in a new universe. Probably after the next Big Bang or the next big crunch or whatever we designate it. Take your choice but humankind will never understand or know. It is just the end.'

He felt her leave him. A whisper in the air that caressed his face before the spirit followed its path to God only knows where. He held her all night, and felt her cold body under his blanket. A rigid block untouched by the heat of the sunrise as dawn passed his eyes and gave him closure.

★ ★ ★

He couldn't bury his lover, he had no strength left. She had gone and soon so would he. So he left her on the veranda with an eternal view. His purpose was to survive, to be the last man on earth. His energy must live to counteract Hers at the end. He thought about the conversation he might have with Her but his thoughts stayed inside his mind and she would never know them. Elemental characterisation of biological material in your spores has shown me your weakness, Lily. You have a lower charge, lower interconnections at the particle level. You were there at the start of time and will be there at the end, but Man has created a new energy field with His particles. We are one; our new particles have joined together. We are one but the opposite to you. We are one but we are complex and you are simple. You were antimatter and we were matter but now our roles are reversed in the succeeding multiverse.

★ ★ ★

Bert went to his laptop and clicked on the broadcast link to CCOW. He wondered if he was now officially the last man on earth who was still alive. He started his broadcast. 'I don't think you can't hear me now. In fact, I know you are all dead or dying in the Deeps and anyway, you didn't really want to know the truth, did you? It was an impossible dream of course. That humankind would exist forever.' He sobbed gently. 'I told everyone the truth but no one believed me. So what have I gained? That is my fundamental question to you all. And rather not what have I lost.' His voice grew stronger: 'I have gained immortality, I have gained divinity! There is only Lily and I left.' He suddenly laughed like a maniac. 'To chat, to argue, to deny and to approve.' He pressed the on/off button and watched the red light of the PC dim and die.

Slowly he inserted the earpieces for his iPhone beneath his bobble hat. He listened to music as he walked towards the etang. It was a modern piece but classical. A piece that Natalia and he had always loved. The pianist was Yiruma, and the tune "River flows in you". On arrival at the etang he walked around to the lowest point, where the rusted Victorian sluice gate beckoned. There was a grinding sound as he turned the handle. Three turns was all he could manage but it was enough. The tinkling of water created a complementary interval to Yiruma's masterpiece as he watched it flow out of the pond.

'*That won't kill me, Bert. Neither did ripping my heart out.*'
'Of course not.'
'*But you do want me dead?*'
'I do.'
She was scared. Did he know? '*Why?*' she asked gently.
'Because you are not you, so tell me who you really are.'

'*My spores will repopulate the earth and I will create new life. I will develop, change and grow and make a better job of existence, dedicated to my way.*'

'Who is my Lily? Who is "I"?' He didn't expect her to reply. He trudged back to the house in the darkness. It was cold and dreary. His universe contracted and the world turned more slowly for him alone as death crept across its surface towards him.

★ ★ ★

The day began and ended the same way: a tribute to Walser writing in the Victorian epoque. "It snowed and snowed, whatever the heavens could let fall, they let it fall in considerable amounts. It did not stop, there was no beginning and no end. There was no longer any sky, everywhere there was a gray, white snow. There was no longer any air, even that was full of snow. The earth no longer existed, it was also covered in snow and yet more snow."

Bert walked slowly across the white grass fronting the infinity swimming pool. To his right was the iced lost pleasure of the basin, the cover with its deep blanket of snow. To his left the snow hung off the beech and pine trees reaching down to the town of Montreux, anxious to melt and join the lake. He retreated slowly, keeping his feet wedged in his penultimate footsteps, the tracks behind were single and solitary. Within minutes they were filled and the surface reconvened to powder. He shook his head and shoulders and watched a small cascade of white join the freshness. He took a breath and inhaled a second time to completely fill his lungs with the stinging air before turning and continuing his walk. Clear thoughts, resolute and pure, announced his arrival back at the house.

The final view before disappearing inside was the slow moving curtain, silent and cloaking the world behind. White, pure, good, clean; each word slipped across his mind and crystallised his thoughts. Now he had the answers, because Bert Leinster never failed.

★ ★ ★

Bert felt the time arrive; the gravitational waves in some part of distant space had reached earth. He was watching the cold air sink off the face of the Rochers de Naye and slide as a visible mist down the Chauderon valley to join the grey curtain over the lake. The fog had been in situ all morning. It was a good day for The End of The World because Bert was finished now. Mentally and physically spent. Thought out and not out thought. Another day and the magic that sparked his spirit would be gone and his life would leave with it. He pressed the ignition of the GT Merc and slammed his foot down on the accelerator to generate a gigantic roar that reverberated out of the garage and ended in France. Man and machine in ultimate harmony sent a message to the surrounding nature. The development of Man had been the fastest of all the species, an exponential clamour to become the best on earth. But the definition of best had been lost along the way. He reversed out of the garage and headed gingerly up the slippy lane towards the mountains. Each turn of the wheel was an effort; the pressure of his foot on the accelerator gave an equal and opposite reaction and pain up his right leg, through his hip and into his side.

Bert knew that his destination was almost impossible to reach in his condition. Every second was borrowed now. On the main route through the village above was a small farm, a few buildings of dishevelled wood. But whenever he had walked past, there were always trials bikes, tractors and other vehicles parked in the lean-to, and sheltered by the rusted corrugated roof. By the back door to the house were a few old milk churns, made redundant by the modern tanker that had called every morning. Also a set of old scythes, big and strong with solid wooden handles. It was a scythe that he used to lever open the back door. In the dark of the entrance hall he saw the numerous sets of keys hung on ancient hooks. There was one marked AEBI, the writing barely legible after 30 years of use. He grasped the key and made his way towards the lean-to where the AEBI six wheeler tractor was waiting to be stolen. It took him ten minutes to stagger the one hundred metres and climb inside the cab. The engine coughed into life and stuttered for a few moments until he gunned it. A second defiant roar fled down the valley before he set off towards the Dent de Jaman. It was bitingly cold in the cab, the old heater had failed years before and each one hundred metres higher the temperature fell by a degree. The ride was hard; each bounce on the metalled road made him grimace with pain. Three times he stopped to retch into the passenger footwell; wave after wave of nausea gripped him and clouded his thoughts.

He crashed the tractor into first gear on the all wheel drive and veered right at the col. Following the forestry path he crossed the funicular railway and kept heading upwards. To his left were the steep cliffs of the Dent de Jaman and as he circled the tooth of rock he saw the narrow trekking path etched beneath the snow as ever-changing shadows presented to the sun. His grip on the wheel had failed. Now he could only steer by laying his chest on the top of the steering wheel to lock it into a straight path. Gradually he worked his way up the east side of the rock, the only side with an accessible grass slope. The AEBI had chains on four of the six driven wheels and by keeping to a constant five kph he crept up the snow covered mountain. High above him he could see the wooden cross that marked the summit and focussed his will on climbing to it. But no machine could have got him there and with two hundred metres to go the tractor stopped, slipping and sliding. He opened the door and fell out. The snow didn't break his fall very well but its cold caress encouraged him to lie still. It would be easy to remain prone and die quietly. The sun inched across the sky and dispersed the shadow across his face that was cast by the tractor. Its brightness penetrated his closed eyelids and urged him to wake. Dragging his body through the snow he crawled towards the cross, a few metres at a time. Only his willpower pulled him upright to stand with his arms embracing the rough wood. Below him was the most beautiful sight of his life. White slopes of crystallised snow shone with a myriad of diamonds and merged into the shining tiara of the lake.

Bert stood with the sun burning away the last of his soul. He could feel the 0.1% of him that mattered, that was the essence of matter. Every particle was agitated and ready to leave. He challenged Her out loud but his physical voice carried to nowhere. His question reverberated around the world to the remains of the dead. 'Declare yourself, Lily! I understand black matter and energy and what happened. I know what you aren't and what you never can be.' He sobbed because of his pain.

'I think you know who I am.'

'You buried us, didn't you? In the Deeps of hell. But not me, Lily. Not me. You thought I would give up. And the human race succumbed to you.'

'*You fool, it was my chance to unbalance and control the fifth world. All the universes would have been mine.*'

'Yes, and now by my living they are still balanced, as everything remains in perfect symmetry. So you failed, Lily.'

'*This time, Bert.*'

Bert had spoken to Natalia in death. 'You never really die, Natalia.' He had looked into the waxwork face and gently stroked the cold cheek. He had hugged her closer and covered her with his blanket. 'You only pass to somewhere else. A particle being accelerated into "somethingness", a place we cannot predict nor understand. Different to here and now. No better and no worse. Probably the same, a mirrored existence in a different time and space that will be repeated forever in an endless and infinite cycle.'

Lily chided him. '*Listen, mere mortal, and learn. God created the earth in seven days. Man's allegory was pretentious as it took billions of years. You can argue about good and evil, positive and negative, in your tiny little minds but we were created in the first millionth of a second. You and I. Do you understand that now?*'

'So by default you can be extinguished in the same short time. My advantage is I have calculated the end of this world, not the earth. The earth is unimportant. The end of this time and entry into the fifth world. I know what happens.'

'*Tell me your story before you die.*'

'Before we die together, Lily. You and me and no one else. Nothing else, as God created and so God is destroying.'

'*God is weak, you humans are weak.*'

'But it's not just us, is it? It is the universe, this one alone. My thoughts are vibrating my particles and will convey the elements of humankind into the beyond, into the fifth world.

I think that you will not be in that new world so therefore providing I don't think of you, well, you are dead. Dead in my thoughts, my particles and my energy. You cease to exist with me.'

She whined. *'But Bert, life without plants in a new universe, it could never function.'*

'No, life without you, I said. You, the one who has been prompting my demise, constantly asking me to die before you.' He crossed his arms and tilted his head to listen. After a few minutes he spoke aloud. 'Why I kept asking myself?' He smacked his head until the skin burned. 'Thinking, always thinking since you contacted me. Why? But I always think why. Why would a plant talk to me? But you cannot be a plant, your particle structure must be more complicated to be able to contact me. You said you came from beyond time and you have made certain you want me dead before the end and definitively before you. So that means you were created at the start, with and by the same thing that we humans call God. By default, you are the opposite.'

Lily spoke slowly, the hate in her voice made his frail body quake as he clung to the wooden cross. *'Save your suffering, you poor demented fool, jump off this cliff and join your wife.'*

Bert looked across at the Rochers de Naye. The gleam of the restaurant windows set into the west facing cliff drew his gaze. Strewn at the foot of the cliff was a disorderly pile of angled clothing, reds and yellows, greens and blues. The 600 metre fall from the viewing platform had been the easiest exit for the imprisoned inhumanity.

She screamed at him. *'Give into your emotions, human!'*

Bert started to crumple and fell to the foot of the cross. He lay on the snow. 'No emotions, not now, not ever again. I was given a gift and understood nothing about why this gift was given to me, but now I know.' He had stopped talking hours before, only his thoughts truly flowed to be heard by no one except Lily. 'It was for the end of the world, this moment.'

'*You are merely human and you must die first.*'

'I was created to defy you. To be your opposite. That was my life's work.' Bert scrabbled his fingers into the ice crystals and pushed himself up. He raised his face to the sky for a final time. The cross reared above him, stark against the purple sky. He felt the burst of HBs, the last pulse of the burnt out universe that died to give life to a newer version. A rewriting of the same events. It took a micro-second to turn him to particulate dust, smaller than the HBs that tore him particle from particle. But she died at the same instant, evil and opposite, diametrically opposed and always there in any future.

The fifth world began and God and the Devil created the new universe with the Big Bang, a dipolar implosion of energy from everything to nothing and back again.

NOT THE END – A BEGINNING FOR US ALL

AUTHOR'S NOTE
[CERN]

T HE SPRAWLING CAMPUS of the European laboratory for particle physics was conceived between 1949 and 1951; a way of enticing the top European scientists to remain in Europe after World War Two instead of joining the brain drain to the USA. It is a contemplation of the interiors of atoms with a peaceful mandate and with a shared resource to benefit mankind. The antithesis of the pursuit of superiority and war in nuclear Russia and America. It is a good reason why CERN had been created in the neutral and stable country of Switzerland, betwixt the superpowers of the Cold War.

In the reception area of the main building, the floor glows blue, red, and green. "Cosmic song" created by Serge Moro is a strange melange of contorted steel and bronze defying the dull metallic shadows of the campus buildings. Outside, there are 1950s Nissan huts interspersed between high tech glass boxes sculpted across many "intellectual" square kilometres.

It is the place where the world wide web was born in 1989. A free gift to humankind that was followed by "The Grid"; a new computer networking technology for scientists that has developed across the globe. A brilliant concept linking tens of thousands of computers to maximise the power required to handle the huge amounts of data created each year by the four underground colliders. Data that is far greater than a twenty kilometres high pile of now defunct data CDs. Inter-related facts that are now held in a gigantic and nebulous data cloud. The first cloud of many that now serve the normal population in a positive rainstorm. The information mists dispersed substantially with the advent of the artificial retina algorithm in 2015. The invention had reduced the data analysis time four hundred fold.

Over many hours during a collision experiment, a particle travels ten billion kilometres, that is to the planet Neptune and back. The niobium/titanium magnets for steering the particles are supercooled to near absolute zero at -273 degrees Centigrade. A point when molecules cease to move, or so we believe. This ensures there is no resistance to the electricity passing through the magnets, and makes for a stronger magnetic force to bend the particle streams. Then there are two particle streams; one is sent clockwise around the torus and the other anticlockwise. When the bunches are collided by diverting the streams using the magnets there may only be twenty collisions. A nothingness hidden amongst 200 billion particles. The new colossal power creates up to 600 million collisions every second. A vast quantity that is minuscule compared to the natural collisions breaching this universe.

The scientists at CERN research particle power in the order of one Tera-electron volt. That is the energy of a flying mosquito. Even by accelerating the particles, they could still only reach seven TeV, even after sending them around millions of circuits of the torus. Massive energy fields, a vacuum comparable with space, high and low temperatures and a hole in our earth is a dangerous brew. And after sixteen hours of an experiment, the energy must be eliminated. So the collider torus resembles a catherine wheel with the excess particles spun into safe side tunnels, where the particle beam can indiscriminately decay into the earth and beyond.

Synopsis:

4 friends play a new game on Facebook called world domination. But the secret intelligence services believe that the evil Madame Musseine, MM, is using the game to control the world's stock markets. They are are recruited by MI6 and the CIA to join MM's neural network of 100 youngsters in her hideout under Mount Kilimanjaro. Objective – stop MM's evil plans and save the world.

No.1 bestselling author, David Edwards, has created an adventure story for 9 – 14 year olds that combines action and pace with technology and social networking in an epic event.

[1]

The volcano

T HE LIGHT WAS intense from 1000 computer screens. A white light interspersed with patches of colour. The light blue of Facebook and the pink of a child's face, usually smiling in the profile photos that were aligned in a horseshoe shape around the silent black hulk.

There were 10 screens mounted vertically and 100 horizontally, creating a modern glass screen suspended from cables of reinforced steel that reached into the darkness above.

But some of the screens had dark grey backgrounds with a black hand turning anti-clockwise at their centre. 30 degrees at a time and twelve times each minute to make a complete revolution. At the midnight position, the hand implied stop! Danger! A signal warning you away from the blackness beyond, where you would be lost in the bowels of the internet. The hands resembled a reversing set of clocks with three fingers and a thumb etched in the blackest of black. On each hand, the little finger was missing, creating a terrifying claw that reached out from the depths of the screen. The glass wall had hundreds of hands that relentlessly revolved until it was their time to disappear, as a screen saver was de-activated to admit another electronic victim for an online chat with the faceless MM.

Madam Musseine, or MM as she was known to the children playing the game on her global domination website. It was an electronic game with no consequences, a bit of a laugh with a couple of letters to identify your foe. Word of mouth had made it a popular game to play via the sponsored online app within Facebook. The automatic translation between English and Chinese, Spanish and French and every popular language in the world made your distant new mates appear stupid as their sensible comments were mistranslated for you but that made it even more fun. It was a fabtastic game because it could be played 24 hours a day, 7 days a week, in real time across the globe. You against the world; a prime motivator in its appeal.

The huge leather chair creaked as Madam Musseine leaned backwards, her giant legs and feet supported on a padded hydraulic rest, barely wide enough to hold the splayed fat and muscle. Her arms were resting either side of the giant keyboard, especially designed for her massive fingers to feverishly jab at the keys as she messaged the junior gamers. Her teeth reflected the variety of colours emitted by the screens as she smiled, but the colours were stained by the brown rot. She was the ugliest person on this earth with bulbous lips and a fat nose, she had no left ear only a gaping hole. MM was dark skinned apart from the lighter coloured scar down her left cheek, a memory from her first knife fight in the dock area of Marseille, Southern France, at the age of ten. Her greasy black hair clung to the headrest until she shook her curly but lank locks in frustration as someone beat her on the game. It was the first child to win in that week and that made her snarl with anger as drool dripped from her lips.

'Techno!' She howled the name and listened to it echo off the hidden walls of the volcano. 'Techno, come here now!' A shadow of a man slipped into the pulsing light of the screens and grovelled beside her. Techno was 20 years old and had served his mistress for five years as her geeky lap dog. Born in East London, he had run away from home at age 15, leaving his younger brother and mum to fend for themselves. His dad had run away years before and Techno was too scared to assume the responsibilities of running a house, of being a man, and so he had run as well. It was in Marseille whilst earning a paltry living mending equipment in a gaming arcade that Twip Twop had found him. Twip Twop was one of the first of Madam Musseine's henchmen, a short and vicious albino from Greece. But Techno was tall and gangly, with a mop of red hair above his thin white face. He kept his eyes to the floor as he spoke.

'You shouted me Madam?'

'No you stupid man, I shouted you twice. Where have you been you lazy piece of scum?' He kept his head bowed and moved slightly away from her side but it was too late as her huge hand slapped across the side of his face. He was hit so hard, that he felt the imprint of her stunted hand on his cheek as it immediately glowed red with pain.

'I'm so sorry Madam Musseine, please forgive me. I was redesigning the new stealth gyroscope. So sorry madam.' He grovelled in front of her as she eased her bulk out of the greasy chair and towered above him. At 160 kilos and 3 metres tall, she scared everyone she met, so it was lucky the real world never saw her now.

'Fix the program geek. I never want to be beaten again.'
After kicking him harshly, she lumbered away into the darkness
and headed for the distant light pouring through a metal door
set in the granite rock. Squeezing through it, she rolled her
way down the long tunnel that led to her quarters located 700
metres below the summit of Mount Kibo, the dormant volcano
that made up Mount Kilimanjaro. She made a mental note to
see the gyroscope the next morning and demand that Techno
should resolve the issue with the hydrogen engines or else...
Tests had shown that water droplets created within the twin
exhausts were visible on radar defence systems and that was
unacceptable. She would give him a week to resolve the issue,
and after that? Well, in The Black Hand Gang there was no
'after' when a gang member had failed to meet her wishes.

★ ★ ★

Jack George sat with his long legs outstretched and perched
above his head as he slumped in the red IKEA chair. Each foot
lay either side of his PC screen, alternatively tapping to the
beat of The Ebb and Flow, the cool new San Francisco based
band that all of his friends hated. He brushed the wire of
his iPod headphones away from his keyboard and messaged
Roger, also called the splodger, since tipping a can of emulsion
over his parent's best carpet. The boys chatted every evening
using Facebook, as they saw very little of each other during the
school term but that would end shortly when Roger Ponsonby-
Smythe returned home from Eton, the Public School, to the
pretty village of Christleton in Cheshire. Jack lived at the end
of the village in a small red brick cottage with a central blue
door. It was set into the hillside near the golf course where

the old sandstone quarry had closed in the 1930s. This was the working class end of the village, whereas The Ponsonby-Smythes resided at the old manor house at the centre of the upper classes, adjacent to the large pond with its ancient ducking stool. Roger's dad Rupert could afford it, as he was 'something' in the city. Dealing in shares and all that, whilst his mother Maria went to the gym and 'did lunch' with her many acquaintances, usually for this or that charity. Jack never called them Rupert and Maria, they were always The Ponsonby-Smythes to him, Mr or Mrs, this respect was given by most of the poorer locals including Jack's parents. They were defined as poor because they lived in a house worth less than 150,000 pounds as opposed to those of the rich worth more than one million.

'What time do you get home on Saturday splodger?' Jack turned the volume up on his IPod as he waited for a response. The screen was blinking, informing him that his mate was typing.

'Luncheon, old chap. See you then what!' Splodger always wrote and spoke like this, even before Eton. Jack typed quickly.

'Luncheon? You great woosy. Is that a nice ham sarnie or caviar and champagne mate?' Jack tapped the keys harder, Facebook was slow tonight but the extra force could not budge the electronic congestion. Maybe his dad was using the wifi again? Silly dad, he had no idea what he was doing on the internet, he could barely find the football reports on the BBC website until his boy had shown him how.

'Look Jack, one doesn't eat caviar on a Saturday. It's like fish – one only partakes on a Friday or Christmas day. By the way, has one seen the app for the global domination game?'

'Huh?' Jack kept it brief as usual.

'MM's app, I sent it to you as a game request last week. I tell you what, it is absolutely excellent.'

There was a knock at the door and dad's face slowly appeared as he gently pushed it open. The top of his bald head came first before the green eyes and smiling but apologetic face.

'Hiya, just a warning. Mum will be home in ten minutes so I suggest you get ready for bed before she arrives. You know what she's like!' Jack arched his back making a bridge from the top of his chair to the shelf of the PC table. At the age of 12, he was strong and athletic. Already over 2.3 metres tall, he resembled Alex Strider in the films. A handsome boy with blonde spiky hair cut to a number three and gelled. Jack pulled his headphones from his ears with a pop.

'What?' His dad shook his head as he replied kindly.

'I said mum will be home soon so get ready for bed mate.'

'Okay dad, love you, night.' Dad was dismissed and the head retracted as the door was shut softly. Jack loved his dad Jonathan, and spent most of the week in his care. Jonathan stayed at home as a househusband whilst his mum lived away all week whilst she was working on contract as an IS consultant. But the loss of his mum made Jack love her more. It also made him more rebellious and so he opened the app for global domination instead of going to bed.

"Challenge other children across the countries of the world by selecting opponents and trading the assets of your country. Gold and currency, kilometres of motorway and acres of forest, your fishing or naval fleet. Every asset in your country is available to you to defeat your global opponents who will use theirs. Be clever and use them carefully in this ultimate challenge. Only

*the best will progress through 1000 levels of dominance to be the
ultimate leader of our known universe."*

The computer graphics were fabtastic as Jack quickly flicked
through the asset lists and names of the competitors in France.
He knew some of the cities like Avignon since his school visit
at Easter and recognised some of the names from the exchange
trip. "*Sur le pont d'Avignon*", the song rang in his head as he
scrolled down the screen. There was tall Thierry, Jean-Claude
in his red jeans…I heard a car door as it was loudly slammed
outside the cottage and so he rapidly hit the off button on the
PC and scampered across to his bed. Quickly, he took off his
'Man U' T-shirt and pulled the duvet over his Adidas tracksuit
bottoms. A minute later, his mum Jennifer gently opened the
door and walked smiling to sit on the side of his bed. She
leaned towards him and kissed his cheek. Jack resisted the
temptation to wipe the slobber away.

'Hi mum, did you have a good week?'

'Yes my love and tonight is the best part. Coming home to
you and dad.'

'And Timmo the dimmo.' She tucked the duvet tighter
around his shoulders as she reprimanded him.

'Timothy is your brother Jack. He's not dim, just four years
younger than you. You know that makes a big difference.'

'Whatever.'

'Whatever, whatever or fabtastic, you have a way with
words young man.' She said this in the patronising way that
mums did when they thought they were cool. 'Both of you
boys talk a foreign language to your dad and I.' He smiled
at her. He desperately missed his mum during the week but
would never admit to it.

'Not foreign, just the way kids talk like when they are at PGL.' Jennifer patted his short hair and immediately he smoothed his hands upwards to re-do it and look good asleep.

'Mum!'

She sighed heavily. 'See, I give up. What's PGL?'

'Parents Get Lost – you know after the adventure holiday company.' Jack constantly dreamed of a week at PGL. Kayaking, sailing, climbing and abseiling. It would always be a dream as he knew they were lucky to have a single week's family holiday in a caravan in Wales. She leaned forward.

'Remember to clean your teeth PGL man and remember how much I love you when you go to sleep.'

'Yeah, yeah. Wider than the sky and bigger than the sea.'

'Precisely lovely. Now go to sleep and give your dad and I, our time. Nightie nightie.'

'Pyjamas, pyjamas.' He replied whilst grinning.

As mum left the room, Jack had a quick bout of guilt. He had cleaned his teeth two days earlier, surely that was enough? Reluctantly he went to the bathroom but on his return the temptation was too strong to resist and so he rebooted his PC and started to play the game. He knew his parents wouldn't bother him again. His first adversary, naturally enough, was Roger the splodger. Within ten minutes, Roger had trounced him by trading five cruise missiles for Jack's starting assets that had been assigned by the gamemaster – a mere two bazookas. As Jack turned off the PC and crept quietly back into his bed he vowed two things. Firstly, to beat Roger and secondly to become the best player on this new game called 'the world of domination'. He turned on his side and closed his eyes remembering the awesome graphics. It was so realistic; it certainly looked like the greatest game ever.